THE
RAVEN
AND THE
DOVE

A NOVEL OF VIKING NORMANDY

K.M. BUTLER

First Firsthand Account Press Edition, November 2021
Philadelphia, PA

Library of Congress Control Number: 2021921524

ISBN 978-1-7376-3911-4 (paperback)
ISBN 978-1-7376-3910-7 (ebook)

Cover design by Cutting Edge Studios

Printed in the United States of America
10 9 8 7 6 5 4 3 2 1

For my wife Shelby,
whose editing strengthens my stories
as much as she enriches my life.

THE
RAVEN
AND THE
DOVE

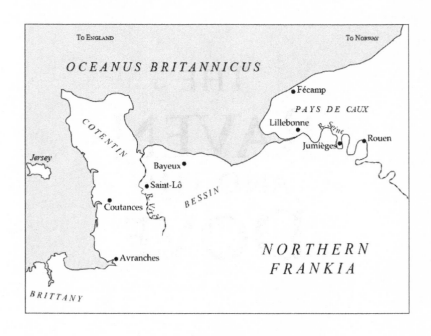

MAP OF NORTHERN FRANCE, AD 890

HISTORICAL NOTE

In AD 911, the Frankish king recognized the Norse warrior Rollo's claim to all lands between the city of Rouen and the mouth of the Seine River. However, historians believe this treaty acknowledged a *fait accompli* of Norse settlement rather than its beginning.

In actuality, the king had lost effective control of this region several decades earlier, and Norse settlers had been living beside the isolated Franks for many years.

Their descendents—the Normans—would reshape the world.

I

THE COMING OF NORTHMEN

AUGUST, AD 890

CHAPTER ONE

HALLA

HALLA TINGLED WITH excitement as she surveyed the column of wagons escorted by her fellow Norsemen. Jarl Rollo would divide this plunder—crucifixes, silver goblets, beads, bolts of cloth, weapons, iron tools, fine clothing, and fistfuls of jewelry—among his warriors when they returned home. Her share would easily pay for new silver brooches to clasp her aprons and that fine linen overcoat in the market of Rouen. The other shieldmaidens and warriors' wives would writhe in jealousy.

Halla released a satisfied sigh. This was a good day.

She lifted a roll of cloth an *ell* wide, a little more than the distance from her elbow to her fingertips, and tossed it to Revna on the deck of one of the jarl's longships. The other woman's black braids danced as she caught it and twisted to stow it beneath the deck planks.

Halla stretched, enjoying the freedom of motion after so many months in armor. She spared a glance for the precious mail coat she'd laid across a nearby tree stump. With the campaign over, she could finally wear a dress again.

Nearby, a goat's bleat ended abruptly as a warrior flashed a knife across its throat and collected its blood in a silver chalice taken from

Saint-Lô's cathedral the day before. Halla made a reverent gesture that circled her head and ended before her face. The gods deserved many more such offerings for granting this victory.

The Franks evidently enjoyed honoring their carpenter god, too. Frankish craftsmen had probably believed the knotted woodwork, fine sculptures, and gilded filigree adorning the fine-grained church door of Saint-Lô would glorify their faith forever.

Halla grinned at the memory of the flames rendering all their work to ash. She had enjoyed watching it burn. The sack had marked a satisfying end to a long campaign stretching over two full summers. The true gods surely cried out in joy.

Between the edge of the forest and the bank of the narrow Vire River, warriors and shieldmaidens laughed and joked as they guarded rows of fresh slaves. Someone opened a stolen cask. With a resounding cheer, a few warriors retrieved goblets from the pilfered chests and filled them with wine.

The young men's muscles rippled beneath their armor as they worked. Halla eyed them each in turn, debating which one offered the best prospect of an entertaining distraction from the long march. A slender blond warrior lifted a series of chests onto a longship with surprising speed. That boded well for an energetic performance in bed. On the other hand, a burly redhead guarding some of the captives had strong thighs that suggested he could generate power with his hips. Even if he tired quickly, she would almost certainly enjoy herself.

Atop the longship, Revna released a guttural cry. She pointed past Halla, her eyes widened in alarm.

"Behind you!"

Pulse leaping, Halla turned. A horseman bore down on her. The large black cross on his white cloak danced as his horse galloped forward. A Christian. His fresh face, blemished neither by scar nor wrinkle of age, bore a wild mix of terror and fury.

And he wasn't alone. Dozens of others erupted out of the forest behind him.

The Christians should have been along the Loire, far to the south.

His sword came down toward her midsection. She leapt to the side too late to avoid it entirely. A sickening rip accompanied the tip of his sword slicing through her padded tunic and into her stomach.

The pain didn't follow until she stumbled to her knees.

She clutched at the wound with shaking hands as the rider passed. This was it. This was her deathblow. She felt none of the joy in the skalds' poems. No one would remember her or sing about such a meaningless death, received on an insignificant shore the day *after* a great sack.

Twenty-two years was too short. Gods, she didn't want to die!

Her next tentative breath came as a wheeze. Though her muscles screamed in pain, she could still breathe. Eyes widening, she pushed aside the fabric, searching for the wound itself. Her fingers felt warm and sticky. She couldn't tell where her tunic ended and her rendered flesh began. The blade had definitely broken the skin, but she could still hold herself upright.

She gasped despite the pain. She could still fight. This wound wouldn't kill her after all.

All around her, men screamed as mounted Christians hewed at them. Several groups of horsemen had pushed her fellow warriors into the river's shallows. Eddies of water swirled around the falling bodies and stained the pebbles on the shore red. A few of Odin's warriors even fled, glancing back in cold terror as another half-dozen horsemen ran them down.

She shuddered in disgust at their piercing cries. Cowards.

Several of the riders tossed torches through the air. They sailed in gentle arcs before landing on the decks of the nearby longships. A few landed amid the stowed plunder. The cargo burst into flames along with the furled sails, filling the air with cindered flakes of floating cloth and the stink of burning oak and singed tar.

This was a disaster, a humiliation.

Why hadn't the scouts and outriders warned of Frankish horsemen?

Had they started celebrating, as well? They were fools to think themselves safe in hostile territory.

An unfamiliar horn blew three times. The Franks disengaged and began to withdraw toward the forest.

Her attacker struggled to maneuver around a warrior tangled in his horse's hooves. As he turned, the flames glinted off the length of his sword, except for a section at the tip smeared dark red with blood.

Her blood.

Halla raised herself to her feet and drew the axe from behind her back. She clenched her jaw at the fresh stab of pain but refused to whimper. The blood had seeped down toward her pelvis, leaving her legs slippery beneath her leather breeches.

She howled in fury at this fresh-faced Frank's arrogance. She would not die this day, not by his hand.

His horse charged, its head bobbing up and down. She gauged the rhythm for a few strides before releasing the axe end-over-end through the air. It sank deeply in his chest with a satisfying thunk.

She beamed in delight. A beautiful throw!

He slumped forward but remained in the saddle until his horse's stride knocked him off balance. Clutching her stomach, she staggered to where he'd fallen. Each step gave her more strength.

Still alive, the Frankish horseman shifted a knee beneath him, struggling to stand. Halla kicked him backward, her growl mixing with the splash of his back against the shallows of the Vire.

The head of her axe stuck out of his chest. She didn't see his sword anywhere. Bracing her foot on his shoulder, she worked the axe back and forth. He screamed and twitched with each tug until it finally came free.

She jumped aside to avoid the blood squirting out of the wound. This time, the motion caused her to whimper. She pinched her stomach to keep the wound from opening further.

He looked up at her with wide, terrified eyes, raising a pale palm toward her. She recalled that Christians believed in mercy, in forgiveness.

She did not.

The stroke of her axe ended with a vibration that ran up through the handle and into her arm. His hand fell to the mud with a wet slap and moved no more.

Around her, some of her fellow warriors formed a defensive line with their backs to the shore. Others waded into the water to save as many longships as they could. A few abandoned horses ran wildly between the bloodied Norse. One group of warriors had captured a Frank and had begun to interrogate him by carving his skin with knives. Though his mouth contorted in a scream, Halla heard nothing but the shouting of the surprised army.

But the Frankish riders who had struck with sudden brutality had melted back into the forest. Though they had failed to save Saint-Lô, the Christians had nonetheless given the Norse one last taste of Frankia: the choking taste of ash, smoke, and defeat.

HALLA

Though the forest hid the conflagration, a thick gray smear on the horizon proved that the ships still burned.

Halla had always thought fire was beautiful. Fire purged false gods and maintained order in Midgard. Only fire could hold the spirits of the dead at bay. Though burning Saint-Lô had taken hours the previous day, she had considered it time well spent. No warrior wished to risk Frankish ghosts following them back to Rouen.

The fires didn't seem so beautiful after consuming a dozen clinker-built *snekke* longships. Each one had been carefully constructed from oak, ash, and spruce over a year with the techniques the All-Father had taught them.

This day, the fires meant defeat.

"Shieldmaiden, move your ass." Bjornolf nudged her aside as he stormed toward the front of the column. As he passed, the battle fury shone in his pale blue eyes despite the streaks of soot and mud caking his eyelashes.

If they hadn't both been *hirdmen*, he would have shoved her a lot harder. Two mornings earlier, she had deliberately woven her chestnut hair into a net of braids to outdo him after he had gloated over the luster of his own locks.

But wounded pride wasn't causing his lingering irritation now, not when the army trudged to the Seine overland when they should have sailed. She felt the same shame and outrage that he did.

Shivering, Halla rubbed the late autumn cold from her shoulders. A fresh stab of pain shot across her stomach. Poking her fingers through the rings of her mail shirt, she exhaled and tested the makeshift bandage for dampness.

"He's just angry he didn't kill more Christians." Her broad-chested jarl had approached without her noticing.

Of course, massive Rollo, jarl of Rouen, walked. His arms dwarfed her thighs. No horse could bear his massive frame, but he led one, nonetheless. Atop it sat Poppa, a blonde, delicately featured Frankish girl hiding within a thick fur cloak. Rollo's cloak.

Halla envied the warmth of that cloak. The scraps of hers bound her injury. The cool air seeped through the few layers of armor and leather wrappings around her wrists and ankles. At least she had looted a pair of fur shoes from Saint-Lô to preserve her toes.

"Is your wound deep?" He studied her with a degree of concern he reserved for his closest companions.

"Others have worse." A glance down the column suggested otherwise. Those with worse injuries still lay at the river's edge.

She could still recall the rending slice of the sword cutting through her tunic. Had the Frankish rider leaned forward a little more or waited an instant before striking, she would have died like the others. She hadn't been afraid at the time. Now, she used every scrap of self-control to hide her shaking.

No. The Norns had woven the skein of her fate long ago. Nothing she could do would extend her life one moment. Everyone knew that.

The warriors who had fled—including one of Rollo's *hird*—were in

Helheim now. Would the stink of so much cowardice keep the Valkyries away? Eyeing the horizon, Halla couldn't decide whether she saw jotuns or Odin's chosen moving amid the smoke. She might very well have dodged the fate of those dishonored dead by a fingerspan. That thought distressed her more than her wounded midsection. She rubbed her shoulders, but the effort only caused her abdomen to scream in pain. No, the Valkyries would come. They had to. "The rest will revel in Valhalla tonight." She needed them to.

Rollo stroked his beard in silence. Any other man would have praised the fallen so he might one day join them. But Rollo was first a jarl, and each dead man reduced his strength for the next raid. "They're getting smarter."

It took her a moment to realize he meant the Franks. "This was our fault. We were lazy. Overconfident."

"We have no reason to be. Not after Paris."

Despite a fourteen-month siege several years earlier, Rollo and her father had failed to take the city. "The Franks paid you well and allowed you to pillage Burgundy. That isn't a defeat."

"Sacking Paris should have been our great achievement. Now the Frankish defender is their king and Berengar resists us to the west." Rollo lowered his eyes and tilted his head ever so slightly toward Poppa, whom he had captured at Bayeux the previous year.

Before he had died, one of the captured riders had revealed he was a Breton, not a Frank, and that he served Berengar of Rennes, Poppa's father.

"We judge the Christians by their farmers and monks, dependent on others for safety," Rollo continued. "But their warriors are learning."

Halla gestured to the wagons behind them. "The loot from four towns says otherwise."

The remaining ships had all gone back to Rouen brimming with captives for the markets. Each warrior—and the families of those who had died—had earned a fortune. She had nearly died for that plunder.

"It was a good haul," he agreed. "But a decade ago, we'd have taken this much from one town." He set his jaw. "North Frankia—the Pays de Caux, they call it—is wrung dry. We've sacked all the Christian god's monasteries and holy places. Whole areas lie abandoned."

Halla's father had told stories of the piles of gold and silver in the early days. She hadn't yet seen plunder like that.

"Perhaps it's time to move on," she ventured. "Bjorn Ironside revealed a world of riches for the taking."

Rollo smiled with the same condescension he always gave when someone spoke of their legends. She wanted to punch him when he gave her that look, but she had sworn her oaths to Týr and Thor to protect her jarl. She adjusted her arm ring.

"And go where? Our brothers pillaging the Loire should have kept Berengar occupied to the south. He obviously defeated them if he was here this morning." He gestured to his right. "In East Frankia, they resist. Even in England, Alfred compelled my friend Guthrum to become a Christian." Scowling, he spat to the side. "They're getting stronger."

"You complain too much." Why was Rollo talking like this? "We attack where we please and they pay us tribute to spare them. That is enough."

Rollo raised his eyebrows. "Ah, but have you ever wondered how they can afford all that tribute?"

"That's what's on your mind?" He should have been worrying about the dozen burning ships or the riders who had ignited them, not where the Christians got their gold.

Anxious and uncertain, Halla cast her eyes across the horizon, searching for danger. Outriders on both sides of the army passed in and out of view through the trees. Revna and a few other warriors walked the column, searching the distance.

Halla forced herself to breathe again. At least Rollo hadn't neglected to assign scouts while he pondered Frankish finances.

"Yes, they're getting smarter," Rollo repeated. "Perhaps we should, as well."

HALLA

The Norse marched well into the night, stopping only when they were certain no one followed them.

A scar running along the left side of his face twisted as Jorund, Rollo's *stallari* and chief advisor, scowled. "We should double the watch tonight."

"Sensible, though I don't expect another attack," Rollo said. "Berengar has what he wants. Attacking again would only cost him lives. He knows more longships will arrive next year."

"So you will raid them again?" Sandy-haired Sigrun, a Danish jarl who had joined the previous four raids, stroked his evenly trimmed beard. He owned half the burned ships. Rollo had already offered some of his own to replace them.

"Oh, yes," Rollo purred. "He challenges me with his defiance. I must answer it."

The army set to work hewing trees to encircle the campsite with a perimeter of sharpened stakes in case their jarl was mistaken. The blacksmiths set up forges while Halla and the other injured began building fires.

Halla was nudging some burning tinder beneath a pile of kindling when Poppa halted beside her. Round of face and fair of complexion, Poppa showed neither the severity of the Christ-women in the nunnery nor the weathering of those in the fields.

"No tasks yet?" Halla asked the girl.

Her deep blue eyes danced. "I'm but a prisoner of you vile heathens."

Halla laughed. Those fine wrists had never known rope or chain. "I keep forgetting. It must be the clothes." The girl wore the same pale blue linen as when Rollo had captured her in the sack of Bayeux the previous year.

Halla blew again, and this time the tinder caught. As the flames grew to caress the firewood, Poppa rubbed her hands together above it.

"It pains you, doesn't it?" She eyed Halla's stomach.

"I haven't had time to treat it properly."

"Let me help." Poppa gestured to her mail. "Take it off."

"Here?" She glanced at the men working nearby.

"I didn't think such things bothered your people." Poppa rose and crossed to one of the supply wagons. Over her shoulder, she said, "Best to have it done with."

Despite having conversed with her regularly over the previous eleven months, Halla hesitated. They passed through Frankish lands owned by this woman's father. Did she really trust her enough to let her inside her armor?

Yet, already the *læknar*—kohl-stained healing women—had attracted a crowd at their tents. Obediently, she slipped an arm out of her mail shirt.

Poppa returned with some cloth wrappings and a bowl of water. Kneeling, she helped Halla lift the padded tunic enough to see the wound. In the distance along the camp's perimeter, a few of the men paused to stare. Halla appreciated their disappointment when she exposed only her ribs.

Poppa studied the tears in Halla's tunic. "The blade was sharp. It made an even cut."

"A boy wielded it. Probably a new sword."

She craned her neck to peer closer. "I don't see any fabric in the wound."

Halla arched an eyebrow. "You were trained in healing?"

She shook her head. "Only by these past few months."

"How deep?" Halla winced when she leaned forward to check for herself.

"A light trace." Dipping a scrap of fabric in the water, Poppa dabbed at the dried blood on the wound. Had she tended to Rollo late at night this same way? "You were lucky."

Halla's thoughts rushed back to that moment when a pointless death had terrified her, a shieldmaiden of Odin. She swallowed and glanced around self-consciously. Revna drove stakes into the ground on the perimeter with most of the other warriors. Even Poppa busied herself smearing a healing mixture of honey on the wound.

Halla released an anxious breath. Only the gods would notice her fears.

Her people wouldn't understand. All they cared about was facing death courageously, not the reasons leading to it. And Halla refused to speak of these fears to a Frankish countess who worshiped a strange god.

"Your father led the Franks."

Poppa's fingers halted in their work of binding the wound with the remaining cloth. "I am sorry for it."

Halla frowned. "Why?"

"Many of your companions died." Poppa tied off the cloth and leaned back, satisfied with her work.

"He defends his lands." Halla flexed, but the wound hurt less than before. "Why did you not escape during the battle?"

A jumble of emotions passed over Poppa's face too quickly for Halla to identify them. Poppa kept her eyes fixed on her hands, tucked in her lap.

If Rollo tired of her, he'd ransom Poppa back to her father. If Berengar didn't pay, she'd go to the slave markets with countless others, then to a distant shore to serve the pleasures of her master. Yet she had stayed despite that danger.

When moments stretched into an enduring silence, Halla shrugged and reached for her mail coat.

The Christian spoke only when Halla had settled the mail over her waist. "I was jealous of you at first."

"Jealous?" The thought struck Halla as absurd. "Of me?"

Poppa tucked her legs beneath her and sat on the grass. "I am the daughter of a count. Nobility. That means—"

"I know what that means."

She nodded, swallowing. "The Bible tells us to obey our parents."

"How does that answer—"

"They expect me to marry a suitable nobleman of their choosing and produce children. I'm supposed to be obedient and silent." She lowered her eyes.

Subsiding, Halla crossed her legs and settled down to listen. "You describe the life of a thrall."

"A thrall…" Her voice was soft.

"A slave. They do as they are told and no more."

"Yes. Yes, that's right. That's what awaits me in Bayeux."

Halla scowled at such Christian barbarism. Her father had begun training her to use the sword when she had turned four. "Do all Franks treat their women thusly?"

"Not all," Poppa admitted. "But those who my father would choose for me certainly would."

"And your god condones this?"

"Those who speak for him do." Inhaling, she met Halla's gaze again. "So imagine my surprise to see a pair of women leading the heathen raiders approaching my keep."

Halla remembered that day well. It had been her first sack. She and Revna had broken through the gates of Bayeux. That day, Rollo had elevated both of them to his *hird*, the elite group of his loyal warriors, in recognition of their courage.

"At the way he honored you, I thought perhaps you and Revna were his favorites, his…"

"Lovers?" Halla's eyes widened.

Poppa blushed, lowering her eyes in a surprisingly demure expression. Halla could understand some of Rollo's affection for this creature.

"That's absurd." Halla shook her head. "He's a decade older than me."

"He's seasoned."

"And so thick-boned, with no grace at all."

"Manly," Poppa nearly purred. "So well-groomed. Sweet-smelling."

"Too pretty," Halla sniffed. "And condescending. I sometimes doubt he believes in the gods."

"Well…" Poppa's face carried the lingering echo of a smile.

She truly cared for Rollo; she was no threat for his *hird* to dispatch. "Understand my confusion. In my country, men and women must be chaperoned before marriage and lead almost separate lives afterward." Halla rubbed her shoulders to banish the night's chill. "That must make sex difficult."

"I…" This time, the blush spread to her ears, and Poppa drew her knees up to clutch them. "Halla!"

"It is no shame to speak of such things." These Christians were a mystery. Did their religion not speak of love? "Sex is merely a way to pass the time."

Poppa picked at the edge of her sleeve, avoiding Halla's gaze. "Of course, now I realize Rollo doesn't view you as an object of desire."

Halla frowned, her good mood dissipating. "Why not?" Her chin might have been a little too sharp and her eyebrows too thick for some, but her deep blue eyes had ensorcelled more than one young man.

"He respects you as a trusted companion. And that makes me jealous for an entirely different reason."

The protest on her lips faded into a spreading glow of satisfaction. Rollo respected her? She smiled despite herself. Yes, it must be true, for this Frank to observe it.

"Do you wish to train as a shieldmaiden?" Halla asked.

"Me?" She gasped. "Heavens, no!"

"Then why does it make you jealous?"

"Because, dear Halla…" She sighed. "You have never known the restrictions I've felt my whole life." She picked at a blade of grass beside her. "There was a moment by the Vire, when Rollo went to confront my father's horsemen. I had a free path to the forest. I could have left."

"Why didn't you?" Halla shifted to sit on her knees despite the pain it caused. "Why stay?"

"Because I could choose, for the first time in my life. And I did," Poppa said. "Months ago, Rollo made it clear I am neither prisoner nor slave."

She hadn't thought Rollo cared about this girl so much as to grant her freedom. Yet he had led her horse as if he cherished her. They had often exchanged affectionate glances. Seeing such feelings for a Christian through to their end would cost him supporters.

And yet... Why shouldn't he enjoy himself? What value was life without the things that made living sweet?

"As Poppa of Bayeux, I must obey. But as Poppa of Rouen, I can do as I wish."

If the life of a Frank was one of submission, Halla could not blame her for choosing another path. "I know something of your beliefs. Your god wishes you to deny your worth, yes?"

Poppa considered. "We are meant to be humble."

"Our gods wish us to be strong so we may aid them at Ragnarok. We must seize opportunity and take what we can to prove our worth."

"Even if others suffer?" Poppa asked.

Halla rubbed her stomach, recalling the feel of the blade slicing into her flesh. "Suffering is a gift, a source of growth."

"I doubt the people of Bayeux or Saint-Lô would agree."

Halla shrugged. "Their ignorance changes nothing. You harden a person as you do steel, by burning away the indecision, the doubt, the fear. Thor is god both of strength and blacksmiths." She jutted her chin toward Poppa. "You know something of this."

Her jaw fell open. "What do you mean?"

"You chose the uncertainty of remaining with us over the protection of your father. There is Norse in you."

A smile spread across Poppa's face. When it touched her eyes, they danced in delight.

CHAPTER TWO

TAURIN

TAURIN BARELY FELT the chill in the air or the hardness of the church's stone floor as he silently debated whether God would approve of his actions.

The villagers had hailed him as a hero for capturing the bandits who had burned their farms and stolen their livestock. His father, God rest his soul, had always insisted the aldermen had an obligation to protect their neighbors. Taurin had fulfilled that duty this day.

But the consequences tormented him. He had killed a fellow Christian and had seriously injured another.

Taurin glared down at the man responsible for the raids. Arbogast knelt before Father Norbert as the priest harangued him about wrath and greed. How could this fellow alderman stand in council with them, listening in silence as the victims reported the devastation caused by these attacks, knowing he had secretly ordered them? Knowing his actions would force his fellow councilmen, his friends, to pursue him?

Taurin's heart thumped in his chest. The muscles of his sword arm twitched. For the first time, he resented his authority. At twenty-five summers, Taurin was one of only three individuals both fit enough and permitted by law to bear arms. He used to think that law prevented civil discord. Now, he hated it for staining his soul.

He raised his eyes to the carved oak cross hanging from a precious iron chain at the apse. A crucifix of sanctified silver liberated from the heathens in Al-Andalus had hung in Lillebonne's church in his grandfather's day. But the Northmen had carted that away along with many of the townsfolk and their valuables when they had burned the town fifty years earlier. In less than an hour, they had destroyed the work of generations.

Now, a fellow Christian had raided them. Taurin inhaled a cleansing breath of the holy air. He could endure the burden of sin to preserve what precious little they had left.

Red-faced with overspent breath, Father Norbert finally paused his diatribe to recover.

Taurin leapt on the opportunity. "Thank you for your wise words, Father. May we rely upon you to lecture this man further while we decide his punishment?" He needed to send riders to assemble the other aldermen and couldn't wait while the priest launched into another speech.

Norbert bobbed his head, apparently unbothered by the interruption. "The Church will provide." He turned to Arbogast. "Do you swear upon the cross and scripture to remain in this holy place?"

Arbogast sighed. His voice, when it came, was a mere whisper. "I do swear it."

Taurin bowed to the priest and turned for the doors. He didn't need to set a guard. Should Arbogast break a holy oath, Norbert would deny him the Eucharist. The disgraced man might risk his fortune and life by raiding his neighbors, but he wouldn't risk his eternal soul.

Taurin stepped out into the town square, facing the shore of the tiny Bolbec River. He cast his eyes downstream, as every father in Lillebonne had taught his children, to the bend in the river that led to the distant Seine. Clear waters meant no raiders, no pillaging, and no suffering.

A good day.

For the past fifty years, that bend had protected them from the endless stream of longships a few miles to the south. In his grandfather's day, the town had hugged the Seine where it met the Bolbec. His people had enjoyed good fishing, whaling on the coast, and trade to distant lands.

And then the Northmen had come and burned it all to the ground. The nobles and agents of the emperor had fled and never returned. Left on their own, the landowners—like his grandfather—had rebuilt farther up the Bolbec so they might quietly endure, hidden from the heathens in the isolated wilds of the Pays de Caux.

Taurin inhaled the cool air. The Northmen might have severed them from the rest of Frankia, but his people had survived. He had a duty to preserve that safety.

A man with short, carefully trimmed black hair waved as he wove through the surprisingly thick midday crowd. Taurin broke into an easy smile. "Orderic!"

They clasped hands before the blacksmith's shop, an open frame with a thatched roof that smelled of coal and heat.

"My friend!" Leaning in, Orderic received Taurin's kiss on his cheek and offered one in turn. "Peace to you this day, this joyous day." His hazel eyes danced in delight.

"And to you." Taurin wondered whether a new paramour or a new horse caused his happiness, but he had other business first. "Seeing you saves me a rider. I've caught our brigand leader."

"How long was the heathen's hair?" Orderic barked a laugh. "Did you find his longship?"

Taurin lowered his eyes. He had made the same assumptions. "He wasn't a Northman."

"What?" Orderic's face darkened. "A Frank?"

"Arbogast."

"Impossible! We dined together just last week."

"I saw him burn the stable of one of Dagobert's tenants." Taurin swallowed. "Orderic…" Though he hesitated to reveal his shame, he could not contain the urge to confess. "I killed one of Arbogast's men."

Orderic placed a hand on his shoulder. His eyes carried none of the condemnation in Taurin's heart. "I am sorry, my friend."

The warmth of the soothing touch thawed the ice gripping his soul. Orderic, who might have been his brother-in-law, always understood him.

Taurin sighed. "What sort of desperation would lead him to this? Surely, he knew he couldn't hide this kind of attack for long."

"It's these Northmen…" Orderic glowered. "Each season, we hear rumors of more attacks. When their depredations go unpunished, others believe they can do the same."

"The nobles weren't so very different," Taurin reminded.

His grandfather had told tales of the lords' brutal tax-collecting and wanton rape of local daughters. Taurin suspected Lillebonne had benefited more from their abandonment than it ever had from their presence. They had stolen Lillebonne's prosperity every season, while the Northmen had raided only once in fifty years.

"It's the Northmen," Orderic maintained. "They sow suffering and desolation."

Taurin subsided to avoid an argument. "I'm sending riders to summon the other aldermen to discuss a punishment." He sighed. "They won't welcome these tidings."

"Oh!" Orderic's face brightened. "I have tidings of my own! We've had a visitor."

"A visitor?"

Beyond a few miles from town, the roads degraded into muddy paths through the foliage, prowled by outlaws. Other than a few seasonal traders from nearby villages, everyone who visited town lived within a day's ride.

Orderic nodded eagerly. "A whaler who lives beyond the Seine, along the Vire River."

"The Cotentin?" Frankish lords still held sway in that area, far to the southwest.

"He found this lying in the remains of a great battle." Orderic fished around the pouch hanging from his belt and retrieved a length of twisted bronze wrapped in an almost complete circle with the head of a wolf at either end.

Taurin drew a shaking breath. He had never seen a Norse arm ring before but recognized it from the descriptions. Every child of Lillebonne feared those rings.

"The Norse burned Saint-Lô." Orderic crossed himself. "But then Berengar of Rennes repulsed them." He whooped in delight. "He burned their longships!"

"Our fishermen saw longships on the Seine two days ago," Taurin reminded.

"Those were the survivors." Orderic shook the arm ring. "He did it. This Berengar, whoever he is, drove them into the river." He gripped Taurin's arm. "This is it, Taurin. He'll push them out, once and for all."

Taurin considered the river again. The Franks had defeated the Northmen at Paris, and now the Bretons had halted them to the west. Yet every spring, fishermen saw more longships travel the Seine. Did one more loss really matter?

He pushed his doubts aside. So far, they had remained hidden, safe from further attacks. Fewer raiders could only benefit them.

Taurin clasped his friend's shoulder, sharing in his delight. "God be praised."

HALLA

Two days after leaving the burning longships along the Vire, the Norsemen reached the mouth of the Seine. The Danish trader Oleg Ygrinsson awaited them in his anchored *knörr* trading ship. He always followed the army at a distance to offer warriors quick gold for their share of the plunder. Annoyed that most of it had gone with the surviving longships, he was only too happy to salvage the trip. For twenty-four handweights of silver, he ferried them across a few dozen at a time, sparing the weary warriors a long trip home along the wrong side of the mighty river.

Halla found Oleg, Rollo, and several of his *hird* on a nearby embankment, watching the first ship unload. "The water depth increases quickly," she explained. "The ship can come right to the shore. We'll be across in four hours."

"Good," Jorund said. "The sooner we're back on our side of the river, the better."

Halla sighed, imagining the relief of even a half-hour in the sauna and a good night's sleep in a real bed.

"I say we burn our way back to Rouen," Bjornolf growled. "Punish these Christians for their cowardly attack."

"Agreed." Revna strummed the hilt of her sword.

"No," Rollo said in a tone of finality. "We've stayed too long in Frankish lands."

"Is this cowardice?" Bjornolf hissed.

Everyone—including the soft-handed Oleg—stiffened at his words. Berengar's horsemen had certainly frustrated Bjornolf, but would he truly challenge the man he'd sworn to guard?

Halla took a step back and turned to Rollo. He had to resolve this now. Simmering resentment was the Frankish way, not theirs.

Rollo tended to slump when he feasted or walked. But now, he straightened, surprising her with his size. She had seen him strike as if Thor himself had possessed his sword-arm. The subtle shifting of his shoulders suggested he was preparing to do so now.

The silent confrontation lasted only a moment before Bjornolf relaxed and spat to the side. He had his answer about his jarl's courage, at least.

Rollo's voice sounded almost pleasant. "They've had time to hide or bury their valuables. And after the haul at Saint-Lô, and Bayeux last year, we don't need a few more bronze trinkets."

Bjornolf shrugged and subsided.

Only then did Halla relax. "The anchorage is good here. I'm surprised they don't have a port town nearby."

"I've seen fishermen working another river that joins the Seine to the east." The two braids of Oleg's beard and the one at the back of his head twirled as he turned toward the far side of the river. "The boats always look the same, though the fishermen change."

"That suggests a carpenter working from a standard design," Jorund said.

"And a carpenter means a town." Rollo stroked his beard, meeting Jorund's eyes until the *stallari* nodded. Rollo continued, "I want to see this settlement."

Halla narrowed her eyes. He and Jorund had decided something in that moment. "Fishing interests you?"

Rollo shrugged. "No, but towns do." His reaction seemed too casual.

"What aren't you saying?" Halla pressed.

The jarl sighed. "Jorund and I have been discussing something."

"And you don't want to share with us?" she asked.

"Maybe on the way."

"You can't go," Jorund declared.

They all fell silent and stared at the *stallari*.

"Why not?" Rollo's voice carried more surprise than anger.

"We've been gone from Rouen for over a year." Jorund crossed his arms, looking as unmovable as Heimdall himself. "The men are tired and expect you to distribute the plunder." He lowered his chin and stared at the jarl. "They burned our ships, Rollo."

Bjornolf spat and strode away, shaking his head.

Jorund nodded toward the departing man's back. "If you don't deal with Rouen, you may lose it."

Rollo glared at the river. Despite sacking four cities and pillaging the countryside, Berengar's charge would almost certainly raise questions about Rollo's leadership. Bjornolf's intemperate words might only be the start of trouble.

"Fine." Rollo sighed. "Jorund, go with Halla and Revna. See if you can find this settlement and talk to the villagers. Learn what they produce, what they need, who they trade with."

Halla repressed a sigh of her own. She had pledged to obey his commands, but this task would delay her return to the warm bath she so desperately wanted.

"And if there's trouble?" Revna asked.

Rollo jabbed his finger at her. "Don't kill anyone unnecessarily."

Revna frowned with a disappointment so complete that Halla broke into laughter.

They chose horses and crossed with the next group on Oleg's *knörr*. Leaving the army behind, they skirted the northern shore of the Seine, looking for the tributary Oleg had reported.

At some point in the past, a cobblestone road like those within Rouen and leading to Paris had run along the river. Vegetation had dislodged the stones, creating an uneven patchwork. The party decided to ride through the wild grasses beside it rather than endanger the horses' hooves on the cobbles.

Tall trees with thick trunks sprouted out of the shattered marble and limestone remnants of an abandoned structure near the river's edge. She guessed no one had lived in it for generations. And yet, here and there Halla noticed signs of recent activity: damaged fishing nets caught in the shrubs near the shore, abandoned fire pits, and patches of chewed grasses and dried horse manure.

An hour later, they found Oleg's river where it converged with the Seine. Along the western shore sat the blackened ruins of a size-able town.

Dismounting, the three Norsemen led their horses through the wide street passing through the ruins. While a few weeds sprung up amid the empty dirt, an army could still navigate it six abreast without difficulty. The burned remains of wooden buildings with solid stone foundations flanked either side.

Halla appreciated the subtle signs of a thorough raid. Broken doors and objects scattered outside the buildings had survived the fire. Discarded chests and disintegrating satchels littered the path from the buildings to the main square. Broken barrels, overgrown with mud and thick grass, sat in a ragged pile in the center square.

"Is this the town Oleg mentioned?" Revna asked.

Halla shook her head. "This happened decades ago." Rain over the years had caused the thick ash to run, leaving gray waves in the dirt. She saw no bodies or bones of either people or livestock. Someone had buried them.

They continued walking until they came upon a large, half-fallen structure. One side remained tall enough to suggest it had once stood at least five man-heights. Though the top had collapsed in on itself, she could not mistake the shape.

"This was their church," Halla announced.

A substantial set of docks clung precariously to the shore of the intersecting river. It bore no blackening of fire, but time had rotted the wood in several places. Halla suspected it would collapse if she tried to stand on it.

Jorund gazed at the far shore. "I see no settlement on the other side."

"This isn't the town we're looking for," Halla decided.

Revna soothed her horse with a gentle pat. "Are we supposed to wander all Midgard?"

"Only until we find this town," Halla chirped. "The jarl gave us a task. Let's do it and get back home."

The tributary river was much narrower than the Seine, and as they penetrated farther north, Halla felt the darkness of the forest closing in on her. She cast anxious glances every few strides. This region resembled the Vire immediately before Berengar's riders had attacked and almost killed her. But this area held no great Frankish lords or cities or monasteries worth sacking, only a silent landscape dotted with ancient ruins.

As the three mailed riders carefully followed the snaking path of the river deeper into lost country, the woods gave way to open stretches. Crops grew in long strips and farmhouses dotted the tops of the gradual hills.

"This is no wasteland," Halla muttered.

And then, rising up from the horizon, she saw columns of thick gray smoke that indicated a forge, beloved of Thor. A blacksmith's fire meant a settlement. Jorund nodded and they dismounted in silence. Spreading out, they guided their mounts forward for a closer look.

They discovered the edge of a town of several dozen buildings just north of a small marsh. Halla could distinguish not only the looming church, but the central square as well. Though large for a wilderness town, it was smaller than even a single neighborhood in Rouen. Its size suggested a number of people lived there year-round, though.

When they gathered on Jorund again, he asked, "Did you see any soldiers?"

"Some wore swords, but I saw no mail," Revna said.

"Wooden market stalls," Halla added, "probably serving farmhouses like those we passed coming in."

Jorund ran his fingers over his whiskers. His gaze settled on Halla. "Are you well enough to fight?"

"I'm fine." She refused to sit back while others risked their lives.

Jorund nodded. "Then let's introduce ourselves. Revna, guard our flank. Halla, watch for archers."

"They'll be surprised and terrified," Halla assured. The Franks were always terrified and often surprised.

"That's what concerns me," he replied. "I mean to talk to them, not frighten them into doing something stupid."

"Stop worrying." Revna grunted. "Whether they will attack us or not was written long ago. Go boldly to your fate."

How often had that sentiment preceded recklessness? Halla resisted the urge to cradle her wounded stomach. The setting sun painted the walls of the buildings in bloody red and deep purple. An ill omen.

No. She refused to live in fear until her final day.

The three warriors led their horses through the grass and down the main street. Almost immediately, a Frankish woman began to scream as she rushed toward the church. Revna fell back a step and checked behind them while Halla searched the distance for mustering soldiers.

Several townsfolk fled into the buildings, but a few gathered before their church as Halla and her companions approached. The town's blacksmith drew a hammer from his apron and repeatedly adjusted his grip. Upon seeing Thor's instruments, Halla gestured reverently. That seemed to confuse and frighten him further. His discomfort made her smile.

They stopped twenty paces from the church door in front of the largest group of Franks.

Halla saw few women. Perhaps the rest waited nearby with bows. Eyeing the buildings, she saw no movement behind the cracks of the sealed shutters.

Off to the right, a man wearing the robes and plain cross of a Christian monk strode forward, accompanied by two others. The first of his companions had short black hair, neatly trimmed, and a bare chin. The rich blues, reds, and greens of the brocade edging his wool tunic suggested considerable wealth. He glared at Jorund with obvious contempt but ignored both Halla and Revna.

The second man walked with the purpose and efficiency of a warrior, but it was his deep blue eyes, not his motions, which intrigued Halla. They carried intelligence and curiosity rather than anger. He had a distinguished face—handsome, even—despite the lack of a manly beard, with a defined but not bulbous nose. And the nakedness of his chin revealed firm muscles beneath, not the flapping excess of a life of luxury. She wondered if the rest of his body was equally sculpted.

His eyes widened when he noticed her studying him. After a few heartbeats that sounded in her ears more loudly than she would have expected, he shifted his gaze to the landscape behind her.

He was searching for further danger, just as she had! Who would have expected such wisdom from a Christian? She felt a pang of regret that she would have to kill this handsome man first in case of trouble. He had already demonstrated too much presence of mind to let him linger in a battle.

"Jorund?" Revna clenched the hilt of her sword.

"Easy." Halla placed a hand on her shoulder as she assessed the crowd. Only the two men beside the monk carried swords.

"Odin, guide my tongue." Jorund stepped forward and extended his hands, palms up. He began in slow, deliberate Frankish. "Hail to you, people of the Caux. Who is your chieftain?"

TAURIN

Northmen.

These were Northmen standing in the middle of the village. The moment his people had feared for decades had finally come. Taurin cast his eyes over the terrified faces of his friends and neighbors. How many of his people would die before dawn?

They wished only to be left alone, but the arrival of these three heathens made that impossible.

Beside him, Orderic fell still. While his fingers hadn't yet reached for his sword, Taurin read the naked fury on his face. He wanted to kill them where they stood.

Taurin saw only three heathens. Where were the others? And why would they announce themselves? In the stories, they always attacked with surprise. Always.

Taurin swallowed and studied these barbarians. The man had broad shoulders and thick muscles that strained his mail shirt as he moved. A deep scar running along his face, interrupting both his eyebrow and beard on the left side, suggested he had survived many grievous injuries. If Taurin ever faced him in battle, he'd have to move quickly to avoid taking the full brunt of an attack.

The two women were younger, but their features and the shape of their faces suggested they weren't the man's kin. Both wore mail shirts and moved with the fluidity of skilled fighters. He'd heard rumors of female warriors among the raiders of Paris, but he'd never seen them before. One of them kept glancing behind, searching the oncoming darkness. Two braids that began at the temples and joined at the back bound her nearly black hair. The blue-black ink ringing her hazel eyes and the symbols drawn on her round cheeks and forehead gave her an otherworldly appearance.

And then there was the other woman. She had also edged her eyes in the same blue-black, but the effect didn't seem as harsh or strange. Her deep blue eyes held a strange mix of curiosity and suspicion. She watched him with an intensity that suggested she would either mount him or murder him. Both prospects terrified him.

She had bound her delicate chestnut hair in a net of interconnecting braids that caught the fading light and threw back a riot of browns and reds. Her nose was a little more pointed and her features a bit sharper, but she stood with a stillness unmarred by fidgeting.

These Northmen weren't the giants of legend; they stood no taller than him. Not one of them showed a speck of dirt on their skin, and their hair was straight and free of debris and knots. He hadn't expected heathens to look so...tidy.

He stirred when Norbert began praying. Someone needed to answer this heathen's Frankish greeting. Perhaps he could stop the slaughter before it began.

He stepped forward. The Northman had stretched forward his hands. To show that they were empty, perhaps? Taurin did the same. "I greet you in the name of Almighty God. I am Taurin, alderman of Lillebonne."

The Northman flashed a smile to his companions. The sight sent a shiver down Taurin's back.

"I am Jorund hinn Hrafn." Jorund the Raven—an odd name—gestured to the coal-haired woman. "This is Revna Viksdóttir." He indicated the chestnut-haired one. "And Halla Skidadóttir."

At least they're not called 'Franksplitter'.

Taurin lowered his gaze to their sheaths and scabbards. They all carried swords except Halla, who bore two axes. One hung limp from a hoop at her right hip, while the other peeked out from behind her in a lateral sheath at her waist.

"Where did you learn our language?" Orderic demanded.

Jorund offered a toothy grin that only made him look more menacing. "Since conquering Rouen many years ago, we've had occasion to…interact with your people."

Taurin swallowed before he could stop himself. He could well imagine the nature of those interactions. "These men are Orderic and Father Norbert, our priest." He paused to take a steadying breath. "What brings you to our town?"

"We are investigating the area north of the Seine, what you call the Pays de Caux," Jorund explained. "On behalf of Jarl Rollo of Rouen."

Murmurs of recognition spread among the townsfolk. They didn't speak Norse, but they did recognize that name. Rollo commanded thousands, any number of which could be linger nearby.

Orderic answered first. "I'm told Berengar defeated Rollo mere days ago. Are you all that remains of his army?" His voice carried a dangerous sneer.

"Quiet," Taurin hissed. "You'll doom us all."

Halla slid her left foot forward in a defensive stance. "If you offer a challenge, declare it like a man. Don't sneer like a cur." She spoke with a deadly calm and lowered a twitching finger closer to her axe.

Orderic smirked but appeared unconcerned. "There are three of you."

"If they frighten you," the woman continued, "I can ask them to leave before I send you to your god."

Orderic huffed. "Fight a woman? It would hardly be a contest."

She shrugged. "I'm sure we could find a child somewhere if you wish a fair fight."

As a flush rose to Orderic's cheeks, Taurin stepped forward. He had to stop this before it deteriorated further. "We will not aid you if you mean to scout for a raid."

"That is not our intent." Jorund lowered his hands. "We only wish to learn about your community. We ask for hospitality."

Taurin hesitated. Would kindness or violence better protect them from another disaster?

Perhaps there really were only three of them, after all. Two dozen townsfolk watched from nearby, along with one of Dagobert's men hovering near the periphery. His people could rush and kill these heathens. None need ever know they had arrived.

Could he trust his people not to gloat to passing traders about dispatching three Norse warriors? If Rollo had sent them, he would send more, and next time they might scourge the countryside with ash and flame. If Rollo's warriors fought in the Cotentin far to the west, he could easily sack a town much closer to Rouen. The Frankish emperor had abandoned them. Unless God came down from Heaven, no one would spare them from ruin.

"What you ask is impossible," Father Norbert said. "Honest Christian households cannot admit godless heathens." He made the sign of the cross in their direction.

"Godless!" Revna evidently understood Frankish as well. Turning to Halla, she shook her head. "I thought they complained we had too many!"

"Your gods are soulless demons," Norbert countered.

Halla flashed her hand down and withdrew the axe from her waist.

"Stop!" Jorund snapped in Norse, extending a hand to halt her.

Though Taurin hadn't heard the language in many years, comprehension flowed back as the Northman spoke. "We did not come for this."

She replied in the same language. "He can worship his carpenter all he likes, but I will not listen to him slander the true gods."

Beside him, Orderic lowered his hand to his hilt and narrowed his eyes.

Taurin pinned him with a glare. "Don't," he whispered in Frankish.

"I say we kill them and be done with it," Revna said in Norse. "Halla can throw an axe at the lead one. I'll slit the mouthy one's throat, then we can burn this irritating village to the ground."

"Rollo won't object if we share the spoils with the army," Halla added.

"Wait!" Taurin cried in Norse. "Let me calm them."

The foreign words felt strange on his lips, but they had their desired effect. All three Northmen gasped.

"What did you say?" Orderic asked in Frankish.

"Do not speak that heathen language," Norbert demanded.

Taurin waved them off and continued in Norse. "Do you swear by your gods that you intend no harm?"

Jorund straightened his mail coat and licked his lips. "By Odin, by Thor, by fair Freya and Sif, I swear it."

"Where did you learn our language?" Halla's hostility had given way to surprise.

"My father's slave taught me, though I've had little chance to practice."

"I would speak with your father if he took one of our warriors as a slave."

Taurin crossed himself. "He died two summers ago."

She made an elaborate warding gesture around her face. He sucked in a breath of surprise. Piety in a heathen?

Orderic tugged at his shoulder. "What are you telling them?"

"I'm preventing violence."

"I see only three. We can kill them easily."

"How many will come next time?" Taurin asked. "Rollo could send his entire army if they don't return."

"If he still has one," Orderic muttered.

"They said Rollo's army survived before they knew I understood them."

Orderic grimaced. "Then what do you suggest?"

"I will not condone heathens in our midst," the priest warned. "Any who welcomes them will be excommunicated."

Taurin scowled at the priest's intransigence. An envoy from Rome hadn't come for decades. While he didn't know if God would honor a priest's condemnation, he wouldn't risk his soul to find out.

Eyes widening, he turned to Norbert. "What if they agreed to primsigning?"

"Taurin..." Orderic began.

He waved him off as the priest rubbed his bare chin. "Think carefully, Father," Taurin warned. "Your answer may decide the fate of our town."

"What is this primsigning?" Jorund asked.

Taurin turned to him. "A holy right that allows you to receive hospitality, enter into agreements, and receive the protection of our law."

Jorund narrowed his eyes. "A mere ritual accomplishes this?"

Halla sighed. "It's a welcoming by their god, Jorund. If we must endure a few words by this weak man"—she gestured to Norbert—"to honor Rollo's orders, what's the harm?"

It was, Taurin reflected, much more than that. It was the first step on the path of becoming a Christian. But sharing that information might make them hesitate, particularly the pious one, this Halla.

"Yes, something like that." Taurin turned to Norbert. "Long ago, other towns used it to trade with heathens."

Norbert exchanged glances with Taurin and Orderic before eyeing the Northmen. Halla still wielded her axe. Sighing, he waved a hand limply. "God does not reject those who wish to embrace him."

"They must follow our laws while here," Orderic warned.

Taurin exhaled in relief, yet still his fears tormented him. After all this time, why had they come now?

The priest retrieved a vial from the church. Dipping a little oil on his fingers, he made an exaggerated sign of the cross over Halla, then swept his hand around her as he whispered a soft prayer. Taurin drew a silent breath when she dipped her head reverently as the priest's hand passed over her.

Norbert welcomed the heathens into the faith, one by one, before returning to stand beside Orderic.

Taurin licked his lips. "On behalf of Lillebonne, I extend my hospitality to you, Jorund the Raven. God protect you."

With effort, he extended his hand without shaking. Jorund clasped his forearm with a grip that continued to sting long after the Northman released him. He prayed he never needed to face this man in battle.

Taurin hesitated. Would he give offense if he welcomed the women as well? He stepped past Jorund with an indrawn breath; if this man intended harm, he would strike now.

But Orderic shouted no warning and the moment passed without an attack. Belatedly, Taurin remembered that Northmen treated women strangely and that both of these women were warriors.

Revna frowned as Taurin approached and extended his hand. She clasped his forearm for less than a heartbeat. Releasing it as if it burned her, she withdrew to stand beside Jorund.

With a shrug, he turned to Halla. She studied him as he approached, but her posture didn't suggest annoyance as Revna's had. Red stained the tunic beneath her mail coat. Blood. She had suffered a recent injury, perhaps against Berengar.

Swallowing, he extended his hand.

She clasped his forearm tenderly, neither challenging him with her strength nor shrinking from his touch. Her fingers twitched ever so slightly, tickling his skin.

These people were supposed to be demons spawned by Satan, but he found himself reluctant to let her go. "Be welcome in our town, Halla Skidadóttir."

She inclined her head without breaking her gaze. "Well met, Taurin of Lillebonne."

Revna grunted. "Are you two going to stare at each other all night? It's getting dark."

He released Halla with a start, remembering the stakes of these few moments. He ran a hand through his dark brown hair. "Forgive me. You must be tired from your travels. Will you join us for a meal?"

Jorund offered a toothy smile. "I never pass up food."

Halla gave an abrupt laugh.

Orderic sidled up to him as he led their guests to the town hall. "Why did you invite them to dine with us? We need to consult with the other aldermen first."

"I couldn't leave them standing in the dark," he grumbled. Their guests' mail rattled as they walked. "And I wager dinner with them may benefit us more than a hundred consultations with our brethren."

HALLA

The walls near the entrance to the town hall bore the unmistakable signs of past scorching. Halla suspected the builders had repurposed the stone from the devastated town she had passed along the Seine.

Inside, large fires crackled within hearths at either end of the room and offered a pleasing wood smell. A series of sconces held torches that further illuminated the long table already prepared with plates and goblets. Platters contained a roasted boar, piles of bread, seasoned fish, a range of vegetables, and some hard cheese. The spread reminded her of meals in the great hall of Rouen during the cold winters.

Four additional men, whom Taurin identified as aldermen, joined them. The Christians quieted as Father Norbert babbled a few soft words and then set to work on the food without further ceremony.

Halla recoiled and raised a hand to her mouth at the revolting scene.

But Jorund was Rollo's most-trusted advisor for a reason. He cleared his throat. "Do you have a bowl with some clean water?"

Eyebrows knitted together, Taurin nodded and signaled one of the servants to produce it. The frightened man splashed some on the table as he set the bowl down before backing away.

Halla removed her belt and laid her axes behind her while the others rinsed their hands and faces. When Revna passed it to her, Halla put a little up her nose to clear the dirt thrown up by the long ride.

When she set the bowl aside, she looked up to discover the Franks were staring at her.

"What in God's name are you doing?" asked the priest in a shrill voice.

"We are cleaning our faces and hands before eating," Jorund said.

"Why would you do such a thing?"

"Why would you not?" he countered.

"Water washes away holiness and leaves the body open to sin." The priest's lip curled in disgust.

Revna smirked and turned to Halla. "Perhaps that's why the Christians fear us. Our evil use of water."

"Or because you're all murderers and villains," Orderic muttered.

Halla stiffened and glared at him. "We are not murderers."

"Those killed in your raids would claim otherwise," he continued.

"We grant them passage to meet their gods. That should be celebrated, not feared."

"That's murder," Norbert insisted.

She scowled. "Murder is a crime that denies a man of the chance for renown by defending himself. Trial by combat, battle, feuding… They are not murder. Death is merely the consequence of a choice."

"A distinction without a difference." Taurin's eyes were distant. "Inflicting death, even for just cause, is sinful."

"To your god, perhaps," Jorund said. "Ours evidently better understand the intricacies of the world."

Shrugging, Halla reached for the nearest goblet and sniffed the contents. "Wine," she reported to the others. "Skol!"

She drank deeply, appreciating the hint of cherry embedded within the spicy taste. With a satisfied sigh, she slammed the cup on the table. She hadn't enjoyed good wine since Bayeux.

Revna wiped her mouth with the back of her hand. "Where are your women?"

An elderly man with long hair choked from behind his goblet. A few drops of the red wine spilled down his chin.

Taurin leaned forward. "Most remain at our estates."

"How far away?" Jorund asked.

Taurin's eyes darted to Orderic. He leaned back and scratched his bare chin. "Within a day's ride."

Halla recalled Poppa's account of Frankish husbands. "And you keep your wife at home as well?"

His pupils dilated, and he again glanced at Orderic. Clearly, these two men were friends. "I have no wife."

Jorund flashed his knife and speared a piece of roasted boar. The sudden motion caused the closest Frank to jump and bang his knee on the table.

"We know little of the lands west of Rouen," Jorund said between bites. "How many estates are nearby?"

Orderic answered first. "A few."

Halla suspected a much larger number, based on the size of the town, but she wasn't going to let Jorund to change the subject. "Why don't you bring your women with you? Don't they enjoy coming to town?"

"I'm sure they do," Taurin answered.

"It's being ravished by heathens or bandits on the way that bothers them," Orderic muttered.

Since their arrival, this man had said nothing without scorn. If he wished to challenge them, he could at least do so openly. "Are you sure?" She pinned him with a stare. "A good ravishing might be exactly what they need."

Revna grinned. "I can attest to that."

Orderic went still. Slowly, he turned to Jorund. "Your woman's mouth is running away from her. Attend to that."

Halla gasped at Revna before bursting into laughter that began deep within her chest. Revna joined her, bracing herself on the table. The sound echoed through the hall. Tears came to her eyes before she finally stopped.

"His woman!" Halla gasped. "Do you hear that, Jorund?"

The *stallari* chuckled. "I prefer softer women."

"Soft in the head, perhaps," Revna added.

This brought another round of laughter. Beside them, the Franks squirmed.

"Silence her wagging tongue," Norbert bristled.

Halla stopped laughing and glared at the monk.

"Why?" Jorund asked with genuine surprise. "She is *hvatur*."

The others turned to Taurin, but the blue-eyed alderman shook his head helplessly. "What is *hvatur*?"

Jorund furrowed his forehead. "We divide our people by their deeds. Those who are *hvatur* are vigorous, aggressive in achieving renown for themselves. *Blaudur* is weak, reliant on others. *Hvatur* commands, *blaudur* obeys."

"But…" Father Norbert's mouth hung open like his widened eyes. "She is a woman!"

Though Poppa had explained how poorly her people treated women, the priest's words left Halla speechless. They were barbarians. She drank deeply from her goblet to occupy her mouth before she said something that would end in bloodshed.

Revna was not so quick to check herself. "You filthy—"

Jorund clamped his hand down on her forearm, halting her in mid-insult. "Gender matters not. I'd rather stand beside these women in a shield wall than a"—the hint of a scowl tugged at his lips as he eyed Norbert—"weak and fragile man incapable of guarding my back."

Into the sudden silence, Taurin reached forward with his own knife and hesitantly poked a slice of meat. "Our ways are different, and we must show some patience." Only after he had swept his gaze over the Franks did Halla realize he was addressing his own people. "Nonetheless, some topics are inappropriate for polite company."

Halla found herself admiring this strange man. His smooth movements suggested strength beneath that tunic. She began to picture the slopes and firmness of his muscles, up his arms, across his shoulders, down his chest...

Beneath the table, Revna jabbed her in the knee.

Halla cleared her throat. "Which things do you not discuss?"

"Matters of carnal relation," Blue-Eyes answered, tight-lipped.

"Among other things," Orderic muttered into his goblet. He took only a small sip.

Jorund studied the Franks. "We meant no offense." He raised his goblet. "Will you drink to friendship?"

"Is that what you desire?" Taurin challenged.

Jorund bowed his head. "It is."

He and Jorund locked eyes for the span of a deep breath before the Frank reached for his glass. "What is it you say when you drink?"

"Skol," Halla said. "A wish for the blessings of the gods."

"God," Norbert corrected as he chewed on a piece of fish.

Revna grunted.

Halla smirked, raised her goblet, and drank.

"Well, then," Taurin murmured. "Skol. And peace be with you."

Jorund smiled in smug satisfaction. Though Halla still didn't understand what Rollo hoped to gain, he'd be pleased by this start.

The nearest Frank relaxed enough to reach for the closest platter. Others joined him a moment later, but none used their knives as Taurin had. Halla suspected he had done so as a gesture to his guests.

"What are your intentions in coming here?" Orderic asked.

Halla turned to Jorund. He owed them all an answer.

The Norseman leaned back in his chair. "Before I answer, why did you welcome us into your town?" He gestured to his mail shirt. "We are obviously not traders. As he crudely said"—he pointed to Orderic—"we are warriors of Jarl Rollo's *hird*, the very people who have raided these coasts for many years."

"You speak very plainly," Taurin muttered.

"I know of no other way."

The Christian nodded. "Then I shall do the same. We could have killed you three easily enough."

Revna bristled. "Are you so certain?"

"Yes, I am." The words carried neither boast nor pride, only the mere assessment of fact. "But could we counter the full force of Rouen that would follow?" Nodding to Orderic, he added, "Even diminished as it may be from recent setbacks."

One of the aldermen rubbed his chin, clearly considering these consequences for the first time.

Halla's first, favorable impression of Taurin's intelligence hadn't done him justice. While they had eyed each other in the square, he had been contemplating months' worth of potential ramifications. This man both intrigued her and left her feeling strangely unsettled. Not even Rollo thought so far ahead.

"I welcomed you not because I forgive your brutality." Taurin raised a finger toward Norbert. "Nor because I believe in your gods."

The priest raised his chin and blessed himself.

"I did so to protect our people from further harm."

Jorund stroked his chin. "We knew the Frankish king had abandoned the lands north of the Seine, but we didn't think any towns had survived. I spoke the truth when I said Jarl Rollo wants to learn about this region."

"To plan further attacks?" Orderic asked.

Jorund turned to face him. "I already said that is not our purpose. Even if it was, we've already taken anything worth plundering."

Taurin narrowed his eyes. "Why do we interest you?"

Halla shifted to face Jorund, eager to hear the answer herself.

He looked at her for a heartbeat before returning his attention to Taurin. "This river outside… What do you call it?"

"The Bolbec."

He nodded. "Rouen lies hundreds of miles inland. The Bolbec meets the northern shore of the Seine near its mouth on Oceanus Britannicus. The warriors and traders who supply us sail past you every season. You are too well-positioned for us to know so little about you."

That was a lie, of course. Rollo had expressed curiosity about these lands and its people, not the strategic position of any settlement.

Taurin studied him. "Is that all?"

"Come to Rouen and find out. The jarl would appreciate meeting you."

Norbert gasped, while Orderic restrained himself to a look of horror.

"Excuse me?" Taurin asked.

Rollo hadn't said anything about this offer on the shores of the Seine. He and Jorund had some deeper intention than a mere scouting mission.

"Jorund…" Halla began.

He raised a hand to silence her. "You offered us hospitality. Let us return the favor." He cast his eyes around the room. "All of you are welcome."

Norbert gasped. "You would lure us into a den of heathens."

Jorund raised an eyebrow. "I invite you to learn more about your neighbors."

A rapid sequence of emotions passed over Taurin's face as he gnawed at his lip. The offer clearly tempted him. Was it because of the Norse slave his father had owned in his youth, or something deeper?

Halla only wished she understood why Jorund had proposed it. Why did Rollo care about these farmers?

"It's a trick," Orderic hissed.

"What would we gain by deception?" Jorund asked. "Rollo knows of your town."

Halla restrained her surprise at the lie. He was trying mightily to persuade them.

He continued, "If we wished to destroy you, nothing could stop us."

"You will enslave us once we reach your city," Orderic insisted.

Halla made a warding gesture in front of her face. "Such deception is the vilest treachery."

"Your people have lied many times in the past," Orderic maintained.

"But not when extending hospitality." Jorund said. "Consider my offer. We trusted our lives to your courtesy. Are you brave enough to do the same?"

TAURIN

Taurin marveled at the additional questions the Northmen asked during dinner. Not once did Jorund, who had revealed himself as Jarl Rollo's closest advisor, inquire about precious items or abbeys. Instead, he asked about the town's influence and interactions with other communities. He pressed them about the lawless wilderness between towns and how they dispensed justice. They were not the questions of a barbarian raider, but of a man interested in their way of life.

But while his curiosity justified Taurin's decision not to kill them, a doubt lingered. Why did a heathen whose livelihood rested on plunder and theft care about their crop yield or where they found eligible spouses?

His thoughts dwelled on Arbogast. Like the Northmen, he had attacked his neighbors because he could. If others followed Arbogast's example, the careful order the aldermen had preserved through decades of isolation could crumble.

As the Northmen prepared to depart for Rouen, Taurin wondered whether the Franks who surrounded them might influence the heathens, as well. The future of their town might rest upon that possibility. So, rather than fear their return, Taurin prepared his own mount to accompany them. His steward, Leubin, could manage his estate for some time, and the aldermen would have to assess the damage from Arbogast's raids before punishing him. That would take weeks.

He swallowed a wave of apprehension. If he didn't return by then, he wouldn't return at all.

Orderic huddled close. "If I can't convince you to see sense, at least take my wishes for your safety."

"Come with me," he invited. "You heard their questions. Frequency of our prayers? How we distribute information to the estates? This Rollo has a plan."

"I suppose..." Orderic frowned. "But what do you hope to learn?"

"At the very least, how much danger we face. We could be worrying for nothing if Berengar annihilated them. But if he didn't—"

"Then find out the truth." Eyes dancing, Orderic studied the Northmen as they checked their mounts. "And if their women are so free with themselves, perhaps you can learn what lies beneath that armor, as well."

"Orderic!" His eyes flew to Halla, the flare of her hips, the slopes of her breasts, not quite constrained by her mail coat. His face flushed with embarrassment. But he couldn't tear his eyes away when Halla bent over to check her horse's hooves.

"Come now, my friend. Your betrothal died with my sister." Orderic crossed himself. "Isn't it time you enjoyed the feel of a woman? And you'll offend no fathers by bedding a heathen."

He forced himself to look away when his groin began to stir. "It's not a father I fear, but the hundreds these three represent."

"My thumb senses trouble, too." Orderic flexed his fingers to a faint cracking sound. "Be careful. I don't want to lose you."

"As always." Taurin embraced him. "I'll do my best to preserve us."

Taurin crossed to the bay mare he preferred when traveling from his estate in the west, with Orderic following.

"Hello, Seraphim." He patted the horse on its shoulder. Hopefully, she wouldn't mind a longer journey this time.

"Do you trust their promise of safe passage?" Orderic asked.

His travel companions glanced at him as they whispered together. These strangers knew nothing of civilized behavior. They spoke publicly of sexual acts, exposed themselves to sin with excessive washing, and justified murder. They were brutish and crude.

But Arbogast, a friend and careful landlord, had stolen from his neighbors and tenants, not strangers as the Northmen had.

"They trusted in our hospitality enough to abandon their weapons at dinner and drink enough to fall over. I believe they will hold to their word."

He refused to believe the world was hopelessly sliding into ruin. Even the heathens had to hold something sacred.

CHAPTER THREE

HALLA

THEY RODE ALONG the bank of the Seine through the day, stopping only when the light began to fade. Taurin set off to cast a fishing line along the river while the Norse prepared camp for the night. Halla had just ignited the first flames of the campfire when Jorund approached with Revna.

Studying Taurin in the distance as he placed a salmon on the ground and reset his line, Jorund whispered to the women, "Talk to him. Find out what he and his people think of us."

Revna sighed. "Haven't you learned enough?"

"About the land, but not his people. He's growing suspicious of my questions. You two might have more luck."

Halla bent to stoke the rudimentary flames when they dimmed. She tended them until they spread to another branch. "Why won't you tell us Rollo's intentions?"

"The jarl will explain when he's ready. But he needs to know how these people will react to seeing us every day."

Halla wrinkled her nose. Perhaps he intended to use the town as a staging area for future attacks against Berengar. Starting a raid

45

at Lillebonne instead of Rouen would give Breton spies less time to report their movements.

Shrugging, Revna squeezed Halla's hand. "I hope Freya is listening."

Halla grinned, recalling the last time Revna had tried to make new friends. She had started a brawl that had broken a few ribs and one of Rollo's feasting tables.

Her friend returned a scant few moments later amid a string of curses. "You deal with him. I don't understand these Franks." She would say no more, but Taurin didn't look at her even once when he returned a short time later with half a dozen fish.

The next day, as the party rode through an overgrown field, Halla fell back to join him. She shifted her mail away from her wound to relieve some of the discomfort. Though it was starting to heal, itching had replaced the pain.

He gave her a curt nod.

How should she approach him? She couldn't command him to obey as she'd done with Franks in the past. Nor could she threaten to harm him. Only consenting to a duel or committing a crime would cancel the jarl's protection.

"I'm impressed by your skill with a fishing line."

He grunted. "For a Christian, you mean?"

She arched an eyebrow. "I didn't realize fish took notice of a fisherman's beliefs."

He gestured roughly toward Revna, riding beside Jorund some distance ahead. "Your friend disagrees."

Halla chuckled as she imagined the flow of the previous day's conversation by the shore. "I wondered why she returned so quickly."

He raised an eyebrow. "She has a talent for insults."

"She doesn't really impress until after a night of mead." Halla laughed again as she recalled a particularly naughty night from before the army had left for the Bessin.

Still in profile, Taurin cracked a smile. Well-worn creases at the corners of his mouth suggested frequent laughter. She had never met a man with such soft lips. She wondered what it would feel like to run a finger over them.

Her horse shifted at a sudden tensing of her thighs, and Halla soothed it with a pat. "We ate well because of you. Do you fish on your lands?"

He shook his head. "My estate is far from the river, but all men should know how to find their own food."

"Words everyone should live by."

"And yet, few do." His words came quickly and with too much passion. A disagreement among his people, perhaps?

"On your estate, do you use a three-crop or a two-crop rotation?"

He turned in surprise, stirring his horse. "You have an interest in farming?"

"Not particularly, but my people know more than raiding."

"Really?" He adjusted his grip on the reins. "That's all we hear about."

She would remember that fact for Jorund. "Our warriors raid after planting their crops. Most of us know how to farm or fish, as well as how to trade."

"That explains why we only hear of attacks in the late spring and summer." Taurin nodded slowly. "I always wondered why so many ships sailed west in the fall."

"They're returning home with their plunder."

"Where do your people come from?"

"Danes, Geats, Swedes, Norwegians… We have many northern tribes, but we all speak Norse and honor the gods."

"Which tribe is yours?"

"I am a Dane, as are Jorund and Revna. Some among us, like Rollo, are Norwegians. None among his *hird* are Swedes or Geats."

He lowered his eyes. "So everything looted from our town is long gone, to many different lands."

His words carried an edge of sorrow. Never before had Halla wasted a thought on those too weak to defend their wealth.

"Some, but many sell their share to traders in Rouen before leaving for home." When he remained silent for some time, she noted, "This seems to bother you."

He turned to the river. Their track took them close enough to hear the bubbling of the water near the shore. "I wonder how many houses in Rouen contain treasures from Lillebonne."

"A fair few, I wager."

He faced her again. "I admire your honesty."

"I have no reason to lie." The vivid blue of his eyes threatened to swallow her. Warmth spread over her cheeks. "I wouldn't repay hospitality with deception."

"I'm relieved to hear that." He swallowed, and for a moment his gaze dipped.

To her mail coat? Or was he, a Christian among dreaded Norsemen, actually stealing a glimpse at her breasts?

The thought excited her. All during the night, she had debated how best to carry out Jorund's instructions. After their icy reception, she hadn't even considered seducing him. Perhaps Christians could act like men, after all.

The untended field gave way to a stand of trees that narrowed the path and forced them closer. Their horses sniffed at each other as they traversed the uneven ground. Taurin controlled his mount with admirable skill, but her horse reared as it brushed against Taurin's mare.

Distracted by thoughts of her companion, she lost her balance. Casting a desperate hand out, she grasped something firm and sturdy enough to prevent her fall. At first, she thought she had found the neck of Taurin's horse. But once she stabilized her seat, she turned to find her hand wrapped around Taurin's upper thigh.

And her fingers were grazing a growing bulge between his legs.

She withdrew and stared ahead, repressing a smile. She was right; his loose clothing did conceal firm muscles, all the way up. This was no weak Christian, but a virile man in every way except his bare chin.

Taurin soothed her horse with whispered words. Stealing a glance, she noticed a distinct reddening of his cheeks. He was blushing.

She felt a desperate need to comprehend this strange man. "Why did you accept our invitation?"

The blood drained from his cheeks and banished his blush. They had passed beyond the stand of trees before he answered. "What do you know of the Pays de Caux?"

The sudden formality triggered a pang of regret. She had never bedded a Christian before, and it seemed she wouldn't do so now, either. "I know the abbeys at Fontenelle, Montivilliers, Fecamp, and Wandrille."

He gave a long, hissing sigh. "All are gone, as are our bishoprics, many of our towns, and the great estates of the counts and dukes." He turned to meet her eyes. "Pillaged, burned, or abandoned for more defensible areas."

"You and the other landowners did not claim them?"

"We already have enough land to keep us busy. Why cultivate lands we must surrender if the nobles return?"

"We passed the ruins of a town when we arrived." She recalled the overgrown square, the pots and chests strewn across the streets.

His jaw tightened. "That was our original settlement. The first time Northmen visited, hundreds died or were taken." His voice sounded husky. "We have nothing left for you to steal. Even the emperor's agents don't consider us worth visiting."

If he was waiting for her to express Christian regret, she would disappoint him. "You showed us around your town so we could see that with our own eyes."

He shifted his weight. "You'd never trust my words alone."

He was right.

They emerged into another field. This one showed signs of cultivation. Fields of wheat grew high, nearly ready for reaping. Halla smiled as a breeze rippled over the stalks and shook them in flowing waves.

Taurin called his horse to a stop and jutted his chin at the blackened stone ruins of a crumbling manor, engulfed in wild grasses poking out of the horizon. "My great-grandmother's family built that manor. It burned in one night." He lowered his eyes. "Beyond a day's ride from Lillebonne is a lawless wilderness of abandoned lands like these. We're so close to being swallowed up by desolation."

Building a manor house like that would require much more work than the thatch homes in Denmark. Where would one even find enough stone? Losing it must have been ruinous. "Yet you rebuilt. I would have left."

He shrugged. "That wasn't an option."

Jorund cast a questioning look from up ahead, but she waved him off. "Why not?"

"Travel is too dangerous for trade, so our estates grow only what we need. If we migrated, we'd have very little to sell for food or supplies."

She could see the sense in that judgment. Very little in his town would interest a raiding party. The townsfolk would make useful slaves, but she suspected the Christians wouldn't sell their own people.

He straightened his tunic. "My father and mother are buried in the graveyard by the old town. I'm part of this land. My blood is in the stone of my house and each strip of field."

He was strong and could earn great wealth as a warrior. Yet, he remained in the wilderness, alone and unknown. What a waste. "Estates are a weakness. They encourage raiders."

"But a home you can pass on to your descendants is the only legacy that endures."

He was wrong, of course. Stone crumbled, crops failed, and wealth went to the strong. Only fame from impressive deeds worthy of the skalds endured. But arguing would only stop his tongue.

"And so you travel to a Norse city to avoid further raids?"

"Something like that."

Despite Taurin's prior confidence, she was certain her companions would have defeated the townsfolk in a battle. They had risked very little by introducing themselves. But Taurin was walking into danger alone, with no hope of escape. What loyalty could compel a man to do such a thing?

"That is a brave act."

"Braver than you expect from a Frank?"

She laughed. How could Revna not appreciate his tongue? She wondered whether it had other uses. "Something like that."

His eyes danced at the familiar words. "I've been assured of safety, haven't I?" He goaded his horse to walk again.

She fell into stride beside him. "Christians don't trust us."

"Trust is difficult."

"And yet you're here."

"You invited many more of us," he reminded.

"So we did." She turned again to the field and the rippling wheat. "I wonder if I could ever live as you do, tied to farm and land."

"Do you have no home?"

"Rouen is my home," she answered more sharply than she'd intended. "I'm a member of Rollo's *hird*."

He looked at her without understanding.

"We are his personal guard and stay with him throughout the year."

"Ah." His eyes fell to her mail.

A flare of anger narrowed her eyes. "Does a jarl trusting a woman with his protection offend you?" Poppa's assessment of her prospects among Frankish men flooded her mind.

He shrugged. "Your ways are different. Who am I to judge?" Again, his eyes lowered, but now they carried something hungry and primal.

She rubbed her fingers along the reins, recalling the feel of his thigh. "You did not answer my question."

"I suppose I didn't." His lips creased in an impish smile. "No, your being a warrior does not offend me."

She noticed no facial ticks, no wandering eyes, no clenched jaw muscles to indicate deception. "Your friend Orderic and your monk would disagree."

"Priest, actually."

"Is there a difference?"

He considered briefly before shaking his head. "They fear the influence of your ways. They fear your people will corrupt what they couldn't destroy. Turn us into you."

"And you do not?"

He shrugged. "Perhaps a little change is useful. Our ways left us unprepared for your arrival fifty years ago. Our traditions should preserve us, not lead to our ruin."

She wondered how he'd react to learning he sounded just like Rollo.

They rode along for some while in silence. The path swung north with the curve of the great river. A group of farmers watched them from a hill far to the north for a few moments before disappearing down the far side.

"You aren't what I expected," she admitted.

He arched an eyebrow. "How so?"

She adjusted her posture to relieve an ache in her leg. "We think of Christians as simple-minded and easily fooled."

His smile filled his entire face.

"This pleases you?"

"It's not that." He chuckled. "We think of you as brutish heathens who slaughter priests and eat Christian babies."

She supposed that was the way of things. "Well, you aren't simple."

He inclined his head at the compliment, but his eyes again swept across her shoulders, her chest, her hips. "And you are in no way brutish."

Reddening, she raised a hand to check her braids. "Perhaps our people can learn to live together." Her voice came out with a faint purr noticeable even to her own ears.

He inhaled as if to speak, but subsided in silence. Instead, he gazed at her without judgment or offense. She doubted his abandoned words would offer anything of value for Jorund, but she hungered for them, nonetheless.

After several dozen steps, he finally answered. "I can't speak for all my people, but I think I could."

She only realized she was smiling when she saw the delight reflected in his face. She felt strangely at ease with this Christian. Why did Revna find him so insufferable? He exuded an alluring confidence that reminded her of any Danish or Norwegian warrior.

Her smile faded. That comparison filled her with a strange unease she didn't quite understand.

TAURIN

They arrived at Rouen, nestled among gentle hills and wide fields on the northern shore of the Seine, as the evening sun faded on the third day. Orange light reflected off the river and cast the stone walls encircling the city in a fiery glow. Candlelight peeked out from the windows of hundreds of buildings, occasionally blocked by passing figures.

As a boy, Taurin had thought himself fortunate to live in one of the largest surviving estates for miles around. The first time he'd come to town, he'd been amazed by so many living and trading within its boundaries. But Rouen was beyond his reckoning. Thousands could live here in comfort.

His people could never resist so many.

Along the river, dozens of ships hugged the wooden docks covering the city's waterfront. Some resembled the fishing boats working the Bolbec, while others boasted high sides, triangular sails, or long prows unlike any vessel he'd seen before. Their owners must come from distant lands, indeed.

A pair of vessels—Norse in design but with wider beams—began to sail downriver toward the ocean. A part of Taurin longed to follow them to the comfort and security of home. But he had come to this heathen city for a reason. He patted Seraphim's neck, thankful at least for her familiar presence.

Even at this late hour, carts and travelers entered through the western gate. Two dozen long-haired and braided mail-clad warriors searched the arrivals, letting them pass once they had deposited coins in a massive chest.

Halla sidled closer. Ever since their conversation, she had become his guide to all things Norse. In fact, she had explained they referred to themselves as Norse, not Northmen.

She gestured at the chest. "Travelers pay arrival fees. Rollo taxes all imported goods."

Considering the size of that chest, he now understood her surprise that his people would choose to rebuild. Rollo's wealth came not from the land, but from commerce and the passage of traders.

"I didn't bring anything of value."

She smirked. "No need. You are a guest of the jarl."

The guards greeted Jorund with a rousing cheer as the party passed through the thick wooden gates and onto the main street. Halla and Jorund exchanged a surprised glance whose meaning eluded Taurin.

They dismounted at a stable just inside the walls. As Taurin removed the rolled blanket holding his extra provisions, tent poles, and fishing line, Halla gave instructions to a stable boy to keep his horse in a separate stall. He followed Halla reluctantly, neck twisting to watch Seraphim until the boy led her out of sight.

He was alone.

Jorund led them down the main road, saluting time and again to acknowledge cordial greetings. As the crowd shifted, Taurin caught his breath as he glimpsed the full length of the street.

Pine and ash market stalls crowded the sides of every building on both sides of the street as far as he could see. A riot of colorful canopies held aloft on wooden supports shaded the hundreds of traders and customers. As they walked, the group passed baskets and troughs and trays of endless variety. Wine, perfumes, silver goblets, knives, flour, wool, iron ingots, copper pots, lengths of cloth, cooking supplies, a thousand kinds of food, and a dozen different spices he couldn't identify... His head spun at the sight of so many magnificent and exotic things.

Beside him, Halla asked, "Is it as you expected?"

"Beyond imagining." he breathed, head twisting to absorb it all. "Where are they from?" He pointed to a group of traders wearing trousers beneath brightly colored *dalmatica* tunics and large muslin capes.

"Byzantium, far to the east." She pointed at a trio of dark-skinned men in colorful robes and hats that seemed to wrap around their heads a dozen times. "Moors from Al-Andalus. They have yet another god from yours." Another group approached the Moors. "And Spaniards greeting them."

"Spaniards?" He recalled his tales of Charlemagne. "Don't they hate the Moors?"

Halla shrugged. "Not here, they don't."

Taurin had never expected to meet someone from Rouen, let alone from halfway across the world. Wonder tangled with outrage. While Lillebonne had barely survived the past fifty years, Norse-controlled Rouen had absorbed the wealth of a region. Why should his people remain isolated while those who had inflicted this misery traded with distant lands?

Hearing a few Frankish words, he wheeled around to find the source. He almost struck Halla with his elbow, but she dodged it with remarkable agility. Two stalls down, a Norseman argued with a farmer in a rough wool tunic and trousers over the price of a scythe. Though the conversation grew heated, Taurin saw only anger in the farmer's eyes, not fear.

"Franks live here?"

She followed his gaze. "Mostly tradesmen. Weavers, blacksmiths, carpenters, carters. A few farmers risked returning after we claimed the city." She tugged his arm. "Come."

Picking her way through the crowd, Halla led him to a massive stone building that reminded him of a Frankish keep. It bore scorching from fire and the smoothing of erosion. Taurin suspected it predated the Norsemen themselves. The sounds of a very loud gathering spilled out of the main entrance, along with the intermittently broken light of a large fire. Small groups of laughing men lingered near the entrance.

"We've returned in the middle of a feast celebrating the campaign," she chirped.

The building didn't seem so jovial anymore. They were celebrating Christian deaths.

"That's fortunate timing," he offered through a dry mouth.

"Not really. Our feasts last several days. This one will probably be on the longer side."

"Why do you say that?"

But Halla only gestured to his pack. "You can bring that inside. You'll sleep in one of the side rooms tonight."

"And after?"

"That depends on Rollo." Placing a hand on his shoulder, she led him into the hall.

A wave of heat struck him as they entered through a door along one of the wide sides. In addition to the large fire in the center of the room, hearths anchored each end of the hall. Bearded Norsemen in dyed woolen tunics and breeches pressed in on all sides. Nearly all were drunk or on their way to it. Yet they laughed with perfect contentment, gesturing wildly and spilling their drinks on each other without taking any noticeable offense.

Yet, it was their composition that amazed Taurin. Nearly half the assembled revelers were women. Dressed in linen shifts with woolen aprons attached by intricately carved bronze or silver broaches, they laughed as heartily and imbibed with the same reckless abandon as the men.

Taurin suspected those broaches could easily unfasten to expose breasts and enable every kind of debauchery, yet he saw nothing of the sort. These men and women drank together in perfect harmony and decorum. Where was the orgiastic lust and wanton lasciviousness in Father Norbert's sermons? The parade of flesh and debauchery that everyone knew Norsemen practiced?

And then he noticed the scents. Aromas of roasting meat and cooked vegetables battled with seared fish and strong wine. Yet he could smell nothing at all of the many bodies packed so closely together, as if they had all bathed this morning.

Of course, that was absurd.

"Skol!" The salute came from the other end of the hall.

As everyone joined in, the cry reverberated in his ears. For a moment, the room fell quiet as goblets and cups and drinking horns met lips. Briefly, he heard the plucking of a lyre. When they finished guzzling, the noise rose even louder.

"The jarl's been busy," Halla murmured.

"I don't understand."

She shook her head. "Nothing."

Beside him, one man urinated along the wall until two others dragged him roughly past Taurin and threw him outside. When they returned, they were laughing.

"—better than to do that in here," one muttered, slapping Taurin cheerfully on the shoulder as he passed.

The force of their greeting propelled him forward a step. Straightening, he turned to see Halla laughing at him. She didn't even bother to hide it.

Removing and slinging her cloak over her shoulder, she leaned toward him. A sweet and fresh aroma tickled his nostrils. Was that the scent of her skin, beneath the earthiness of the long ride?

"Follow me." Her cool breath tickled his ear and sent a tantalizing chill down his back.

She led him down the left side of the hall. Every man and woman they passed greeted her before eyeing him. He forced himself to meet their gaze for as long as he could. They were judging his worth, assessing his position. Now was no time for meekness.

They approached a large walnut chair at the back of the hall. Carved ravens sat atop the high back on either side. Within sat a man in a tunic edged with an intricate knot pattern made of gold thread. A matching gold chain hung around his neck. This had to be Jarl Rollo.

Though he sat, his head of slicked-back hair rested squarely between the ravens. Taurin had thought Jorund a mighty man, but Rollo's chest and arms were thicker than the arms of the chair itself.

And yet, this imposing man's face brightened like a child when he recognized his absent friends. Rising, he chortled and surrounded first Revna, then Jorund in his broad arms.

"Have something to eat and drink," Halla instructed Taurin. "Don't challenge anyone to a fight and you'll probably be fine."

His stomach churned. "Probably?"

She waved a hand and began to walk away. "You'll be fine."

He watched her follow Rollo and Jorund to a room behind the throne with regret. After their pleasing conversations on the ride, he felt at least comfortable with her. But she was still a heathen and might well enjoy tossing Christian babies onto rocks for entertainment.

Taurin felt suddenly exposed. He cast his eyes around for a friendly Frank, but the moving sea of bodies wore Norse aprons or braids or beards. If Rollo disagreed with his *stallari's* offer of hospitality, Taurin would be at their mercy. He reared back from the shifting crowd of far too many heathens. Fumbling beneath his tunic, he clasped the cross hanging around his neck.

Home smelled of fish, smoke, and wildflowers, far different from the perfumes and dominating aroma of roasting meat here. His mouth watered even as his stomach threatened to churn at such overpoweringly foreign smells.

A man rose from the table to refill his goblet. As he stepped aside, Taurin saw a blond-haired woman in the distance behind him. She wore no apron or broaches, but rather a long blue dress partly concealed by a charcoal gray *chlamys* cloak pinned at the left shoulder.

Frankish clothing.

Delighted, Taurin circled Rollo's empty throne and picked his way toward her.

Noticing his approach, she glared and charged toward him. He barely had time to execute a bow before she clasped his arm with a surprisingly tight grip.

"I'm not going back," she hissed as she pulled him away from the table. "Tell my father to leave me be. Go before they discover your intentions."

"Who are you?" He pulled his arm free. "What do you mean by this?"

The woman eyed him. "Don't you work for my father?"

"I work for no one. I am Taurin of Lillebonne. I came with three Northmen who visited my town a week past."

Her eyes widened. "The town to the west." Her shoulders relaxed. "Forgive me. Franks don't attend our feasts. I thought…" She shook her head. "It is no matter."

"Who are you?"

The woman straightened her hair and inhaled a calming breath. "Poppa of Rennes, though here I am Poppa of Bayeux, since I was taken from that city last year."

"Rennes…" He narrowed his eyes. "Are you Count Berengar's daughter?"

She drew her lips tight and offered a polite curtsey.

"But, Bayeux fell last year. Have you been a prisoner this whole time?" He considered this woman's fine Frankish clothing and soft skin. She was no slave laboring for the Norse.

"Not exactly a prisoner." Her lips curled into a smirk. "And I only just arrived here. I was with the army."

Taurin gasped, mind swirling with the shameful acts a heathen army would inflict on a Frankish woman.

"Oh, nothing like that." She crossed herself. The gesture offered a soothing familiarity amid so much strangeness. "Rollo would never allow that to happen."

Taurin searched her face for several moments before realizing her meaning. "You…and he?"

Her eyes danced despite her blush. "Indeed!"

He took a step back. Frankish women did not act thusly, especially with heathens. She should be at home, safe and secure from their corrupting depredations, not attending a feast celebrating Christian deaths.

He eyed the celebrating Norsemen. Could he blame her for attaching herself to the jarl if the alternative was rape and slavery? He had only just arrived, and already he felt lost and uneasy. What would he do after spending a year with them, as Poppa had? He had no right to judge her decisions. Already, he faced some difficult ones of his own.

"They know about my town."

She folded her hands over her waist. "I was there when Rollo ordered them to investigate it."

Rollo's feelings for this Frankish woman might very well have led to the visit of those three Northmen. He lowered his voice. "From one Christian to another, can I trust them?"

Poppa drew her lips tight and guided him farther from the crowds, almost to the wall. "No more than you can trust all Christians."

Taurin thought back to Arbogast, raiding his neighbors.

"But you can trust Rollo. He has never forced anything upon me. He loves me."

He could not conceive of such a thing. These people felt no guilt at massacring good Christians. He would never understand them. His own guilt over the death he had caused still gnawed at him.

"Do you love him?"

"I do." Her lips curled into a smile as she glanced at the throne.

"And Jorund?"

She barked a laugh. "I do not love him."

He scoffed, in no mood for humor. "Can I trust him?"

She sobered and clasped her hands together. "He would do anything for Rollo, including any sort of crime or horror."

Taurin nodded slowly. "And Halla?" His voice sounded huskier than usual.

Poppa raised an eyebrow. "She is a dear friend."

"Friend…" He had never imagined a Christian woman could befriend a Norse shieldmaiden or love the jarl of a stolen city. And yet, the woman who had guided him here to Rouen was no heathen demon. She spoke with a thoughtfulness Norbert's sermons said was impossible. She had killed Franks, yes, but those same Franks would have enjoyed nothing more than seeing her and her kind dead.

Well, not the Frankish woman before him. "Forgive me, but if you love him, how can I trust your words?"

Her lips dimpled into a wry smile, but she showed no signs of taking offense. "I have some personal interest in peaceful relations between Frank and Dane." Her gaze shifted to somewhere beyond him. "But I must go. I have work."

"Work?" Perhaps she was a slave, after all.

"Rollo must know the thoughts of his people. They'll share with me what they don't share with him." She curtseyed again. "It was a pleasure to meet you, Taurin. Have some mead. It will calm your nerves."

She glided across the room, deftly circling flailing limbs and laughing feasters. More than a few men and women saluted her with a raised goblet. They might have captured her at Bayeux, but she was no prisoner in Rouen.

He reached for an abandoned goblet on the table. Sniffing the contents, he offered a silent salute to Poppa's receding back and took a sip. He winced at the sickening sweetness and intensity of alcohol. It tasted flat compared to the rich bouquet of the wine from home. Mead was a dreadful drink for a violent people.

Stomach growling, he approached some carved boar fanned out on the table closest to him. As he reached for a piece, a knife flashed and stabbed the meat, narrowly missing his fingers. Recoiling, he turned to confront a grinning man with a braided beard.

"Watch out," the man spat in Norse, "or we'll be eating parts of you tonight."

He had forgotten to use his knife. Thinking quickly, he curled a lip. "I don't recommend that. Christians are stringy." The man gawked as he flashed his own knife and speared a slice. The riot of flavor tasted of foreign spices, but in a way that pleased his tongue. Someone here was a master cook. "And this really is delicious."

The man cackled and clasped him about the back of the head. Taurin twisted to free himself in growing panic. No, by God, not like this…

"Skol!" He jumped at the clang of the Norseman's goblet striking his own. Mead spilled onto his sleeve and began to soak into the fabric as he pulled free.

Taurin steadied himself with a hand on his chest and a few deep breaths. Feeling the Norseman's eyes upon him, he forced enough of the sweet mead down his throat to satisfy his new companion.

Barking a laugh, the man dragged him away to introduce him to a group of six Norsemen. There, he drank again, and not for the last time that night.

HALLA

The sounds of the feast carried through the stone walls of the antechamber Rollo used for planning his raids, but Halla hardly needed to scrutinize his every word to realize her jarl had no intention of sharing his plans. Dismissed after revealing her discoveries about Taurin and his people, Halla sighed and left Jorund and Rollo to scheme privately.

Despite the roiling of the thick crowd, Halla had no trouble spotting Taurin by the wild boar. His clean-shaven face reflected the light like polished metal. A group of Jarl Sigrun's Norwegian farmers were laughing heartily at something he had said.

He clearly needed no rescue.

Revna approached and extended a goblet. "You need this."

"Gods, yes." Her tongue danced at the sweet Danish mead she preferred, rather than the exotic Norwegian variety that Rollo usually served. She smiled her thanks. "Skol." She drained the goblet before wiping a drop off her chin with the back of her hand. She looked behind her. "What's Rollo planning?"

"Stop fretting." Revna smirked. "Why worry about tomorrow?"

Halla sipped again, but the mead did nothing to loosen the gnawing concern in the pit of her stomach. "Doesn't it bother you? If not for Taurin, we'd have had to fight our way out of that town."

"Taurin." The single word dripped with annoyance. "Do you trust Rollo?"

Rollo seemed to recognize the importance of the attack on the Vire, albeit for his own reasons. "I do."

"Then let him do the fretting." Revna looped her arm around Halla's and led her toward the crowd. "Don't ruin this feast with your pouting, as alluring as it may be." With a wink, she pinched Halla's lip.

They walked arm in arm along the wall. A few Danes who had wintered with the army in the Cotentin leered as they passed, their thoughts written in their hungry eyes. She ignored them and instead glanced at Taurin. She could still recall the firmness of the parcel between his legs.

Distracted, she stumbled out of stride with Revna and hurried to catch up. Why was she thinking of the Christian when she really wanted a belly full of meat and a few goblets of mead?

Bjornolf waved from a spot in the corner. Beside him, Oleg and Jarl Sigrun were singing about Thor dressing as Freya to recover his hammer from the jotuns. As the women approached, the men finished the final few lines:

> When the hard-souled one his hammer beheld;
> First Thrym, the king of the giants, he killed,
> Then all the folk of the giants he felled.
> The giant's sister, old, he slew,
> She who had begged the bridal fee;
> A stroke she got in the shilling's stead,
> And for many rings the might of the hammer.
> And so his hammer got Odin's son.

"Skol!" Sigrun cried.

Laughing, they raised their goblets. Their smiles caused mead to dribble down their chins, which provoked another round of laughter.

While they cleaned and composed themselves, Halla cast her eyes around the room. She saw no signs of anger or mistrust, no undercurrent of unease. Sigrun drank and laughed with contentment despite the loss of his ships. Rollo had evidently calmed the discontent from the Vire.

That wasn't surprising, she supposed. He had won his fellow raiders over twice before: first when they had elected him jarl and again after the humiliation at Paris four years earlier.

"Fair shieldmaidens, you return to us from heathen lands." Bjornolf rested an affectionate hand on Revna's arm. "Tell us of the Christians you slew."

"No loot this trip," Revna muttered, "though a few deserved to meet my sword."

"Well, you've earned plenty from the past year," Bjornolf continued. "Rollo divided his share among his *hirdmen*."

It was an unfathomably generous offer; Halla's share would almost be enough to buy a longboat of her own. No wonder his people celebrated.

"That's news worth drinking to," Revna said. "I'm glad I didn't complain about visiting those Christians."

"Too much, you mean," Halla corrected with a wink.

Revna grunted. "Yes, well, I can't imagine how you dealt with that insufferable man for three days."

As Oleg asked Revna about Lillebonne, Bjornolf turned to Halla. "How is the wound?" The words carried genuine concern, lacking the annoyance from the march.

"It itches, but it heals."

He frowned. "I acted poorly the last time we spoke."

She had never known Bjornolf to apologize.

Halla gave a curt nod, and he did the same. No bad blood would remain for his gruffness. As *hirdmen*, they needed to trust each other with their lives.

"—lost their sense when they realized we weren't Jorund's women," Revna finished with a laugh.

"Well, I can't blame them," Sigrun said.

"What does that mean?" Revna demanded.

The jarl smirked. "They're not used to seeing real women, only the docile things they beget." Chuckles spread through the group.

Revna took a drink. "They spend so much time around their livestock they start to resemble them." That brought a fresh laugh from the group. "I need to bathe after three days with them."

Bjornolf grinned. "You really do."

Revna shoved him, but her eyes carried mirth. Halla suspected they'd continue that exchange later in private.

"You both do," he added, including Halla in a wave of his hand.

Halla could smell the long ride sticking to her. "Perhaps we will, after the feast." She ran a hand along Revna's arm. When the men fell into an awed silence, the women tilted their heads back and cackled, drawing the attention of a few others nearby.

Sigrun grinned. "Perhaps I'll join you."

"We did tell them Frankish women might benefit from some time with Norse men," Revna said.

Another round of laughter sprinkled through the group, more easily this time.

Oleg raised a hand. "In fairness, they can be cunning traders."

"I doubt that." Bjornolf grunted. "They always fall for our tricks."

Sigrun's eyes narrowed. "Almost always."

"Ask Halla," Revna said. "She spent more time around the one we brought with us than either Jorund or I."

Halla resisted the urge to find Taurin in the crowd as the others gave her their attention. "Their stories describe us as demons."

Bjornolf beamed. "They tell stories of us!"

"Demons?" Sigrun asked.

"Like jotuns or the children of Loki." Halla continued, "They know how far the Franks range, but haven't traveled past the nearest towns in many years. They know little of us." She recalled the burned farmhouse. "They live among the relics of the past. They know how to endure."

"If they fear us, why did Berengar attack?" Sigrun asked.

Laughter bubbled up again from a nearby group of women listening to a warrior's particularly raunchy poem.

Now she did jut her chin in Taurin's direction. "That one knows more about us than the others. He came with us, though his neighbors did not. Knowledge cures fear, as the All-Father teaches." She gestured reverently around her face.

Bjornolf did the same a moment later. "Then we'll have to teach them fear again." He gave a feral grin.

"Or make them a better offer," Oleg suggested.

Halla thought she detected hints of a deeper meaning in his expression, but it vanished before she could be certain.

Rubbing her eyes, she recognized the first signs of intoxication from the mead. She had spent too much time around Franks this past week. She needed some food, the company of her people, and a good bath. Then, everything would return to normal.

CHAPTER FOUR

TAURIN

TWO DAYS LATER, Rollo gathered his *hird* and the jarls who had joined the year's raids. While Taurin's exploration of Rouen had confirmed that Rollo suffered losses on the Vire, the jarl still commanded more than enough warriors to flatten Lillebonne.

The great hall had changed since the end of the feast. Rollo's thralls had removed the tables and cleaned the shattered goblets, spilled mead, and rotting meat. Over a hundred men and women had already assembled when Taurin entered. No one carried axe or sword, but knives dangled from nearly every belt. The men Taurin had feasted with stood with their jarl, a man named Sigrun who matched the fearsome description of marauding barbarians he'd heard since childhood. Hushed chatter contained an undercurrent of excitement.

When he'd issued the invitation to this meeting, Jorund had given the distinct impression that these assemblies rarely happened so late in the year. His invitation worried him. It suggested Rollo had more than a passing interest in his town.

In the front of the crowd, Halla stood beside Revna and two of the men she had conversed with at the feast. She had removed her net of braids. Now, her hair, bound by a simple copper ring, cascaded over one shoulder. In place of her mail shirt and leather breeches, she wore a white shift with a pale red apron held by a pair of silver brooches shaped like wolf heads.

That shift clung to her curves in the most alluring way. To muster the strength to look away, he had to remind himself she'd intended to kill him the first time they met.

In fact, everyone around him would probably prefer to kill him. He was alone in an unholy place. He placed a hand to his chest to feel the comforting cross beneath his tunic.

Jorund waved him over from a trio of chairs beside the outer wall. Poppa sat in the first, picking at the edge of her *chlamys*. Her eyes darted back and forth, a stark contrast to her previous poise.

"My lady, are you well?" He seated himself on the chair Jorund indicated.

"Only a little anxious." She drew her lips into a tight smile.

Breath quickening, he scoured the room for a hidden threat, a hostile gaze. Only now did he realize he and Poppa occupied two of only three chairs in the room, excepting Rollo's throne. Rollo was deliberately singling them out.

"Anxious?" he whispered. "About what?"

Jorund settled next to him in the last chair.

Poppa met the Norseman's eyes before promising, "You'll see."

"What in God's name does that—"

Rollo thumped the arm of his chair three times, silencing the chatter and drawing the crowd's attention. His imposing frame dwarfed the throne itself when he stood. "These past two raiding seasons, you have done great deeds and fought glorious battles. We've pillaged enough Frankish cities to fill twelve longboats with treasure. We've sent countless slaves to the markets of Hedeby, Uppsala, and Trondheim."

Anger flared through Taurin's nostrils. That treasure belonged to his people. Those slaves were good Christians.

Rollo rubbed his hands together behind his back. Taurin noticed the anxious gesture only because of his position off to the side. He doubted the assembly saw it.

Beside him, Jorund stirred.

Rollo's eyes darkened. "In fact, we've been too successful. Abbeys and towns provided rich plunder a generation ago, but instead of rebuilding, the Frankish nobles abandoned the lands north of the Seine. The abbeys of Jumièges and Lillebonne lie empty. Saint Wandrille and Fontenelle are ruins. Fécamp and Montevilliers contain desperate farmers, not riches."

Taurin had said many of these same words to Jorund a week earlier. He spared a glance at the faces watching Rollo. Many of them murmured in agreement. They suspected a new migration, too, one that would take them far from these shores. He'd dreamed of this moment his whole life: the moment the Norse decided to leave his people forever!

He leaned forward to hear every word so he might repeat them in Lillebonne. Good-bye, Norsemen!

Rollo raised his chin. "For this reason, I will claim the lands the Franks abandoned as a Norse kingdom centered around Rouen."

Gasps of surprise and shouts of outrage competed for dominance in a room suddenly too small for the emotion. A few stilled, like Halla and Bjornolf, while others chattered and fidgeted.

Head falling into his hands, Taurin repeated the pronouncement to himself. He clenched the ears that had betrayed him by hearing such terrible words. The Norse were thieves, not lords. They destroyed. They didn't rule.

At least, not until a Frankish landowner had shown three of them how the people of the Caux lived.

He raked his hands through his hair, clenching fistfuls of his brown locks. Anguish squeezed his heart, thumping the blood through his veins loudly enough to echo in his ears. What had he done? He wanted to preserve his people, not forge their chains.

He jumped when Poppa laid a hand on his shoulder. "Hear him out."

He released his hair and rounded on her. "You knew?"

"Hear him out," she repeated.

"And you," he hissed to Jorund. "After hearing me recount the suffering of my people, you thought they deserved more? You are a monster."

"You believe he does this to make you suffer?" Jorund raised an eyebrow. "How foolish you Christians are!"

"What else could it be?"

Jorund nodded to the throne. "Close your mouth and open your ears."

The man with the single braid who had been conversing with Halla the previous night shouted over the rest. "Rollo, this is a poor jest."

These Norse were strange, indeed, for a jarl to allow his men to openly question him without reprimand.

"I am quite serious, Bjornolf." The other listeners fell silent. Rollo extended a hand in Poppa's direction. "And to prove it, I intend to take Countess Poppa of Bayeux as my wife."

Every eye shifted to Poppa. With rigid control, she bowed her head without rising. When he met her gaze, the jarl's severe countenance cracked into an affectionate smile that wrinkled his nose.

Taurin gaped. Rollo truly did love her.

Now, he understood Poppa's earlier anxiety. She had expected the crowd's dangerous glares and their jealousy and hatred at an outsider.

Beside him, Jorund pushed his weight forward, exposing a small axe in a parallel sheath at the small of his back. Taurin hadn't noticed that before. How many other warriors around him concealed weapons?

Did Halla?

This gathering could devolve into a battle if Rollo's supporters believed his infatuation would risk their lives or fortunes. Taurin eyed the exits, noting their positions in case he had to drag Poppa through one in a hurry. He could not leave a Christian woman at the mercy of these people.

Jorund silenced the murmuring. "The countryside to the west

along the Seine has many abandoned estates. The fields have lain fallow for many years and have good, rich soil."

Taurin glared at Jorund's turned back and clenched his fists. That soil rested because Norsemen had slaughtered those who worked them. He now longed for a massacre, so long as only heathens died.

The bearded meat connoisseur from the feast asked, "And you'll simply give them to us?"

"I need farmers to work the lands, warriors to defend it, and traders to supply Rouen," Rollo said. "Those who settle the countryside will receive estates far richer than any at home."

Taurin gasped. "Those are my people's lands!"

"Which your people do not use," the *stallari* growled through gritted teeth. "Let him finish."

Anger rising, Taurin inhaled to argue further, but a man with long hair bound by small gold rings shouted, "We tried this in the Danelaw. Now, Alfred of Wessex attacks those settlers."

The objection breathed on the embers of Taurin's hope.

"Wessex was a powerful kingdom before we arrived," Rollo continued. "I'm claiming lands the Franks abandoned, as was done in Orkney and Shetland. Those lands thrive."

"Your settlers in the countryside won't have Rouen's thick walls," Revna shouted from beside Halla. "They'll be as vulnerable as the Franks we raid."

"We're already vulnerable when our warriors return to Norway and Denmark for the harvest," he countered. "But if they have farms here, we can muster them to our defense."

"I already have lands in Norway." Jarl Sigrun's words silenced the rest of the murmuring. His *hirdmen* had claimed their lord would have been leading the raiders if Rollo didn't own Rouen. "What do I gain from this plan of yours?"

Rollo straightened. "How many of your warriors die in feuds over land or inheritance? How many younger sons, like me, sought fortune in Orkney, Shetland, or the Danelaw?" Rollo stretched his arms out.

"If they settle here, your ships have many berths—not just Rouen—to stage raids into Frankia. Your warriors won't waste their time collecting provisions before going *víkingr*."

Taurin squirmed in his seat. He didn't want to deal with younger sons or quarrelsome heathens, he wanted them to go away and never return. Why must they force themselves on his people?

"How can any of you consider this?" Bjornolf stabbed a finger at Poppa. "I say the Frankish plaything in your bed has weakened you."

Poppa hissed an indrawn breath and stiffened. Several heads were nodding at Bjornolf's words. Taurin's frustration at her faded into sympathy. A countess didn't deserve such insults.

Rollo's answer, while edged with a dangerous anger, did not address the insult to his future wife. "Only a fool would do what his enemy expects. The Franks have learned to exploit our ways. They surprised us at the Vire and annihilated the raiders along the Loire. They set a strong watch during feast days. Their monks bury their treasures to hide them." He pinned Bjornolf with a cold stare. "We must change with our times."

Bjornolf scowled. While he said nothing further, the anger in his eyes didn't subside. This Bjornolf clearly thought with his fists, while Rollo considered the future beyond his own desires.

That future had destroyed Lillebonne's hopes for obscurity.

"What of raids?" asked another voice. The murmuring ended as hundreds of faces awaited an answer.

Rollo made a fist. "We will raid the Cotentin and punish Berengar of Rennes for his insolence." The motion of Halla turning to Poppa broke the stillness within the crowd. "We will strike the Bessin, the Vexin, and pillage the lands around Paris for their arrogance. Outside of our lands, we will take what we value."

Taurin clenched his fists. This Norwegian jarl would make Taurin's people complicit in the murder of other Christians.

"But"—Rollo raised a finger—"my lands, the lands of the Caux, will fall under Norse law."

Taurin hissed, "What does that mean?"

"He's protecting your people," Poppa whispered.

"What?" His indrawn breath drew Jorund's attention.

"He forbids raids in his lands," the Norseman said. "I told you to listen."

Taurin had come to convince the Norse that pillaging Lillebonne was a waste of effort. Yet, would that ever have truly worked? Their safety depended on their anonymity, but that was gone. Who could better protect them from Norsemen than other Norsemen?

That thought felt wrong, dirty. But doubt nagged at him. Would Rollo truly protect them? Poppa loved the jarl and would defend him. But the fact that Rollo intended to marry her seemed to disturb many of the Norse. Rollo needed this to work; he had ruled Rouen for the past fourteen years and had nowhere else to go if he failed.

Taurin began to see the possibilities. His people could once again look to the horizon without fear. Perhaps they could finally begin trading again, at least as far as Rouen. He could increase the plantings around the estate if he had somewhere to sell the surplus. Lands left fallow from lack of need could bring wealth to Lillebonne after fifty years of watching it slip away. His people could enjoy all the exotic wonders Taurin had witnessed in the markets.

He rubbed his temples. What other choice did they have? The Frankish king had done nothing to protect Lillebonne. Even if the Frankish emperor wished to help, his army would first have to capture Rouen, and Taurin doubted any force could breach these strong, stone walls.

In the crowd, men stroked their beards and gnawed at their lips. With sinking spirits, Taurin realized they wouldn't riot and destroy each other, after all. They were considering Rollo's words.

Unable to restrain himself, he stood. Dozens of faces turned in his direction. He might only be a guest, but someone had to speak for his people. Determined not to show his fear, Taurin clenched his hands against his thighs to hide their shaking.

"What if the Franks who live in these regions object?"

Gasps and whispers bubbled up from the crowd. They evidently didn't expect a Christian to speak their language.

When Rollo turned, his massive frame blocked the light from a side door behind him. "I'll convince them it's better to be protected by us than be crushed by us."

Taurin swallowed and crumpled onto his chair, his mind swirling in despair. He could not stop this thing. It would happen whether he approved or not.

It had taken the Norsemen fifty years to return. This time, they intended to stay.

HALLA

Halla staggered out of the hall in a daze, her mind racing. Settling the wilds along the Seine? Protecting the Franks from raids? She had expected Rollo to use Lillebonne as a winter camp when punishing Berengar, not this.

Ducking down a side alley, she stomped through the muddy street, rubbing her temples.

A man in a clean tunic approached with an eager expression. "What news from our jarl?"

She left him behind with his confusion.

The gods had witnessed her doubts on the march back. They were offering her a chance to help create a new kingdom where they could roam. The All-Father had inspired Rollo to send her with Jorund. It wasn't random, wasn't an accident. This was a gift.

As she turned another corner, she slowed and braced a hand against the wooden exterior of a building. Sucking air in heavy gasps, she twisted to lean against the rough oak.

Chatter spilled out into the street as groups left the hall and spread throughout the town. From the fragments Halla could discern at this distance, most recognized the opportunities in good, rich soil and flat fields. They would have good fishing, plenty of timber, and—if Taurin spoke the truth—tin and iron mines.

The air felt heavy with anticipation, like before a lightning storm. An eerie presence settled upon her. The gods were with her even now, watching her. She'd asked for a purpose, and they'd offered one. She ran her fingers up her neck and linked them behind her neck. Why would they grant her wish? The gods should condemn her fears, not reward them.

Her eyes widened. Perhaps her fear was a sign that she'd been following the wrong path. Even as that Frankish rider had borne down on her, she'd faced it bravely without fleeing. Nor had she wavered when surrounded by pagans in that Frankish town, even though she had expected them to attack. She hadn't disappointed the gods, after all.

This was her chance to change the future of Frankia. Bringing the gods to this foreign land was a deed worthy of song and remembrance. A cause worth dying for.

HALLA

Halla halted outside the carved oak door and glanced behind her. The torches had burned down, but the thralls had kept a few logs in the hearths, more for warmth than for light. A few warriors muttered in the far corner, but most of Rollo's *hird* dozed, scattered throughout the great hall.

She smiled at Vikarr, the coal-haired warrior learning against the far wall guarding his jarl's door. He grunted and shifted his weight, but said nothing. Outside Bayeux, she had pulled him to safety when she'd seen the archers preparing to fire and he hadn't.

She rapped on the door three times.

"Go away!" Rollo's muffled voice thundered from behind the door.

Grunting, Halla hammered three more times.

She heard no footsteps, only the unlatching of the door. It opened enough to reveal a sliver of Poppa's face and her arched eyebrow. Upon recognizing Halla, she offered a tight smile and opened it further. "He's ready for bed," she warned.

"I must speak with him." She pinned the countess with a stare.

Sighing, she glanced deeper into the room before nodding. "Quickly."

Halla nodded.

Poppa allowed Halla inside before locking it again. Rollo poked his head from behind a partition. He frowned upon recognizing her.

"Not you, too." His voice sounded as strained as his eyes looked. He sat on a thick bench that bowed under his weight. He waved limply at the door. "Come back to complain tomorrow, when my ears have had a chance to recover."

"I'm not here to complain, you oaf." Halla inhaled a breath. The tingling of her skin remained; the gods watched her still. "I'm here to help you build your damned kingdom in Frankia."

Poppa gasped behind her. "Truly, Halla?"

"I wouldn't say it if it weren't so." She pointed at Rollo. "But you had better give me a good parcel of land, not a barren strip of worthless dirt."

"Are you certain?" The bench creaked as Rollo rose. "Revna spoke truth. You'll face danger without the glory of a battlefield."

"What can be more glorious than creating a new home for the gods?" To die while defending one's home would guide her to Sessrumnir, Freya's hall in Folkvang. Perhaps this was the goddess's way of claiming her.

And if it wasn't, Halla could change her mind. Other warriors would surely covet authority over these Franks after a night's sleep to banish their surprise. She would have to watch for signs and portents about the gods' plans for her.

Beaming with delight, Rollo raised a finger before disappearing behind the partition. Crashes and the shuffling of a frantic search echoed through the room. Halla turned to Poppa, but the other woman had gone to unlatch the door and whisper something outside. A moment later, Vikarr entered and stood along the wall.

Halla pinned the countess with a questioning stare. Poppa merely smiled, her eyes crinkling with mirth.

Rollo returned a moment later holding a knotted torc of pure gold with a silk ribbon interwoven within it.

Behind her, Vikarr gasped in comprehension.

"What?" She drew an unsteady breath, unable to believe his intentions. "Why?"

"I trust you, you're a skilled *hirdman*, and your father was a dear friend." He licked his lips. "Plus, you're the first to declare your support. I wish to honor that loyalty."

She knelt, placing a hand on the ground to steady her shaking legs. Her heart threatened to thump out of her chest. She had imagined this moment since seeing her first shieldmaiden as a child.

"Halla Skidadóttir." He raised the torc before him. "I name you as my *hersir*, leader of warriors and representative of my authority."

This was no figment of her imagination, conjured as she would listen to her father's stories about the glorious raid leaders of Rollo's army. This was real. The torc felt heavier than she expected when he placed it in her hands.

And it was hers now.

She ran her fingers over this symbol of his authority, eyes beaming with pride. All her hard work and training had led to this triumph, this honor. No longer simply a bound warrior, she would now only answer to Rollo, and Jorund as his *stallari*.

"I expect you to support my authority and enforce Norse law, no matter the cost. Do you give your oath to do this?"

Her voice came out as a thin whisper. "On Freya's necklace, Brísingamen, and on Odin All-Father, I swear." She ran her fingers over the tiny bumps in the knotting of the torc.

Tugging on the torc, she widened it enough to fit it around her neck before bending it back into place. Exhaling from the exertion, she pushed her hair aside so her father might see it from Valhalla and hail her success.

The sword slash that had nearly killed her had elevated her higher than she'd dreamed. The ways of the gods were, indeed, strange.

HALLA

When Rollo summoned Halla the morning after next, she arrived in her freshly repaired mail coat with her axes dangling from her belt. Female *hersirs* were rare enough that she wanted to remind everyone of her skill. Warriors would obey a battle-hardened shieldmaiden, not an unarmed maiden in shift and apron.

But this was no great assembly of Rollo's supporters. Only Revna and a few thralls cleaning the fireplaces from the night before awaited her in the great hall. Her heart leapt at the sight of her dear friend.

Halla clasped Revna's shoulders and leaned her forehead against hers. "I prayed to all the gods that you would stay." She would never choose her companion's path for her, but she did revel in her choice.

Revna wrapped her arms around Halla's waist. Despite the pain as they tugged at her healing stomach, the gesture warmed her.

"Rollo's plans change nothing," Revna insisted. "The raids continue, so I remain."

Halla's smile tapered. "You're not going into the countryside?"

"I answered Thor's call, not Freyr's." Eyes narrowing, she stiffened and pulled away. "As you did, of course?"

Halla shrank from her companion's searching gaze. She could not risk revealing her own doubt and fear, even if the gods had accepted them. Nor could she talk of a life empty of purpose when her friend reveled in battle.

"The gods spoke to me. I cannot ignore them."

Eyebrows wrinkling, Revna studied her for a time before eventually shrugging. "So you go out to rule the Christians?"

Halla nodded.

"With lands to farm?"

"I didn't think about that. I suppose so."

"You'll forget how to throw an axe, I'm afraid." Mischief dimpled the corners of Revna's lips. "You'll spend all your time milking your own cows."

She winced at the common insult. "Then visit often and remind me."

She smirked. "Will you still be part of Rollo's *hird*?"

"*Hersir*, actually."

Revna cackled and grabbed Halla's cheeks, kissing her on the lips. "The gods' path is lined with glory, I see."

"Is there any other way?" She savored her friend's laughter. She would have missed moments like these if Revna had abandoned Rollo. "Have you heard from the others?"

"Three longboats are leaving to raid up the Seine this morning, but they'll be back. Then there's Oleg. He imagines leading fleets of trading *knörrs* up every river in Frankia."

"No surprise there." She paused. "Jarl Sigrun seemed skeptical."

Revna shrugged. "He'll see the advantage of allowing his people to settle here instead of Britain or Iceland."

"Oh?"

Her friend nodded. "Those who live here can identify rich targets and enemy movements. They can swell his numbers without taking seats on longboats."

Revna didn't need to mention the advantage of having warriors with bonds to his own lands should he one day challenge Rollo for Rouen. Such treachery happened all the time back home. Halla would have to watch for it. "And Bjornolf?"

Movement near the entrance drew her attention to Taurin entering the hall. Why was the Christian here?

"You haven't heard?" Revna asked.

Halla faced her again. "Heard?"

Her lips tightened. "Bjornolf cursed Rollo's plan and left this morning with a full longship of warriors. He intends to raid Frankia as his fathers did."

"What of his oath as *hirdman*?"

"Rollo freed him from it but repeated his warning not to attack the Franks under his protection."

Halla raised a hand to check her braids. Bjornolf's defection made her thumb itch. Trouble would follow if more warriors followed his example.

Rollo emerged with Jorund from the room behind the throne. "Welcome!" He approached with arms outstretched.

Halla bristled when she realized he'd directed the greeting at Taurin, not her or Revna. Why did this foreigner deserve attention when she was the jarl's *hersir*?

Taurin approached and inclined his head in a show of respect somewhere between that of an ambassador and a subject. The reaction showed more nuance than Halla thought him capable of.

Rollo gestured for everyone to approach. "Taurin of Lillebonne, you've explored Rouen and have had two days to consider my words." He rubbed his hands together. "What say you about my announcement?"

She narrowed her eyes, irritation building. This was no meeting to discuss dispositions or introduce her as *hersir*. She was here only because she knew Taurin better than the others.

At least the Christian had the good sense to show neither anger nor panic. Though he appeared relaxed, Halla noticed his weight shift to his back foot in a defensive, warrior's posture.

He cleared his throat. "Which lands, specifically, do you intend to claim?"

"The whole Pays de Caux, from the Seine to Oceanus Britannicus," Rollo said.

Taurin drew his lips tight. "Lillebonne as well, then."

Rollo nodded. "Securing Rouen requires us to control the mouth of the Seine. Plus, Jorund says the lands leading to your town are ripe with farmlands, but many lay untended. You can produce more, and we need your food."

Taurin met Halla's gaze. The silent accusation in his eyes unsettled her. The burned estate that had once belonged to his mother's family would soon belong to her people. That was the way of things, but she doubted he'd accept that simple truth.

"Traders from Iceland, Britain, Norway, Denmark, even Hispania and the Mediterranean pass down the Seine," Jorund added. "Think of the wealth. All we ask is a tax on that trade."

Halla almost laughed. Though a fearsome warrior, Jorund had the heart of an administrator, fretting over costs and resources. Bjornolf might blame Poppa for Rollo's plans, but they had undoubtedly originated in the *stallari's* mind.

Rollo added, "I'm told your tenants pay the landowners rents. You may continue to do so. I won't even require you to give me a share."

Taurin swallowed and licked his lips. The gesture banished Halla's lingering resentment at the attention Rollo paid him. He might care for his people, but he didn't neglect himself. Greed was understandable, relatable. He wasn't as strange as she'd feared.

"That is generous." The Frank narrowed his eyes. "But what good is wealth if you cart my people away as slaves?"

Revna gasped. Halla clamped down on her arm to restrain her from advancing on him.

"By Thor, you have balls!" Rollo began to pace. After a few passes, he stopped and stared at the two ravens on either side of his throne. "Franks in my lands will not be taken as slaves for any reason, provided they remain loyal." He raised a hand toward Revna when she bristled. "But, I will not force my people to release their thralls. This is as far as I'm willing to go."

"And you promise your protection of every soul in those lands?" Taurin asked.

"I do."

"Do you swear on your gods?"

Rollo grunted. "Would your people trust that?"

"No, but I would."

Taurin's eyes shifted to Halla for a moment. What did that glance mean?

"Then I give it." Rollo clasped the Thor's hammer hanging from a chain around his neck. "By Thor, by Odin, and by Freyr, I swear to extend Norse law to the land under my control and preserve all those within it from abuse or enslavement."

Taurin crossed himself, eyes shifting back to Halla as he did. The gesture felt like something private between them, not at all condescending like when the priest had done it. The others in the hall faded away, leaving only them. The sensation filled her with unease. Why should a pagan ritual carry such meaning?

"In exchange, I expect your people to trade only in towns in my domain and pay taxes on those goods." Rollo raised his chin. "Will they accept my rule?"

What would the aldermen who had only reluctantly shared a meal with the Norse think? Or Orderic, the landowner who'd seethed with contempt for her? And that fragile priest?

"Would their resistance steer you from this course?"

The Christian's words came too eagerly. He still hoped for a reprieve, even after hearing the jarl announce his intentions to his supporters. Halla admired his stubbornness despite its futility.

Rollo joined his hands behind his back. "I would prefer not to kill and replace them with my own people, but I will if I must."

Taurin stared at the ground between himself and Rollo. A rapid sequence of emotions passed over that beardless face. Transfixed, Halla could not look away, though she recognized only some of them: anger, disbelief, outrage, eagerness, perhaps even anticipation. Her foot began to itch, in an ominous sign.

The jarl crossed his arms and shifted his weight. Less patient, Revna hissed an annoyed sigh.

Taurin's eyes carried a new resolve when he raised them. "A great many will delight in no longer fearing another attack, but some will always view you as heathens." He inhaled a wavering breath. "However, you can win them over."

Halla struggled to accept his words. Taurin cared so much for his people that he'd risked his life to visit Rouen. Yet now, he advised a Norse heathen on how to win their hearts. He was committing himself. The man who had spoken so passionately on the journey would not undertake that decision lightly.

Rollo raised his eyebrows. "How?"

"Norsemen laid waste to every bishopric and monastery, profaned every holy place," Taurin said. "My people will expect you to force them to convert to your beliefs. If you want their support, you must guarantee their right to their faith."

Rollo snorted and looped his thumbs through his belt. "Done."

His assent came too quickly; he must have intended to grant that concession before even entering this hall.

Taurin blinked. "Just like that?"

"I care nothing for their beliefs. If they work the land, pay tariffs on their trade, and don't aid our enemies, they can believe what they wish."

Taurin's throat bobbed up and down as he swallowed. "They will welcome the trade routes." Half a breath later, he added, "But I'm a landowner, not their leader. My words cannot bind them."

"They can bind *you*," Rollo reminded.

His lips drew taut. "So they can."

"Will you support my goals if I protect you from raids?"

Only the chatter of a group of men passing outside broke the silence.

Taurin took a deep breath that rasped like a horn calling to battle. Though he didn't turn, his eyes shifted subtly toward Halla. "If you defend my people, I will support your rule."

"How can we trust him?" Revna snapped before the echo of his words had faded.

"He would swear on his holy book," Rollo suggested.

"No oath would prevent him from doing what he thought best for his people," Halla said.

Taurin's eyes snapped an accusation at her.

"I thought you were fond of him," Revna muttered.

Now, the Christian's eyes widened.

At first, the comment outraged her. But as Halla reflected, her anger faded. Before her, she saw not a strange Christian, but a thoughtful, courageous man. He moved like a warrior and spoke of the land he loved like a skald. How many of her people would walk into a heathen city without even a sword for protection? Yet Taurin had. He was unusual.

In fact, he struck Halla as otherworldly.

She drew an unsteady breath. The gods had led her to that one specific town, with the one man in Frankia not terrified of her people. They'd bestowed overwhelming courage upon him, bringing him to this moment. She could see their intentions so clearly. She had asked for signs, yet she already had them.

"A sign," she murmured.

"What?" Jorund asked.

"They will need a sign," she repeated louder.

The *stallari* frowned. "What do you mean?"

Rollo had asked them to live beside these strange Franks as they created a Norse kingdom. "We have to give the Christians more than mere promises."

The jarl and Poppa had proven it was possible. Now, Halla understood why she had doubted her path on the Vire, why the gods had led her to that village.

"Put Lillebonne under my authority."

Rollo frowned. "How will that help?"

She inhaled a deep, steadying breath and approached Rollo. "It will signal our dedication to live beside them"—she pointed to Taurin—"if I take that one as my husband."

Taurin's throat bobbed as he swallowed. Halla curled her lip, savoring his surprise.

"Do you believe these people would ever obey a woman?" Contempt dripped from Revna's words. "You saw how they reacted to us simply speaking to them."

Halla dared not look back at her. She could not endure her friend's outrage and hurt. But nor could she continue as she had.

"If they don't, I'll demonstrate the error of that mistake." She swallowed. "He's an influential alderman. Marrying one of us would show demonstrate that he believes your pledges."

"But…" Revna clenched her shaking hands. "Why you, Halla?"

"None other can do this for Rollo. If a warrior married a Frankish woman, the Christians would view it as rape and theft." She pointed to the jarl. "I had better still receive a share of plunder if I'm keeping the Franks in line while you go pillaging."

Rollo stared at Jorund in inscrutable silence. She wished Odin would send Huginn and Muninn to their totems on Jorund's throne to whisper in the jarl's ear. He had to accept this offer. She needed him to.

Rollo finally asked, "You would do this?"

"You intend to marry Poppa."

"I love her. You only met this man a week ago."

Halla sighed at his stupidity. Marriage was based on mutual benefit, not love. Every shieldmaiden eventually married and gave up raiding. Why should she not take this opportunity and become leader of a community in exchange? This was her chance for a purpose.

She faced Taurin. True, she had known him only a short time, but he had defied her assumptions about his people. She had witnessed his thoughtfulness and courtesy. He had befriended Norwegian farmers at the feast, had explored Rouen without cowering. That suggested wisdom and an open mind.

"You can know a man for years, yet only meet him when you share danger. He faced uncertainty and death for his people." She turned to Rollo. "That is admirable."

Jorund cleared this throat. "He did speak wisely when he brokered peace in Lillebonne."

She crossed to stand before Taurin and took his hand, calloused like a warrior's. That made her smile. Slowly, it tightened around her own. His touch felt tender but strong.

She had glimpsed his true nature on the ride to Rouen. And if she was wrong, she could always kill him. The gods did not condemn the slaughter of cowards, traitors, or oathbreakers.

Unlike many girls, she had never dreamed of marriage. Her arms bore axes, not needle and thimble. She had always imagined killing

Frankish warriors, not marrying one. But the gods had planned another fate for her. She understood that now.

Filled with a strange exhilaration, Halla smiled as she studied his face. She would have to do something about his bare chin.

"What say you? Will you bind yourself to me and serve both of our peoples?"

TAURIN

Halla's words sounded as if they'd come from a great distance. How could he consider this decision? She was a heathen, a murderer who chose a life of raiding like the rest of the people in this city.

He cleared his throat and licked his suddenly dry lips. "I am at your mercy, surrounded by your people. Do I truly have a choice?"

"We do not choose another's path," Rollo said. "I've already sworn to protect your people and will convey you home safely." Eyes dancing, he curled his lips. "This choice concerns only you and my *hersir*."

Taurin's clarity of mind abandoned him. What thoughts he could muster centered on the strange woman before him.

The two deep pools of blue that gazed at him carried a vulnerability and sincerity that dispelled his suspicions. She had offered this proposal willingly, not at anyone's behest. Her chest rose and fell quickly, faster than he remembered from the ride to Rouen. Anticipation or anxiety? He couldn't tell, but a part of her clearly wanted this.

Her slender hand, stiff with tension, carried the calluses of a warrior. It was nothing like the hand of the woman he'd intended to marry two years earlier. And yet, she radiated a heat that warmed his body, even from this distance. He had felt it during their first touch in Lillebonne. Had she, as well?

She had a wild and dangerous energy unlike anything he'd experienced. In town, she had wanted to kill him, and he had prepared to do the same. Yet on the road, his thoughts had been decidedly less violent, though perhaps just as heated. Halla grasping his leg on the ride had sent ripples of excitement through his body and into his groin. Had she noticed his body rousing at her momentary graze?

Orderic had suggested he avail himself of the Norse women. Perhaps his friend had noticed his reaction to this exotic heathen. But Orderic surely never intended to suggest her should marry one.

But, why not? His people badly needed protection now that the Norse knew of their existence. Rollo would have to send someone to represent him. As wife of an alderman, Halla would live with the consequences of both her successes and failures. She couldn't inflict her will and move on to some other town. Surely that would soften her decisions.

Like all the aldermen, he could profit from markets for the excess his estate could produce. And as the husband of the Norse leader, he would learn of every opportunity first. He would gain some influence to curtail men like Arbogast, who would try to take advantage of this shift in power. That man already shared too many traits with these Norsemen.

Father Norbert claimed all things fell within God's plan. If that included the burning of their town, then perhaps it included this moment. God had presented him with the chance to restrain these Norsemen, preserve his power and influence, and marry a beautiful woman who set his blood burning.

He need only abandon the hushed existence of the past and commit himself, in body and by oath, to take a chance on an uncertain future.

Everything would change, but perhaps it needed to.

"You will safeguard my people and defend their right to worship as they wish?"

She nodded once, slowly. "If you support my authority and convince your people to trade in Rouen."

When this woman had presented herself in the square, he had foreseen many consequences, many dangers. Not once had he imagined this moment.

"Then I accept."

HALLA

Revna's footsteps followed close behind as Halla departed the hall. The moment they reached the street, Revna spun her around and pushed her against the outer wall. Her eyes no longer held tenderness.

"By the gods, what was that?" Her face burned with fury. "You agreed to marry him."

"I know. I was there."

"Why?" Her cry was halfway between a scream and a moan. "I thought I knew you. Why would you bind yourself to one of those people?"

"Rollo did the same."

"Rollo is my jarl, not my dear friend."

"No other shieldmaiden is as respected as you and I. Only one of us could make this gesture. Did you wish to?"

Eyes wild with disbelief, Revna spoke with a voice suddenly bereft of strength. "You never spoke of marriage before."

"Surely you knew it would happen eventually." Halla raised her hands to cup Revna's cheeks. "I treasure you, my dear. You know me like no other. That will never change."

"Of course it will," she whispered.

"Why should it?"

"You will be married."

"I still decide who I spend time with."

"The Christians treat their women as thralls."

Halla barked a laugh. "Let him try! I'll start with a finger, then decide what I sever next based on how his other parts please me."

"He's insufferable." Revna folded her arms across her chest. "At least promise me you'll remember your salt wash after lying with him. You can't raid if you're heavy with child."

"Of course I will."

Revna narrowed her eyes. "Have you fallen in love?"

"Don't be silly." Halla straightened. "He was here and was willing to cooperate. That's all."

"So it could have been anyone, even that detestable Orderic?"

"No." Halla scowled, remembering his arrogance. She supposed she would have to deal with him now, as well. "Taurin has proven himself utterly different from that man."

"You admire him?" Revna breathed. "That's how it starts. Before long, you'll love him."

Halla leaned in and kissed Revna on the forehead. "I do respect his courage, yes. Will that lead to more?" She shrugged. "Only the Norns know the future. But I do this for myself and our people, not for him."

Revna pulled back, shaking her head. "You'll forget all about us and the gods."

"No, I could never forget them." The gods had guided her to this moment. She could never turn her back on them. "Wheat can ripen but cannot become flax."

CHAPTER FIVE

TAURIN

CLEARLY, THE NORSE hadn't learned that bathing exposed a person to evil. Early in the morning before their respective marriages, Rollo invited Taurin to join him in the ceremonial cleansing.

Taurin had learned that when the Norse had conquered Rouen, most of the wooden structures had burned in the sack. Enough centuries-old stone buildings had survived to house the occupying army once they had replaced the charred roofs. But the Norsemen had built one new, wooden structure before the first year had ended.

The bath-house was a fairly uninteresting structure, except for the tar lining the seams where each plank of the construction came together. Squat and square, it looked like a storehouse from the outside.

The heat struck Taurin the moment Jorund opened the door. It felt like a blacksmith's furnace.

"Good, they've prepared it for us," Rollo purred.

"You intend for us to go inside?" Perspiration already beaded his face.

"Yes." Rollo ducked to pass beneath the threshold.

Taurin had never seen fog inside a building. But unlike the haze that sometimes settled over his estate, this fog pressed in on his skin like a heavy weight. Behind him, Jorund closed the doors, leaving them in a darkness broken only by a single torch. After his eyes adjusted to the darkness, he could distinguish benches running along either side of the room, separated by a door in the far wall.

Without a word, Jorund and Rollo stripped out of their tunics and sat on one of the benches. Rollo closed his eyes and allowed a smile to curve across his face.

Taurin averted his gaze even though the fog obscured the jarl's naked body. Perching on the edge of the other bench, he studied the joints of the roof supports, the intricate layering of the heated rock pile in the center of the room, anything that would distract him from the bare Norsemen.

"Take off your tunic," Rollo commanded.

Taurin frowned. Though he had only brought one with him on the journey to Rouen, he would rather soil it with sweat than display his own nakedness. "Is it necessary?"

"When we bind ourselves to our wives, we begin a new life," Rollo said. "The steam purifies our bodies and strips away our past selves. It completes the work of the sword-theft."

He had come to Rouen to restore his old life, not embark on a new one.

But at least this ritual had no power. The Norse gods didn't really exist. Reluctantly, Taurin lifted his tunic over his shoulders and fought to prevent his sudden vulnerability from showing on his face. These warriors could tell much by the placement of his scars and the definition of each muscle.

"Sword-theft?"

Jorund wiped a drip of sweat from his brow. "Last night, Rollo broke into a grave mound to retrieve the sword placed inside. Normally, we'd do it with one of his relatives' graves, but they're in Norway."

"Merciful Jesus!" Taurin crossed himself at the thought of

disturbing the dead. Such things led to vengeful, restless spirits. Yet, suspicion overcame his outrage. "Why did I not have to do this?"

"During the ritual, one of the husband's friends or relatives reminds him of his obligations and family traditions," Jorund explained. "We know nothing of what your people would say."

He released a breath, satisfied that the oversight wasn't an attempt to invalidate his marriage. He and his people needed protection, and despite what the Norse might say, that protection depended on this marriage.

In truth, he appreciated being spared such a ceremony. His people would never understand it, let alone condone it. Already, he would struggle to explain his pagan bride.

They sat in silence for some time. Rivulets of sweat left streaks on his skin. He was glad he had removed his tunic; even the simple contact of his hand resting on his thigh and his skin against the bench seemed intolerably hot.

"Come." A glistening Jorund rose. Taurin had grown accustomed enough to the steam to see mischief in the man's eyes. When Taurin reached for his tunic, Jorund interrupted, "Leave it."

"It's my only one."

"Not anymore."

He led Taurin through the door in the far wall. The room beyond held four basins large enough to fully accommodate even a man as large as Rollo. Water reached to the very top of two of them. The suddenly cool air caught him unprepared and he shivered.

"Submerge yourself in one of the basins," Jorund instructed. "Now! Do it!"

Already Rollo had jumped into one, sloshing water onto the ground. Inspired both by Jorund's insistence and Rollo's unquestioning obedience, Taurin gripped the side of the basin and did the same.

Every inch of his body cried out in agony at the cold. He felt as if he'd fallen through the ice of the Bolbec in the dead of winter and the swirling current was dragging him under.

But there was no current here, only two laughing Norsemen. He dragged himself out of the basin despite his stiffening muscles. Shivering, he barely felt Rollo slap him on the back.

"Now, we're ready for our brides."

A baptism. Now, he understood. Taurin prayed this heathen ritual hadn't purged the sanctified water of his own baptism so many years before. He would have to ask Father Norbert to bless him again when he reached home safely.

New tunics lay folded on a table near the exit. Rollo reached for one in a rare and expensive deep blue. A bleached white tunic hemmed with gold edging at the neckline and cuffs sat folded beside it. Taurin ran his fingers along the smooth material, delighting in the fine grain. The edging consisted of little lines of hammers made with yellow thread interwoven with real gold. Such expense!

Rollo watched him with a smile. "Consider it a gift."

When the group returned to the feasting hall, Rollo presented him with black wool breeches, turnshoes, and a belt that still smelled of new leather. Taurin couldn't remember the last time he'd received so many gifts.

In a back room, a slave rubbed some sweetly scented oil into Taurin's skin and parted his hair down the middle. It felt strange to have another man's hands rub his flesh. He wondered what orphaned children the Norsemen had left behind when they'd captured this slave, just as they'd stolen the people of Lillebonne fifty years earlier.

He caught his reflection in a segment of polished iron. Hair parted, wearing a hammer-edged tunic that almost certainly referred to a pagan god, and smelling utterly unnatural, Taurin hardly recognized himself.

And why should I? he wondered as he emerged from the preparation room. Rollo was right; he had washed away his old self. But he had done so long before he'd jumped into that vat of chilled water. His grandfather would be ashamed of him.

The Norsemen awaited him. Rollo took him in at a glance before nodding in apparent satisfaction. "Tell them we're ready."

Jorund strode to the end of the hall and pushed open the doors. Chatter seeped in from the sizeable crowd outside. Taurin swallowed and ran his tongue over his dry mouth.

This was no dream.

"I almost forgot…" Rollo crossed to a nearby table and returned with a sheathed sword. "Here."

Taurin held the blade for a moment. He had left his own sword back in Lillebonne. His people didn't even know what was happening here.

As he affixed the scabbard to his belt, Rollo blurted, "Halla's father was as a brother to me. Treat his daughter well."

Taurin's fingers froze at the warning. This wasn't the wedding he'd imagined in his childhood, and Rollo wasn't the father-in-law—or the closest thing to it—he'd expected.

He finished securing the scabbard. "As dearly as you treat Poppa."

He raised his gaze to meet Rollo's. The big man was smiling.

"Then we shall be good friends!"

Jorund waved them forward and Taurin fell into step beside the jarl. Rollo's thumping footsteps sounded like the quick beats of his own heart. He needed to scamper to keep pace with the jarl's wide strides.

They emerged into a sea of bodies. All of Rouen—at least, those who had remained to support Rollo's new domain—flanked a path leading from the feasting hall to the main square.

Taurin's doubts about agreeing to this marriage vanished like a mist lifting over the Bolbec. He had never before seen so many people in one place. His town could never withstand so many Norsemen. Wherever he looked, strange faces stared back at him.

Or, rather, at Rollo. Upon seeing their jarl, they erupted into a cheer that threatened to deafen him.

Somehow, Rollo whispered to him alone, "Do as I do."

Taurin fell in stride as Rollo made his way down the path. The jarl deliberately slowed his pace so Taurin could march comfortably beside him. Still, he struggled to keep up.

More than a few faces hardened as they shifted from their jarl to the man walking beside him. He felt their eyes like daggers waiting to plunge into his soft Christian flesh. Swallowing, he set his jaw and looked ahead, refusing to meet their gazes. He needed no further reminder of his isolation.

They turned a corner in the path. Halla waited ahead, facing a collection of people and animals at the end of the path. Two piles of hastily erected stones sat beyond her.

When she turned in his direction, his breath caught in his throat.

She wore no braids now, and her chestnut hair hung freely, draped over each shoulder. A circlet of woven gold that sparkled in the sunlight sat atop her head. Instead of her apron, she wore a coat of faint gray fastened by a single gold brooch. A green shift of linen so airy that the hem rippled in the faint breeze peeked out from beneath it.

She looked magnificent.

Somehow, he reached her without stumbling. She clasped his hands almost immediately.

"You look..." He swallowed, unable to continue.

"The man of many words finds himself speechless? I'm flattered." Her lips spread into a smile as she appraised him. Her eyes flashed with mischief. "You make a fine Norseman," she purred as she turned to stand beside him.

They weren't alone, even excepting Rollo and Poppa waiting beside them. An elderly woman in a black hooded cloak raised her hands. One held a knife. The strange symbols lining her face matched the kohl covering her eyes.

A pair of well-muscled Norsemen with patterns of lines in the same blue-black stood behind her. One held a rope attached to the neck of a goat standing with disinterest nearby, while the other wrangled a bound sow lying on the ground beside him.

He stiffened as he guessed the meaning of those animals. Beside him, Halla and Rollo watched the priestess with stoic certainty. Poppa, though, smiled encouragement as she met his gaze.

How could she, a good Christian woman, endure such a ritual? Had a year with these pagans changed her so much? Would it change him, as well?

"Oh, gods of Asgard, hear us," the woman cried in a strong baritone that echoed off the buildings. "Turn your eye to your children, Rollo Ragnvaldsson and Halla Skidadóttir. They bid you witness their oaths this day."

Lowering her hands, the priestess crossed to the goat and drew the knife over its throat in a quick, smooth stroke. A gurgled cry bleated briefly before it fell silent, but the blood streamed out steadily, filling the air with a metallic smell. The odor threatened to make him vomit.

The Norseman holding the rope produced a bronze bowl to capture some of the blood while still restraining the animal's involuntary twitching. The rest poured onto the dirt and down the street. A few of the assembled Norsemen shuffled their feet to stand within the tiny river of red. One woman raised her hands to the sky as the blood ran between her toes. She was smiling in abject delight.

Squirming, Taurin watched helplessly as the priestess did the same to the sow and the other attendant placed a copper bowl beneath its throat. All around, the assembled townsfolk whispered prayers and made the same reverent gesture Halla had made a week earlier.

The attendants raised their bowls aloft. Droplets spilled down the sides and streaked their arms. Turning slowly, they placed them atop the stone mounds and backed away reverently. Taurin had never heard of Norsemen moving with such humility.

"We call upon you, Odin All-Father. We call upon you, mighty Thor. We call upon you, Freya, fair one." The woman raised her arms again. "We pray you accept this sacrifice and bestow your blessings upon your children."

The slaughtered animals had ceased their twitching. This was a scene for a barn, not a wedding. How could he declare an oath in such an unclean place? Taurin only hoped God would forgive him.

Halla turned to him, seemingly unfazed by the carnage. And why shouldn't she be? She believed this sacrifice drew her gods' attention. She seemed so confident, so certain.

He was purchasing his people's safety. So long as that remained true, he would honor this pledge, regardless of how many animals lay dead at his feet. Pulling his sword from his scabbard, he presented the hilt to Halla and uttered the words Jorund had told him. "With this sword, I pledge to you my loyalty."

Smiling, she accepted and kissed it. "I shall guard this sword for our sons and daughters." Revna approached, and Halla exchanged it for a full scabbard. Unsheathing the blade within, she presented it to Taurin. "With this sword, I offer the protection of my people."

Beside them, Rollo pledged his protection and Poppa her obedience. However, that exchange made little sense in Halla and Taurin's case, since she held the authority and was preserving his people with their marriage.

Taurin wrapped his hand around the hilt, carved with symbols of the moon. The blade, a tempered steel, felt light but strong.

"I bought it from a trader from Al-Andalus," she boasted.

His Norse bride had given him a Muslim sword while standing over a lake of animal blood. More than anything, he wanted to make a sign of the cross.

Halla, still holding his hand, squeezed it gently and brought him back to the moment. She prompted him with a reassuring nod.

Revna stood beside them, scowling as she held a plate with a pair of rings on it. Taking the first one, a simple silver band with tiny beading along both edges, Halla slid it onto Taurin's finger. "I pledge myself to this man under the eyes of Freya."

Swallowing, Taurin reached up and lifted the remaining braided silver ring. He was supposed to invoke Odin or Thor. He could utter the words in good conscience, of course. Oaths before pagan gods had no meaning. He could be swearing by a tree or rock for all it mattered.

Orderic might do such a thing in his place, but Taurin couldn't hide behind the excuse of a false oath. He had given his word in his heart. He couldn't expect her to honor her oaths if he wiggled out of his.

Swallowing, he licked his lips and placed the ring on Halla's finger. "I pledge myself to this woman under the eyes of God."

The Norse near him, even Revna, accepted the words without comment. Only Halla seemed to understand the distinction. Her widened eyes carried not outrage, but something softer and more affectionate.

She was a strange one, this Norse woman who was now his wife. But, perhaps he was no less strange. No other man from his town would marry a heathen in such a ceremony. Whether that credited or condemned his soul, he couldn't decide. But he would discover which with her.

He watched without comprehension as the priestess walked toward them with a bundle of twigs in one hand and the bowl filled with the sow's blood in the other. Slowly, she dipped the twigs in the blood, saturating it. A moment later, she flicked the animal's blood at the newlyweds, sprinkling their heads, faces, and chests in a red mist.

He froze, tightening his throat to avoid screaming in outrage before all these Norsemen. The droplets still felt warm and slippery as they hit his face. Unable to resist, he turned to Poppa. She watched the scene with a blank expression. If she felt similar disgust, she controlled her reaction better than he did.

Demons. They truly were demons. The sauna had stripped away God's protection and this filthy ritual had stained his soul.

Halla smiled with eyes closed, resembling the woman standing toe-deep in the pooling blood. Red dots stained her fine overcoat. He doubted the stains would ever come out.

All his fine reasons for agreeing to this marriage deserted him. He had sold his soul and his people's lives to these heathens. What had he done, to marry a woman so strange as to enjoy bathing in the blood of God's creatures?

TAURIN

The feast lasted well past dark. Every few moments, another Norseman toasted the newlyweds. They respected Halla, and evidently the depth of her gods' marriage blessings depended on how much mead the guests consumed, or some such nonsense.

Though he tried to sip his mead and eat heartily, it had gone to his head by the time three men and three women escorted Halla and himself to her home, a single-story stone and plaster building two streets down from the great hall.

At first, he didn't understand why they followed him and his new wife inside. Nor could he understand why four candles already illuminated the room.

One couple began searching the corners and under the bed. The other two men began removing Taurin's shoes, belt, and breeches while the women helped Halla out of her outer coat and shoes. Eyes widening, the fogginess from the mead dissipated.

"What are you doing?" Rumors spoke of pagan sexual rites involving the entire community.

They completed their work quickly despite Taurin's growing resistance and departed without a word. The last woman to leave offered Halla a wry smile before stepping outside and closing the door.

Stripped except for the tunic that extended to mid-thigh, he felt suddenly cold as the air tickled his groin. Nor did Halla's see-through shift help. His body began to rouse at the gentle curves of her breasts and hips beneath the gauzy material.

She had noticed, as well. "A good beginning."

She fixed her gaze on his waist. Her lips curling into a smile only stiffened him further.

"Do…do they expect us to lie together?"

"Yes." She stepped forward and raised her chin. "As do I."

In every way he could imagine, she differed from the Frankish women of home. "You…you do? Truly?"

She laughed as she slipped her dress off her shoulder. He yearned to kiss her collarbone right where the candlelight met shadow.

"This marriage is an agreement, is it not?" She took another step.

The scent of flowers, probably from her own ritual cleansing, filled his nostrils. His fingers hungered to reach out for that soft skin, glowing in the faint light. "It is." His voice sounded husky, loaded with raw desire.

"Well, I want to enjoy the spoils of it."

His eyes widened. Her confidence, her certainty banished his doubts and filled him with exhilaration.

She brushed her dress off her other shoulder and wiggled slowly. The fabric slipped unevenly, exposing one breast and then the other. He had expected them to rest closer together after seeing them bound in her wedding attire, but now they seemed more natural, softer and wilder. He ran his tongue over his lips.

The shift caught at her hips, exposing the half-healed wound on her stomach. She used her hands then, sliding the garment off the rest of the way, exposing the thatch of curly brown hair between her thighs. His loins pulsed at the elegant curves of her body, the slopes of her breasts. He longed to touch and kiss every wondrous part.

Her hips ensorcelled him as she crossed the remaining distance. Reaching down, she wiggled a hand beneath his tunic and grasped his penis. Her firm grip sent a shiver across his body. Stirred, he tore his tunic off and cast it aside.

This was not her first time with a man, he realized as she teased him with a finger and ran her eyes over him. Taurin wanted to strangle that man, whoever he was. Taurin had kept in good condition and had muscle enough to use both sword and shovel skillfully, but some of these Norsemen dwarfed him. He wanted his tunic back to cover his own inadequacy.

Halla apparently had other intentions. She took his hand and led him toward the bed.

For an instant, he resisted her pull. Could he really lie with a heathen? For years, Father Norbert had warned them not to forget the evil that had spread across their land. God wished them all to resist these vile unbelievers.

She was reclining on the bed, resplendent in her nudity, watching him with curious eyes. She might braid her hair and her skin might bear the memories of old scars, but none of that mattered compared to the rhythmic rise and fall of her excited breathing as she wiggled on the furs.

This was his wife. He had accepted her, despite the pagan ceremony.

Laying down on the bed beside her, he traced a line with his fingertips against her shoulder, up one breast, and down the side of her hip. Her warm skin tickled his fingers with its softness.

With a fluid motion, she flatted him on his back and rolled atop. Candlelight silhouetted her curves as she ran her fingers along his chest. Shifting her weight, she reached down to guide him inside her.

Bursts of pleasure rippled over his body as warmth enfolded him. She rocked slowly, pushing him deeper with each motion. Reaching up, he wrapped his arms under hers and pulled her close. She fell with a gasp, lying atop him with her breasts pressing against his chest.

He had expected not to know what to do, but they fell into a rhythm quickly, naturally. Encouraged by her sudden moan, he thrust in delight. She rewarded him with a tighter grip on his back that pushed him deeper. Pace quickening, he felt the sensation build until he felt he would explode.

Just as he began to pulse, she cried out in delight and squeezed down harder. Waves of ecstasy washed over him. As they began to fade, he realized that she too was pulsing in rhythm with each twitch of his muscles.

They laid like that, her atop him, for some time as they caught their breath. When she twisted to lie against him, cradled in his embrace, he didn't want to let her go.

With a free hand, he pulled himself closer and kissed her. Her lips parted to embrace his. Despite his closed eyes, he could see her. The woman he had met in the town square…his riding companion…the suitor in the feasting hall. Amid this collision of bodies, their marriage had truly begun.

His uncertainty and fear vanished. She was no wild pagan who communed with devils and committed terrible carnal acts. This was his wife, and he her husband.

Straightening her hair with a free hand, she inhaled. "Very enjoyable. I'm glad I suggested this match."

That was, he decided, as good of a description as any. He stroked her back, soaking in the feel of her skin. "Why did you?"

She stiffened for a moment before sliding off the bed. Her bare behind rocked back and forth in the pale candlelight as she crossed the room.

After a moment's distraction, he propped himself on his elbows. "Where are you going?"

"To cleanse myself, of course." She disappeared behind a wooden partition.

This must be another strange Norse custom, he decided, probably an obeisance to one of her gods. But he heard only pouring water, not muttered prayers.

She returned a few moments later and slid back into bed. A salty scent lingered around them.

"Why did you suggest this match?" he repeated.

She settled beside him, though not as relaxed as before. "I gave my reasons."

He rested his hand on her hip, ever so close to that delightful thatch of dark hair. "The reasons you wanted the jarl to hear."

She was silent for a time, but she continued to tease his chest hair with a finger. The moments stretched long enough that he started to question the wisdom of his tongue.

Finally, she shifted the lay of her head but didn't relax her neck. "Shieldmaidens don't raid for their entire lives. We eventually marry."

"Surely you had suitors among your own people."

"Marrying you earned me a region to command. And even among my people, some husbands are brutes." She reached down to cup his testicles. "There is safety in marrying someone who must behave."

Though his body roused again at her touch, his mind lingered on her words. "Is that the only reason?" His voice sounded petty and desperate to his ears.

"No." She released him and placed her hand around his waist. "In you, I saw a thoughtfulness I didn't expect in a barbarian."

He smiled faintly at the word.

"You surprised me in your town," she added. "And again on the road."

He squeezed her hip. This was an important moment. She had shared a part of herself, and he wanted to do the same.

"I meant my vow. I will do everything I can to honor it."

She lifted her head to look at him and offered a wry smile. "Then kiss me and rouse yourself. I want to do that again."

He felt drained of both tension and energy. "I'm not sure I can manage."

She purred and ran a finger down his chest. "We'll see about that."

CHAPTER SIX

HALLA

H ALLA AND TAURIN left two weeks later by *knörr* for Lillebonne with Seraphim and the other horses, a half-dozen warriors, and a host of surveyors. Jorund promised to send the first settlers and supplies to see them through the winter as soon as he could organize them.

Taurin kept wandering up and down the *knörr* during the voyage, searching the distance. Though he was still a stranger in many ways, Halla could nonetheless recognize his anxiety at returning home with the news he carried.

He had recommended they time their arrival to follow Sunday mass so they could greet all the aldermen at once. But as they rounded the bend in the Bolbec, the church bell rang out rapidly over the water. She had heard that quick rhythm many times as she had crested a hill outside a Frankish town.

"Someone saw the sails," Taurin murmured.

Halla sighed. Causing a panic was an ominous way to begin her rule. Why had she agreed not to darken her eyes with kohl or wear her mail armor if these people chose to hide away instead of meeting her? Retrieving her axes from the bench beside her, she slipped them into the loops at her waist.

The town square sat empty by the time the *knörr* drew tight against the pier and Taurin and Halla disembarked. She saw no one within sight of the docks.

"Be on your guard," Halla warned her warriors and surveyors. "These people may react with violence."

Taurin dashed toward the town square, waving his hands. "My people! Do not fear!" He crossed to the church and cupped his mouth with his hands. "You are in no danger!"

His frenzied movements reminded her of the Frankish defenders at Saint-Lô, desperately seeking escape after Rollo's army had breached the walls. Yet she felt an unexpected sympathy for him.

Too late, Halla realized his people probably didn't recognize him. Why would they? He still wore the bleached, gold-edged tunic from their wedding, finer than any attire she'd seen during her first visit. His people had feared Norse ships for decades, and now he was returning home aboard one of them. Of course these cowering people would hide at the sight of Norse sails.

One of the windows to the church cracked open a sliver before shutting again. A few moments later, the door opened. That annoying man Orderic emerged and greeted Taurin before beckoning the others in the church to join him. Slowly, the townsfolk began to emerge, eyes fixed on the longship berthed along their pier.

"Keep your weapons sheathed," she instructed the warriors and surveyors behind her. "I'll go first. If they kill me, return to Rouen."

"You expect us to withdraw?" growled Vikarr among them.

"I expect you to come back with more men and avenge me by burning this town to the ground," Halla corrected.

He peeled back his lips to bare his teeth.

Disembarking, Halla approached the group of men who had gathered to greet her husband. They kept casting their anxious eyes toward the longship. Most had long ago abandoned the virility of even middle age and sported more gray hair than muscle. Other than the priest in his black robes, they all wore fine linen tunics with embroidery along the edges. The acrid bite of incense clung to each of them.

She recognized a few of them, including the detestable Orderic and those with whom she'd dined several weeks earlier. Presumably, the others were the remaining aldermen.

Norbert crossed himself. "God has delivered you from danger and returned you safe from the heathen…" He trailed off as Halla halted beside Taurin. "What is that…that woman doing here?"

Taurin met her gaze and swallowed. During the voyage, he had requested that she allow him to explain the situation to his people, so she bit back her sharp retort and merely nodded to him.

"In Rouen, I saw thousands of Norse warriors," he began. "I saw many traders from distant lands and more wealth than I could imagine."

Orderic shook his head. "But, Berengar—"

"Berengar's attack injured their pride, but killed very few warriors," Taurin said. "Rollo's army remains intact, many times greater than the warriors who attacked us so many years ago."

The aldermen shifted and looked to each other in obvious disappointment.

"We should have killed them," A man older than her father limped forward and peered past Halla at the Norsemen clustered near the pier. His words came in a rush. "When those three first arrived, we should have killed them. They will raid us again." He crossed himself with a shaky hand.

A few of the oldest men nodded in agreement. Halla brought her hand rest at her waist, close to her axes.

"No, they won't," Taurin said. "Jarl Rollo has forbidden his warriors from attacking us and pledged to protect us against other Norsemen."

Halla smirked when a few of the aldermen gasped. She never tired of the look of Christian disbelief and surprise.

Orderic clasped Taurin's wrist. "Is this true?"

"It is, my friend." Her husband smiled. "He offered his word not only to preserve our lives and fortunes, but our faith, as well." He turned to Norbert. "Rollo has sworn to respect our beliefs."

Norbert closed his eyes and crossed himself, muttering something in Frankish too softly for Halla to translate. A few of the men slumped in visible relief. Now, a few of them even smiled, the tension draining from their faces.

Taurin licked his lips, which curled upward in a nascent smile. "And, he offers us access to the markets in Rouen and other nearby towns in exchange for a small tax on trade."

"Other towns?" asked one of the younger aldermen.

"Yes, Dagobert. It seems more towns survived as we did."

"But…the bandits…" Orderic's eyebrows furrowed.

Taurin gestured to Halla beside him. "The jarl's warriors will clear the roads."

The others began to chatter excitedly, peppering Taurin with questions about the markets of Rouen. But Orderic shouted them down and waved his hands.

"Are you saying the Norse intend to stay?"

The others fell silent. Taurin straightened his tunic with a shaky hand. In the distance, Halla heard the muted, anxious murmuring of the other townsfolk, still clustered around the church and studying her warriors.

"His protection comes with a price." Taurin's words sounded strained, like wool stretched to the point of tearing. "He intends to extend his rule over all the towns of the Pays de Caux."

For a long time, they simply stared at him. Expressions hardened, necks tensed, and their eyes narrowed in unmistakable defiance.

Halla's discomfort grew as the silence extended. She bit her tongue hard enough to draw blood, resisting the urge to intervene. She had agreed to let him deal with this matter.

"What did you say to this… intention?" the limping alderman asked. Taurin swallowed, eyes darting back and forth. "I pledged that we would support his rule if he protected us."

"You presumed to speak on our behalf?"

Taurin raised a hand. "By agreeing, I persuaded him to forbid his people from enslaving us."

"You went to Rouen to determine the threat we faced, not decide our future!" The alderman clenched his hands into fists. "And which of these violent pagans is to be our master?"

Taurin hesitated before raising a hand toward Halla. The Franks' eyes widened even before he spoke. "This is Halla Skittadottir, she is Rollo's—"

"A woman?" The alderman cried.

"Not only do you sell us to a pagan, but to a pagan whore?" Norbert spat. "This succubus addled your wits and made you betray your own people."

Halla clenched her fists to restrain her outrage. She could kill any one of these men in combat. How dare they condemn her for her sex!

"I will not tolerate such a comment about my wife," Taurin warned.

His defense of her against his own people made her skin tingle with excitement.

"Your wife!" Orderic cried. "You married this heathen?"

The others pumped their fists and slung insults, accompanied by droplets of spittle.

"Your father would be ashamed—"

"—more foolish than we thought—"

"—ruining the honor of your family—"

"Villain!"

"—betrayed your faith—"

How dare they accuse him of betraying his faith, when he had done so much to preserve them! It mattered not that he worshipped a different god; piety deserved respect, not ridicule.

"Traitor!" The limping man raised his fist as he advanced on Taurin.

Outrage boiling over, Halla sprung forward and threw her hip into the man, knocking him to the ground amid a cloud of dirt. He clutched his hip and gaped at her in disbelief.

She loosened her axes enough to grip the shafts and rounded on the other aldermen.

"I advise you not to mistake me for a meek woman," she warned. "I am a warrior of Odin, like the thousands Rollo can command in Rouen." None of them could possibly know many of those warriors would return to their homelands for the winter in a few weeks.

She straightened and took a step back, calming herself with a few quick breaths. Her rapid reaction had made the aldermen hesitate. She doubted they would attack her now, unarmed as they were.

She spared a glance for Taurin, who was frowning in obvious distress. She felt sorry for him. He had started so well.

"You condemn the only man who witnessed our numbers." She straightened and raised her chin. "You should thank him for his decisions in Rouen, then decide whether you would rather profit from our strength or compel us to crush you with it."

HALLA

Taurin waited to speak until they were leading a column of surveyors, recorders, and wagons west toward his estate.

"That could have gone better." He released a long sigh. "You shouldn't have threatened them."

She rolled her eyes at his naïveté. "They dismissed me when I first visited. I showed them they cannot do so again."

"What if they press your bluff?"

"My bluff?"

"That you would crush them."

She flipped a hand in his direction. "Oh, I left Rouen expecting at least one of your aldermen to force me to execute him."

His head snapped around. "Excuse me?"

"You said some would never accept our authority. If they sow discontent, then I must put an end to it. A little bloodshed may prevent more."

"I never agreed to help you kill my people." He frowned and picked at some stray grass stuck to Seraphim's mane.

"I don't desire to," she reassured. "But I must keep order."

"What if one of your people endangered this town?" He spoke the words as if they were an accusation.

"A Norseman?"

"Yes."

She shrugged. "Then I would punish him according to his crime."

"Even execution?"

"Certainly."

Taurin studied her, eyes narrowing. "I expect you to honor that pledge."

"I wouldn't give it if I didn't mean it."

He turned to regard the landscape through which they traveled. "Just remember that even after the settlers arrive, there will still be many more Franks than Norse. Many times more."

She chose to interpret his words as a warning. She doubted he'd be foolish enough to threaten her after all he'd seen in Rouen. "That's why I show strength now. They must understand that even if they massacre me and all our settlers, Rollo would return and kill every last one of them."

Taurin swallowed. "He said as much in Rouen."

"We do not say what we do not mean." His face twisted with disquiet. She reached out and squeezed his hand. "My people are content to work the land beside yours, so long as it doesn't endanger them. Let us work toward that goal."

Taurin rubbed his bare chin roughly. He had claimed he couldn't grow a beard until he met his people, lest they believe he betrayed them. Perhaps this winter, she could persuade him.

"You accomplished one thing, at least," he said.

"Oh?"

His smile brightened his face as if it had never darkened. "They won't think you're a soft woman."

She barked a laugh, surprising the horse bearing the closest surveyor behind her.

"I'm glad of it. We'll have enough trouble preparing for spring without rebellion."

"The tension will calm when Jorund sends the supplies."

"How so?" She frowned at the strange twists of his mind.

"Food, fresh farm equipment, grain, paper, timber, clothing… My people haven't seen its like. Some of it will find its ways into their hands through trade."

"A taste of what they can expect from working with Rollo?"

He nodded. "And proof of his commitment."

In Rouen before they'd left, Rollo had showed them and his other *hersirs* the room filled with plunder that would buy supplies for the settlers. He had been gathering it for quite some time. Both she and Taurin had marveled at its size. Rollo had intended to emphasize his expectation for a return on his investment, but now Halla realized Taurin had seen opportunity, as well.

His mare sniffed her colt with interest. Once he brought the animal under control, he asked, "How long until the first settlers arrive?"

She rubbed her hands over her thighs to warm them. The weather had turned colder since her last visit. "The first dozen families should arrive in three weeks. They'll want to build homes before the snow begins."

He frowned. "That's not much time."

"More than the others have." It would take time for the other *hersirs* to establish their authority in their regions and begin settling. Come next spring, the Norse who claimed Jumièges, Fécamp, and the rest would plant during the day and build farmhouses at night.

Taurin had made it possible to bring settlers to Lillebonne this fall. Hopefully, those extra months of familiarity would convince the Franks against burning crops or fouling the water supply. They could cause a host of problems, and she truly didn't want to repay her husband's support by massacring his neighbors. Nor would doing so make her job easier.

"Look." He pointed to the fields opening before them as they crested the hill. "You wondered whether you could be happy on a farm."

Before her lay a broad, shallow valley hidden in the slopes of a trio of forested hills. Three wide fields sown in alternating strips filled most of the land and surrounded a collection of buildings marked by rising tufts of white smoke. To the northeast, several groves of trees divided gardens, each clearly marked by wooden fences. A stream wound its way along a faint depression that cut through the valley's center.

She gasped, sweeping her eyes over the vast basin. A horse would tire long before galloping from one end to the other. "*This* is your estate?"

His eyes danced as he smiled. "Welcome home."

Taurin guided them to a dirt road wide enough for four horses to walk abreast. He pointed as they progressed. "My father planted the fruit groves to the northeast when he was a boy. Grapes, apples, raspberries, elderberries, even a few cherries. We intersperse them with the vegetables. Carrots, turnips, beets, beans, peas, cabbage, radishes."

Taurin gestured to his right. "We're letting the southwestern field lie fallow this year. We have barley, oats, and flax to the southeast and rye to the northwest, with a little wheat. Wheat doesn't grow well in the soil here, so we don't give it too much land." He pointed as he spoke. "We're reaping the rye now."

Several heads bobbed in the fields, harvesting the stalks and collecting them in large baskets. A trio of children dragged the full baskets toward a nearby cart.

"The people working that field… Are they your thralls?"

The corners of his mouth turned downward. "Only free men work my *demesne*."

"*Demesne?*"

He rubbed his chin. "I rent most of my lands in parcels—called *manses*—to tenants. They pay rent with a portion of their crop and a certain number of days working my personal fields, my *demesne*."

She shook her head. He owned all of this, and more beyond? When she had agreed to support Rollo, she expected to tend a little farmland, some animals, and a small garden. An estate of this size suggested influence over many families and many items to barter for influence and position. He was a powerful man indeed, more powerful than she had thought.

She swallowed. It seemed too much for one person to control. She hadn't hesitated to command an entire region for Rollo, but the thought of running this estate seemed too great a responsibility. She couldn't do this.

"How do you manage it all?"

He waved the question off. "My steward, Leubin, does most of the work. Crop rotations, managing the workers, arranging supplies."

She forced herself to breathe, uncoiling the knot of tension. Of course he would have help. He couldn't leave for three weeks during the harvest without it.

They traveled farther down the dirt road separating the rye from the orchards. In the distance, animals roamed through the tall grasses of the fallow field.

He followed her gaze. "Cows, chickens, sheep, goats. We have pigs in pens farther up the road."

She began to understand why Rollo wanted to control the countryside. While the land might have little gold or treasure, it teemed with life. They were fools to believe they had destroyed it all.

"Do all of your people have so much?"

He squirmed atop his horse. "A few of the aldermen." He hesitated before pointing to the granaries nestled near a windmill. "But I take care of my tenants. Most years, my stores can see them through bad harvests." He spoke the words with a smug pride, as if he expected them to impress her.

Several of the innermost strips of cultivated land ran short to create a pocket for the estate's buildings. Most looked like homes, with thatched roofs and plaster walls encased by wooden frames that bore the signs of frequent repairs. Wells and barns surrounded them at random, at least to her eyes.

The gabled roof and solid wooden walls of one structure made it stand out. Beyond the strange construction, it was larger, enough for perhaps two rooms. By Frankish standards, she supposed it was luxurious, but it sat frighteningly close to the pig pen.

"Is…is that your home?"

He cleared his throat. "Leubin and his wife, Adella, live there." His voice carried a hint of humor. He gestured her forward, out from the shadow of the steward's house and around the corner. "*That* is my home."

She and two of the surveyors gasped.

The building before her stood two stories. What the massive structure lacked in refinement and straight lines it made up for with size and obvious age. With so much stone, it rivaled only the great hall in Rouen for size and expense. Mortar indicating numerous repairs crisscrossed the limestone walls that ended in jagged lines that someone had attempted to smooth, without much success. Unlike the rest of the buildings, this one had a solid wood roof with exposed rafters poking down every couple *ells*.

"The Romans built it many generations ago. My father believed it originally possessed two additional wings, one on either side." He gestured to the jagged edges. "We continue to find new fragments of stone quite far out when we plant new crops. I think it used to be walled."

She imagined the size of the lost wings, stretching into the fields. "What happened to them?"

Taurin shrugged. "Damage over time. We no longer know how the Romans repaired them. We save what we can, but we've had to make some alterations. Now, only the main building remains."

The eastern wall had collapsed some time in the past, for the stone stopped in a ragged, diagonal line. Stout wooden walls, affixed by mortar, completed the height. Another wall bore the stains of charring from an ancient fire, faded by uncounted storms.

Seeing this strange monster that clung to life despite the weathering of time, she began to understand Taurin's words on the way to Rouen. This building, even this whole estate, had lasted for centuries, defying the forces that sought its ruin. No one who called it home would willingly abandon it.

Their progress had attracted attention. A man and a woman awaited them ahead.

Taurin reached out to squeeze her hand before dismounting. "Welcome home."

Home. On a farm in Frankia among heathens, so far from civilized comforts.

Halla dismounted as a young man approached. The same height as herself, he lumbered rather than walked, with each step taking the full burden of his weight. She doubted he had ever carried a sword.

He dipped into a stiff bow before reaching up to take the reins. With a graceful motion, he easily guided her colt toward the stable in a tight circle. He might not know battle, but he clearly knew horses.

Taurin extended a hand for her to join him. "Halla, come meet my steward, Leubin, and his wife, Adella."

Stocky Leubin looked to be younger than Halla's father would have been. The dark-haired woman beside him wore a Frankish dress that hugged her figure and clearly concealed no weapons. Rounded hips suggested many births. She studied Halla, tight-lipped.

As she approached, both sets of eyes dropped to the axes hanging from her belt. Halla supposed they had never seen an armed woman before.

After summarizing the consequences of his trip to Rouen, Taurin introduced her. "This is Halla Skidadóttir. She will represent Jarl Rollo of Rouen here in Lillebonne."

Leubin's mouth fell open, but Adella merely arched an eyebrow.

Inhaling, Taurin clasped Halla's hand. "She is also my wife."

"Wife!" With the skill of the most capable warrior, Adella leaned forward and assessed Halla's tactical assets: long, braided hair, deep blue eyes, shapely hips, and well-defined legs.

While she had received jealous glares many times before, she puzzled over it now. Adella had a husband and a high position at the estate. Taurin had explained that she and Leubin had only sons, so she couldn't expect to marry a daughter to him. Surely a Christian lady didn't aspire to become a mistress!

Leubin set a hand on Adella's shoulder, a surprisingly gentle gesture that nonetheless soothed his wife. He offered Halla a toothy smile that reached his eyes. "Then I welcome you."

Halla nodded gruffly. At least one person wouldn't cause her trouble.

Leubin turned to Taurin again. "We didn't expect you. I've sent a few of the ladies in to light the hearths." Leubin indicated the Norsemen unloading the wagons. "What about them?"

Halla leaned back and rested her hands on her axes. "The warriors will sleep here until we secure homes in town. The surveyors will return to Rouen once their work is done."

Leubin frowned. "I don't know of any vacant buildings in town."

She shrugged. "Then we'll build them."

He shifted his weight and studied the forest in the distance. "We'll have to start cutting trees and shaping planks immediately."

Halla dimpled her lips into a smirk. She liked this man who carried out instructions without protest. She could appreciate why Taurin valued him. "We left a sizeable stock of wood on our longship in town."

"That will help. The fruit harvest is going to take much of our time." Inhaling, he pinned Taurin with a glare. "Your new husband left before telling me what trades he had arranged with the other aldermen. I can't harvest until I know how much of the crop I can press into wine and cider."

Sighing, Taurin raised a hand. "I know, I'm sorry. I have many things to share." He turned to Adella. "Will you show Halla the house while Leubin and I talk?"

Adella directed an angry glare at her husband. Leubin merely jutted his chin toward the house. Finding no support there, she inclined her head the faintest amount.

"Follow me."

She trudged toward the long oak door with heavy footsteps and nary a glance backward to see if Halla followed. This one had spirit. Halla would either befriend her or kill her before the winter passed.

The musty odor of old fires tickled Halla's nostrils as Adella opened the door to the ugly manor and stepped aside. Beneath the scent of oak and elm, the faintest whisper of roasted meat clung to the air. At first, it reminded her of the feasting hall in Rouen.

But the illusion faded when Halla took a tentative step inside. This building contained no laughter, singing, or fighting. Other than the warriors and surveyors who'd accompanied her from Rouen, she wouldn't find any of her people within a week's ride in any direction.

She had expected a large space with a set of wooden stairs along one wall like the buildings in Rouen. But the main hall, though many strides across, did not extend the full length of the exterior. Stone walls that blended seamlessly with the exterior frame divided the space into distinct rooms.

She had seen such construction only once before, during a raid far to the south. That building had not burned easily, and the foundation had survived the fire despite her and her people's best efforts.

Young women in simple Frankish dresses were stacking logs in the hearths. One of those hearths sat along the western wall, beyond a long table and a pair of benches on either side. The lack of scratches in the stone floor suggested Taurin rarely moved it aside for extra room. She grunted a low laugh. Her Norsemen would bring more bustle than this estate had seen for some time.

Adella pointed to the room near the long table. "Beyond is the pantry and larder. We also have tables for staging prepared food before being served. The actual cooking happens in a building behind this house."

Halla frowned. "Why?" It seemed foolish to carry hot food through the rain and snow.

"To prevent a fire from burning down the manor, of course." Adella pressed her lips together and ran her eyes over Halla again. "Do you cook?"

Halla shrugged. "I can heat meat over a flame."

Adella arched an eyebrow but made no comment. Instead, she crossed to another threshold on the other side of the building beside the second hearth. "A corridor wraps from there, around behind the stairs, and ends at the pantry. Off it lie rooms for two maids, the stable boy, and three other male servants." She raised her chin. "I chose each member of the staff myself."

Halla's thoughts lingered on the layout. "Two doors? Do the servants' rooms have windows?"

Adella's lip twitched in a nascent scowl. "Of course."

Each one gave attackers a means to enter. With so many doors and windows, she could never keep them out.

The solid stone stairs wrapped like a torc around the largest part of the main hall. A cedar banister framed the inside edge. Each step sloped into a depression in the middle, worn away with time like so much of this town.

She almost wished they were wooden so she could replace them. But stone wouldn't burn or take as much damage if she and her warriors ever had to shoot arrows from the second floor. Blood would also make them slippery and further help to defend the old manor. "Show me the second floor," Halla instructed.

Exhaling audibly, Adella began to ascend with footsteps that fell rhythmically but slowly. "Upstairs are the family's rooms," she said as she climbed. "We haven't used most of them since Taurin's father died."

At the top, a short corridor ran to the right, with four other doors signaling the other rooms. "When your servants arrive, we'll lodge them with you and Taurin here on the second floor." Half a breath later, she added, "Unless you intend to eject the household staff to make room for yours."

Such a suggestion seemed unduly harsh. Was this how these people behaved? "I have no staff."

"None?" the other woman breathed.

She nodded. "Nor have I ever managed a household. I wouldn't know where to begin." Cleaning the rooms, stocking the larder and pantry, managing the staff, washing the clothes... The list of tasks seemed endless. "Who manages it now?"

Adella folded her hands together before her. "I do, ever since the old mistress died many years ago." She narrowed her eyes. "Until today."

A wave of relief washed away Halla's tension. This woman's cold reception made much more sense now. She had evidently expected Halla to displace her.

"Taurin explained how he values Leubin's management of the estate," she said. "Are you willing to do the same with the household?"

"But..." Eyes and mouth opened wide, Adella looked like a fish.

Halla restrained the urge to laugh.

"But this is *your* home now!"

This sprawling estate, so far from the bustling markets and streets of Rouen, would never be her home. Nor did she care to learn its management. Governing Lillebonne would consume all her time. "I trust your abilities more than my own."

Adella eyed her for a long time before straightening. "Very well, then."

Halla exhaled a slow breath. What would she have done if Adella had refused?

She had suggested marriage to Taurin surrounded by her people, in her city. She had assumed he would adapt to her people's ways. But sniffing the odors of age in a rural manor, surrounded by Christians, she now understood the depth of her foolishness. She'd come here not only as ruler, but also as wife and mistress of a household. She should have anticipated that. Even Norse women assumed such duties.

The terrible sense of dread began to grow in the pit of her stomach. If she had overlooked such an obvious fact, what else hadn't she considered?

HALLA

Halla stood within the bedchamber and listened to the mooing of cows and the clucking of chickens that seeped through the wooden shutters. Livestock set her heart thumping. Animals meant settlements, and settlements meant battle and plunder.

At least, they used to. Now, she would hear them every night instead of the laughing and shouting and rutting and arguing of Rouen. In this strange land, home meant silence, except for the bleating of accursed animals.

A pair of cows called out to each other again. Oh, how she wished their call warned of a cattle thief! At least she knew how to handle that problem.

Shuddering, she offered a silent plea to the gods for the strength to endure this emptiness. No matter how far she traveled from Rouen, they would never abandon her while she did their work.

Three thumps on the door pulled her out of her thoughts. One of the warriors drinking downstairs had probably forgotten which door was his. The squeal of metal rubbing against metal as she lifted the latch interrupted the livestock and brought a smile to her face. The sound of grating metal, she knew. That sound had always provided comfort.

But no Norse warrior awaited her. Instead, her new husband held a platter in one hand and a clay jug in the other.

"I thought you might be hungry."

Her stomach growled at the aroma of roasted meat. "It seems I am." She stepped aside to let him enter his bedroom.

He set the platter on the bed as she latched the door. In addition to the boar were two bunches of grapes, boiled carrots, and a pair of goblets.

She shook her head as she surveyed the food. "You prepared a meal for me."

"I…but…" He frowned. "I meant no offense."

"No, it's just…" She gave a quick chuckle. "No one has done that since my father went to Valhalla. Usually, the *hird* would eat together in the great hall."

"We can go downstairs, if you prefer. Your men were returning from bathing in the stream when I came up here." He rubbed the back of his neck. "They were dripping on my floor."

"It is *Laugardagur*." She settled onto the bed and reaching for a piece of meat.

He sat across from her and did the same. "Is that some sort of festival?"

She chewed, savoring the shaved salt that tickled her tongue. "Our bathing day. We do so once a week."

His fingers stopped part-way to his mouth. "So often!"

"You do not?"

"Bathing allows evil in."

She grinned at the foolish thought and a piece of meat almost slipped out of her mouth. Hastily, she stuffed it back in with a finger. "I've found that cleanliness puts men in a better temper." Would she truly have to interact with these people and all their accumulated filth? "Perhaps because their wives are more satisfied with the smell," she hinted.

He turned to the shutters, jaw set.

This was impossible. These people were too backward. They knew nothing of the gods, rummaged in filth, and surrounded themselves with further stink by living among animals. Where was the man on the ride to Rouen who had spoken with such ease and elegance?

If not for the gold torc Rollo had given her and the green linen shift that still bore the faded stains of her wedding sacrifice, she would think dark magic had placed her in the life of another.

She looked down at her hands, noting the old scars and calluses. She remembered every one of them. They were real. Being here was real. She had chosen freely and would have to live with her choice. She reached for another piece of meat.

Beside her, Taurin sighed. "I guess I'll go to the stream tonight, then."

She drew a sharp breath and almost choked on her food. She needed a moment to recover. "What?"

His smile creased the corners of both his lips and his eyes. "It's bathing day."

She coughed and swallowed the offending meat. "Would you truly risk leaving yourself defenseless against evil?"

Doubt snuffed the emotion behind his smile even as it lingered in his muscles. "Not defenseless. I can say the Lord's Prayer as I bathe. No demon can endure it."

"A powerful weapon indeed, then." She gestured around her face to ward off evil before reaching for more food. She had satisfied her hunger, but now she ate out of genuine pleasure at the taste.

He squeezed her hand, apparently oblivious to the sticky meat juice on them. "If my bathing more often comforts you, I'll gladly say a few more prayers. This is your home now. I want you to feel welcome."

She doubted such a thing was possible, but his gentle touch soothed her regardless.

He sighed. "In Rouen, I felt pressed in on all sides by the noise, the heat of so many bodies, and not a stand of trees in sight."

His words brought her back to the soothing din of voices, the creaking of cart wheels, and distant laughter and shouting of a bustling city. On the march, cackling fires and hushed stories of great warriors lulled her to sleep. She was never alone, always wrapped in the familiarity of her people.

Here, no walls wrapped her in their comforting strength. If her axe head came loose or a ring in her mail coat tore, she would have to journey to town for a blacksmith. In a fire, what neighbors would grab buckets to haul water from the river? Who would sing to the gods in this distant land?

"It's like that for me here," she admitted. "After how your people reacted today, they won't make my task any easier."

Taurin leaned on an elbow and popped a carrot into his mouth. "You mentioned your father. What was he like?"

She smiled as she rolled a grape between her fingers. She had tasted her first grapes when her father had returned from a raid in Frankia. At the time, she had worried Rollo would punish him for stealing from the spoils. Only when she had joined the raids herself did she realize food wasn't considered plunder.

"He played the lyre, but only at home." She would listen to him play from beneath her fur blankets on winter nights. She had made the mistake of revealing she listened only once; he had stopped and refused to continue. "His playing made me think of my mother." She tossed the grape into her mouth. "She died in childbirth when I was young."

Taurin swallowed and lowered his eyes. "I'm sorry."

She shrugged a shoulder. She recalled little of her mother beyond a few vivid memories. "It was her fate."

Taurin rose and crossed to a trunk in the corner. "My father left his mark on this estate." Lifting the lid, he retrieved a flute made from bone, a femur from a large animal like a cow or deer. "My mother used to play. I taught myself after she died."

He spent a few moments carefully placing his fingers before he began to blow. Though she had expected a song of languid sorrow, he piped a cheerful, bouncing song with a repeated melody that would entertain in any feast. Each time the tone rose, he raised his eyebrows with it, lost in the music. She delighted in the subtle movements of his lips as he controlled the intensity.

He had also used his lips well in Rouen. Warmth spread through her body.

The smile lingered on both of their faces after he had finished.

"Bragi has blessed you, as he did my father." The best warriors often made the finest musicians, a sign of the close friendship between Bragi and Thor. "Father always loved the gods."

Taurin placed the flute back in the trunk. "The slave who taught me your language came to us as a child. He knew only a few stories about your gods."

"Did he die well?"

"I don't know." He settled onto the bed and ate another carrot. "He fled after my father died."

She tried one as well, and found the taste surprisingly pleasing. "You didn't pursue him?"

He shrugged. "If he survived, then God desired his freedom."

A quick chuckle slipped out.

"What?"

"You sound like my people. We believe our fates are fixed." She shook her head. "I did not expect to find such wisdom in the words of a Christian."

He smiled. "Perhaps we are not so different after all." After a long silence, he rubbed his thighs roughly. "This is all very strange to me."

"I doubt that." She snorted. "You are home."

"I wasn't married when I left." He shook his head. "Though I should have been." His voice quavered.

"What do you mean?"

He folded a leg beneath him. "I was betrothed to Orderic's sister for nearly ten years."

"That explains your friendship." Orderic and Taurin were too different in attitude and behavior to be natural friends.

"She was much younger," he continued. "We would have married when she turned seventeen last year."

So young! She was about tease that she was too old for him when she noted his strained expression. "What happened?"

His eyes fell again. "Two years ago, a fever spread, killing many." Shoulders slumping, he shook his head. "I lost my father and my intended bride at the same time." He restored his poise with a slow breath. "This house became very lonely. I suppose I grew to like it that way."

"And now, you return with a wife and her band of heathen Norsemen." In the wake of her words, a round of drunken laughter rose up from downstairs.

He cracked a faint smile. "It's louder than I'd prefer."

Halla was pleased to see a little levity after discussing the dead. She didn't wish to live with a morose man. "While I find it too quiet."

He released a laugh akin to the notes of his flute. "If that's the least of our problems, we are blessed indeed."

"Ah, but by who's gods?" she teased.

He chuckled. "I'm in too good of a mood to even contemplate the sacrilege of that question."

"So am I." To her surprise, it was true. "But I have eaten much and am curious what *that* contains." She pointed to the jug beside the bed.

"Oh!" Eyes twinkling with mischief, he uncorked it and began to fill her goblet. The liquid was a familiar golden color. He passed it to her.

"Aren't you having any?"

He shook his head quickly. "Not to my taste, I'm afraid."

Accepting it, she sniffed the contents. Nostrils flaring, she shot him a silent question. It couldn't be!

His smile grew wider.

Raising the goblet to her lips, she drank. The familiar flavor tickled her tongue and the sides of her mouth. "Mead!" She nearly wept with joy. "Where did you find mead in the wilds of Frankia?"

"One of your warriors gifted me a dagger at the wedding. I already had plenty here, so I traded it in Rouen."

She gasped. "You brought this all the way from Rouen?"

He shrugged. "I thought it might help."

Over her life, she had received many tokens of affection from friends, lovers, and her jarl. None of them had meant more to her than this piece of home in a distant land. A Norseman would think of it, but Taurin was no Norseman. He disliked the flavor and had no use for it. He had brought it solely to please her.

Watching him over the rim, she stirred with anticipation and desire. Rising, she moved the platter to the floor.

"What are you doing?"

"You gave me a piece of Rouen in Lillebonne." She curled her lips into a grin, her eyes dropping to his waist. "Now I want a piece of Lillebonne in Rouen."

His eyes widened as she straddled him and pushed him down onto the bed.

CHAPTER SEVEN

TAURIN

PERCHED BESIDE HIS window, bathed in the silvery glow of the full moon, Taurin listened to the clear trill of a nightingale. Dawn would break soon, but despite the many hours of travel, he felt no fatigue.

He released a contented sigh that dispersed as a faint fog when it struck the chilled morning air. In Rouen, he had feared the season would change before he saw his home again. In a couple more weeks, these nightingales would depart for the winter.

But despite his heathen journey, home was as he had left it.

A faint breeze drifted through the open window, carrying the scents of the nearby herb garden. Sage, lavender, and rosemary tickled his nose, bringing back the memory of the night his father had died. It had been late autumn then, as well.

It felt good having life in this house again, even if a passel of Norsemen had brought it.

Behind him, Halla shifted in the bed with a murmur and pulled the blanket over her shoulder. She must be cold. Quietly, Taurin crossed to the window and latched the shutter. Tiptoeing, he pattered over to the door and slipped into the corridor.

The slapping of his feet on the stone steps leading downstairs echoed like the angry whispers of the aldermen a day earlier. He rubbed his face roughly, desperate to banish the interrupting memory.

It could have been worse. They hadn't stormed out or declared open rebellion. But he hadn't been prepared for the personal insults. Hopefully, in time they would realize their fortunes would only improve.

If Rollo kept his word.

At the bottom of the steps, he tripped over one of the surveyors strewn across the floor and staggered to keep his footing. The man rolled over and continued to snore. A wooden cup lay beside him with a small amount of wine seeping into the stone.

Taurin sighed. That stain would never come out.

"Judas…" he muttered as he surveyed the hall.

Norsemen dozed in the corners, over the benches, and even in empty patches of stone where they fell. Shoes, riding cloaks, and bits of food littered the room. His home resembled the barn outside more than the orderly estate his father had kept.

He continued outside. The first rays of dawn peeked over the horizon to enflame the tops of the apple trees. Crossing to them, he picked a low-hanging apple and took a bite. Juice rolled down his chin. These trees were ready to harvest and not reduced to ash because of his decision in Rouen.

Halla was right; the aldermen should thank him, not sling insults.

He wandered to the stable, his breath following him in a faint fog. A fat cat with thick gray fur—one of several that kept the estate clean of rats—waddled away at his approach. Most of the horses were sleeping, but Seraphim caught his scent and approached her stall door, whinnying softly. The mare stomped at the ground and rubbed her head against his shoulder.

He laughed and patted her. "Hello, girl." Smiling, Taurin rubbed her nose. "Lots of riding today." He and Halla planned to start assessing the abandoned farmsteads.

With a quick tickle of her nose, Taurin glanced at the orange haze peeking over the horizon. Already, some of his servants were gathering by the carts, sharing a loaf of bread. An hour from now, the tenants who owed service this day would arrive.

Taurin crossed to the barn. Inside, he chose a bucket and squatted down by the nearest cow. Did Halla enjoy fresh milk in the morning? He knew so little about his new wife.

He had barely covered the bottom when a gasp from behind interrupted him.

Halla stood in the doorway in her shift, framed in the morning light that threatened to expose her curves beneath the thin material. Someone could see!

She stared at him open-mouthed. "What are you doing?" she hissed in a tone somewhere between disbelief and horror.

The intensity of her reaction left him speechless. He reached behind to check that the seam of his pants hadn't torn. "What?"

"You're milking your own cow!"

He turned back to the cow and the bucket beneath it. "I thought you might like some."

"Don't you have servants for that?"

"I can milk it if I wish." He narrowed his eyes. "It's my cow."

"That's the point." She crossed to him and tugged on his arms. He rose obligingly as she looked over her shoulder.

"What's wrong?"

"Did the other Norsemen see you?"

He shook his head. "They're all passed out."

"Thank the gods." She rubbed her hands together. "Among my people, saying that a man milks his own cow is a grave insult. It implies he's too poor to afford a servant to milk it for him."

Taurin tilted his head back and laughed until tears dripped from his eyes. Between gasps, he gestured to the orchards before spreading his arms to encompass the estate. "Are they blind?"

Halla scowled. "Did you earn it with your sword-arm, by doing great and brave deeds?"

He stopped laughing. Suddenly, her comment sounded a lot more reasonable.

"Yesterday, I had to prove my will to your aldermen. As soon as possible, we must prove your strength to my warriors."

He rose and crossed to her. She was panting. Her eyes carried genuine concern over how her countrymen viewed him.

He took her hand, threading his fingers through hers. "Then that's what we'll do."

She squeezed his hand quickly, but her brow remained knitted in tension. "In fact, we should invite all your warriors to train with my people."

"That might be a problem." He swallowed, suddenly wishing he'd collected more milk to wet his throat. "Our laws only allow the aldermen and a handful of their servants to bear weapons."

She gasped. "None of your people knows how to fight?"

He shifted his weight under her scrutiny. "The nobles feared revolts. When our town burned, our leaders needed every advantage to maintain order."

Her lip quivered, threatening to break into a scowl. "Perhaps if they had trained their people better, my kin wouldn't have killed so many."

He rubbed his hands on his breeches to steady their shaking. She referenced the casual slaughter of his ancestors too easily. "I agree with you." If his people knew how to fight, perhaps he wouldn't have had to kill a man. Nor would he have feared further raids enough to risk traveling to Rouen.

Without that law, he wouldn't be married now.

"Well, that law no longer exists," she declared. "I don't plan to run to Rouen at every difficulty. I expect your people to learn to defend themselves like any Norseman would."

The aldermen would have never abandoned their authority, yet she had freed him from his burden with a casual word. He had feared the changes the Norsemen might bring to Lillebonne, but perhaps they could do a little good, as well.

HALLA

Halla, wearing her mail coat and axes, was enjoying some cold boar from the previous night when whinnying horses and creaking wood drew her attention outside. Still chewing, she swung open the heavy wooden door. Grunting, she shielded her eyes, cursing whichever feeble-minded builder from generations past now forced her to confront a face full of sun every morning.

A servant struggled to control a thickly muscled bay draft horse that chomped its iron bit and shook his head impatiently. Fists on her hips, Adella watched her son tighten the harness connecting it to a two-wheeled cart.

"You're traveling?" Halla asked.

Adella couldn't quite remove her scowl before turning. "If this horse will calm enough to ready the cart, I will." A pouch dangled from a belt at her waist. "I have to find someone in town to trade with for supplies."

"Supplies?" The word conjured images of ladders, rope, hard tack, and waterskins.

Adella turned back to oversee her son. "Your people need plates, goblets, and blankets."

"Goblets, certainly." Halla recalled falling asleep beneath the stars on beds of grass during the summer raids, surrounded by the comfort of a thousand other warriors. "They're used to doing without the rest."

Adella answered without turning. "Regardless, I won't neglect my own standards of hospitality."

Halla adjusted the lay of her mail coat, which jangled as the metal rings shifted. "Then I will come with you."

Adella's head snapped around. "What?"

The hissed reaction gave Halla a moment's smug satisfaction after the woman's veiled insult. "The aldermen are judging the man who attacked your people today. I'd like to observe Frankish justice. If we're both traveling to town, why not go together?"

Her son halted his preparations and stared, eyes shifting from his mother to Halla.

"If…if you wish." The Christian swallowed before dropping her eyes to the mail coat. "I will wait while you dress."

She bit back an angry retort. "I'm ready now."

They alighted and Adella's son slackened the reins, allowing the horse to break into an easy trot.

After the cart passed several of the fruit trees lining the road, Halla asked, "How often do you visit Lillebonne?"

Adella pulled a fold of material out from beneath Halla's thigh on the narrow bench. "Once a week."

"And your son always accompanies you?"

Adella fussed with the hem of her sleeve. "Not always."

Frowning, she tried once more. "Do you ever travel alone?"

"No."

Giving up on conversation with a restrained sigh, Halla turned her attention to the countryside. Taurin might see beauty and history in the endless fields, hills, and forests rolling by, but to Halla, this long stretch of emptiness represented an obstacle between her new home and the town she intended to govern.

When she had first visited, the red glow of the setting sun had imbued the town with a sense of looming danger. But morning was a time for raiding. As the town came into view, the pre-midday light and fragmentary shadows made Lillebonne look like any other Frankish town ripe for looting.

They halted the cart on the outskirts of town.

"My son will remain with the cart." Disembarking, Adella adjusted the folds of her dress. "We can meet here an hour after midday."

Halla leapt to the ground and scratched the horse's ears. It rewarded her with an eager nuzzle that made her smile. "Lead on."

Adella's fingers froze around a fold of fabric. "You wish to accompany me?"

She thought the previous night's conversation had buried the animosity between them, but this woman clearly didn't wish her presence. That only made Halla want to impose herself upon her even more. "Is that a problem?"

"I just didn't expect…" She rubbed her shoulders and searched the area with wild eyes.

The vehemence of the other woman's reaction confused her. What could worry her so?

Adella glanced at the sun before sighing. "Let us go quickly, then."

Unease tickling the back of her neck, Halla fell into pace beside Adella. They followed the western road, a narrower version of the one running parallel to the Bolbec that Jorund had taken during her first visit. The outskirts contained a patchwork of buildings constructed from different woods and using different styles. Some had high eaves with vaulted struts, while others were square-framed with front-sloping roofs. Those with framed doorways and detailed architraves sat beside structures with rudimentary wooden planks blocking holes cut out of the surrounding wall.

From the way the first cross-street curved toward the river, Halla guessed it encircled the entire town to the waterfront. The buildings within that ring showed more uniformity. Though some had two levels, others had only one, and a scant few had workshops open to the street, all looked similar in joinery, texture, and technique. A few showed fresh planking, but in all cases, nearby charring suggested past fires.

"Are these the settlement's original buildings?"

Adella halted. "This land was forest before…" She licked her lips.

"Before my people burned your town."

Adella crossed herself. "You speak very casually about massacre."

With a sigh, Halla squared to her. This woman's hostility was wearing thin. She might have reassured Adella about her position on the estate, but clearly her objections remained. "I was neither responsible for that raid nor your leaders' inability to defend you."

"But your people murdered—"

"Your people consider us evil and torture our captured warriors to death," Halla interrupted. "Your nobles abuse their own people. Yet I do not blame you for their actions."

Creases formed around Adella's brow and chin. That line of thought clearly disturbed her.

Halla added in a low voice, "I am here to defend this town."

"Out of kindness?" Adella set her jaw.

"Of course not." Halla curled her lip and clasped her hands behind her back. "But we can only draw taxes and food from your town if it prospers."

The other woman bit at the inside of her lip for a time. In the silence, a cow mooed from somewhere nearby. "Taurin must believe you. He isn't prone to rash decisions."

The thought validated Halla's own observations. "Lying is cowardly." She shrugged. "My gods admire courage above all else."

"And mine admires forgiveness."

"Then we are agreed!" Halla clasped the other woman's shoulder amid a jangle of her mail.

Adella gave an awkward, uneven smile. As she resumed walking, she adjusted the lay of her thick, luxurious hair, disrupted by Halla's hand. Only then did Halla realize the older women in Saint-Lô and Bayeux had bound their hair with head coverings. Traditions were different in these forgotten hinterlands of the north.

"Your hair is beautiful." Halla hoped the compliment would ease the other woman's resistance. "I would love to braid it."

"We don't braid our hair. Not since…" Again, she trailed off. Halla sighed. It seemed a shame to waste beautiful hair for a decades-old trauma.

Adella led them at a brisk pace down the second cross-street until they reached a simple, single-floored building with a wooden sign bearing a cup and a plate. A pair of chickens clucked in a small enclosure around the side of the house.

When Adella knocked, a young woman in an apron answered. Gray powder, damp in places, covered her hands. From her fine blonde hair, Halla wondered if perhaps she had a Norse ancestor.

The woman smiled at Adella before noticing Halla and stumbling against her door frame. "The Norse woman!"

Halla struggled to release a breath without sighing audibly.

Adella laid a hand on her forearm. "Giselle, this is Halla." She turned to Halla. "Giselle is a very fine potter."

The woman swallowed, her eyes lingering on the axes dangling from Halla's waist. "What do you need, Adella?"

"What cups, plates, and platters do you have? We have a number of guests." She turned her head a fraction toward Halla. "I can trade you eggs, cheese, or meat, if you prefer. Perhaps the last pressing of wine?"

The other woman eyed Halla with obvious disdain. Halla would have much preferred fear. The boldness of this woman's gaze made her fingers twitch.

Adella shifted her weight to position herself between them, interrupting the stare. "Will you show me what you have?"

Though a simple gesture, Halla appreciated it nonetheless. The potter stepped aside and jutted her head for them to enter.

An earthy smell struck Halla's nostrils the moment she crossed the threshold, but beneath it lingered wet straw and mold. Adella detailed her needs as she accompanied the potter to a work table bearing half-finished cups and bowls. Beside it sat crude shelves with stacks of finished items and several colors of clay. A side door near the table divided the work space from the living area of the home: a hearth with a cooking pot, a table for eating, and a wooden partition frame covered by a blanket that partially concealed a bed, trunks, and small tables bearing combs, tweezers and a dozen other personal items. Laid atop a sleeping pallet was a roughly sewn doll with chestnut horse hair.

In Rouen, Halla could find trinkets from a dozen exotic lands in the markets, but all the wood here matched the colors of the buildings she had passed. Everything in this house had been made locally.

The women settled their business quickly and Giselle saw them out after agreeing to deliver the goods to the cart. "Send my good wishes to your husband," the potter bade to Adella. She glared at Halla one last time before closing the door.

The latch slid into place with the squeal of metal rubbing against metal.

Halla watched the closed door for a few heartbeats amid a conflicting sense of irritation and disappointment. She hadn't expected a warm welcome, but she had at least hoped for quiet acquiescence. Didn't these Franks realize the power Rouen could bring to bear?

"God's wounds," Adella hissed.

Halla turned, muscles tensing to confront an attack. But instead of angry villagers, she saw only a trio of unarmed women strolling down the street toward them.

A brunette with a pale green dress snapped her hands out to halt her companions. The others turned to Halla and Adella with eyes wide and mouths hanging open.

Naked disbelief twisted into obvious disgust with the faintest curl of their lips. Each set of eyes studied her with the skill of a priestess searching for a flawless sacrificial sow in the marketplace. Halla hadn't applied kohl to her eyes, yet they looked at her as if she was bathing in their children's blood.

Halla's skin tingled, screaming of danger. They were judging her. How dare these peasants look at her with such contempt? She was a *hersir* and shieldmaiden while they had cowered in obscurity their entire lives. Her fingers slide toward her axe to put them in their place.

No, she had come to rule them, not to kill them. Swallowing, she resolved to stare them down, her usual answer to jealous scrutiny. She was a warrior of Odin and would not allow these women to see her unease.

One of them managed to compose herself enough to make the sign of the cross and tug on her companions' arms, guiding them down the other side of the street. Halla challenged their glares as they passed abreast. Their necks craned to glare at her as they continued down the road.

When they finally disappeared around the corner, Halla sucked in an unsteady breath and made a protective gesture before her face. The intensity of their contempt seemed almost otherworldly.

"Halla?"

She traced her fingers along her neck, rubbing out the chill that tickled the skin beneath her ears. "Yes?"

Adella's eyes hardened with concern. "Are you well?"

She frowned. "I expected hostility from the aldermen but not the women." After Poppa's reasons for remaining with Rollo, she had thought the women of Lillebonne would openly support her authority.

"Are you truly surprised?" Adella arched an eyebrow.

Halla smoothed the lay of her mail over her stomach and hips. "What do you mean?"

Mouth parting a fraction, she swept her hand over Halla. "You come here clad in armor and carrying axes. How did you expect them to react?"

Halla shrugged. "If I don't demonstrate my strength, your people will challenge my authority."

"Oh, poof." Adella waved a hand. "That might work with the men, but that matters little. Us women are far more influential." Her mouth curled into a smug grin. "When they look at you, they see a pagan warrior. You have to convince them you mean no harm."

"I've already told them—"

"Words are empty." She shook her head. "You need to *show* them."

How could she prove her good intentions to a people who cared nothing for strength? "What should I do?"

Adella studied at her for a long time with an unchanging expression. Halla shifted her weight to her back foot. Though the discomfort returned, this time she felt none of the same menace as with the crowd of women.

Finally, the Christian sighed. "Come with me."

"Where are we going?" Only a few moments earlier, this woman had loathed to be seen with her.

"Trust me."

Curious, Halla fell into step as Adella cut a path toward the town square. The woman moved with the determination of a *hersir* leading a raid. They passed a few more townsfolk, but while Halla felt their scrutiny, Adella's pace carried them past before the anxiety could return.

Adella stopped at a two-story building very near to the square. A sign carved with a loom hung above their heads. An older man with thinning hair answered and passed a practiced eye over Halla.

"We need your help," Adella greeted.

Eyes brightening, the man beckoned them inside with an eager wave.

A dozen rolls of fabric sat in piles on a display table near the door. Drawn by the rich blues, greens, yellows, and reds, Halla reached for the closest. Her fingertips tingled as they passed over the scratchy rough wool. The fine wool lay beside them in colors just as rich. She had to run her hands over the material to tell the difference.

And then there were three rolls of earthy, pale-colored linen. Already the edges showed signs of wrinkling, but she didn't care. The smoothness tickled her fingers, and she pressed her entire hand against it to bask in its softness. "Mmm…"

Self-conscious at her outburst, Halla glanced around. Adella and the owner both watched with broad smiles.

"Pick one," Adella instructed.

Her eyes widened. "For what purpose?"

Adella gave a light laugh that contained none of the hostility and suspicion she had exuded during the rest of the trip. "I need cloth to make you a proper Frankish dress."

"A dress?"

She gestured to encompass Halla's mail, axes, and leather-wrapped pants. "That may suit Rouen, but you live in Lillebonne now." Her lips quivered.

Halla hesitated to dress like these people when her own settlers would arrive in a matter of weeks. What would they think? "I brought a shift and apron with me." She also had her wedding clothes.

"But not a proper dress. They won't trust you if you look like a Norse shield lady."

"Shieldmaiden."

Adella waved her off. "Yes, that."

Halla rubbed her arms to banish the chill from their passage through town. If honoring her oath to Rollo required wearing a different dress, then so be it.

Halla studied the rolls of cloth. She wished the linen came in richer colors, but she insisted on comfort. Unfurling a length of pale blue linen fabric, she smoothed it out on the table. The color reminded her of the winter sky over Rouen. "This one." She offered the roll to Adella.

The other woman studied it for a moment, nodding slowly. "Good, good." She unfolded it further. "I have some strips of brocade I can add."

Halla watched her argue the price in growing confusion, but didn't voice her question until she held the fabric on the street. "Why are you helping me?"

Adella settled into a stroll toward the cart. "I don't know if Taurin made a wise decision in Rouen. I certainly wouldn't have done the same." She sighed. "But what's done is done. Your actions reflect on the household now, so I will do what I can to help you succeed."

Halla searched Adella's eyes. "Do you *want* me to succeed?"

Adella brushed a lock of hair from her forehead. "Trouble would endanger my sons and my husband. So yes, I suppose I do."

Halla inclined her head at the distinction. She could work with that attitude.

HALLA

Adella visited some friends, but Halla decided against accompanying her. She had little interest in enduring more glares and hostility from the ladies of Lillebonne.

Instead, she explored the town. She studied the construction and quality of every building, noted which homes had chickens and pigs, and reviewed the rust on the hinges of each door. She spared no detail that might help her understand the needs of her new domain.

When the church bells sounded the beginning of the proceedings against Arbogast, she headed for the square. A large crowd had already gathered. Though the aldermen conversed near the closed doors of the church, Taurin stood on the periphery, separated from both them and the rest of the crowd.

He offered a pained smile as Halla halted beside him.

A breath of wind carried his scent, fresh and clean compared to the odors of the town. She gasped. "You bathed!"

Smiling, his eyes crinkled at the corners. "I wondered if you'd notice."

She leaned in and sniffed again. "Mmm. Perhaps next time, I'll accompany you."

His cheeks reddened, but instead of responding further, he shifted his weight onto his far foot, opening the distance between them.

The odd reaction confused her, but she supposed this was another manifestation of Christian modesty. These people were odd.

"Shouldn't you be with the other aldermen?" She nodded toward the small crowd of finely dressed Franks in the distance.

His jaw jutted out. "I thought the same when I arrived."

She narrowed her eyes. "What does that mean?"

He glanced sidelong at her, but didn't turn from the aldermen. "They preferred that I not participate in today's proceedings." His voice wavered as he exhaled the words.

Now, she understood his strange behavior. "Because of yesterday?"

"They claimed my involvement would encourage you to interfere."

She grunted and crossed her arms. "These crimes occurred before I knew you existed. I have no reason to involve myself. Perhaps if I tell them—"

"I don't think that would help."

Before she could question his meaning, the church doors opened. Orderic and Norbert emerged with Arbogast bound at the wrists between them.

The murmurs rippling through the crowd carried the same dangerous undercurrent as among the Norse warriors on the march back from the Cotentin. Not all were pleased to see Arbogast, but Halla couldn't decide whether their unease stemmed from his presence or his bindings.

Norbert raised his hands. "We gather today to punish Arbogast, caught engaging in banditry."

The prisoner stepped forward. "I admit my guilt, Father, and beg God's pardon for my sins." The murmuring became open chatter, punctuated by more than a few nods.

Halla settled her weight on her heels, content to watch how these people faced death. It seemed this would be a straightforward execution.

Orderic stepped forward. "Regardless of personal punishment, your kin must repay your victims. Any tenants you attacked will receive the *pecunium* to their lands and be absolved of obligations on your *demesne*."

Arbogast raised his chin. "None but God may punish me. I claim the right of trial by ordeal."

Excitement spread through the crowd.

Orderic consulted with the aldermen for a few moments. After a few rapid exchanges, he nodded to the blacksmith, who crossed to his forge and began heating a pot of water over his fire.

"Ordeal?" she whispered to Taurin.

"Rather than submit to the laws of man, a prisoner appeals to God," he explained. "He walks twenty paces with an iron heated in boiling water. In three days, we assess the wound."

She scowled. "What does any of that prove?"

"If it heals properly, God doesn't wish him to suffer further punishment."

She listened with growing horror. "And if it begins to foul?"

"Then God judges him worthy of condemnation."

She gasped. "You believe such a thing?"

"Don't your gods make their wishes known?"

"Of course, but we don't base our laws on whether someone dresses a wound properly."

Wrapping his hands in several layers of cloth, the blacksmith retrieved the pot and set it on the ground before the prisoner. Freed from his bindings, Arbogast rubbed his hands together and flexed his fists a few times.

Norbert raised his hands. "Oh, God, convey to us your divine will regarding your child. *In nomine Patris, et Filii, et Spiritus Sancti.*"

The blacksmith withdrew a pair of tongs from his apron and plunged them into the boiling water. After fishing around for a moment, he withdrew a billet of iron. Tentatively, Arbogast raised his right hand, palm-up, and the blacksmith dropped the billet in his hand.

Argobast's scream pierced the air. He took several steps, changing direction seemingly at random. Though he squeezed his right wrist with his other hand, he neither closed his hand on the scalding iron nor dropped it.

Halla, a veteran of battle, winced and averted her eyes from the twisted agony in his face. This was senseless. It proved nothing.

After twenty paces, he turned his hand over and shook it. The iron stuck to his skin for a moment before falling to the ground. Before anyone could speak, he rushed to a waiting bucket near the well and plunged his hand inside.

The townsfolk and aldermen began to disperse, muttering in satisfaction as if this strange spectacle solved the matter. Arbogast disappeared into the care of friends who began plying him with wine.

Halla gestured to the square. "What in the nine realms was that foolishness?"

Taurin frowned. "How do you judge crime?"

"Our communities host an assembly called a *Thing*, where they discuss disagreements and decide punishments with the advice of a lawspeaker."

He scratched his cheek. "And a wealthy or powerful man has never influenced the result?"

She subsided, unable to recall a king's or jarl's actions ever being judged in the *Thing*.

He faced the square again and sighed. "Hopefully, Arbogast need suffer no further punishment."

"You captured him, yet you wish to spare him?"

"He won't be spared, even if he lives." He gestured to a few of the houses around them. "Some will refuse to trade with him, and others will fleece him. His children will struggle to find husbands and wives, while he will lose influence. He will pay his neighbors, not the council of aldermen."

"You seek to avoid a feud?"

Taurin frowned. "Feud?"

Had she mistaken his intelligence all this time? She explained as if to a child, "Retaliation by the criminal's kin against those who captured him."

He shook his head. "Such a thing would be a crime against God. It isn't done."

Halla gaped. Accusations routinely led to feuds; otherwise, frivolous charges would abound. "But you want yourself and the other aldermen to remain free of the blame, yes?"

He sighed. "We've been on our own for a long time. We can't afford to needlessly incur animosity."

If his people called this justice, she could win them over with simple, fair decisions. "Then be pleased we discovered you."

"Oh?"

"My people don't fret over offending our subjects."

Though his face twisted in obvious unease, Halla couldn't imagine how her response had prompted it.

CHAPTER EIGHT

HALLA

"RAISE YOUR ARMS."
As Halla obeyed, Adella wrapped a strip of cloth around her chest and pinched where it overlapped the edge. Once again, she bent to line the strip against the fabric stretched out across the manor's dining table. After clipping the edge of the fabric with her spring scissors, she straightened again. "Now hold your arms out. Bend at the elbow."

Halla studied the flow of the Frankish woman's dress. It didn't move easily enough. A Norse shift allowed a good range of movement, while an apron held up by brooches at the shoulders kept the material from getting in the way.

"How am I supposed to fight in a dress like that?" she whined.

"With a proper dress, you won't have to fight."

"That makes no sense."

Adella sighed as she dropped the edge of the strip and returned to the cloth at the table. "Did your mother teach you nothing?"

"She died when I was four summers."

Adella frowned. "I'm sorry. I didn't know." She clipped another edge. "A good-fitting dress provides all the protection a shapely woman needs. No man can withstand her curves." She wrapped the strip around Halla's hips. "And you have nice curves."

Halla straightened a little, pleased at the compliment. "But I may eventually have to fight."

Adella sighed again and waved a hand. "Stretch and the seams will rip. Then you can do your axe swinging."

"Is that what you do?"

She laughed. "Don't be ridiculous." She snipped the cloth again. "I don't fight."

Halla gasped. "You're joking."

"The men handle all that. Hold this at your shoulder." She handed Halla the end and knelt, carefully positioning the strip. "All that sweaty work? No, thank you."

"But what if someone attacks the estate?" Even in the homelands, women mastered a weapon to protect against outlaws.

"That's different." Adella planted a shoe on the bench and hiked her dress up enough to reveal a sheathed dagger strapped to her thigh by a ribbon. "Stabbing a man with a dagger isn't a fight."

Halla barked a laugh, throwing off Adella's measurement. "And what of riding? Just hitch your skirt up to mount the horse?"

"Why not?" Adella asked.

Norbert had wanted to keep her silent and docile. Surely he would object to her exposing what lay beneath her skirts. She could fathom no sense to these customs. "Because your men lock you away."

Adella gaped, her hands halting again. "Who told you such a thing?"

"The daughter of a Frankish countess."

"Oh, perhaps among the nobles," she conceded. "I suppose countesses don't do much of anything, but we have far too much work to tolerate such nonsense."

Adella had impressed her at the market, and the work she did every day to run the estate terrified Halla. "I can believe that."

"But I don't ride much. Horses are filthy beasts."

Clearly, she hadn't journeyed through hostile country where speed meant survival. In truth, Adella probably had never left Lillebonne. That was a shame. Travel required endurance and a strong will. Adella had demonstrated both.

"Will it at least stretch enough that I can remove it by myself when I bathe?"

"You won't need to." Adella rolled her measuring cloth in a tight coil. "Next month, all the women will go to the Bolbec together and pray as we cleanse ourselves."

"Oh, no." She shook her head. "I'm not waiting that long, and neither are you. If I'm wearing a dress to soothe your people's eyes, then you're going to bathe to soothe my nose."

At Adella's look of horror, Halla erupted in laughter.

TAURIN

Taurin spent the next week accompanying Halla as she recorded every abandoned estate, farmhouse, and barn. Each day, they started with the entire corps of surveyors. Once they confirmed the suitability of a site and the group staked out the boundaries, they would move on, leaving a surveyor and warrior behind to record the useable equipment and measure the amount of farmland, forest, and stream.

"We'll have to split some of the larger estates," she commented as they returned home on the fourth day.

If the Frankish king ever returned, the nobles would want their land back. Dividing those estates among Halla's settlers would allow the nobles to eject all the Norse at once.

No. Taurin had made a promise to support her and would not undermine her efforts here. "Parceling out estates kept intact for centuries will upset my people."

"Clustering the settlements together would give them friendly neighbors." She didn't need to add that it would also help to defend against Frankish insurrections.

But Taurin shook his head. "We need to encourage familiarity between Christians and Norsemen. Besides, that's quality land. Giving it to your settlers will cause jealousy and anger."

She frowned. "We'll have to distribute it eventually."

"When you do, offer everyone the chance to trade their plots for those parcels."

She eyed him. "You spoke with such passion about your land. If others feel the same, would they truly trade it away?"

He smiled, eyes dancing. "No, but they'd appreciate the offer, nonetheless."

Each night, the Norsemen reconvened at his manor, drinking, feasting, and telling tales of their gods. Adella had started listening with rapt attention despite not speaking a word of Norse. What she took out of them, Taurin couldn't fathom.

On the eighth day, Halla expected the first settlers from Rouen. Though she had intended to greet them herself, Taurin shook his head. "I'll go. One of us must accompany the surveyors, and I can calm my people if there's trouble."

His wife raised an eyebrow but offered no objection.

Taurin rarely traversed the road to Lillebonne before full sun. The angle of the light hitting the fields left them half-shadowed. The wholesome rye that grew soothingly at midday looked threatening so early in the morning. Every few steps, the dew glistening on a stalk reflected the light and sent his senses firing with warning. Shaken, he crossed himself.

Whatever dark force lingered in those fields had evidently decided to let him pass, for his sense of dread lifted as he reached town. He only realized how tightly he was squeezing Seraphim with his thighs when the mare whinnied and nipped at him. Apologizing with a friendly scratch between the ears occupied his attention for those first few steps into town.

When Taurin looked forward again, a farmer who had sold him a bull two summers earlier looked away and trudged in the opposite direction. At first, Taurin thought he'd imagined the reaction, but as he walked, few pedestrians met his gaze. Those who did wore sneers or scowls, and two groups of women crossed the road at his approach.

Taurin dismounted and tied Seraphim up at a nearby hitching post, ignoring the glares of a pair of men watching from nearby. It seemed the townsfolk shared the aldermen's outrage at his actions in Rouen.

Heart thumping in his chest, Taurin searched for an alternative explanation for their hostility, but the morning felt like any other. The townsfolk drew water, milked cows, and retrieved eggs from their chicken coops. The chilly breeze carried the unmistakable aroma of fresh bread, smoked fish, and the odors of morning cooking fires. Already, Huebald the blacksmith's hammer clanged in rhythm with the cadence of muted conversations.

They were glaring at him and him alone.

Orderic was speaking with Father Norbert by the church. Noticing Taurin's approach, the priest offered a grim expression before shaking his head and trudging away.

Taurin leaned in to exchange kisses on Orderic's cheeks, but stopped when his friend didn't reciprocate. He swallowed. "God bless you, my friend." He jutted his chin at Norbert's receding back. "Did he leave on my account?"

"Rather on account of your consort."

The sound of Taurin's swallow echoed in his ears. "My wife, you mean."

"Yes, your wife." Orderic accented the last word. "He thinks you've betrayed us for that woman." He gestured to a pair of farmers glaring from across the square. "They all do."

Hearing his friend utter such words banished the other townsfolk from his mind. Orderic knew him better than all others. "Do you believe that?"

Orderic hesitated. "They burned our town and raided our shores." It wasn't a refusal. "These Norsemen haven't attacked us."

"But they have attacked Christians, or am I wrong that your new wife burned Saint-Lô only a week before you met her?"

He scowled, unable to argue that fact. "They haven't attacked us."

"It's only a matter of time. They'll corrupt us."

"They already have." Taurin stabbed a finger at the church. "Arbogast pillaged his own people."

"He didn't kill anyone," Orderic defended.

"It's only a matter of time," he countered, smirking. "We can't continue as before. It's too late for that."

"But collaborating with those heathens—"

"What help have our own people been?" His words came out higher-pitched than usual. The threatening ride, the glares of the townsfolk, and now the intransigence of his friend finally boiled over. "No Christian lord or bishop has visited in decades. What would you have me do?"

"Still, I—"

"What would you have me do?" Taurin spoke loudly enough to startle a few passersby into changing their course to avoid him. "Their thousands would cut through us like scythes through rye. Rollo offered me a way to preserve us, and I took it. Do you condemn me for that?"

Orderic shifted his weight but didn't break his gaze. After several long moments, his expression softened. "If you say we could not resist, I believe you." He set his hands on Taurin's shoulders. "I couldn't have done it. If I had been in your place, our town might be ash now."

His anger quenched by the unexpected admission, Taurin sighed and accepted Orderic's offered embrace. "This isn't the help we wanted, but it's the help we have." He shrugged. "And we can profit from this, if we're wise and cautious."

Orderic patted him softly on the shoulder. "I know. I see it, too. I just…" He shook his head. "We should have discussed this as a group."

"I had little time. Rollo was already planning to send his people here. I sealed the best agreement I could."

"I believe you." He pointed to Taurin. "Just recall your own words. The nobles abused us, and these Norse may do the same."

His eyes widened. "I didn't think you listened when I spoke."

"I always listen, my friend. I just don't always agree." Orderic shifted his attention to something behind him and swallowed.

Taurin turned. A dragon-headed *knörr* slowly glided up the Bolbec. A mast on the horizon meant danger.

"As you say," Orderic said through a scratchy throat. "They are here, and we must confront that fact."

HALLA

They had given the same answer all morning. "We have nothing to spare for your people."

The way the Frankish farmers had emphasized the final words grated on Halla. Bjornolf had foreseen this aggravation and had chosen to sail away rather than endure it. She felt a similar urge.

Several ships had arrived over the past two weeks, bringing settlers in woolen caps who sniffed fistfuls of Frankish soil with delight. The Franks couldn't decipher their strange language, but they couldn't possibly mistake the implications of those reactions. More than once, she had overheard loud whispers and dangerous muttering as she turned a corner. Raiders moved on; conquerors settled.

A scant few townsfolk had delighted in the newcomers. Jorund had sent wood for longhouse frames and a few animals and grain to help each family survive the winter, but little else. Enabled by raised fingers and gestures, the Norse settlers had purchased every piece of the carpenter's timber and all the hammers, chisels, augers, and bow drills Huebald the blacksmith could spare. Weighed down by bags of coins, the craftsmen celebrated.

But Lillebonne simply didn't produce enough excess for a dozen new farms. So Halla's and Taurin's rides assumed a new purpose. Two Frankish farmers had already refused—with smug delight—to trade their surplus to help their new neighbors establish farmsteads.

A rough path of crushed grass marked the recent passage of a cart through the uncultivated field before her. At the end sat the half-erected wooden frame of a farmhouse. As Halla and Taurin approached, a woman standing in front of it turned to them and shielded her eyes from the sun. A moment later, she waved.

Halla waved back, delighted at the warm greeting after so much hostility already this morning.

While they dismounted, a pair of children briefly emerged from the tall grass before ducking back inside. The girl chased the boy with a snake, threatening to feed him to it.

"Hail, *høvding*," the woman greeted before turning to a man carving a notch into a cross-beam. "Steingrim, come greet Halla,".

"Audhild, how's the house coming?" Halla asked.

The woman turned to study the growing structure. It would be a small building, but sufficient to keep them warm when the weather turned. "I don't think we have wood enough for all the rafters."

Halla sighed. "I'm working on finding more. How are you for thatching?"

"The children collected more than enough grass."

"Yours is taller than most," Halla said. "Can the others draw from your field?"

She barked a laugh. "By all means. It'll save work this spring."

The woman's husband, Steingrim, approached with a raised hand. "Hail, *hersir*."

Halla grinned. "I see your arm's feeling better."

He rubbed where he had taken a slash during the debacle on the Vire. "To think, a little more than a month ago, we were killing Franks. Now we live beside them."

Taurin shifted and crossed his arms. "It's strange for everyone."

Steingrim shrugged. "The Norns move us in unexpected ways." He jutted his chin toward Halla. "Will you hold a *blót* this winter?"

She nodded. "I will."

The Norseman relaxed and offered a tentative smile. "Good. Shouldn't start a farm without the gods' blessing." All the Norse made a gesture before their faces, and Steingrim raised his eyes to the sky. "What brings you here?"

"I'm just checking on your progress."

"Where can I get some beehives?" Steingrim grinned, revealing that he had lost one of his canines since Halla had last spoken with him. "My mead won't last forever."

"I'll do what I can." She would also have to find some for the *blót* this winter. Bees had just become a priority. "Have you spoken to your new neighbors?"

Audhild said, "I saw a rider yesterday and another the day before, but they kept their distance."

"Give them time," she reassured.

Audhild shrugged. "I'm in no hurry. Let them keep to themselves."

Halla, seeing Taurin shift out of the corner of her eye, pressed her lips together. "I'll leave you to your work. Contact me if you have any trouble."

"Thank you, *høvding*. Gods protect you."

They mounted and retraced the matted path in the grasses since it was easier on the horses. As they circled the field and entered a stand of trees leading to the next farmstead, Taurin asked, "*Høvding* means chief, doesn't it? I thought your title was *hersir*."

"*Hersir* is when I'm with the army. *Høvding* is the leader of a community."

"Steingrim is a warrior, then?"

She nodded.

They passed the trees and continued riding until they reached the sloping crest of a long, shallow hill. Below, light tufts of gray rose from the smoke-holes on either end of a wooden-roofed farmhouse.

After exploring so many dilapidated parcels, she recognized the signs of prosperity around this farm. The vestigial roots of harvested plants and bare fruit trees dotted the long, even stretches of cultivated land. A pair of cows, several pigs, and a pen of chickens all looked tidy and clean. While they didn't approach Taurin's wealth, only the worst of famines would threaten these farmers.

Most importantly, a sizeable pile of wood sat beside the farmhouse. Hopefully, she'd have better luck here.

Seraphim trotted to a stop beside her. Taurin gestured with a nod. "Tescelin and his wife Rosamund. They grow excellent pears."

"It's wood that interests me." She tugged at her skirts to smooth the new pale blue Frankish dress. Adella was a talented seamstress, but the brocade running down either side snagged on the axe-heads and money pouch near her belt and bunched when she rode.

"I can't request rent in lumber," Taurin warned. "They hold the *pecunium*."

"Then they have no excuse for being miserly."

Tescelin and Rosamund waited in their open doorway while Halla and Taurin tied their horses to a nearby fence. The woman wiped her hands on her apron as Taurin raised a hand to greet them.

"Peace be with you."

Taking one last bite of an apple, Tescelin tossed the core to the side. "And also with you."

"Allow me to introduce my wife, Halla, the representative of Rollo of Rouen. Halla, this is Tescelin and Rosamund, freeholders of honorable status."

The farmer straightened at Taurin's introduction and met Halla's gaze. Rosamund, though, lowered her eyes to assess her dress. Halla resisted the urge to adjust the lay again. Doing so would only draw attention to the axes dangling from her belt.

"Why have you come?" the man demanded.

"Husband, greet our guests properly." Rosamund offered a strained smile. "Come inside. Let us refresh you after your ride."

"Yes, please." Halla exhaled a tense breath at the encouraging reaction.

Their home was airy compared to many Halla had reviewed these past weeks. Ten strides wide and perhaps twenty long, the building had solid wood frames, including the rafters and slanted roof panels. Though it consisted of a single large room, support beams offered natural divisions. A thin sheet of wool slung over one fluttered as Rosamund closed the door, exposing a fur-covered bed behind it.

The warm air, heated by a stone-lined hearth inlaid into the ground in the middle of the house, made Halla thankful she wore her new dress. She would have sweated in her mail and padded tunic.

Rosamund removed the wooden plates bearing the remnants of breakfast from a trestle table. She returned with a jug and an armful of wooden goblets as the guests sat on the surrounding stools.

Halla reached for a goblet once Rosamund had finished pouring the yellow liquid, but Taurin cleared his throat. The others had joined hands. Instead of drinking, she clasped his hand and offered him a smile in silent gratitude.

"Oh, Lord, we thank you for your bounty," Rosamund intoned into her lap. "We ask that you bless this house and its guests. Amen."

"Amen," the men intoned before reaching for their goblets.

The watery ale brimmed with a fruity taste that quenched Halla's thirst from the long ride. She released a contented sigh. "This is delicious!"

Rosamund beamed. "I add pear during the brewing."

"Keep doing it." She took another sip. "Thank you for your hospitality and the blessing of your god."

Tescelin squirmed on his stool. While Rosamund's eyes signaled alarm, her smile never faltered. "How may we help you?"

Halla leaned forward, resting her elbows on the table. "The first Norse settlers are working to complete their homes before winter."

Rosamund glanced at Taurin, eyes darkening. "Autumn has been warm, but winter arrives quickly."

Halla nodded. "So Taurin says."

"They better hurry," Tescelin mumbled into his goblet.

"They don't have enough prepared wood," she explained. "Rouen didn't anticipate them needing to hew trees and shape planks."

The farmer scoffed. "We prepare for several seasons before building anything."

Halla continued, "My husband speaks of your prosperity and thinks you may be able to help."

He glared at her. "You cannot simply take what we have."

Taurin raised a hand. "That is not our intent." He shifted his weight, using the delay to take a breath. When he spoke again, his voice had calmed. "This summer, you mentioned wanting to build a new granary. Is that still your desire?"

Tescelin narrowed his eyes. "It is."

"It seems late in the year to start work."

"Not for next year. I've already gathered the lumber."

"We saw," Halla said. "I was hoping I might convince you to let the Norse farmers use that wood."

"Out of the question." He leaned back and folded his arms. "My sons and I can only fell and shape a few trees each month. If we have to start over, I won't have enough until this time next year."

Halla leaned forward. "What if I promised you'd have your wood when the ground thaws?"

He snorted. "How can you guarantee this?"

"If you let the Norse use the wood you have now, they'll replace it by spring."

He raised a smug eyebrow. "If they're so skilled at cutting wood, why do they need mine?"

"Time. They have to finish their houses before the first snow or they'll freeze."

"Perhaps they should go back home, then."

Taurin leaned back, eyes widening.

During her first two visits this morning, the Franks had refused

Halla outright. She had hoped for better when Rosamund had invited them inside. But this man had no intention of aiding her.

No. She refused to leave empty-handed again, not when the wood she needed sat just outside.

She took a slow drink of her ale. Over the rim, Tescelin shifted. He had clearly expected an immediate reaction. Halla grinned into her goblet, delighted to disappoint him.

Setting it back down, she first met his gaze, then Rosamund's. "They could return to Rouen. Return to a life fighting Franks and pillaging those who refuse to welcome them as neighbors." Both sets of eyes dilated. "But in their hearts, they're farmers. They want good, rich soil and clean water. Cows and goats to give sweet milk. Fat chickens and plump, ripe fruit." Remembering Taurin's words, she added, "Something to pass down to their children."

"Children?" Rosamund breathed.

Halla's heart quickened at her interest. "Rollo is only granting land to families." She faced Tescelin. "Right now, you can decide whether they become warriors in Rouen or farmers in Lillebonne."

The farmer swallowed. He found and held his wife's gaze. "Norbert."

Halla could guess at his meaning. The priest must have said something to discourage cooperation.

Rosamund took his hand. "To help children is no sin."

They were silent for a moment longer before Rosamund cleared her throat. "Your offer is generous, and God teaches us to help our neighbors." She eyed her husband one more time.

With a sigh, Tescelin took a deeper drink from his goblet. He scowled and ran his tongue along a tooth. "Very well." His face showed every drop of his uncertainty and discomfort.

Halla smiled unabashedly, excitement surging through her veins. Finally, some success!

Taurin met her eyes before flicking his gaze to the door. Rising, he offered his thanks for the drink.

Rosamund escorted them out, followed by her husband. "May the lord's blessing speed you on your journey."

"And may your god bless you." Meeting her eyes, Halla whispered, "Thank you. You've saved lives today."

That wasn't quite true; Halla would have ordered the Norse to finish what homes they could and group together for the winter. But the sentiment made Rosamund smile and kiss Halla's cheeks. Revna had embraced her the same way, but the lips of this heathen Christian felt strange on her skin.

It presented an opportunity though. "Come by the house tomorrow. Bring some of that pear ale. I'll introduce you to mead, and we can discuss how much wood you'll need in spring."

The men gasped beside her, and Taurin stepped back from the farmer. She had made some sort of misstep but couldn't fathom what. The ale had proven that Frankish women could drink, at least.

Rosamund beamed. "I would enjoy that."

They returned to their horses. The animals were more interested in necking each other than eating the grass by the fence. After another wave, Halla and Taurin set out for the next farmstead.

Taurin's straight-backed posture caused Seraphim to shake her head in irritation. "That isn't done."

"What isn't done?"

"Landowners don't invite tenants to dine with them." His eyebrows nearly met from the severity of his frown.

"I didn't. I invited her to drink."

He glared at her. "A distinction without a difference."

She rolled her eyes. "You said your people must grow used to us. To do that, I have to interact with them, show them I don't feast on their children's bones."

"Not at the expense of control over my tenants."

She pulled her horse to a stop. "I thought you take care of your tenants."

He snorted. "If their landlord helps them, they're appreciative. But they expect a friend to soothe every difficulty."

"Is that a problem?"

"I have many tenants. I can't fulfill every request. If they feel entitled to help, it would breed discontent." He shook his head. "We survive by avoiding such trouble."

She rolled her eyes. "Authority lies with Rouen now. You no longer need such tricks."

"Tricks?"

"Keeping your people at a distance to ensure obedience."

"You did the same. Audhild referred to you as chief and you did nothing to correct her." He snorted. "You value your customs, yet you undermine ours."

She straightened her dress again, shifting the lay of the axes. "My authority keeps the settlers from looting and pillaging what they need when your people refuse to help."

"You're not treating us the same."

"Perhaps," she admitted. "But that doesn't mean I'm wrong. I don't need to be fair, only effective."

Most of the time, she understood her new husband. In this moment, however, she could not decipher his thoughts from his pinched expression.

CHAPTER NINE

TAURIN

WITH SINKING SPIRITS, Taurin reviewed the pitifully few townsfolk willing to learn combat from the Norsemen. The majority of the volunteers came from his *manses* or the estate itself, including Tescelin and Leubin and his sons. No aldermen had come, not even Orderic. Several days earlier, he had learned some had threatened to deny their tenants access to mills, streams, or forests if they participated.

When Taurin fumed to Halla, she simply laughed. "What did you expect? Your aldermen enjoy their rights too much. Men used to power do not lightly surrender it."

He privately wondered whether they objected more to their loss of privilege or to Taurin himself leading this effort. Despite the passage of many weeks, his people's animosity hadn't slackened.

The one exception to their intransigence was Guntramm, a *pecunium*-holder with a farmstead on the Bolbec, who had come representing his alderman.

"Dagobert gives his blessing. He hopes—his words—others might do the work of fighting brigands so he can sleep in."

Taurin could appreciate that sentiment, though for slightly more spiritual reasons. He would have to send a bottle of wine to Dagobert for his support.

Huebald the blacksmith was one of the few who had even held a weapon before. Beholden to no landlord for his livelihood, he brought not only his willingness to participate, but the skill to forge the iron Taurin had scavenged over the previous month into proper swords. The Norse warriors approaching from the stream would have laughed heartily if the Franks had to share blades.

Halla, in her vambraces and padded tunic, led a mix of two dozen settlers and warriors. Most carried swords, though they all bore different combinations of thick wool, leather, and iron armor.

"A woman!" Guntramm pointed to Halla. "You expect us to train with a woman?"

Some of the Franks murmured in agreement.

Halla rested her axes over her shoulders. "Does an armed woman bother you?"

"It's unnatural!" the farmer scoffed.

"Your holy book disagrees," Halla countered. "Or do you not know the story of Judith the shieldmaiden, who decapitated her people's enemies? Or Deborah, who led an army?"

Taurin gaped. "You know of them?"

"Female Christian warriors?" She barked a laugh. "Of course. My people have traveled these lands for many decades."

"Father Norbert would not like hearing a pagan speak of the Bible." The muscles in Tescelin's neck tensed. "And his dissatisfaction may have consequences."

His wife raised an eyebrow.

"You're here because our ways need to change." Taurin placed a hand on Guntramm's shoulder to steady him. They couldn't afford this, not now. "They can teach us."

"We don't need them," the other man maintained.

Taurin gritted his teeth. "Any one of them has fought more battles than all of us combined." He turned to the warriors and offered, in Norse, "Thank you for sharing your experience."

Halla gestured both groups with her axes. "Pair up. Let's see what each of you can do."

The farmers working Taurin's *demesne* stopped their labor and gathered around the periphery, and some of the wives and children of his servants gathered outside their homes, watching the exercises. Even Adella emerged from her home with her youngest children, clapping as Leubin broke through his opponent's defense to earn a begrudging nod from his bearded partner.

While some of Taurin's men managed to hold their own, the Franks spent most of their time on their backs. Despite not speaking Frankish, a Norseman adjusted Guntramm's stance and moved his arms and sword to demonstrate a more efficient slash.

The advice seemed sensible to Taurin, who observed the pairings with Halla. "I wasn't sure whether your people would mock them or help them."

"They're getting better." Halla looked from one group to another. After a few moments, she turned to study him. "What did Tescelin mean, about Norbert and consequences?"

The change in topic caught him unprepared. "Your arrival has upset many."

"I understand that, but why mention an unarmed priest? Why not threaten me with the aldermen and their guards?"

"I don't know." His thoughts returned to the unsettling way the priest had avoided him in town. "We look to Norbert to show us the way to God. He has our respect."

She nodded and returned to watching the pairs train. "Speaking of respect..." She smirked and sauntered forward.

"What does that mean?" he called after her.

"Hold!" She waved her hands to draw their attention. Once all eyes turned to her, she announced in Frankish, "You show skill. You can learn much from us, but I think we can learn from you, as well."

Steingrim grunted and brandished his sword. "You give them too much credit, Halla."

"And you sell them short." She turned to Taurin and gestured to an open space between several of the pairs. "Husband, why don't you demonstrate?"

All eyes turned toward him. While the Norse shook their heads and chuckled, the naked hope and pride in the faces of his trainees threatened to break his heart. They had come to learn from him. He couldn't refuse and keep their respect, let alone earn it from the Norse.

Heart hammering, he selected a shield laying on the ground and slipped his hand through the straps. He fired a glance at his wife, only to find her smiling. Did she know something he didn't?

The others formed a rough circle around them as Steingrim swung his sword a few times and rolled his head around his neck.

Taurin unsheathed his sword. The hiss of the blade against the wooden sheath concealed his uneven sigh. The pairings thus far had been casual, but this felt different. Steingrim neither smiled nor blustered as Taurin slid his rear foot back. Halla had installed him as the Frankish champion, and Steingrim would not hold back. Not now, with so many watching.

He raised his shield so it almost covered his eyes and laid his sword flat against the top edge, pointed forward. "I am ready."

Steingrim bolted forward with surprising quickness. Instead of raising his sword before bringing it down again, he twirled it back and upwards. Eyes widening at the strange flourish, Taurin misgauged the timing of the attack and barely angled his shield in time. The point scraped against the wood with a grating screech before deflecting to the outside. Steingrim easily deflected his follow-up slash.

Taurin's pulse thumped in his ears and he backed up and repositioned his shield. He had never faced such a quick opponent before.

"I almost had you with that one," the big man taunted in Frankish.

Taurin narrowed his eyes. "Almost," he answered in Norse.

Steingrim shifted his grip. "Should I go easy on you?"

The other warriors laughed.

A flare of anger tightened Taurin's neck muscles. "You'll regret it if you do."

Steingrim curled his lips to reveal his one remaining canine. Without another word, he rose onto his toes and chopped down.

Taurin dodged the first attack and deflected the second. When the third came, he sidestepped and slashed upwards. Surprised, Steingrim barely pulled his shield around in time. Taurin's attack nicked the rim and forced him back.

A round of cheers erupted. In the background, the Franks pumped their fists.

Though neither of them aimed to kill, a wrong move could inflict a nasty wound, and Taurin didn't intend to shed his blood before all these people.

When the pagan charged again, Taurin fell back, letting Steingrim expend his attack before reaching him. As his momentum died, Taurin shoved with his shield but couldn't budge the Norseman. His maneuver having failed, he scrambled to twist aside in time to avoid the subsequent chop.

Nose hissing as he sucked in deep breaths, Taurin adjusted his grip. Both his sword and shield felt heavy, dragging his arms down. He hadn't trained nearly enough for a fight to last this long.

Steingrim lunged again, but this time, he lowered his shoulder, fully committing himself. Taurin slid to the left over rocks that cut into his knee through his breeches. He angled his sword upwards as the Norseman's weapon passed overhead.

It stopped a hand-span from Steingrim's side, where both combatants stared at it in disbelief for a silent moment.

He had won. By God, he had proven that a Frank could equal a Norseman in combat!

A roar of frenzied excitement rose up from all sides.

Barking a laugh, Steingrim hauled him up by the shoulders. "Good move!" He slapped Taurin on the back so hard he felt it in his teeth.

But despite the throbbing of his arms and shoulder, he raised his shield in salute. "Well fought, Steingrim."

While the others resumed their training with more excitement, Taurin shambled over to the manor. Halla joined him as he rested his back against the exterior and slid to the ground in exhaustion. She handed him a goblet.

He put it to his lips, only to wince and run his tongue along his mouth to banish the taste. "I think the wine went bad."

She settled beside him. "It's mead."

That explained it, then. He drank just enough to wet his throat before setting the goblet in the weeds.

"You did well, though you're too cautious. Raw aggression keeps your opponent off-balance."

The advice ran contrary to everything his father had taught him about combat.

He rubbed his shoulder where Steingrim had congratulated him. "Calling me out like that was too a great a risk. I could have embarrassed myself, and then your—"

"I knew you wouldn't." She met his gaze and raised a hand to pat his cheek. "I know the man I married."

TAURIN

The *blót* began at noon. While Halla insisted the gods needed every ray of life-giving sun to see them on the edge of Midgard, Taurin wondered how they could miss five dozen Norse men, women, and children standing on an unbroken field of snow.

She stood beside a cow, a pig, a goat, and a boar. Though she had promised not to sprinkle blood on the celebrants this time, Taurin ventured no closer than the threshold of his manor. While he acknowledged the value of his presence, he wouldn't risk the taint of a pagan ritual more than necessary.

With kohl runes across her face and a stripe over her eyes, she looked frighteningly similar to the priestess at their wedding. Beneath all that unholiness, he couldn't find the woman he'd made love to the previous night. The thought unsettled him.

No *gythia* would oversee the sacrifices this day. From how often she had mentioned the fact, he could infer her anxiety about conducting this first *blót* correctly. While her people had endured the snow months within their warm, newly finished farmhouses, she had ranged far and wide collecting unblemished animals and the few available barrels of mead.

"I've already missed the proper timing," she had said as she prepared herself that morning. "But I will give the gods a proper offering."

Raising her hands, Halla's clear voice echoed through the still February air and over the unbroken snow. "Freyr, lord of rain, master of the shining sun, we beg you to bless these new lands with the fruits of the earth so we may honor you and all the gods."

Curiosity had induced several of Taurin's servants and farmhands to cluster outside their doors, close to the safety of their houses. They watched in grim silence as Halla raised the curved ceremonial knife high. Their faces showed the same unease he had felt during his first sacrifice. Strangely, their reactions comforted him.

Halla flashed the knife across the throat of the bound boar before the animal could react. It thrashed wildly despite its restraints and the Norse farmer holding the jug beneath its neck had to jump out of the way to avoid being gored. Little tufts of steam rose up as the blood touched the snow beneath before he repositioned the jug to catch the hot liquid.

The other animals reacted to the squeals of pain and began to struggle. Halla went down the line, gently soothing the animals before slitting their throats. Once the final twitches had stilled, Halla dipped her fingers into the jug and ran them along her face, leaving red streaks before her.

Taurin swallowed and looked away. The similarity between her and the *gythia* at their wedding sickened him. Instead, he turned to his people. They were watching in amazement with expressions torn between outrage and disbelief.

All except Leubin, who was eyeing the horizon.

Father Norbert was approaching at the head of a procession of townsfolk that included Orderic and the other aldermen.

He couldn't tell whether Halla noticed the approaching mob. She raised the heavy jug over her head without spilling a drop and looked to the sky. He sometimes forgot how strong she was. "Gods of Asgard, hear my pleas on behalf of my people. Witness our devotion to you. Bless this offering so it may nourish the land."

"Stop!" Father Norbert jogged forward with his Bible held before him like a weapon. Now that they had come closer, Taurin noticed swords hanging from the hips of each of the aldermen. A score of other townsfolk carried scythes, axes, and knives.

They could have only one purpose.

Meeting his wife's gaze, Taurin gestured to his face. As she bent to place the jug on the ground, she wiped off the blood with a fold of her dress.

He took half a dozen strides toward them before realizing he had no weapon of his own. No matter. Even if he could bring himself to raise a sword against his own people, he couldn't overcome so many.

Norbert halted seven strides from the Norsemen, who parted to expose a clear path between Halla and the priest.

She stepped forward. "What is it you wish me to stop?" Her voice rose and fell with a melodic cadence, free of anxiety.

"We will not tolerate the sacrifice of children or wanton orgies of licentiousness." The crowd behind him nodded and pumped their fists.

"Nor would we."

Her words silenced the nascent fervor with the deadening certainty of a storm's first thunder crack. Norbert's mouth fell open as a sequence of twisting emotions crossed his face. The only motion breaking the stillness came from foggy puffs of the mob's hot breath.

Taurin regretted not visiting town more frequently, despite the brutal snows of the past two months. His people's hostility had grown into something truly dangerous. He should have seen this coming.

"In any case, the sacrifice is over," Halla explained.

The priest narrowed his eyes. "Where are your victims?"

Halla gestured to the animals at her feet. "All are welcome to join our feast." More than a few townsfolk craned their necks for a glimpse of the offerings.

Norbert glared at her. "We will not participate in your orgies."

Halla smirked. "We would never profane this sacred rite with wantonness." Behind the kohl, her eyes carried mischief. "Our god Freyr mistreated no maiden and harassed no wife."

Axes and scythes lowered as the muttering began. Even Norbert's expression drained of its confidence in his cause. "You merely feast?"

Of course, that wasn't all this sacrifice entailed. When she met his eyes, Taurin had no secret guidance to offer. He was torn, uncertain whether honesty or a careful lie would ease the danger.

But Halla, he now knew, did not lie. "Our farmers will sprinkle this blood on the corners of their fields." At Norbert's widened eyes, she added, "Freyr, god of the harvest, bestowed these animals upon us. We return them to him to honor that gift."

Off to Taurin's right, Leubin shuffled his youngest son inside the house. The thump of the door closing sounded like the chop of an axe in the silence.

Taurin studied the anxious faces around him. He had known most of them his entire life. The wrong decision could see many of them dead.

He stepped forward. "After being so long abandoned, doesn't the land need a blessing?"

"Certainly not by a pagan ritual," Norbert hissed.

"Would you like to offer the blessing of your god?" Halla asked.

Norbert snapped to face her. "Excuse me?"

"Would you like to bless these lands?"

"Do not mock my faith, woman."

"I would never insult your beliefs." She met the priest's eyes. "We are working land that has lacked the plow for many years. We would not scorn the blessing of any god."

The hand holding the Bible fell limply as a wave of helplessness washed over Norbert's face. The aldermen shuffled behind him. He had come expecting to find licentiousness and villainy. By neither defending her beliefs nor insulting his own, Halla had robbed him of his vigor.

Orderic broke the silence. "Perhaps you should give the Blessing of the Farms."

Norbert gasped. "You were loudest in demanding we punish this devilry."

The words sent a chill down Taurin's spine. His friend had summoned this mob? They could have harmed his wife, or even himself.

"I see no devilry, Father," Orderic said. "We were mistaken in our suspicions."

"They taint the land with this blood."

"Is it not better to purify it with Christ's blessing than leave it profaned?"

"Will you offer the blessing of your god?" Halla repeated in Norse, then again in Frankish.

The townsfolk began to murmur. While they still held their weapons, they no longer wielded them. One leaned his scythe against his shoulder and exhaled foggy breath on his hands to warm them.

Orderic rested a hand on Norbert's shoulder. "Imagine what you'll gain if all farms provide equal bounty."

Norbert stilled and cast his eyes over the Norse farmers. The priest would bless the Christian farms in the spring just before planting. If all farms grew equally well, then clearly Freyr possessed no power of his own.

Taurin licked his lips. Norbert could convert these heathens. Others had done the same elsewhere. Wouldn't that solve all their problems?

"I will offer the blessing of Christ," Norbert decided.

Taurin relaxed as the Franks leaned on their farm tools and Norbert recited the prayer. The Norse listened in reverent silence, with some even raising their hands to the heavens. When he had finished, most of the Norse made the same gesture before their faces Taurin had seen Halla make. A few even emulated Norbert and the Franks in an approximation of the sign of the cross.

Norbert watched their reaction with wide eyes.

Taurin crossed to the priest. "Once again, your actions saved lives. Thank you, Father."

Halla sidled next to Taurin. "The meat will take time, but we have nuts, vegetables, and mead, if you wish to feast with us."

"Mead?" Norbert arched an eyebrow.

"An alcohol made from honey. The finest gift of the gods." She led him through the corridor of Norsemen toward the house.

Norbert shuffled in her wake, his forehead wrinkled in consternation. Dagobert, a couple of the aldermen, and a scant few of the townsfolk followed him.

Orderic hovered on the periphery, but Taurin confronted him before he could slink away. "You led this mob against my home? Against my wife?"

The other man crossed his arms. "Against a minion of the warlord who stole Rouen and murdered uncounted Christians."

"She now protects us from further raids. Orderic, I gave my word. Did you think about the position you put me in?"

"You are responsible for your position, from the moment you married her and gave your word to the Northman." Orderic raised his chin and met Taurin's gaze boldly. "We heard rumors about sacrifices of children. We had to investigate them."

Disbelief left Taurin able only to exhale a guttural scoff. "Do you think I would allow that on my estate?" The pain of such an accusation stung his eyes and burned his cheeks.

"I didn't know whether I could trust you anymore." Gaze falling, Orderic picked at the edge of his tunic. "I feared she had corrupted you."

"We've known each other all our lives." Taurin jabbed his finger to emphasize each word. "You should have asked me."

Orderic raised his hands before him and released a heavy sigh. "You're right. I'm sorry." He extended his hand. "Will you forgive me?"

Taurin eyed the subtly twitching fingers before him. Traveling back from Rouen, he had hungered for Orderic, of all people, to accept the reasons for his marriage. More than all the others, he valued this man who would be family but for a season of fever.

And now, his dear friend extended his hand in friendship and contrition. Taurin clasped and squeezed it, willing himself to release his lingering resentment. "I have always spoken truth to you."

Orderic's smile creased the corners of his lips and the skin near his eyes. He pulled Taurin into an embrace so sudden that Taurin had to gasp for air.

Once released, Taurin asked, "Will you join us?"

The other man spared a glance for the receding Norsemen. "I don't think so."

"Orderic…"

He raised a hand. "I was wrong to question your integrity, but I still don't trust them."

Taurin scratched his eyebrow over his right eye. "I tire of this same conversation, Orderic. They've kept their promises."

"For this winter, yes." He raised a finger. "But a fair spring doesn't guarantee a good harvest. You don't know whether they'll keep faith. Only time will prove which of us is correct."

Orderic's words lingered in Taurin's mind long after his friend joined the snaking line of Franks returning to town. He prayed Orderic would one day realize that these Norsemen weren't monsters.

He followed the final guest into the warmth and noise of the house. They had already begun feasting. A cluster of bearded men stood near the open barrel of mead, distributing sloshing goblets. Three Franks and two Norsemen stood nearby, debating the virtues of barley versus rye in broken Frankish. Taurin listened for a time with his weight on his toes, ready to intervene. But though the cadence of their argument rose and fell, no one reached for a knife or started a brawl. After a few exchanges, they parted amid mutters of disagreement.

He released his breath.

Father Norbert stood by the dining table telling Bible stories to a dozen rapt Norse children sitting on the benches, with Audhild repeating his words in Norse. Gesturing wildly, he paired the rhythmic rise and fall of his voice with the exaggerated expressions Taurin remembered from his childhood. He smiled at the fond memory.

"He's speaking of your Jesus." Halla threaded her arm through his. She had removed her kohl, but some smudges lingered around her eyes.

"Is that so?"

"He was surprised to learn that while your Jesus hung from a cross for three days, Odin hung from Yggdrasil, the world tree, for nine."

"Surprised, or annoyed?"

She tilted her head. "Intrigued by the similarity."

He watched the priest answer a question from the young daughter of Norse farmer. "He intends to convert your people." Why did he tell her that?

Halla shrugged. "What's one more god? At least he won't cause any more trouble."

He shifted his weight, but the motion pulled him away from Halla enough that she abandoned his arm and straightened. He missed her touch already. "He no longer concerns you?"

"He knows his worst fears are false. Orderic worries me, though."

"Orderic?" He raised an eyebrow.

"He goaded the priest to act, and I don't see him among his new neighbors now. He's trouble."

That wasn't a fair assessment of the kind man Taurin knew. "He only wants to protect his people. You will see."

She made no reply. A Northman pointed a platter of fruits and cheese out to a nearby Frankish fisherman. After trying a nibble, the fisherman popped a chunk of goat's cheese into his mouth and brightened. The Norseman slapped him on the back and barked a laugh.

Halla gestured to them. "Important things are born in such moments, though no one ever remembers them."

He nodded slowly, contemplating the narrow margin by which they had avoided a riot. "Your quick thinking out there made this possible."

She shrugged. "The gods have already decided what will be." She leaned closer and whispered, "I had forgotten the blood. Thank you for the warning."

The night would have gone quite differently if Norbert would have confronted a blood-soaked heathen.

A man wearing a Norse farmer's tunic and pants approached. On a second glance, Taurin recognized him as Vikarr, one of Halla's warriors. "Now, *hersir?*"

Halla studied the crowd before nodding. "Be discrete. Store them in the larder."

Vikarr nodded and ducked through the door.

Taurin frowned. "What was that about?"

"I suspected we may have trouble, so I hid swords and axes in the underbrush by the *blót*. If we don't recover them, they'll start to—"

"You did what?" His voice rose above the chatter in the house, attracting attention.

Clasping his elbow, she forced him outside and closed the door behind them. The sudden chill of the winter air did nothing to calm him.

"You had weapons ready to use on my people?" His frosty breath formed tiny clouds around his head.

"Of course. I heard rumors they might interrupt the *blót*."

He barely contained the scream clawing its way out of his throat. Rumors! Would he never be rid of rumors?

"First Orderic and Norbert exclude me, and now you?" He jabbed a finger at her. "I've sacrificed too much for that. Every alderman joined them. Every. One. They don't trust me anymore. And now, I learn you don't, either."

She crossed her arms. "You muttered about my inviting Rosamund to the house for weeks. You accused me of treating my people better than yours. You clearly don't agree with my ways. How could I expect you to understand this?"

"You didn't give me the chance."

"If you knew my intentions, you'd have tried to stop them. I couldn't risk that. I need to know which of these people are enemies and how far they're prepared to go. Your sentiment would deny me vital information."

"Sentiment?" He gaped at her before finding his voice again. "Did I act out of sentiment when I risked the anger of my people to marry you? When I argued with Orderic about cooperating with you? When I convinced my tenants to supply your settlers this autumn?" His hands shook with anger. "I've done more than enough to earn your trust, yet you brushed me aside as if none of it mattered."

He stormed off toward the orchard, leaving a trail of sloppy footprints in the snow. She called after him, but he ignored her. Orderic's words echoed in his ears. A gnawing pit in his stomach began to grow along with the fear that he had, indeed, sold his people for a lie.

He recalled the tender vulnerability of his nights spent entwined with her. The advice he had given on winning over his own people. The loneliness of the angry glares of the townsfolk. He rubbed his eyes hard to banish the memories.

He had opened his home to her. God help him, he had allowed a pagan sacrifice on his land. And still she didn't trust him.

Perhaps he shouldn't have expected so much. She'd never sworn to trust or speak truth to him, either before Rollo or at their wedding.

He was a fool for thinking he could ever live with a heathen.

HALLA

The last celebrants didn't leave until well past sunset, smiling and flushed with intoxication. Near the end, the Franks even clapped along as the Norse drummed their goblets against the table and sang a song of Thor slaying the jotuns. Though it might have started with the threat of violence, the night ended in perfect accord, at least for those who chose to stay and feast.

But though a Norseman plucked at a lyre, Taurin's flute didn't join in, and Halla didn't see her husband for the rest of the night. Like Orderic and most of the other aldermen, he did not attend.

Halla dragged her feet up the stairs and shuffled to her bedchamber, leaving Adella to direct the servants and warriors as they cleaned the manor. Stripping off her clothes, she fell onto the bed, exhausted and naked, and burrowed beneath the blankets to keep warm.

Though her body yearned to succumb to the blessed relief of sleep, her mind couldn't stop churning. She recalled each of Taurin's words and the fury on his face. He had left before she could explain further, and she would not allow him to do so again. She composed and recomposed an explanation of her reasons, determined to convince him he was acting like a fool when he came to bed.

Downstairs, the latch sounded on the door. Soon after, one of the servants offered a humble greeting to whoever entered, soon followed by a low voice she instantly recognized as her husband's. The unmistakable cadence of his footsteps—rhythmic and sure, indicative of a man who felt confident in his ownership of this house—echoed up the stairwell.

Pushing herself upright, she briefly regretted not remaining in her shift. And yet, perhaps having this conversation nude would serve her better. Men rarely thought clearly in the presence of a naked woman.

The footsteps stopped at the top of the stairs, just outside her door.

She ran through the points she intended to make one last time. More people would suffer if she allowed troublemakers to spread discontent unchecked. Besides which, she had merely planned for the worst possible result. She hadn't sought it out. She hadn't spread the rumors that had terrified Norbert. Her actions had alleviated the tension, not caused it.

He was an intelligent man. Surely, he would understand.

But the footsteps, when they resumed, receded down the hall, growing fainter with each step until they ended with the unlatching of a door at the other end of the house.

Outrage battled with disbelief. Surely he wasn't angry enough to abandon their bed all night!

Out in the hall, the other door closed with a quiet thud that vibrated through Halla with the finality of Thor's hammer striking the dwarves' strongest anvil.

II

WHERE THE RIVER MEETS THE SEA

APRIL, AD 891

CHAPTER TEN

HALLA

HALLA RUBBED HER hands together. The days had finally begun to warm by noon, but the morning chill still numbed her fingers. Winter in Rouen was different, surrounded by fires and hearths and protected by the winding rows of buildings. Here, the frigid wind blew uninterrupted over the fields. The Franks were hardier than she had imagined if they endured such a freeze year after year.

The docks upon which she stood still smelled of Norwegian oak. Though Frankish animosity had diminished after the *blót*, the town carpenter had still objected to the prospect of building three new piers to strengthen the connection with Rouen. But when the fresh hardwood had arrived, he had run his hands sensuously along the smooth wood and quietly agreed.

The warriors jumped out of the approaching longship and waded toward her. She could only imagine how cold those men must be as they pulled on the guide ropes to tug the longship closer to the dock.

Beside her, Taurin rubbed his shoulders. His breath came out in a faint fog.

"You should wear the cloak I bought you."

He grunted. "I'm not cold."

She gave a loud sigh.

Two weeks earlier, the first trading *knörr* had visited the new docks. She had bought a fur-lined cloak from a trader from Oslo and presented it to Taurin as a peace offering after the *blót*. Yet the cloak remained in a trunk in their bedroom, untouched despite the plunging temperature. Sometimes, she couldn't follow the twists of her husband's mind.

His shivering filled her with a smug satisfaction. He could freeze, for all she cared.

Christians were a strange group. Their spring festival approached, but instead of celebrating, they deprived themselves of everything in life worth having. Their ways made no sense.

As the ship settled beside the docks, a *hirdman* lowered a gang-plank from the longship.

Beside her, Taurin straightened his tunic.

She grunted. "He'll be judging me, not you."

"He considers you an equal. I'm just his subject."

"You have all the rights of any Norseman."

Arms dropping, he gaped at her. "I do?"

"When we married, you gained legal standing among my people." She frowned. "I thought you knew this."

"I did not."

The gangplank flexed under the strain of Rollo's weight, and he quickly stepped onto the pier with a glance back at the slab of wood, muttering. Weighing it down with his foot, he offered Poppa his hand. She looked pale. Evidently, the Frankish countess did not enjoy sailing.

Halla suppressed a smile.

Though he towered over her, Poppa set the pace as they walked down the pier hand-in-hand. With a practiced rhythm, Rollo took one step for every two of hers. Both wore fur cloaks like the one moldering in Taurin's trunk, and Halla suddenly felt self-conscious in her Frankish overcoat. She looked like the outsider and Poppa the Norse woman.

"Halla!" Poppa approached with outstretched arms.

She took her hands, but Poppa kissed her on either cheek in the Frankish way. Her breath smelled of a mint that matched the scent on her neck. "Hello, Poppa."

Taurin bowed and offered a courteous, "My lady."

Halla dimpled her mouth into a frown. She should have greeted the woman as the wife of her jarl, but it was too late now.

Rollo presented his thick arm and Halla clasped his forearm. His shake rattled her teeth. She had forgotten his strength after all these months.

"Halla, it's good to see you."

"And you, my jarl."

He turned to Taurin. "And the brave Christian." His eyes settled on Taurin's still-bare chin.

She gestured to the horizon. "Where are the rest of the ships? Did you call off the raid?"

"Certainly not. Berengar needs to be taught a lesson. They're coming later this week. I came early to see the town." Rollo stomped on the wooden pier. "Good construction. Feels new."

"It is," Halla confirmed.

"The surveyors put this together?"

She shook her head. "A Christian."

"Is that so?" He ran his foot along one of the planks before casting his eyes over the other two piers. They could accommodate six long-ships at a time. Lillebonne had become the best safe port in Frankia, excepting only Rouen itself. "Very good. Any visitors yet?"

Some of Rollo's warriors began to alight and crowd the pier, so Halla led them into the town. They fell into step, with the Norsemen in the center and the Franks on either side.

"Three *knörrs* so far."

"To resupply or trade?"

"Trade."

"Excellent. Tolls?"

"Rollo!" Poppa slapped him on the chest. "He carries on endlessly about those tolls."

"It's the whole point, dear," he reminded.

"At least ask if poor Halla is well."

Poppa had changed since they had last spoken. She moved with more certainty, like a Norse woman. Halla would have to inquire whether the girl had adopted their gods as well.

"I'm well, truly." Halla smiled at the countess. "And yourself? Sailing doesn't seem to agree with you."

"I've resolved to endure it." She reached out to Rollo and he cradled her hand. As he met her eyes, a smile brightened her face.

He turned to Halla. "The tolls?"

Poppa sighed.

"Collected and awaiting you," she answered.

His tender mood changed to one of wonder as Halla led him through town. Townsfolk milled about, no longer scurrying in fear at the sight of a docking longship. In fact, more than a few hovered nearby, bearing heavy pouches that weighed down their belts. They hadn't yet learned the difference in draft between a *knörr* trading vessel and a *snekke* longship.

Rollo had noticed them, too. "Under guard, I hope?"

Taurin stumbled, shuffling his feet to keep pace.

"That's why only we greet you," Halla explained. "My warriors are guarding the coffer."

Rollo stroked his beard. "Strange, isn't it?"

She frowned, not following his meaning.

"*Your* warriors," he repeated.

When had she started talking like that? "Is it wrong for me to think so?"

He shook his head. "This is your town. You have every right to your own *hird*."

Her own *hird*. The thought exhilarated her as much as her appointment as *hersir*. Only the most powerful, most successful warriors ever accumulated the respect necessary to assemble their own warriors. It couldn't be granted, only earned.

And after the confrontation during the *blót*, she had earned the distinction in the eyes of the Norse. Her lips curled upward.

"Welcome to Lillebonne." She spread her arms to encompass the market.

Freshly built stalls contrasted with the dull, weathered wood of the old ones. Some spilled out into the side streets. Normally, the stalls would remain bare until late spring, but Norse traders occupied four of them. The carpenter whose docks had impressed Rollo was haggling with a braided man in a Danish tunic. Taurin greeted him when Poppa stopped to admire a glass-beaded necklace on the table, and the carpenter smiled in return.

They had begun to change how they treated her husband after the *blót*, but of course Taurin hadn't thanked her for that. She clenched her jaw but pushed that thought aside.

Rollo perused the goods with a growing smile. "This comes from Uppsala." He gestured to a bronze dragon pendant. A moment later, he gasped and pointed at a silver crucifix. "I remember that from Saint-Lô!"

"Last week, a *knörr* arrived from Rouen," Halla said. "They must have brought some plunder."

"Excellent." Widening his gaze, he studied the new buildings and the smoke rising from the forge. The blacksmith's hammering interrupted the rhythmic sawing from the carpenter's workshop. Both had hired assistants, who suffered the occasional shouted correction, to keep up with the work.

The jarl gestured to the shore beside the docks. Fishermen were preparing to depart, loading half a dozen boats and checking their nets. "I'll send a shipwright. Travelers will pay dearly to avoid traveling to

Rouen for repairs." As Taurin and Poppa rejoined them, Rollo offered his wife his arm.

"I'd welcome it," Halla said. A shipwright would give every passing vessel a reason to stop. Every ship needed some amount of maintenance. The markets would swell, more settlers would arrive, and taxes would increase. "We'll plant more oak saplings this spring to supply him. The Franks will appreciate another item to trade."

"How are our settlers?"

She sighed. "The land is overgrown and difficult to clear. But they're ready to plant when the frosts end."

"Did you sacrifice this winter?"

Taurin's jaw set as he looked away.

She swallowed. "Of course I did."

"Of course you did." Rollo offered an easy smile. "And Christians caused no trouble?"

Though Taurin stilled, he didn't draw attention to himself. Halla noticed his reaction only because she expected it.

She lowered her eyes. How much did her jarl need to know? "I had some trouble from the priest a few months back."

"I said so," Poppa said to Rollo.

Rollo patted her on the hand. "You did, my dear."

"But I've dealt with that," Halla assured.

"You have?" He arched an eyebrow.

"He understands I don't threaten his beliefs, and he is content."

Rollo stroked his beard. "Good. A rebellion led by their priest would be harder to crush."

Taurin frowned. "You still expect trouble?"

Rollo glanced at Halla before answering. "In other regions, some view my protection as conquest."

"Isn't it?"

Poppa gasped, but Halla simply sighed. She shouldn't have informed him of his rights as a Norseman; he'd never shut his mouth now.

Rollo's eyes carried admiration. "Perhaps, but lacking the slaughter, enslavement, and plundering that usually merits objection."

Taurin smiled without humor.

Rollo pointed to Halla. "You've fared better than some. Gordrun executed a handful of landowners and their families to halt a rebellion."

Taurin blessed himself quickly, with Poppa following soon after.

"Did it stop the rebellion?" Halla asked.

"Oh, yes."

She glanced at Taurin. "My husband encourages me to use a lighter touch."

Rollo shrugged. "We'll see if it works."

Recalling Taurin's words after the *blót*, she had to admit that without his help, she'd have fared no better than Gordrun.

As the group passed by the church, Father Norbert, standing outside conversing with a pair of Norse farmers, nodded to Halla. She offered one of her own in return.

Poppa dipped into a curtsey and pushed aside her cloak to kiss a crucifix at her neck. As she rose, she crossed herself before bringing her hands together.

But it wasn't the Christian woman who interested Halla, but Rollo, who raised a hand in a limp, circular gesture roughly following his young wife's motions.

Halla kicked her own heel and nearly fell over. She offered a sheepish smile and fell into stride again, but her thoughts lingered on the display. Jarl Rollo of Rouen had saluted the Christian god. Disbelief competed with panic. No one had ever accused Rollo of piety. He obeyed the gods only because his people expected it. Had these Christians truly seduced him, as Bjornolf had accused?

"In any case," Rollo continued, "we'll have plenty of pillaging in the Bessin, once the ships arrive."

Halla clung to the words. It would mean killing and raiding those very Christians whose church he saluted. "Will we?"

"Lessons must be taught," he replied with a wolfish grin.

"How many are coming?" Taurin asked. When Rollo narrowed his eyes, her husband stammered, "We can only feed large numbers for a short time. The winter rye won't be ready for a couple more months."

"He makes a good point," Halla admitted, swallowing her unease at Rollo's salute. Perhaps he had simply acknowledged his wife's religion. He would still raid. She had no reason for alarm. "Will you sail once the other ships arrive?"

"You mean, 'Will we sail'. I hoped you'd come with me."

Beside her, Taurin rasped an indrawn breath.

Her eyes widened. "I didn't..." Thinking her responsibility would keep her in Lillebonne, she'd negotiated a share of plunder from Rollo's raids. "The town—"

"You said all is calm," he reminded. "Many chieftains raid. Why not you?" He chuckled. "Revna is desperate to see you again."

Poppa added, "She talks of nothing else."

Revna was well, then, or at least well enough to join the raid. A smile tugged at the corners of her lips at the thought of seeing her again.

Her fingers still itched to wrap themselves around the haft of an axe, to feel the exhilaration of battle. The gods needed warriors, not administrators. And she could safeguard Lillebonne best by fighting the Bretons on the other side of the Seine, rather than waiting for them to attack here.

She met Rollo's eyes, but she saw only the memory of him gesturing reverently at the church. She refused to become like him, saluting this Christian god.

Her own gods no longer spoke to her. To hear them again, she needed to live as her people did. Her faith had led her to Lillebonne. It now called her to raid.

TAURIN

Kohl stained half of Halla's face and pagan patterns covered the rest. She looked as strange to Taurin now as the night of the *blót*.

With the deftness of familiar tasks, she adjusted the lay of her mail coat and slid her axes into the loops affixed to her belt, shifting them around until they fit comfortably. She frowned as she tugged on her mail coat.

"Is something wrong?" he asked.

She pinched the rings, struggling to grab the material. "Nothing."

But for the gold torc signifying her rank as *hersir*, she looked like any of the hundreds of Norsemen loading their ships with provisions for the long journey.

Like those of the townsfolk who weren't selling their wares to the departing army, Taurin could only stand and watch the spectacle unfolding before him. But he didn't share his people's awe at this demonstration of strength. He had already experienced that in Rouen. He cared only that his wife was departing to murder Christians. The part of her that hungered to spill blood unsettled him. He would never understand it.

She could be sailing to her death. Despite her behavior at the *blót*, he didn't wish that. "I ask you once more. Do not go."

Fingers halting, she pinned him with an irritated glare.

"You're needed here."

Finished with her adjustments, Halla rested her hands on her axes. "This is our way. I must go."

"I don't understand."

She sighed. "Oh, I know."

He ignored her irritation. "You said you'd protect my people. What if we're attacked?"

"By whom? We'll keep the Franks busy in the Bessin."

He frowned. "We spotted longships nearby."

She gestured at the dozens of ships waiting along the river and the six berthed at the piers. "Of course you have."

"You know my meaning."

"The settlers are thriving," she said. "Your people are trading with them. Last week, Audhild and Rosamund walked through town together. You'll be fine."

He raised his gaze to the ships on the water as they aligned themselves to sail south, toward the Seine. One of the remaining longships undocked and moved to join them.

"Do you have enough warriors? Rollo said some went east."

She followed his gaze, but her lips drew tight. "We're better off without them, if they ignore the chance for revenge."

"Revenge?" A chill ran down his neck as the sense of strangeness returned. The scriptures warned against such base urges.

She placed her hand against her stomach and grimaced.

He jumped on the gesture. "And are you well enough to raid? I heard you vomiting today."

"It's this deprivation before your festival. I cannot endure any more fish."

Any excuse that kept her from joining this heathen violence would suffice. "Shouldn't you stay and recover?"

"I'm healthy enough." More softly, she added, "And we have plenty of raiders from Norway and Denmark. Six longships even came from the Danelaw in Britain."

As she spoke, Rollo and another Norseman approached. Both wore fur-trimmed cloaks above steel mail coats. The other man's hazel eyes lit up as he approached Halla. He had spoken out during the assembly in Rouen. Taurin remembered being terrified of him then.

"Jarl Sigrun." Halla clasped his arm in a gesture that, Taurin had learned, signified friendship. So, she knew this man. "It is good to see you again."

"And you, Swift-Axe."

"Swift-Axe?" Taurin asked.

The man peeled back his lips to reveal clean, fine teeth. "She has the fastest blade I've ever seen."

Visions of her embedding it in the skull of a Christian monk or a landowner like himself came unbidden. He lowered his eyes in shame that he couldn't prevent this ugliness.

"Sigrun brings us eight longships filled with warriors." Rollo spared a glance for Taurin before adding, "And three more with settlers. Some will go to the other settlements, but I understand you have enough plots for at least ten families, yes?"

"We have the land." She bit at her lip. "When?"

Rollo offered a casual wave. "They won't arrive in Rouen until later this month. I won't send them to you without the lumber you asked for, probably another month from now."

Taurin sighed in relief. She couldn't join the raid now. Ten more homesteads' worth of Norse settlers would re-ignite Frankish anger and require daily rides to soothe.

Taurin spoke as soon as Rollo and Sigrun left earshot for their respective longships. "We should choose plots close to the other Norse, but still beside my people. Encouraging them to cooperate has worked so far."

"I agree. You shouldn't have any problems."

He must have misheard her. "You're still going?"

"Of course. I've already instructed the surveyors and my *hirdmen*"—she smirked at the word—"to obey you as they would me."

He gasped. "You're leaving me in charge of settling your people?"

"You said I don't trust you. I wish to prove that I do."

He could still feel the winter chill from when he'd paced in impotent rage after the *blót*. She had betrayed the intention of their marriage oath, if not its words. Stomach roiling from the memory of that hurt, he swallowed down the bile that threatened to erupt.

That was then, he reminded himself. Now, she was trusting him with something of equal importance. She had heard him that night, after all.

Her words transformed his anger into something far worse. Even through the kohl, he saw his wife again. He had squandered these past two months with cold distance and wounded mistrust. He wanted that time back. But it was gone, and he could do nothing but regret its waste.

Her eyes were the familiar ones he'd gazed into when they would lie together. Those lips were the same ones that had curled into that mischievous, candlelit smile on their wedding night.

"What if something happens to you?"

She shrugged. "No one threatens the lords near the Loire, so they won't rally to Berengar this year. Besides, I doubt he expects another attack after repulsing us at the Vire."

"No…" Taurin clasped her hands. "What if something happens to *you*."

Eyes softening, Halla pressed a hand against his cheek. Her touch felt soft and tender, banishing the last of the morning chill. Oh, how he had missed it!

Grazing her fingers against his bare chin, she frowned. He realized she hadn't complained about his lack of a beard for some time.

Her smile returned as she met his eyes. "Then recount my deeds and toast to my memory."

She leaned in and his lips met hers for the first time since the *blót*. Sticky kohl smeared against his skin. He didn't care. He had missed too many kisses of late.

Wrapping his hands around her waist, Taurin felt her chest rising and falling beneath the metal rings of her armor. If felt strange to hold an armored warrior in a tender embrace.

He drank in the scent of her hair, imprinting the memory of her body in his arms. He might never see her again. He had wasted so much time this winter; he wanted to remember every detail of these final, precious moments.

His sight began to glisten and he fought back the tears. Neither Halla nor the other Norsemen would respect him if he cried as his wife sailed away to battle.

When they parted, she held his gaze. "Will you wish me luck for a successful raid?"

Behind her, another longship began to sail away. Despite his regrets for these wasted months, he couldn't bring himself to wish her success in killing Christians.

"I wish you a safe return."

The moment of tenderness shattered. She stepped back and lowered her hands to rest on her axes. The muscles in her neck tensed as she clenched her teeth.

She had caught the distinction in his response.

When she spoke again, her voice was drained of affection. "Prepare for new settlers at the end of next month."

She marched to the nearest longship without another word. Taurin watched her go, silently pleading for her to turn back.

She did not.

Orderic slid up next to him after Halla's longship had undocked. "I'm glad to see the end of them."

The fleet began the slow crawl down the Bolbec, carrying his wife toward the Seine. Even if she returned, he couldn't say who she would be when she did. The memory of killing Arbogast's companion still haunted him. How many times could she kill before it changed her?

Orderic grunted. "Now, they go to intimidate someone else."

He turned then. "You think Rollo brought his army here to intimidate us?"

"They want us to know our place." Orderic snorted. "How have they helped us these past six months? By sending a few traders?"

Taurin glanced back toward the busy market. His friend's words rang hollow. The Norsemen had paid good coin for every scrap of surplus food, tool, and available resource. Even Orderic had planted extra crops to sell to Rouen.

"Now they use our town to make war on our neighbors," Orderic continued. "Oh, they definitely meant to show us who commands here now."

"She left me in charge." Taurin clung to that proof of her trust.

"Only to carry out her instructions. Does she offer you trust or the chance to prove your obedience?"

Taurin turned back to the longships. The last one had disappeared around the bend in the river. Surely Halla trusted him. She wouldn't be leaving otherwise.

But memories flashed in his mind. Halla covered in blood at the *blót*. The strange look of the braided, bearded warriors. The *gythia* dragging a knife across the throat of the sacrificial animals at his wedding. The sickening warmth of the blood sprinkled on his face.

Norse ways were foreign. Perhaps her mind worked in strange ways, as well. How could he make any assumptions about her motivations?

Taurin stood facing the water, caught between hope and doubt. But he could not deny one simple fact: this relationship with the Norse was not an equal one.

CHAPTER ELEVEN

HALLA

WHILE HALLA HAD expected to stir with emotion at raiding with her people, she didn't expect to feel indignity most keenly.

Never prone to seasickness before, she spent the first two days doubled over the edge of the longship, sharing the contents of her stomach with all the fish in the sea. Bouts passed quickly but returned often. The warriors murmured their mockery loudly enough for her to overhear as she stumbled back to her seat like a girl drunk on her first mead.

Many warriors had passed through Lillebonne, eyeing the busy town and the many goods for sale. More than a few might hope for the fame of ruling in Rollo's name. In their place, she surely wouldn't have allowed a vomiting, unsteady *høvding* to stand in the way of her desires. She would have to be careful, or she might lose the position for which she had paid such a high price.

The thought of her judgmental, temperamental Christian husband sent her to the railing again.

The longships disgorged on the western shore of the Cotentin, south of Coutances. Halla exempted herself from encampment duty and visited the hastily constructed forge in the center of camp. By the time the warriors had completed the hedgerows of perimeter stakes and erected their tents, the blacksmith had widened the waist of her mail coat with two more rows of rings.

She scowled as she held the mail before her. A male warrior would need to expand his mail as he grew fat with age. But a shieldmaiden raided for less time, certainly not into her wide years. She had tightened it after her father had died. She should have never needed to widen it again. A long winter of comfort in a Frankish manor, filled with all the food she could enjoy, had plumped her waist.

"Not good enough for you?" The smith folded his arms before him.

She bit off a sharp reply. "It's fine." It no longer caught at her waist as she donned it. Pride had to give way to efficiency.

The night came quickly as the sun disappeared into the western sea. On her way back to her tent, she stopped to warm her hands at a nearby fire already occupied by a pair of warriors. They nodded when they eyed the torc around her neck.

She had arrived in the middle of a conversation.

"They refused to remove a dam that dried up the stream running through my father's farm," said the first, a tattooed man who spoke like the Norwegians of the northern hinterland. "My father demanded they restore the stream, but they refused. The *Thing* sided with my father."

Halla rubbed her hands over the fire, listening with a smile of satisfaction. Families traveled great distances to resolve conflicts and vote on laws at the *Thing*. She supposed Rollo would hold one now that his people had spread throughout the Caux.

"Did they obey?" asked the second, a bald man with a braided blond beard who spoke with a Danish accent like her father's.

"No, so my father burned their farm." He sniffed and wiped his nose. "They retaliated while my father fed the chickens. He only had a sickle, but he killed one and punctured the lung of another before he died." He smirked with pride.

The Dane grunted. "A good death."

Halla raised two fingers to the sky. He had died defending his home, just as Halla wished for herself.

"The next night, I led my brothers back to their farm," the Norwegian continued. "We bolted the doors to their longhouse and burned it to the ground, killing every last man, woman, and child."

The Dane barked a laugh. "Glorious."

Halla nodded. The Franks would call his actions monstrous, but a feud could endure for many years. Those sensible steps had preserved his family from retribution. She cleared her throat, constricted by the cold. "How did the jarl react?"

The Norwegian grinned. "He was pleased to have the matter resolved and gave us their lands to compensate for my father's death."

Her thoughts returned to the mob at the *blót*. At the time, she had celebrated her victory in avoiding a confrontation and in soothing Norbert. Now, she wondered whether she had simply delayed even greater trouble. Should she have killed them all at once?

Amid dredged regrets, Halla abandoned the fire and headed to her tent. No decision was permanent. Though she had preserved Norbert and Orderic that winter, she could always correct that error later.

Halla ambled along, soaking in the delights of camp life. Laughter. The scraping of swords on whetstones. The aroma of roasting meat. Behind it all lay the crackling of fires and the low exchanges of scouts relieving each other. Everywhere, burning elm, cherry, and maple tickled her nostrils and stung her eyes. She preferred that sting to the stench of animals on Taurin's estate. Fire purified and smoke anointed their purpose here.

A young warrior with blond, braided hair ground an iron file against his teeth to create deep grooves. She had seen this before; later, he would fill the grooves with dye to terrify his enemies. She sighed in disappointment at such intentional mutilation. Despite his youth, the way he wore his armor hinted at tight muscles beneath.

Before an open canopy, a gray-haired warrior painstakingly

tattooed a stylized wolf onto the shaved head of a younger man. Halla made a warding gesture before her face. She would not want Fenrir, the wolf who would devour the world at Ragnarok, permanently inked on her body, regardless of what strength it imbued.

Ahead, a large group of warriors that included Jarl Sigrun surrounded a fire too small to accommodate them. No one spoke. All eyes watched a skald standing near the flames. Thickly muscled, he differed from the others only in his attire. Instead of leather or mail armor, he wore a mere pale blue tunic embroidered with silver runes stitched into the edges, invoking the blessings of the god-poet Bragi. His beard stretched far longer, down beyond his waist in honor of the god he served.

Halla halted next to Sigrun to listen to the recitation about a warrior wading into battle against impossible odds.

> *Borvi the brazen knew no fear*
> *Widow-weaver high to lift.*
> *Hungry he was to hasten his foes*
> *To death, a glorious gift.*
> *Death be a glorious gift.*
>
> *Behind he left his fearful friends,*
> *Bold-strided and furious-faced.*
> *Cowed by his courage, they followed his charge*
> *To death, lest they lose their place.*
> *They charged to claim their place.*
>
> *Three warriors claimed by widow-weaver,*
> *Two more ran from his fist.*
> *The former will dine in Valhalla;*
> *The cowards none shall miss.*
> *Cowards none shall miss.*

Through axes sharp and spears he rushed
Out-pacing his followers few.
Each enemy shook at his splendor,
Each unfriendly sword did hew
Many swords did hew.

Though voices in victory rose that day,
Brave Borvi beheld them not.
Skewered on shafts, lost in lake red,
Borvi earned the death he sought.
Song-worthy, the death he sought.

The tale ended to a silence broken only by the crackling fire. Somber faces stared into the flames. Halla joined them, entranced by the magic of the skald's words, worthy of the rune-tongued god whom he worshiped. Her heart swelled with memories of honor and glory. They would remember Borvi. Perhaps, one day, warriors would remember her, too.

Someone shuffled, clinking a scabbard against a piece of armor. The moment passed and the crowd began to chatter.

"Such a death stirs the blood."

Halla turned. Sigrun studied her with gentle eyes that hinted at a thoughtfulness so like her husband's. But this man didn't judge her. He simply waited for her response with those thick muscles and that carefully combed, sandy-brown beard.

Taurin had no manly beard.

She sighed. "I've missed the stories of our people."

Sigrun placed a hand on her shoulder. His touch felt warm, sending ripples of anticipation down her chest. "Though surrounded by Christians, you will always be Norse."

She recalled him asking about the Christians at the feast. Unlike Bjornolf, Sigrun clearly had an interest in these non-believers. A part of her hungered for his thoughts about her experiences in Lillebonne. As a Norseman, he would understand her unease at the Franks' strange ways. She hungered for that comfort.

But one of his *hersirs* called him away to solve a conflict between two of his men. When he released her shoulder to leave, she watched him go with sinking disappointment.

Revna sat before the small fire in front of their tent. While Halla's new rank entitled her to privacy, she had wanted to spend more time with her friend during this campaign and had invited her to camp with her.

"Vomiting again?" Revna smirked as she poked the fire with a branch.

"You heard as well?" She settled down beside her.

"Everyone's talking about it."

Face reddening, she gazed into the flames. Word traveled fast on the march. "Mocking my soft life among the weak Christians?"

"Something like that." Revna grinned. "Are they wrong?"

Halla recalled the long rides to regional farms and the endless squabbling over boundaries and promised trades. She had spent more long nights with the surveyors than she cared to recall, and mornings had started well before dawn. But Revna wouldn't consider any of that hard work. She had dug no ditches, built no fortifications, and rarely found time to train with her axes. She had grown soft along with her waist.

"I suppose not."

She had achieved *hvatur* with the speed of her axe and skill on the march as part of Rollo's *hird*. But ruling Lillebonne threatened to squander it all. Mockery of her soft life could cost her her position.

Revna reached out and tucked a strand of hair back behind Halla's ear. Though the Franks often kissed cheeks in greeting, it lacked the reassuring comfort of this single touch.

"It must be hard," Revna said, "living among those cowards."

The simple sentiment filled Halla with warmth. No one in Lillebonne would describe Halla's existence as lonely. At the estate, servants and farmhands surrounded her at all times. Adella attended her throughout the day. Rollo's surveyors and her warriors—her new *hird*—accompanied her when she made her rounds. And then there was Taurin.

She set her jaw, recalling his final refusal to accept her nature by offering good wishes for victory.

Yes, she often felt isolated, despite the crowd. None of the Franks heard Thor's cries of joy in the thunder or understood that winter came because Freya left to search for her husband. Only the settlers might understand, but they looked to her for leadership. She couldn't risk losing their respect by sharing her feelings.

But Revna understood. Without Halla having to say a word, Revna understood how every day left her exhausted from guarding her words and actions. Only here, among her people, could she relax.

"Sometimes." She reached up to clasp Revna's hand. "No one understands me like you."

"Even your husband?"

"Especially him." Halla grunted. "He asks about our ways, but cringes at our differences. He sees only the wild heathen in me."

"That sounds exhausting."

Halla smiled with relief. Revna always understood.

"If he doesn't accept all of you, then he doesn't accept you." She threw her arms back in a wide stretch. "I have an early watch tomorrow. I must sleep."

Revna's final words echoed in her ears, though not for the reason she intended. How could Taurin accept her if she had never shared herself fully, without reservation? She hadn't revealed that her fears of a meaningless death had brought her to Lillebonne. Could she blame him for searching the depths she deliberately concealed? Perhaps she demanded too much from her husband after only a season of marriage tainted by mistrust.

She raised her chin and surveyed the warriors sprinkled through the camp. These were her people. She belonged here. She had promised

Revna she would never forsake the gods who had answered her prayers. She would not change her ways for her Christian husband.

Perhaps half a hundred *ells* away, Jarl Sigrun watched her from the entrance to his tent, standing like the warrior in the poem, tall and strong. He had evidently solved the quarrel quickly. When she met his gaze, his eyes carried a desire not fully concealed. He curled his lips faintly in a silent invitation.

She drew an unsteady breath as she realized he wanted her despite her growing waist from a winter of idleness.

An idea began to blossom.

She had worked hard to earn her position and refused to watch it slip away. She had to silence those who might take it from her. Sigrun had earned the renown and respect of his people. Taking such a man as a lover would prove to everyone she remained *hvatur*, virile and strong.

She pictured Taurin's face, irresistible and yet so mulish. They hadn't lain together since the *blót*. She refused to remain celibate like his monks because her husband couldn't accept her for the woman she was.

Besides, her marriage was an alliance. She provided protection and Taurin supported her rule. His wife sleeping with a jarl, so far above his status as a landowner, would not dishonor him.

She carefully slid first one arm then the other out of her mail and set it beside the flap of the tent. No one would steal in a Norse camp, and she didn't want to disturb Revna's sleep.

The gods wished men and women to enjoy themselves, to explore the pleasures of the world. Any day, Ragnarok could reduce the world to ash. Until then, the wise would drink deeply, eat richly, and revel in desire.

And just then, she desired to run her fingers through that sandy beard.

She crossed to Jarl Sigrun's tent, eager for a release from the cares of a winter spent among a weak people. She could think of worse ways to spend the night than being impaled on a strapping Norse warrior.

TAURIN

An endless parade of wagons brought tables and stools from the surrounding estates to the town square throughout the day. Barrels of ale and dozens of bottles of wine sat beside crude wooden and clay mugs on several of them.

The food had come this afternoon: fruit, eggs, cheeses, stews, and the meat—the blessed meat. Salted and smoked and boiled. And especially the roasts. A group of women tended the roasts, basting them every few minutes with ladles filled with succulent drippings. This evening, they would feast. After forty days of fish, bread, and fruit, Taurin's mouth watered at the teasing aroma of roasting boar, venison, and mutton.

Taurin saw no fish. That pleased him immensely. Halla wasn't the only one sick of fish.

Easter had finally arrived.

Raised bonfires at each corner of the square and torches on poles every few dozen feet illuminated the hundreds of men and women celebrating and dancing together in the cool night air. An aldermen plucked at a lyre as a farmer played a lively tune on a flute. A third man kept beat with a drum made of stretched pigskin and affixed with sinew. Taurin wished he'd brought his flute so he might join them.

Children chased each other through the shifting crowds, giggling. A rowdy group of boys that included Leubin's youngest son took turns evading each other while carrying a stuffed sack to the laughing delight of their fathers. Two girls sat at a nearby table, feigning disinterest but sneaking glimpses of the boys every few moments.

Taurin smiled at the simple pleasures unfolding before him. Despite fears of rampaging heathens, they had survived the tense, uncertain winter. The Norsemen had passed without attacking a week earlier. That alone deserved celebration.

The weather had turned so that even the mornings felt warm.

Spring crops would have a good, long growing season, leaving plenty of time for reaping.

The wife of one of his tenants, laughing with a group of friends, raised her cup and called his name. The drops of wine she sloshed only set them laughing again.

Taurin saluted in return, thankful for the change in reception. While some townsfolk still glared, those who traded with the Norsemen and invited them for meals had begun to greet him warmly again.

The dancers threw themselves about with reckless delight. They could celebrate the Resurrection without fear because Rollo had kept his word. Taurin had made the right decision, after all.

A hard winter, with the promise of a good spring.

Reaching the food, he sliced off a piece of boar from the roast and nearly burned his fingers before spearing it on the tip of his knife. Fat melted as his teeth sank into the tender meat, dousing his tongue in salty bliss that left it tingling after he swallowed.

A ripple of surprise passed over the crowd, dampening but not silencing the good cheer. He turned in the direction of the apprehensive gazes. Shielding his eyes from the glare of the bonfires, Taurin saw the silhouette of a group approaching from the shadows.

Norsemen.

They clustered together in three groups. A Norse farmer who had cleared and planted a field that had never been cultivated before eyed the food with a toothy smile. Steingrim stood in front, placing a protecting hand over the shoulders of each of his children, while Audhild hunched over and whispered to them. But their expressions were curious rather than anxious.

No one moved for a few heartbeats.

Taurin swallowed. A confrontation now, with Rollo's army mobilized nearby, could see them all massacred.

Sidestepping surprised townsfolk, he maneuvered closer to the newcomers. He had to move quickly to prevent the wrong word or an offensive action.

One of the Norse whispered something to her husband and gestured back toward the darkness.

Before he could reach them, a young Frankish girl with long blond hair skipped into the open space. She was the daughter of a fisherman who lived on the edge of town.

"Cerila!" her mother cried, but her husband restrained her from rushing ahead.

The Franks watched in collective silence as Cerila stopped before Audhild's daughter. The girls smiled at each other.

"I'm Cerila."

"I'm Bera," the Norse girl replied in Frankish, eliciting gasps from the crowd. After six months of lessons, she spoke the language well, albeit with a discernable accent.

"I like your hair." She raised her hand to touch the Norse girl's braids. "Can you do that to mine?"

The Norse girl turned to her mother, eyes bright. "Mama?"

Audhild inhaled a ragged breath and gave a curt nod.

Delighted, Bera clasped Cerila's hand, and they skipped off toward an open table by the church.

And, just like that, the anxiety and tension melted away. Before Taurin could resume his approach, Rosamund broke free from her husband's restraining hand and greeted Audhild with outstretched arms. One of Dagobert's tenants introduced her sons to one of the Norse families. A fisherman who had needed wood to repair his boat this winter clasped hands with the grinning Norse farmer who had provided it from trees he had cleared from his fields. Even Father Norbert made the sign of the cross over them, which one of the Norse children faithfully reproduced.

The usual murmurings of discontent bubbled up, but they were quieter than before. Taurin relaxed and took a slow breath. Good, common sense could still hold sway. Scarcely a family in town hadn't bought something from the merchants visiting from Rouen and the

Norse homelands, from tooth scrapers and new bone combs to fresh cooking pots and cloth.

Orderic and Dagobert approached as the music resumed and the crowd returned to its revelry. Dagobert shook Taurin's shoulder eagerly with one hand without spilling the goblet in the other. "Blessings upon you this Easter."

Taurin smiled as he steadied himself. "And upon you."

The alderman swayed to the side, dodging a trio of boys—one Norse and two Frankish—who darted past. "You should have told me you invited the Norse."

"I didn't. Someone else must have."

"And why should they not?" Orderic asked. "They own this town and all of us in it. Look!" He pointed to a large, bushy tan and white cat running off with a piece of meat from one of the tables. "Even their monstrous cats steal from us."

Taurin sighed. "Orderic…"

"I know, I know." He raised his hands in surrender. "Easter is no time for discontent."

"I recommend taking advantage of Arbogast's good wine," Dagobert suggested.

Orderic raised an eyebrow. "He's buying forgiveness?"

The other alderman shrugged. "I suppose so."

"Is it working?" Taurin asked.

"No." The other alderman finished his cup and grinned. "But I'll tell him after I've drunk my fill!" With a salute, he tottered off toward the casks.

One of the Norsemen was leaving the wine table as Dagobert arrived. Taurin briefly wondered whether Halla's people lacked the lands to cultivate grapes or whether mead simply tasted better to Norse palates.

A pair of Franks from east of town, far from the Norse settlements, walked deliberately into him, knocking him off balance.

"Interesting." Orderic jutted his chin toward the incident.

Taurin stiffened. The Norseman would demand an apology. The Franks would refuse. A quarrel, a brawl, perhaps even an injury. The townsfolk would blame the Norse and set upon them. If someone should die...

But the Norseman merely snickered and raised his cup. "Skol!" His salute was loud even from this distance. Patting one of the farmers on the shoulder, he sidestepped and continued on his way.

Taurin exhaled. "Easter miracles."

"Indeed."

Taurin caught the scowl before it faded from Orderic's lips. Time. Time would heal his friend's suspicions. Orderic was a rational man.

Orderic tilted his head. "Your wife was ill before she left, wasn't she?"

It was kind of him to ask. Taurin offered silent thanks that marrying a heathen hadn't cost him his friendship. "She was."

"Have you heard from her since she left with the raiders?"

"No, not yet." He chewed on his lip.

Orderic placed a hand on his shoulder. "I'm sure she's doing the killing, not being killed."

Taurin dreaded either prospect. That departing fleet meant death to someone. He had never met the Christians in the Bessin, yet he would rather see countless dead Bretons than see harm come to his wife.

A flush raced across his cheeks, and he scratched the stubble growing on his chin.

Her deception at the *blót* couldn't diminish his feelings. Reason mattered not at all. He didn't care whether she'd placed him in charge to show her trust or to prove his obedience. Their months together had wrought a change within him. A marriage of mutual interest had become something more, at least for him.

So, this is what love feels like.

TAURIN

The festival lasted well past midnight. The sliver of a crescent moon cast far too little light for travel. A horse could easily stumble and throw its rider on the uneven roads and pitted paths. Taurin, soothed by the gentle rain slapping against the thatch roof, spent the night as a guest of the carpenter and his wife.

The roosters woke him at first light, but he rolled over until the smell of baking bread made his stomach growl. He had drunk more than usual the previous night, and not even a cup of weak ale, a pair of fresh rolls, and a chunk of cheese could banish his hunger.

Offering his gratitude to his hosts, he dragged Seraphim away from the feed trough on the third try and began the long ride home.

Leubin, eyes as ragged as Taurin felt, meet him outside his manor. He couldn't have possibly arrived home much earlier. The mud retained fresh ruts from the cart he'd lent Leubin's family the day before.

The steward wore a severe frown. "Emeline's son awaits you." She rented a northern parcel with a small stream.

"Is she ill?" Her eldest boy was ten winters old, too young to travel alone.

Leubin's frown deepened. "She returned home this morning to discover her farm had been pillaged."

His final warning to Halla about longship sightings echoed in his mind.

Seraphim needed a rest, so Taurin rode out with Emeline's son and two of Halla's *hird* as soon as his steward could prepare another mount. Hopefully, Emeline had simply misplaced a few items and was overreacting to seeing the Norsemen at the celebration.

The scene at the farm convinced him of his error.

Smoke puffed from a ruined granary that still smoldered despite the morning rain. Its roof had burned away, and the heat had disintegrated enough of the daub to expose the wattle and collapse one of the sides. The jagged shards of the farmhouse door littered the ground beside an open chest sitting upside down in a patch of mud. Someone had attempted to burn the barn, but the rain must have doused it. A black smear ran from half-way up the support to the roof. A young boy tended a few chickens and a pig within a makeshift pen beside the farmhouse, but at least they—and he—still lived.

Emeline threw her arms around Taurin the moment he dismounted. Her dirty cheeks bore the streaks of tears.

"Dear woman," Taurin soothed. "What happened here?"

"They stole all our farm equipment," she blurted. "All our spare grain and food. My cooking pot. Look what they did to our cow!" She pointed to a headless animal lying in the fields that Taurin had somehow overlooked. A young girl carved meat from the corpse.

Taurin swallowed. This attack was more brutal than Arbogast's the previous year.

He took her hands. "Are you and your children safe?"

"For now. But without our cow and spare grain, we'll never—"

"I'll provide grain from my own stores and can loan you a cow until we discover who did this."

"I thank you," she breathed, "but nothing can replace my silver brooch."

"Where did you get a silver brooch?" Taurin asked more sharply than he'd intended.

"It was my great-grandfather's. He served in the army of Charlemagne."

He could do little to recover the rest, but silver was rare enough that it might attract attention. "What does it look like?"

"It's as big as my fist and shows an eagle surrounded by a circle of braided silver." She raised her hand for comparison.

"Dull, burnished, or shiny?"

"Shiny." She straightened as she inhaled a deep breath. "Did Alderman Arbogast do this?"

"I intend to find out." A simple search of Arbogast's home would reveal his guilt.

"Norsemen," declared Vikarr—one of the *hirdmen* who had a tremendous tolerance for wine—in Norse.

A cold hand gripped his heart. "Why do you say so?"

"They took food they could eat and metal they could sell. Things of value." The warrior led his horse toward the barn. "They tried to steal the cow, but it wouldn't cooperate." He pointed to tracks in the mud. "Frustrated, they killed it."

"You can tell that?"

"The shape of their footprints matches our turnshoes."

"My people wear the same kinds of shoes," Taurin reminded.

"Franks would ride. We raid on foot. I see no hoof-prints."

Taurin studied the ground. He was right. When Arbogast had raided his neighbors, he had always done so on horseback.

"What does he say?" Emeline tugged on his sleeve.

Taurin halted her with a raised hand. "Are you certain?" he asked the warrior.

Vikarr scowled. "I wouldn't have spoken otherwise."

His grandfather's stories flooded his mind. The little girl found wandering beside the burned-out remnants of her family's farm. The shattered marble floor left over from the Romans that no one living knew how to repair. The mourners in the half-filled church standing where they always had out of habit, despite the telling gaps of dead relatives. It would all happen again, all because he had collaborated with Rollo.

Taurin rubbed his forehead. Norse raiders. He had warned Halla. She never should have left. She had dismissed his fears, but he had been right, after all.

And now, Norse raiders were attacking his tenants, scant miles from his own manor.

"What did he say?" Emeline demanded.

"Norse raiders did this," he answered in Frankish.

"Norse…" Her eyes hardened. "You said they would protect us, that they went south and would leave us alone."

"They did," Taurin assured.

"How do you know?"

"If Jarl Rollo did this, he would have attacked all of us at once. He has thousands of warriors." He turned to Halla's *hirdman*. "How many raiders?"

Vikarr studied the ground. In Frankish, the man asked Emeline, "How many animals are missing?"

She glanced at Taurin before stammering, "T-two chickens, three pigs...a pair of goats."

"How many sacks of grain? Any meat?"

"Five sacks, a few pieces of salted meat."

He stroked his beard. "No more than a dozen, then."

One of the longships must not have joined Rollo's raid. Taurin squeezed Emeline's hands. "I will find these raiders."

"And see them punished?"

"I did so with Arbogast, I will do so again."

With a pledge to send Leubin to see about the woman's needs, Taurin led the warriors back to his estate, his eyes fixed on the ground before his horse.

He would need to scour the area quickly before signs of the raiders' movements disappeared. A dozen warriors might have attacked Emeline's farm, but he doubted he faced less than a full longship. Halla had said they could hold thirty men. And unlike Arbogast, they would fight to the death.

Halla. Did landowners in the Bessin contrive to trap and kill his wife as he did these raiders? Rollo wouldn't turn back until the plunder satisfied him. Halla would return in triumph, or not at all.

For the entire ride home, he gnawed over the uncomfortable truth that he wished for one raid to succeed, yet schemed to thwart another.

CHAPTER TWELVE

HALLA

R OLLO HAD HOPED to surprise the town of Avranches by attacking during Easter mass, but he found the wooden gates shut tightly. By mid-day, Halla's squad was struggling to scale the walls near the western tower.

Her first two attempts to raise the ladder had claimed three warriors. They lay at her feet with arrows sticking out of them like stalks of wheat rising from the earth. Her arm already ached from holding the unfamiliar double-planked shield between herself and the nearby tower. Two others bled from where a skilled archer had struck exposed thighs and calves.

Another arrow impacted her shield near the edge. She peeked around the side. The archer sheltered behind an embrasure atop the tower that stood perhaps fifteen *ells* high, close enough for her to hurl her axe if he revealed himself.

All along the wall, the Franks made obscene gestures. One of them bore a gash across his forehead from a gray-haired Norseman who had managed to ascend the ladder briefly. That warrior now lay still at the bottom of the wall with an arrow in his throat and his lips curled back in a final smile.

He was in Valhalla now.

Her warriors rushed forward in an attempt to recover the ladder, discarded beside the wall. They would all die before withdrawing. Once, she had thought that noble.

The tower archer shifted, giving himself more clearance to draw his bow. Atop the battlement, the Franks pelted her men with rocks that clanged against shields with rhythmic thuds.

She adjusted her grip on her axe, waiting.

Her Norsemen reached the wall and raised the ladder. A fraying rope that reinforced a damaged rung fluttered in the breeze. This time, they leaned the ladder against the wall at a shallow angle. One of her men circled to the other side to weigh it down, the wood creaking from the strain. Halla grinned at the ingenuity. The Franks wouldn't push it aside as easily this time.

As her warriors began to climb, the Frankish archer finally rose to his full height and drew his bow.

Halla sprung up and released her axe. She watched it glide through the air, turning end-over-end in a graceful arc toward the top of the tower.

The archer drew back the bowstring, his eyes fixed on her warriors.

He didn't notice her axe until it embedded itself in his chest. He offered a gurgled scream and misfired his arrow before falling back out of view.

She whooped in triumph. And Revna had said she'd forget how to throw an axe!

Her delight faded once she shifted her attention back to the ladder. The Franks had set it aflame before casting it down again. Her warriors scrambled clear as the Franks shouted in triumph.

But something was happening to the east. Norse warriors were abandoning their attacks along the walls and surging toward the gatehouse amid shouts of delight. She had participated in enough sieges to understand the meaning of that behavior. Halla offered a silent prayer to the gods.

Rollo had breached the gates.

As she led her squad to join the attack, she marked the position of the tower. She'd have to return to recover her axe from the body of that archer.

The fighting had swept deeper into the city by the time she reached the gates. Bodies of Frankish townsfolk and guards and broken doors and barricades lay everywhere, cast aside as if the gods had smote the defenders with their own hands. Every few moments, screams of new victims echoed down the ravaged streets.

She raised a hand to protect her nose from the acrid stench of smoke and charred flesh. The world would end in fire as the nine realms burned. The city of Avranches was simply experiencing that fate first.

A few dozen warriors guarded the gate, but they had already begun to strip the dead of rings, swords, metal armor, and even the iron rims around shields. Others checked the ground for disturbed earth where the townsfolk might have buried their valuables. Extracting a city's wealth took hard work and a keen eye.

Her warriors rushed past her to join the looting. Halla picked her way over the islands of dirt framed by streams of blood with a caution her men showed no sign of sharing. This was the most dangerous time. Franks could be hiding in any building, waiting for her to pass before ambushing. She didn't intend to die in this Frankish town.

At the first intersection, wounded warriors guarded huddled masses of prisoners. A group of Danes escorted a collection of old women and children up one of the side streets to join the rest. Even from a distance, Halla smelled the sweat and urine of their terror.

A bald warrior with a braided beard sorted the women who would satisfy the army later that night to one side and the children destined for the slave markets to the other. The men, of course, were already dead. They only caused trouble or tried to escape.

With a swift stroke of his axe, the warrior beheaded one of the women too old to be a profitable slave. The others whimpered and cowered as her head rolled to a rest beside them.

A young, dark-haired woman broke free from the rest and rushed forward. Halla slid a leg back and drew her axe. Captives should have already been checked for weapons, but warriors sometimes made mistakes. Everyone ultimately had to protect themselves.

"Please, help me!" She clasped her hands together and fell to her knees before Halla. "My husband is an archer at the western tower. Let me go and I can tell you where they're vulnerable."

Recalling the skilled archer she had killed, Halla struck the woman in the temple with the haft of her axe, knocking her to the ground. "Your husband was a brave warrior, and you betray him?" She curled her lip into a scowl. Even Taurin's people condemned traitors to their version of Hel.

A pair of warriors jogged over and dragged her back by her hair. One nodded in gratitude.

Halla met his eyes. "Make sure she lives to be of use tonight." She would rather die fighting than cower like that. These people merely knew how to exist, not how to truly live. Pathetic.

A few warriors ran past, shouting about the Franks making a stand at the church. She ignored them. Rollo's army would make short work of any resistance now that it had breached the walls. It'd end before she could reach them.

Because Rollo had attacked during Easter, the market stalls were empty. They would have to go through each building to find the town's valuables. She could have first choice, up to her share from this raid, from anything she personally looted. If some armed Christians hid in one of the buildings, that would be fine, too.

She continued walking until she reached a neighborhood with a few unbroken doors. A sign bearing a needle and thread hung from a wooden bracket above one of them. It reminded her of home.

She frowned. When had she started thinking of Lillebonne as home?

The door had no lock and creaked when Halla pushed it open with the head of her axe. Thin beams of light seeped through the cracks in the shutters. Inside, four large tables held rolls of cloth, half-sewn clothing, shears, thimbles, bone and bronze needles, and precious patterns that Adella could use to make a chest full of new dresses.

The Franks might be weak and cowardly, but their dresses draped nicely on her frame if she didn't wear her axes.

She studied the corners and behind the furniture and pushed the door open until it struck the wall, leaving no room for an attacker. A low-burning fire still tickled the charred logs sitting within the fireplace; no one could hide there, either.

After a quick glance outside, she approached the tables. They held not only rolls of the muted shades available in Lillebonne, but also deep reds, bold blues, and vibrant greens. Someone had soaked these fabrics in dye tubs for a long time.

Her drifting eyes stopped on one rich purple bolt of cloth with an exceptionally fine grain. She reached out to touch it but halted before ruining it with the grime and blood covering her fingers. Suddenly, all the cloth seemed dangerously close.

She returned to the door. Holding her axe by the head, she carved Brísingamen around three dots in a triangle to claim the contents.

Outside, the cries had diminished, but a thick gray cloud ascended from the direction of the church. Halla smirked, recalling the Norwegian's story about the longhouse burning. The army could sift through the embers to collect the gold and silver from inside once they cooled.

Most of the nearby buildings were squat single-story houses with shuttered windows and thatched roofs. Evidently considering them not worth the time to search, someone had tossed a few torches to burn them. The flames hadn't taken, but no one cared enough to give them a second thought.

She picked a building at random and tried the door. Locked.

Arching an eyebrow, she stepped back and kicked the door once, twice. On the third try, the hinges finally gave way and broke inward.

Wrapped around the haft of her axe, her fingers tingled with excitement. Locks guarded valuables.

But inside she only saw cooking pots, an iron ladle, and a few ceramic jugs. One contained an acrid spice of some sort. Someone would pay for such a pot in Rouen, but Halla couldn't decide whether the profit would justify its space on the longship.

A wooden bed sat in the corner beside a pile of furs. A linen dress hung from the bedpost, wrinkling from neglect, near a man's tunic and a wooden toy sword leaning against the wall. A couple lived here with at least one child, probably a son. Halla doubted the Franks would teach a daughter the sword.

She grunted. The women in the square would suffer after sunset for not knowing how to defend themselves.

The rafters sat too close to the ceiling to hang lengths of cloth from them, so the owners had settled for a wooden screen to divide the room into sections. One of those stood directly in front of the door, concealing the rear quarter of the room from view.

Halla adjusted her grip on her axe and took a few tentative steps to the side, eyes watching the hidden space. Above a table and a pair of long benches, wooden mugs hung from pegs hammered into the gaps between the log planks of the far wall. The hearth sat along the other wall, directly facing her but concealed by the screen.

This house had nothing of value to the traders of Rouen, nor seeds or tools that Leubin could put to good use. She understood why her companions had tried to torch this neighborhood.

But the hearth caught her attention. Fresh footprints from someone with a lazy, dragging gait had smeared the soot and ash of countless fires. After a few feet, they became swirls of alternating soot and clean patches, as if someone had circled the area.

Crouching down, she studied the grain of the floor planks. Compared to the rest of the house, the wood here contained a great many joints. With the haft of her axe, she tapped the floorboards on one end of the collection of joints. *Thump. Thump.*

She moved to the other side. *Drum. Drum.* The legs of the table ran on either side, but did not pass over a section four planks wide.

A secret compartment. No wonder she'd seen nothing of value!

Wedging the curved tip of her axe between planks, she leaned her weight against it. After a moment, the plank and the three others attached to it rose enough for her to squeeze her fingers in and lift.

It contained no horde of valuable coins or precious metals, only a woman clutching a little boy to her chest and gazing up in terror.

Halla gasped and nearly dropped the plank. The shape of her face, the slope of her chin, and even the color of her eyes reminded her eerily of Adella. Adella, whose youngest son was the same age as this little boy. Adella, who had helped her win over the women of town by sewing her a Frankish dress. Adella, who could drink a whole cup of mead without tottering even once, defying all of Halla's expectations about Frankish women.

Did Taurin have a secret compartment in his manor? Had his father hidden there as a child, when her people had last pillaged his home? How many of Leubin and Adella's ancestors had died during that raid?

Something moved outside. Startled, she dropped the plank back into place. She scrambled to her feet as one of Jarl Sigrun's Norwegians stepped through, wielding his axe before him. He offered a perfunctory shout before recognizing Halla's braids and kohl.

She raised a hand in greeting. "Hail."

"Hail, shieldmaiden." A splash of blood formed a ragged line across his face, an arterial spray from a victim. "Anything worth looting?"

With a word, she could expose that woman and her son. They would fetch a good price at the slave markets; the boy was young enough to forget his life before this attack.

But Halla could still taste the choking air of the smoke-filled night as the longships had burned. Visions of those flames crawling up the sides of Taurin's manor and his servants strewn lifeless across the road haunted her.

"Nothing," she answered. "But I haven't checked the other homes."

The warrior nodded and raised his axe in a curt salute before ducking back through the door.

Only once she heard him kick in another door down the street did she raise the floorboards again. The woman flinched at the sudden light but softened when her wild eyes recognized Halla was alone. She would have heard a man's voice and probably expected the worst.

"Stay here. Stay quiet," Halla instructed in Frankish. The woman's eyes dilated at the familiar language. "I'll mark your door to keep other warriors away. When you hear a horn sound three times, wait a hundred breaths before leaving through the eastern gate. Only the eastern gate. Don't delay, or you'll burn with the town."

The woman adjusted her embrace of her son. "Why are you helping us?"

Halla swallowed her surprise. She even sounded like Adella.

She shouldn't be doing this. Cowards and weaklings would only breed softness, and the gods needed strength for Ragnarok.

And yet, strength had many varieties. Could she blame a woman for hiding beneath a false floor to protect her child? Halla would have grabbed a knife and fought, but she had no one to protect. What if she did?

She couldn't endure seeing Adella each day if she killed this woman. Was that weakness?

"Do as I say." She removed her axe and replaced the planks, sealing the woman in darkness again.

Crossing the room, her footsteps echoed in her ears. At the door, she carved a large X into the door. She closed it enough that her people would notice the mark, but not all the way. A closed door required investigation.

She had many more closed doors to investigate, and now she had at least one more warrior to compete with for the best plunder. She hurried to the next house.

HALLA

A knife-wielding Frank surprised Halla during her looting. She ducked at the last moment but took a slash in the forearm before driving her axe into the man's neck.

Ransacking a town was dirty work, so with a sigh, she trudged off to find a healing woman before the wound soured. She had uncovered more than enough plunder for her share, and the rest of the warriors could do the hard work of hauling all the goods back to camp.

The *læknar* had converted the buildings nearest to the gates into healing huts. Warriors growled and screamed from wounds as serious as cleaved skulls and lost limbs. The healing women had assigned some of the uninjured to remove the dead, one heavy body at a time.

The smell of blood filled the square, and her stomach couldn't endure the stench from the denser concentration of wounded. She bit down the bile that threatened to erupt as she crossed to a *læknir* farthest from the square. Hopefully, anyone who saw her pale would assume she suffered a grave wound. She had already endured too many indignities to add to them by vomiting at the sight of a little blood.

Shelves covered the far right wall of the building she entered. Jagged exploratory tears spilled wheat, rye, and barley from several sacks sitting upon them. Molested crates sat in the corners, their sides hacked open and their lids pried off to gauge the worth of their contents. A large counter ran from the far wall to the center of the room.

Revna sat upon it, tended by a *læknir*.

Halla rushed forward, slipping on a smear of blood at the last step. Hands flashing out, she grasped the counter to stop herself from falling. The sudden motion sent a tear of pain through her arm. Out of breath, she searched Revna for wounds, terrified of what she might find.

"I'm fine." Revna waved her off with one arm while cradling the other. "I only bruised my shoulder."

"How?"

Revna scowled. "The door didn't give when I shoved it. I thought I broke it."

"She didn't," the elderly *læknir* reported. "But next time, kick the door." Arching an eyebrow, the woman turned her crinkled eyes toward Halla's arm.

Halla endured her probing for a few moments before sighing. "It's only a cut."

"So the goddess Eir speaks to you now, does she?" The woman glared at her for a moment before returning her attention to the wound. "With what sort of blade? Rusted or sharp? Clean or dirty?"

Halla frowned, trying to recall. "A knife. It cut cleanly through."

The healer placed a hand on Halla's forehead. Frowning, she felt Halla's cheeks. "Have you felt nauseated?"

"A little, yes."

"Did it start with the wound?"

"No, it's been some time. Several weeks, perhaps?"

Withdrawing her hands, the old woman narrowed her eyes. "Lift your mail shirt."

The request made little sense, but with the *læknir*'s earlier berating still ringing in her ears, she obeyed.

The healer squeezed and pressed on her stomach, pausing occasionally to gauge her patient's reaction. When Halla gave none after several iterations, she lowered her hands.

"When you joined the raid, did you know you were pregnant?"

Revna gasped.

"Impossible!" Halla's body, suddenly heavy, seemed to fall away from her neck and shoulders. "I can't be pregnant."

"When did you last bleed?"

She counted the days to refute the ridiculous suggestion, trying to recall the phase of the moon during her last bleeding. She supposed it had been some time, but that didn't mean anything. She missed cycles all the time.

As she finished her calculations, she swallowed. "No, it can't be."

This couldn't be happening now, not when she had finally rejoined her people. "I cleanse myself with saltwater. I have never forgotten."

The *læknir* shook her head. "Such methods don't always work."

Why had no one told her? How, in all the dark corners of Helheim, would she know that? The shieldmaidens all swore by the salt cleanse, and it had always worked for her in the past.

Pregnant. Eyes widening, she recalled Sigrun's firm body beneath her a few nights past. "When?"

The healer shrugged. "The firmness in your belly suggests some time ago."

"Some time ago?" she hissed.

"Two months, perhaps."

Then it was Taurin's. This child would blend both Christian and Norse. She had asked the gods for another path, and they had sent her a man with a body built for wielding a sword. But she had never dreamed intended this.

Ignoring Revna's cries behind her, she stumbled through the door. She placed a hand to her chest, suddenly too small to contain her breath. Her heart pounded through tunic and mail.

The sudden brightness outside blinded her. Rubbing her eyes, she nearly fell as her foot came down on the edge of a rut in the road.

Arms caught her. "Sit, sit." Revna guided her to the stone step of the house across the street.

She rubbed her palms into her eyes. "Gods... What do I do now?"

Revna squeezed her shoulder. "You wipe your nose, sacrifice a goose to Frigg, and go home."

"Go home?" She reared back. "I'm not leaving until the raid is over."

"You must," Revna insisted. "A child is a gift from the gods. You cannot endanger it. Go home to your husband."

She swallowed. Of course, she was right. Any one of the tower archer's arrows could have killed her child. She couldn't risk harming it in another battle. This was her fate. She would have to return home.

To Taurin, who mistrusted everything she valued.

"But, Revna, you hate him."

"Oh, I do. He's annoying and his people are weak." She continued to rub Halla's shoulder. "Yet he clearly cares for his own. If he would risk his safety for his people, I suspect he would die for his child."

"Perhaps," she mumbled, still unconvinced. That man clung to a grudge with an irritating stubbornness.

"And if he doesn't treat its mother well," Revna added with a smirk, "he will."

TAURIN

Taurin focused on Father Norbert's words as the priest offered a Latin invocation for divine mercy. Sunday mass felt more somber than usual. Instead of gossiping about the scandalous cut of a dress or who conversed with whom, the celebrants bowed and clenched their hands with increased sincerity, desperate to manifest the priest's blessing with their own prayers.

Taurin had hoped those who had attacked Emeline's farm would move on, but two more attacks had occurred within the week. Each time, the raiders had ransacked the farmhouses for valuables and burned the outbuildings while the farmers were either visiting town or tending their fields.

During the fourth attack, a farmer fought back. His wife, hiding with their young daughter in a storage compartment beneath their floor, listened in terrified silence to the agonized gurgling of her husband's final moments. Dagobert, investigating the smoke of the burning farm, had found her several hours later.

His people had begun glaring at him again. Even now, as he listened to the priest's words in church, he felt their scrutiny and caught furtive glances out of the corner of his eye. Nor could he blame them. He had given his pledge that the Norse would protect them. Every further raid called that promise into question.

The priest completed the concluding rites and the townsfolk filed out of the church. The moment Taurin reached daylight, he felt a hand on his shoulder.

Guntramm straightened to his full height. "Have you found the raiders?" He didn't even bother with a greeting.

Perhaps training the townsfolk to defend themselves had been a mistake that had merely encouraged insolence. Taurin kept his voice low as the parishioners filed past. "We suspect they're Norse."

"And what do you intend to do about them?" His loud question drew the attention of Tescelin and Huebald, who sidled closer.

Too late, Taurin realized Guntramm intended to attract a crowd. "I intend to find them and stop them."

"How long will that take?"

"Not a moment longer than it must," Taurin reassured, desperate to end this confrontation before the gathering swelled. "The Norse search for them as we speak."

"And you trust them?" The farmer lowered his eyes to study Taurin's whiskered chin. "You said Rouen would protect us. Where are they now?"

He knew very well that they were killing Christians to the south. Taurin raised his hand to stroke his whiskers but caught himself before drawing more attention to his short beard. "It was one of Halla's warriors who first blamed Norse raiders."

The man scowled. "While they take their time, our farms burn."

A few townsfolk had stopped their progress to listen.

Taurin searched for a path of escape. More spectators gathered to watch the brewing altercation, hemming him in on all sides.

Fine. If they wanted to discuss this, then he'd discuss it. "What would you have me do?"

"We should search for ourselves," Guntramm declared.

The pair of men behind him nodded in agreement.

"Are you prepared to face a full longship?"

The man frowned. "Do you question our courage?"

Taurin shook his head. "Only your numbers. A longship can carry thirty veteran Norse warriors."

The disgruntled men shifted their weight and glanced at each other. At least they tempered their bravery with common sense. Though his people had improved with the sword, the Norse settlers still routinely trounced them.

Their caution offered him an escape. He placed a hand on Guntramm's shoulder. "The *hirdmen* know Norse ways better." He leaned forward. "Let them risk stumbling upon the raiders by accident."

The man's eyes widened. Taurin suspected he hadn't considered the danger a scout faced alone in the wilds.

"But prepare yourselves in case we must fight to defend our home."

Guntramm swallowed and stepped back, signaling an end to the interrogation. But instead of slinking away quietly, he and his companions headed off together, muttering. Taurin had only bought himself some time.

Halla should have been handling this mess, not raiding in the Bessin. He would have rather done anything but hunt down Arbogast, but had done his duty. She thought like those raiders and could probably find them in a day. She might even convince them to raid elsewhere. Anywhere would be better than here.

He glanced over his shoulder at the cross atop the church. He couldn't lie to himself, not so close to the house of God. He desired not her skill, but her touch. She had warmed to him in their last moment together, but he had offended her and snuffed that flicker of intimacy. He hadn't been able to sleep the past few weeks, imagining her lying in a mass grave far to the south. He needed her to return so he could make up for all that wasted time.

Would Rollo even inform him if she died, or would he learn of her fate only when another *hersir* arrived to replace her? He brought a hand up to his chest to steady the hammering of his heart.

Shame and regret weighing him down like a sack of grain, Taurin shuffled past the market stalls. Before Halla had come, farmers would use these stalls only occasionally to barter extra supplies. But now, traders occupied all of them, calling to the procession leaving the church. A Norseman with a braided moustache brandished an inlaid goblet and halted a passerby with a few heavily accented words in Frankish. A few women stopped before another table with silver hair pins, earrings and brooches of bone, horn, copper, and bronze and over a dozen beaded necklaces. A group of townsfolk clustered around another stall as a dark-skinned Moor rattled off the features of a dagger with a strange, mottled pattern to the metal.

A Frankish farmer brandished a bolt of rough wool cloth, shouting to the congregants. Both the carpenter and blacksmith took up the cry, gathering crowds as they displayed their wares. As a boy reached out to touch the blade of a woodcutter's axe, Huebald slapped it away. Before Halla's arrival, craftsmen would never have wasted material on anything but bespoke commissions, yet each displayed several sample pieces.

Had Lillebonne looked like this in his grandfather's time?

Distracted, he stumbled into a pair of women halted beside one of the stalls. He bowed and mumbled an apology. When they continued on their progress, his eyes fell upon the stall behind them, and he froze.

Atop a shelf sat a silver brooch in the shape of an eagle, surrounded by a circle of silver.

Emeline's brooch.

He wiped his hand over his chin. The rippling of his whiskers springing back into place convinced him he wasn't imagining it.

A clean-shaven man behind the counter clasped the gold cross around his neck. "God's blessings upon you on the Lord's day," he greeted in accent-free Frankish.

"And upon you."

He pretended to study the man's wares while he worked through his doubts. Perhaps Halla's *hirdman* had made a mistake in blaming the Norsemen. This Frankish trader had first visited town during the winter, long before the attacks began. And while the brooch matched

Emeline's description, it might simply be a coincidence. Many had served in Charlemagne's armies.

He had to be certain.

Taurin feigned a cheerful smile that felt awkward on his face. "I seek a gift for my wife. What would you recommend?" He studied the wares in earnest now but carefully avoided glancing at the brooch.

"Wouldn't you prefer some new turnshoes for yourself? Buying gifts for your wife will spoil her."

Taurin suspected Halla would spoil this man's face with her fist if she heard him speak thusly.

"She prefers jewelry," Taurin lied. "Silver or gold."

"Very expensive." The man ran an appraising eye over Taurin. "Do you have coin to pay?"

"I am Taurin, the alderman."

Eyes widening, the man bobbed his head up and down. "Then allow me to show you what I have." He reached into a chest behind him.

Taurin took advantage of his turned back to eye the brooch. The silver bore some dirt within the crevices of the braids. Weathering along the eagle's beak suggested age. It matched Emeline's description perfectly. But was it hers?

When the trader turned back, he presented a burnished silver ring set with pink stone and a smooth ring with a small emerald on two of his fingers. His other hand carried a gold chain with a ruby pendant and a necklace of silver-beaten leaves. All of them were genuine treasures, and Taurin didn't want to imagine the circumstances that caused them to be sitting in this man's stall now.

He had once overheard Adella tell her husband silver matched everything. "What do you have to pair with that silver necklace?"

Finally, the man reached for the brooch. Taurin exhaled a breath he hadn't realized he held.

"A lady can always use a brooch to pin her cloak."

Taurin accepted the offered item and turned it over. He had never seen craftsmanship like it. The individual eagle feathers and the careful shaping of the eye would require tiny tools wielded by a steady hand. "It's breathtaking. Where did you find it?"

The man's tongue darted over his lips. "From a trader in Cherbourg. He told me it was one of a kind."

His tone carried the strain of a lie, but whether he lied about its origin or uniqueness, Taurin couldn't decide.

If the *hirdman* was right, this man had received this brooch from the Norsemen responsible for the attacks and would know where to find them.

Haggling long enough to convince the trader he only cared about the jewelry, Taurin paid three fur-trimmed cloaks for the necklace and brooch together.

Two hours later, he rode up to Emeline's farmstead. The teary-eyed woman pointed out the tiny scratch on the eagle's leg made during a brawl with her younger brother years earlier. It was hers, after all.

Sidestepping her effusive thanks, Taurin mounted Seraphim and rode hard for home, brow furrowed in thought. If this trader led him to Norse raiders, he'd need help to subdue them. His fellow Franks were too inexperienced to defeat veteran warriors. Even if they did, Taurin doubted he could convince them to spare the raiders' lives. And spare them, he must. Unless Rouen condemned them, others would simply replace them.

He would have to use Halla's *hirdmen*. She had claimed that she had instructed her people to obey him. He had no choice but to test that promise, but he resolved to have at least one person to rely upon if they didn't.

And he knew exactly whom to ask.

TAURIN

Taurin lifted his ear from the ground and wiped a patch of dirt from his cheek. "He's still moving."

Orderic doubled over, resting his hands on his knees. "If we keep running like this, we won't arrive in any condition to fight."

Vikarr and three other Norsemen stood nearby, breathing rapidly but not sucking in breaths as Orderic did. They had been traveling for four hours. Fortunately, the trader's cart moved slower than they could jog. When they came close enough to hear the grinding of stones beneath the wooden wheels, Taurin halted them until the cart opened more distance.

So far, Halla's *hirdmen* hadn't complained. Then again, he hadn't asked anything difficult of them. Yet.

Breathing more evenly now, Taurin rose and adjusted the positioning of his sword, the one Halla had given him at their wedding. He might use it to shed Norse blood this day.

"Let's keep moving."

A thin road, little more than a dirt track used by the local farmers, hugged the slope of a hill that ended in a winding defile. Taurin didn't dare follow the easier route of the path. If the trader stopped suddenly, they might venture too close and expose themselves. Instead, he led his men through the thin forest along the defile. It hadn't rained in several days, but a thin stream of runoff collected at the bottom. They picked their way over the uneven ground, avoiding the water lest their splashing footsteps announce them. Taurin's calves burned from the extra exertion of jogging on an angle, and the short breaks he risked weren't sufficient to banish the pain.

At the next pause, Taurin no longer heard hooves. Gesturing for his companions to crouch, he led them forward slowly, staying low to shelter in the nearby bushes.

Up ahead, the trader had halted his cart in a widened clearing on the opposite side of the road where the hill leveled out. Three others with long, braided hair and wearing mail shirts faced him beside a second cart.

Norsemen. The raiders were Norsemen, after all.

Taurin signaled for the *hirdmen* to halt with a tightened fist.

As many as thirty could fit on a single longship, but Taurin saw no other movement.

"Where are the others?" Orderic whispered.

One of the Norseman with a single braid down the side of his head and crisp blue eyes stood a few steps in front of the others. When he turned, Taurin recognized him: Bjornolf, who had protested Rollo's plans in Rouen. Halla knew him.

He and Orderic halted behind a hawthorn bush, close enough to overhear their words. With a nod, Vikarr signaled the *hirdmen* to split off and encircle the raiders.

"We pillaged a few more estates up north," Bjornolf was saying. "We have some gold necklaces and fine linen cloth."

The trader craned to study the contents of the second cart. It looked much like the carts in Lillebonne. He had probably looted it from a nearby farmstead.

"Not bad," the trader said. "I can move jewelry. How about thirty silver pieces for the lot?"

"Thirty?" Bjornolf scowled. "The gold alone would go for fifty." His hand reached for his sword. "I didn't spare you in Cherbourg for you to cheat me in the Caux."

The trader cackled. "No, you spared me because you need someone to supply your men. And without me"—he jabbed a finger at the warrior—"you'd have to sail to Britain to sell your plunder, and you probably wouldn't earn enough to keep your men loyal."

While Taurin admired his courage, he expected Bjornolf to draw his sword and slay him right there. Yet, the Norseman merely scowled and clenched his fist.

The exchange resolved one question, though. "He brings only those warriors he trusts fully," he whispered to Orderic.

"You hope."

"If they knew of this trader, his men could betray him. Halla spoke of such things." Watching for it, Taurin noticed an unmistakable twitch of Orderic's cheek at the mention of his wife.

"We should wait," Orderic insisted. "They can lead us to the others."

Taurin shook his head. "He's their leader. He's the one who matters."

Frowning, Orderic nonetheless nodded. "If you say."

Taurin inhaled a slow breath and gripped the hilt of his sword. *Calm. Steady.* He met Orderic's eyes. "If the *hirdmen* don't obey, we'll make for the stream."

The other alderman swallowed and nodded.

He glanced at Bjornolf again, arguing with the trader now.

It was time. He shifted his weight, prepared to rush back the direction he had come if Halla's warriors did nothing.

God, watch over us.

He gave the birdcall.

The *hirdmen* surged from their hiding places amid snapping branches and rustling leaves, rushing for Bjornolf and his companions.

Bjornolf rounded on the bewildered trader. "You betrayed me?"

"No, I swear, I had no—"

The Norseman drew his sword and slashed the trader across the throat with a single motion, silencing his protest. The man crumpled to the ground in an awkward pile.

Taurin's men reached a redheaded Norseman first. He landed a glancing blow on Vikarr's vambrace before taking a stab to the shoulder and recoiling back into the tip of another *hirdman's* sword. He collapsed backwards, pinning his killer beneath him.

Bjornolf's other companion screamed Odin's name and charged for the nearest enemy, a young *hirdman* of eighteen winters. Eyes wide, the *hirdman* raised his sword a little too late, and the raider's axe knocked him to the side.

Orderic, circling to the left, brought his sword around in a wide arc intended to draw the raider's attention. It worked, but instead of deflecting Orderic's slash, the raider charged and knocked him to the ground. Orderic's sword clattered against a stone off to the side with a metallic clang.

Taurin rushed forward, eyes fixed on his friend's face. Orderic raised his hands before him, as his attacker shifted his weight to strike.

The Norseman raised his axe. "By Thor!"

As the warrior began his downward swing, Taurin slashed. His sword traced a path across the man's forearm. The Norseman screamed in pain and recoiled, dropping his weapon. Before he could turn, Vikarr speared him through the back. Blood gurgled from his lips for a moment before his gaze lost focus and he slumped to the ground.

Hauling Orderic to his feet, Taurin whirled around, searching for Bjornolf, convinced the big Norseman would be upon them.

But he saw only the *hirdmen*, two dead raiders, and the trader, lying in the soggy mud of his own blood. Bjornolf had vanished.

"Bjornolf, you coward!" Vikarr wiped his sword on the tunic of one of the fallen raiders. "Face me!"

Only the birds, warbling in the distance, responded to his challenge.

One of the *hirdmen*, bearing a gash on his forehead above his left eye, approached leading two horses by their reins. Mud dripped off the back and sides of his pants. "He escaped," the man grumbled. "Knocked me to the ground and mounted a horse past these bushes."

Escaped.

Taurin cleansed his own sword on his tunic before slamming it into his sheath. He had failed. Halla had trusted him, and he had wasted his one chance to capture the raiders' leader.

CHAPTER THIRTEEN

HALLA

POPPA GUSHED WITH excitement to learn of Halla's pregnancy, but Rollo scowled at losing his *hersir* so early in the season. Yet, neither of them objected when Halla departed on the longship heading to Rouen, bearing Rollo's instructions for Jorund. The gods had made their wishes known, and none would dare to challenge them.

The voyage involved an unbroken bout of seasickness, interrupted only by her very creative and shockingly graphic string of curses when she learned they would press on for the Seine instead of stopping at Jersey. Knowing of her condition, the crew didn't mock her queasiness this time.

Disembarking on the southernmost pier in Lillebonne, she gagged at the odor. A farmer had brought several cattle to market but had forgotten to hire a carter to haul away the excrement. She yearned for roasting meat and the scent of muscled men in camp, for the fresh aroma of ripening berries and blooming flowers as they marched to Avranches. Instead, she was home, pinching her nose from the stink of cow dung.

Nonetheless, the farmer's oversight benefited her. She doubted she could ride a horse with her stomach still roiling from the voyage. Taking advantage of the unemployed carter, she climbed into the back and settled in for a long ride to the estate.

The jostling cart offered only a marginal improvement from the rocking of the waves. She grasped the sides for stability, but each rock the wheels struck caused her stomach to roil. The countryside crawled by too slowly and seemed too confining in its frustrating sameness.

The invigoration of marching with her people had begun to fade. Before her waited a man who refused to learn her ways. His face, in those final moments before they'd parted, suggested Revna was right and he would never truly accept her.

That could be mended. Dissolving a marriage was no great difficulty. The Franks would object, but she could manage their anger as Gordrun had—with executions.

Still… The gods had connected them forever through this child. She drew a slow breath to settle her stomach. Provided he remained loyal to Rollo, they could coexist. And she would find a wet nurse so she could raid again next year.

The manor was bustling with activity when the cart arrived. Some laborers were planting late-spring crops, while others repaired fresh damage to the barn. Adella sat on a stool near the well, scrubbing a tunic clean with a basin of water. When the cart approached, she bolted to her feet and waved.

Lips curling into a smile, Halla thought of the patterns, safely stored in the army's baggage wagons somewhere to the south. Adella would be delighted.

Far to the left, Leubin and a bearded man leaned on a long wooden pole, levering up a wagon as the town's wainright replaced a wheel. She initially mistook him for one of the Norse farmers who had arrived from Rouen in her absence, but his beard was too short for him to be one of her people.

When he turned, she realized the unfamiliar man was her husband. By the gods, he had grown a beard!

He had said his people deemed it a sign of their heathen past, cured by Christ. He had claimed his people would call him a traitor after his agreement in Rouen. And yet, there it was, clinging to his chin.

He had grown a beard for her! This man, whom she had spent weeks thinking cared little for her, had done this thing for her.

A warm glow spread over her as his eyes met hers and widened.

He offered a parting word to his companions before running to the cart. Skidding to a halt before her, he clenched the sides of the cart for support. "You're home," he gasped between recovering breaths. "Is the raid over already?"

She shook her head. "I returned with some of the wounded and the messengers."

"Wounded?" He turned her wrists over and felt her thighs and shoulders, searching for injuries. The unmistakable fear in his eyes filled her with tender affection. "Where?"

She remembered the first time she had seen the depths of those eyes. They weren't the eyes of an ideologue, but a kind man.

"I'm fine." She reached down to squeeze his hand.

"I had visions of you bleeding beneath some tower." Raising a hand, he hesitated before brushing his fingers across her cheek. "I feared you wouldn't return."

She closed her eyes, soaking in his unexpected tenderness. Her own news yearned to burst forth, but a new question, now conceived, would not wait.

"Would you not prefer that after the *blót*?" After the awkward winter, she hadn't expected the answer to matter so much to her. Yet, it did.

He hauled himself onto the cart beside her. His eyes carried a softness she would have disdained in another man.

"I can't sleep without you beside me at night. I see something during the day and turn to comment to you, only to find you gone." He squeezed her hand. A ripple of exhilaration ran up her arm. "I may never understand you ways or beliefs, but I'd rather spend my life trying than live with another woman. If that's sacrilege, then so be it."

His words tickled her ears with delight. Raising her hand, she ran her fingers through the whiskers on his chin. Her smile widened as they pricked her skin. They showed the truth in his heart, dissolving her worries.

"I have something to tell you."

He lowered his chin a fingerspan, the way he did when he expected bad news. That she could interpret his expression pleased her.

"I returned early because gifts from the gods must be preserved and treasured, and there is no greater gift than the coming of a child."

His lips parted in disbelief. "You're...pregnant?"

"I am."

He gave a whoop and jumped from the cart. Beaming, he cupped her cheeks and kissed her, then ran a few steps toward the house. "I'm going to be a father!" He thrust his hands skyward.

A few of his people turned at the sound, but he had already returned to Halla. "Praise be to God." Ever so slowly, he raised his hand and rested it on her belly. His touch was delicate, as if she were one of those glass bottles for sale in the markets of Rouen. If only he knew how she had charged into battle a week earlier outside Avranches!

Fears unknotting, she leaned her forehead against the top of his head. His weren't the reactions of an uncaring heathen. She had been so very wrong about him.

"The gods," she corrected, flashing a mischievous smile.

"All of them, if it keeps this child safe and healthy."

She couldn't disagree with that sentiment, though she had learned other Christians would consider it blasphemy.

"What must we do now?" After a moment, he snapped his fingers. "A cradle. I have some extra wood from repairing the barn." He shifted his hand to her shoulder. "Do you need any special food? New clothes?"

"Always." She smirked. His fluttering filled her with a lusty delight. "Speaking of clothes, I find myself wanting to rip yours off."

Reaching up, he took her cheeks in his hands and leaned in to kiss her. His lips tasted like sweet berries. The raspberries must have ripened in her absence.

He pulled back suddenly. A shadow veiled his eyes.

"What?" She repressed his irritation that he would taint their happy reunion with troubles.

He pursed his lips. "Much has happened since you left."

She listened with growing discomfort as he explained the raids, the brooch, and the failed ambush. While Bjornolf's continuing to raid didn't surprise her, she hadn't expected him to attack Rollo's territory after the jarl's warning in Rouen. Why would he risk outlawry to burn a few pitiful farmsteads?

Bjornolf, you fool.

"Are you certain?"

Taurin nodded. "Vikarr recognized him."

She rubbed her wounded arm, frowning. Whatever his reasons, he had violated Rollo's edicts, and that required a response. "Rollo will hold a *Thing* this fall. We will charge Bjornolf there and the people will punish him for it."

"But I didn't capture him."

She shook her head. "That doesn't matter. Between you and Vikarr, we have two witnesses. They don't know you, but they will remember Vikarr. It should be enough."

Taurin jutted his lip out in an almost-frown. "Should?"

She squeezed his hand. "You'll see. Rollo will honor his word."

HALLA

Halla was practicing her axe technique against the trunk of a dead apple tree when a rider advanced down the road. At first, she mistook him as one of Taurin's tenants, but the braided locks flowing behind his leather cap suggested otherwise.

She wiped her hands on the new, pale purple dress Adella had crafted to accommodate her pregnancy. The waistline was far too wide, but Adella had insisted it would feel tight before she gave birth. The possibility terrified her. Already, her belly had grown enough that riding left her sore.

"Hail," she greeted as the rider pulled himself free of his stirrup.

When he turned, his eyes carried a tension that wrinkled the skin around them.

"Oleg!" She stretched out her arms to embrace him. "Please tell me you aren't here about Bjornolf."

"Bjornolf?" He clasped her shoulders but did not embrace her. "What do you mean?"

Halla explained about the raids. When she reported the fate of the Frankish trader, he frowned, but the strain around his eyes remained unchanged.

"That isn't why I've come." His beard twitched as he gnawed on his lip.

She narrowed her eyes. "Then why?"

"The longships returned from the south," he said with a tight voice.

"All of them?" Not another disaster like the Vire...

"This time, yes. They took great plunder and ended the raid rather than risk losing it."

She exhaled, satisfied that her patterns and cloth were safe. Rollo could ill afford further losses after the previous year's disaster.

"My *knörr* joined them as they rounded the Cotentin." He took her hand gently between his own.

The delicacy of his grip sent a shiver down her back. "Oleg, tell me." She adjusted her stance. "Is Rollo injured?"

"No." His eyes fell to the ground before her.

At least the jarl was safe. He had no sons, and Jorund was no raid leader. Everything she was working toward would collapse if his warriors began fighting over control of Rouen. They might even lose the city if the Franks took advantage of the quarreling. Sigrun had the men to claim the city, but would he abandon his own lands back home?

But Oleg had said that hadn't happened.

"Then what?"

Sorrow and pain filled his eyes. She remembered that look from many years prior, when Rollo had come to tell a girl of fifteen that her father had died. Only one person in her life could justify that look. She brought her hand to her mouth even before he uttered the words. "Revna is dead."

HALLA

Halla felt cold despite the heat thrown off by the pyre. The yellows and oranges blended with the dark backdrop of night into a single, sparkling mass of prismatic light through the lens of her tears.

She hadn't cried when she had learned Revna died raiding a smattering of buildings barely worth the name of village. But the tears came now as she watched the sacrificial goat burn in her honor. Revna's body and arm ring had already burned along with a pair of warriors who had succumbed to their injuries from Avranches. Halla had missed it.

Only three weeks earlier, they had sheltered together in the same tent on the march.

Halla thought of her friend's scowl when some warrior would woo her with an awful poem. The gentle tug on her braids as Revna ran her fingers over them. That barking laughter of utter abandon. Halla would miss them all. Those moments of joy would never come again.

She wiped the tears from her cheeks, not caring that she was probably smearing the kohl around her eyes. If she hadn't left the army, would Revna still be alive? The question sent a shiver down her back.

Surrounded by Franks, she was starting to think like them. The Norns had decided Revna's fate long ago. Her time had come, and she had died as a warrior.

She took a deep breath. The flesh of the sacrificial goat had started to char. She fluttered her cloak, finally feeling the heat from the flames.

Bits of memory from the past day returned. Despite understanding none of the significance, Leubin and Adella had handled all the preparations for the ceremony. A year earlier, Halla wouldn't have expected such courtesy from Christians.

And Taurin. He had remained at her side since finding her on the ground outside the house beside a frantic Oleg. He had led her toward the pyre erected in the space before their manor with a gentle hand. Grief and sympathy knew no religion or language.

A laugh escaped her lips as she remembered how Revna had stormed back from that river, grumbling about the Frankish man who irritated her so. How strange that this same man should honor her now with reverent silence.

They watched the pyre until the carcass matched the black of the burned wood and the flames faded to a faint red glow beneath the cinders. Only then did she lean her head against her husband's shoulder. Her cheek rubbed against his cloak where her tears moistened it.

"I first met her the day I learned my father died," she began in a voice that surprised her with its strength. "I thought it was a mistake. I ran to the docks, certain a ship would appear with him at the masthead. She found me there and stayed with me until twilight."

He raised a hand to caress her head. "Orderic did something similar for me once. I don't know how I'd react if he was taken from me."

"I wasn't there when she died. Because of this child."

"I'm glad of it," he breathed.

She rounded on him. "What did you say?"

"Call it God's will. I don't even care if you mean yours or mine. This child kept you safe, and for that, I'm grateful. Otherwise, I would be performing this rite for you."

His words quenched her nascent anger. "You would do that?" Conducting a pagan ritual would have rendered him unclean in the eyes of his people.

He caressed her cheek. "I pray that I never must."

His eyes carried the same vulnerable sincerity as when he had spoken of this land on the ride to Rouen. But now, that look was for her. Her kohl didn't matter, nor her language, nor her gods who celebrated the death of his ancestors. He saw only her, and he did not look away.

She began to tremble. He would burn an offering to gods he didn't believe in. He would profane his very soul. For her. Tears welled in her eyes that someone would risk so much for her.

Revna had walked the path of her choosing with neither fear nor doubt. She must do the same. But she need not walk alone.

The previous year in Rouen, she had thought Taurin had agreed to a partnership. Now, standing over a sacrifice to Thor announcing her dear friend's arrival among the gods, she understood how much she had underestimated him. His heart would walk through life with hers. She hadn't understood the enormity of that pledge until now.

They had squandered so much time. But it was never too late to start again.

She lifted herself onto her toes and brushed her lips against his. They felt moist, welcoming, despite the drying heat of the pyre.

He offered a surprised moan. "My darling."

The words tickled her ears. "Beloved." Her lips formed the word under their own power.

Her sudden vulnerability terrified her. But the feeling also thrilled her, and she yearned to explore it more with this man beside her. Taking his hand, she led him toward the door of their manor so they might begin that exploration.

They were alive, and life should be enjoyed.

TAURIN

Taurin repressed an irritated sigh as yet another farmer interposed himself and reached for his hand.

"Thank you, sir, for killing those monsters."

He mouthed a quick, "Anyone would do the same," before pulling his hand free and sidestepping the man.

The aldermen waited in the first row of the church for Father

Norbert's sermon to begin. Taurin made his way toward them, evading a pair of women who curtseyed as he passed and putting off another farmer who tried to approach.

The previous year, those pleased at Arbogast's capture had very narrowly outnumbered those who remembered his family's past contributions to the town. Exposing him as a bandit had raised unsettling questions. But now, the people of Lillebonne could express undiluted joy and hail the heroes who had defended them. They cared only that he and Orderic had killed two raiders.

But each expression of gratitude reminded Taurin of his failure. An entire longship of raiders still lingered somewhere in the hinterlands. Their leader had escaped, and he had squandered his only chance to capture him.

Orderic squeezed his shoulder when he finally reached the other aldermen. "Is this treatment not glorious?"

He simply grunted.

As Norbert began his opening benediction, Taurin's previously repressed sigh escaped. He wished only to put this threat behind him, but that wouldn't happen until the *Thing*. What an insignificant name for such an important meeting! As Halla's husband, he could participate. In the eyes of the Norse of Rouen, he was one of them.

Once, that thought would have unsettled him. But now, it reminded him of Halla leaning against his shoulder, lifting her lips to kiss his before the pyre. He hadn't expected to ever feel that kind of contentment.

An anxious whisper rippled through the nave of the church. More than a few townsfolk turned to stare at him. Had he inadvertently voiced his private thoughts?

But not all eyes faced him. A great many had turned to the back of the church. Following their gaze, he gasped in disbelief.

Halla stood in the doorway, a shadow framed in the surrounding daylight. Instead of braids, a simple ribbon bound her hair. She wore the pale purple dress Adella has sewn for her pregnancy, the same dress as when she had sacrificed to Revna. It probably still contained some of the cinders from Revna's pyre that had floated on the warmed air to rest within the fibers.

Draped around her neck, she wore the necklace of silver-beaten leaves Taurin had bought for her. It looked beautiful against the background of lightly shaded purple, but it didn't quite lay properly over her gold torc.

His wife was standing in a church! He wanted to run to her and take her in his arms, despite the scandal of such a public display.

The murmurs began again, breaking the silence.

"—in a house of God—"

"—is she converting—"

"—already primsigned—"

"—blood-soaked blasphemy—"

He smiled his encouragement when she met his eyes and began to pick her way through the crowd of muttering Franks. Though she endured their stares with a rigid smile, her eyes carried the strain of their scrutiny. He remembered feeling the same back in Rouen.

She shouldn't do this alone.

With a few measured strides, he met her halfway and offered his arm. Her iron grip threatened to numb his forearm below the elbow, but her smile never faded.

Surprised chatter tinged with the faintest edge of outrage accompanied them as they progressed. More than a few of the stunned onlookers crossed themselves. Though the other aldermen whispered with the rest of the faithful, Orderic, the man with whom he most wanted to share this triumph, vanished before they reached the front of the congregation.

The chatter ended when Father Norbert raised his arms and restarted his greeting. If the priest saw no reason to object, no one else would. In fact, excitement shone in the priest's eyes.

Taurin's fingers tingled with the same excitement. He stood in church, arm in arm with his wife. They had shared strange blood-soaked rituals and grief and carnal pleasure. Now, they would share the warm shower of divine regard.

Together, as it should be.

TAURIN

After mass, Taurin tethered Seraphim to Halla's cart and sat beside her as they returned home. "What made you come?"

She chewed on her lip. "Do you know why I married you?"

"You said my people would accept you more readily." The effort had assuredly worked on Dagobert and some of the others.

"That was part of it." Her shoulders slumped with her exhaled breath. "The Vire changed everything."

"Was Rollo truly surprised that Berengar fought back against him?"

"That's not what I meant." She lifted her eyes to the sky, but her gaze roamed without settling. "I nearly died on that shore."

Did she want sympathy, compassion, or something else? "I didn't know."

She cradled her stomach. "My people revel in the moment they fall in battle." The words came slowly, reluctantly. "I felt only regret. My death would have had no meaning." She swallowed. "I would have earned no glory worth remembrance, made no mark on the world."

She had never expressed doubts about her beliefs before. He had never expected to hear such things from any Norseman.

"That must have been...uncomfortable."

"I asked the gods for another path, one that would give my life purpose. They answered. I met you, Rollo announced his plan, and I decided to help create a kingdom here in Frankia for the gods."

He squirmed at the thought that his marriage depended on the will of heathen gods. "It is no less dangerous a path."

"I don't seek safety," she insisted. "But my death would at least have significance. It's what I thought I wanted."

He clung to that word. "Thought?"

"I now see there's more to life than a meaningful death. I have a life to lead, and I want to live it with you. How can I do that and ignore something as important to you as your faith?"

He smiled and reached for her hand.

"But I want you to accept me in the same way," she continued. "I can't endure your constant searching for the wild woman in me. You're not more enlightened than I am."

The words struck him like a slap. He snapped his head forward to stare at the road before them, cheeks burning.

The truth of her words cut his heart. Memories sprang to mind. The sprinkling of blood at their wedding. The disgust at her excitement to murder innocents during the raid. How her appearance at the winter *blót* had reminded him of Father Norbert's tales of witches and demons. He'd been a fool to think he had concealed his thoughts. She had seen it all.

He could offer neither denial nor defense. Yet even amid his shame, he realized she had confided in him for a reason. "Something changed your mind."

Her smile stretched to her eyes. "You grew a beard for me."

He exhaled a puff of air. "Such a little thing!"

"Is it, though?"

Ambushing Bjornolf had banished the townsfolk's suspicions that he had betrayed them to his pagan wife, but still they whispered about his heathen appearance. Yes, he had grown a beard for her, and that was no small thing, after all.

"That showed me perhaps we could be more than allies. The least I could do is to visit your church."

He reached out and threaded his fingers through hers. The smile she offered carried the warmth of the sun.

"That means a great deal to me."

"As did your staying with me as I honored Revna."

Swallowing, he gestured behind them. "What did you think of the service?"

She shrugged. "Long."

He laughed. "Did it speak to you?"

"No more than our *blót* did to you, my husband." She squeezed his hand again before releasing it. "While I want us to accept each other, I would never choose your path—or your beliefs—for you."

He had never met a Christian woman like her. Something wild lived in her people, molding them from raw passion. "I can respect that."

"You can?"

Leaning toward her, he pressed his lips against her forehead. "You are my wife and will be the mother of my child. That's all that matters."

CHAPTER FOURTEEN

TAURIN

A N ENDLESS STREAM of trading *knörrs* sailed up the Seine toward Rouen for the *Thing* in mid-September. While most passed without stopping in Lillebonne, a few, including a fleet of three from Norway, made the short journey up the Bolbec. A dozen traders disgorged and occupied the market stalls, announcing in Frankish that they wanted to buy all the food their longships could carry.

Taurin and Halla arrived an hour later in one of Taurin's carts. Nearly every other farmer in the region had already arrived. The usually passable streets were thick with carters and shouting pedestrians. Their passage blocked, they dismounted and decided to walk, despite Halla's condition.

Some of the residents took advantage of the traffic to peddle meat pies and wine from their front doors. Huebald, the carpenter, and the other craftsmen had erected rickety tables with their wares outside their workshops. So many customers prodded their offerings that the dust thrown up by the additional traffic didn't have a chance to settle on the items.

Through it all, Father Norbert droned on about the evils of greed from an overturned crate in the market, though no one paid him much attention.

Taurin saw Orderic negotiating with one of the traders and waved when he caught his eye. "Perhaps we should go back and gather some of the harvest to sell," he suggested to Halla.

She shook her head. "Sell it in Rouen. You'll get double what these traders are paying."

He gaped at her. "How can you be sure?"

She chuckled. "That's the way of things. Rouen needs food and will pay dearly for it." She patted his stomach. "In fact, you should buy from your tenants and bring that, as well. As *høvding*, I can claim as much space on the longships as I need."

Taurin could certainly use some extra coin for repairs around the estate, and it only seemed right to benefit from Halla's position. Yet the idea of risking his precious wealth on the hope of better prices elsewhere seemed dangerous, unpredictable.

"Perhaps next year," he muttered.

Halla shrugged. "Your choice, but you're missing an opportunity." She braced her hand against her belly and grimaced, but the discomfort passed quickly.

When they reached the docks, Halla departed to speak with the sailors, leaving Taurin to watch the frenzied trading.

Almost as soon as she departed, Orderic approached and clasped Taurin's arm in greeting. "So you mean to go again, do you?" He scowled as a cart dragged by a servant of one of the traders brushed against him.

"Come and represent our people with me."

Outrage battled with consideration within Orderic's growing frown. "Do you truly expect to find justice at this assembly of theirs?"

"Rollo warned Bjornolf personally not to raid these lands," Taurin reminded.

"A warning he disregarded." He turned and spat. "I wish we had killed him."

Taurin shook his head. "They value glorious death in battle. Killing him would only encourage others. But if Rollo condemns him, others will learn the price for attacking us."

Orderic gasped. "You mean to test the jarl?"

"Yes!"

"And if he exonerates this man?"

His thoughts dwelled on that possibility more as the *Thing* drew closer. "Then we'll know he won't honor his word."

Choking off a cry, Orderic gaped and took a step back. "I didn't think you had doubts!"

"Of course I do. But doubts can't prevent me from making decisions." He rubbed his hand over his beard. "How Rollo reacts to Bjornolf's crimes will prove whether we can rely on his protection."

"Now *this* is the man I remember." Orderic's smile stretched to his ears. "Your words delight me, my friend."

"So you'll come?"

Orderic shifted his gaze to study the closest *knörr* along the shore. "Yes, I'll come."

He pulled Orderic into a tight hug and barked a laugh of triumph. This was how he'd convince Orderic to put aside his animosity.

He released his friend. "If Rollo punishes this raider, will you finally support Halla?"

Orderic turned to face the church and inhaled a long, slow breath. "If he orders this raider's death, I will swear an oath to support him."

Taurin clasped his friend's hand and smiled, giving into the joy lightening his heart. Halla had soothed Father Norbert's animosity at the winter *blót*. Now, he would soothe Orderic's.

Provided that Rollo honored his oath and the *Thing* confirmed all of Halla's trust.

TAURIN

Taurin spent most of the trip to Rouen comforting his wife at the side of the *knörr*. The little passenger in her belly didn't favor sea voyages.

Between bouts of vomiting, Halla explained how the few short days of the *Thing* would resolve a year's worth of quarrels and extract punishments. Frigg's day, the very best day for a marriage, would keep the *gythias* busy on the final day.

Orderic's expression slowly shifted from awed silence as they approached the city to apprehension as the Norsemen hemmed them in on all sides at the port. "Is it always so busy?"

During his first visit to Rouen, Taurin could at least navigate the streets. But now, the smells of pack mules and oxen and shouting in many languages battered their every step. Twice, they had to shove the crowd aside to avoid being separated from the ox-cart carrying their goods.

Beside him, Halla laughed. "The *Thing* is a serious matter. All who can attend will discuss new laws."

"Laws?" Orderic asked. "They come to hear Rollo's edicts with their own ears?"

Halla scoffed. "My people aren't slaves to their leaders as yours are. All may speak for or against proposed laws. They pass only with the assent of the majority."

Orderic again pushed aside a pedestrian who ventured too close. "Does that include us?"

"Taurin may speak as he wishes."

He snorted. "But not me?"

She smiled without mirth. "Don't be ridiculous. You aren't one of us."

"And Taurin is?" The edge of annoyance in his voice shifted to something more dangerous that Taurin couldn't identify.

"As my husband, he may even join the raids if he chooses."

"He would never…" Orderic hissed, crossing himself.

Taurin repressed a shudder as he recalled his own revulsion at the suggestion. He had killed a fellow Christian once before and never wished to do so again.

Halla rolled her eyes. "I must report to Rollo." She turned to her husband. "Come to the feast hall once you've finished in the market."

Leaning over her growing belly, she took his cheeks in her hands and kissed him deeply enough to scandalize the people of Lillebonne, if they had been present. The warmth of her lips stirred a growing desire to run his fingers over her naked flesh. They had enjoyed no privacy on the voyage over.

But she stepped away and waded into the crowd, her belly leading the way. Most deferred to her once they noticed her condition, but she harangued the occasional pedestrian who didn't until he gave way.

Orderic shook his head. "She's unbelievable."

Taurin smiled. Yes, she was remarkable.

Before they reached the warehouse, a Norseman offered more for his goods and the cart holding them than Taurin could have ever hoped for in Lillebonne, so he accepted.

As the trader led the cart away, Taurin noticed an elderly, clean-shaven man studying them. "Can I help you?" he asked in Norse.

The man raised an eyebrow but remained silent.

"Why does he stare at us?" Orderic whispered.

"You speak Frankish?" The man brightened. Fumbling beneath his tunic, he withdrew a wooden cross on a string.

Orderic's eyes brightened. "God bless you, sir! This is Taurin, and I am Orderic, of Lillebonne."

The other man crossed himself. "Philbert of Fontenelle."

Taurin had seen the town in the distance the first time he had traveled to Rouen with Halla. The Norse had pillaged it more than once over the decades.

Philbert bowed his head. "Forgive me. Had I known you were Christians, I would have intervened."

Taurin frowned. "Intervened?"

The man's eyes darted between Taurin and Orderic. "Not three streets away, that man will sell your goods for double the price he paid."

Orderic shoved Taurin's shoulder. "Trust them, you say?"

"It seemed a fair price," he grumbled.

Philbert scowled. "It always does."

"You speak from experience?" Orderic asked.

"Not mine, as much as others'." Philbert huddled against their wagon and beckoned them close enough to feel his breath on their cheeks. "Do you know Fécamp?"

Taurin had to strain to make out the soft words. "I hear they had some trouble. What happened?"

The man licked his lips. "The Norse leader heard rumors of rebellion. His men swept through the countryside and ransacked ten farms." He lowered his eyes. "When the people sheltered in the church, he burned it. Forty-five dead, including many children."

"Blessed Jesus." Orderic crossed himself.

Taurin did the same. Rollo had said Gordrun had killed some rebels, not a church filled with families. How could he so casually reference a massacre?

"How has your town fared?" Taurin asked.

Philbert straightened his tunic. It was made of the finest linen, not rough wool. A thin, embroidered line of crosses ran along the edge. His breeches were fine leather, not the cheaper rough material.

"We haven't suffered as Fécamp, but pagans surround us. We can do nothing against their numbers."

"Indeed," Orderic muttered.

Philbert saluted someone in the distance and clasped Orderic's forearm. "Take my advice. Don't trust these Northmen. They don't think like us." With a wave, he waded into the crowd.

Orderic grunted after he had departed. "We aren't the only ones suffering."

"He doesn't suffer as badly as he claims. Did you see his fine clothes?"

"They burned people alive, Taurin. Do you want to see our church in flames?"

He imagined the scene, the screaming, the ash floating on the wind as the flames touched the sky, destroying the cross his grandfather had installed. How much resistance would Halla endure before deciding to do the same?

No. Halla might execute rebels, but Taurin would not—could not—imagine her slaughtering children.

"Perhaps the wrong man ruled Fécamp. All the more reason you should support my wife. She wants our peoples to live together."

"Under her rule," Orderic corrected.

"To protect us from the kind of raids that devastated Lillebonne, Fontenelle, and all the others."

"What happens if she dies?"

He gasped. "Orderic, don't you dare—"

"God forbid!" He placed a hand on Taurin's shoulder. "But you must consider the possibility."

Taurin frowned, recalling his own fears. He valued Halla for all the ways she differed from the rest of her people. Yet, she had wounded her forearm during the raid. Who would Rollo send to replace her if she died? What suffering would a *høvding* like Bjornolf inflict?

"That she alone stands between us and devastation should terrify you," Orderic said.

For the first time, it did.

TAURIN

As Rollo rose from his raven-headed chair, he stood head and shoulders above the hundreds of sweaty bodies filling the feast hall, including Jorund and the lawspeaker standing on the dais with him. The latter looked much like Norbert both in age and in the black robe that hung from his narrow frame.

"Jurgur will reimburse Snorrun at market rates for the crops his goats ate," Rollo declared.

The disputants standing in an open space before the jarl shook hands and melted back into the crowd as dozens of others had already done that afternoon. The observers began to chatter. A few stretched or reached for food.

Taurin leaned toward Halla. "I don't see any mead horns."

"I thought your people always drank," Orderic said.

Halla exchanged a glance with Vikarr, standing nearby, before answering in a voice without mirth, "One does not drink during battle or the *Thing*."

"Aren't they the same?" Taurin smirked.

The corner of her lip quivered. "Perhaps so."

Two thick-set warriors glared at each other as they approached the open space between Rollo and the assembly.

Rollo seated himself as Jorund stepped forward. "Next, we have a claim by *hirdman* Audfinnr against *hersir* Thorwold."

The crowd's murmurs quieted as one of the men in the center, thick-muscled with a single braid down the back of his head, stepped forward.

"After the sacking of Avranches, my warband raided a church where Christians sought safety. Though we took much plunder, my *hersir* denies me my share of the spoils."

Taurin ignored the crowd's scoffs. He imagined those poor, terrified townsfolk retreating to the one place they believed God would protect them. That plunder belonged to his people.

The other man in the open space scowled, twisting the thick scar running across his eye and down his cheek. "While Christians shot arrows from windows, he turned his back to the enemy." His thick red beard muffled his voice. "He cannot profit from his cowardice."

Jorund turned to the black-cloaked man beside him. "Lawspeaker?"

The lawspeaker stepped forward, thumping his raven-headed, oak staff with each step. He looked slight and frail. Taurin doubted he had ever carried a sword. Halla had led him to believe her people respected only strength of arms, but the crowd fell into revered silence before this strange man.

"The law is clear." His voice was surprisingly clear. "A coward must die."

"I did not run!" Audfinnr shouted.

"Did you turn your back to the enemy?" Jorund asked.

"Yes."

Shouts of outrage spread across the hall.

Audfinnr whirled on them. "But not to flee. I circled to the other side of the building while our men occupied them at the front."

"What he says is true." A third man stepped out of the crowd. Taurin gasped at the extravagance of a burnished length of gold that circled his arm four times. "I witnessed this."

"And I," another announced.

"How do you respond to these words?" Jorund asked the *hersir*.

Thorwold straightened his beard. "If these warriors vouch for him, I withdraw my charge of cowardice. But he still disobeyed my command to attack. I needed his strength, only to find him missing." He pointed to Audfinnr. "Do you deny this?"

"I do not." The other man folded his arms. "I sought a path to victory. What man may question that?"

"One of our warriors took an arrow in his shoulder," Thorwold countered. "You left your brothers unprotected."

A surprising number of heads now nodded. Even Audfinnr had fallen silent. How quickly the mood had shifted!

Taurin only wished his own people would fight with the vigor of the Christians in that church if the Norse ever attacked them again.

"Did this wounded man die?" the lawspeaker asked.

Thorwold shook his head. "He will recover."

"Will he raid again?"

Again, the *hersir* nodded.

The lawspeaker swapped the staff to his other hand as he shifted his weight. "The gods write our fates, but a man must still answer for his actions. Leaving a brother vulnerable and disobeying one's war leaders are offenses against the gods."

Jorund raised his hands. "What say you, free men of the *Thing*? Should Audfinnr be punished for his actions or receive a share of the plunder?"

The chorus of voices filled the hall. While a few near Taurin dissented, the vast majority shouted for punishment, including Halla and Vikarr beside him.

"Why don't more women voice their opinion?" he asked.

"Many do not have the right to speak." She raised her chin and gave a smug smirk. "I am a *hersir* and shieldmaiden."

Once again, Rollo rose. "The *Thing* has spoken. Audfinnr will be punished. Lawspeaker, what punishment does the law demand?"

"Disobeying one's war leader in battle requires ten lashes with a sapling no thicker than the thumb. Because his negligence harmed a fellow warrior, Audfinnr's share of the plunder must go to the wounded man."

"Then it is settled," Rollo announced.

"What happened?" Orderic asked. After Taurin explained the result in Frankish, Orderic grunted. "This isn't over. Audfinnr will retaliate against the other man."

"You are wrong." Halla pointed to the litigants.

Thorwold whispered something to Audfinnr before the men clasped arms.

"How can he be pleased?" Orderic asked. "He'll be beaten for showing intelligence."

"He left his brothers undefended," Halla said. "Yet he retains his position, so he is content."

"I would not be so forgiving," Orderic murmured.

"That's because you care only for your selfish desires, regardless of your circumstances." She met Taurin's gaze. "We're the final ones today." She jutted her chin toward the space behind Taurin.

When Taurin last stood in this room, Rollo had pledged to protect his town. Now, he would see the value of the jarl's promise.

Jorund was waving her over. Swallowing, he squeezed Halla's hand before she stepped into the clearing. They had agreed she would lay the charge, even though he had ambushed Bjornolf. The law might consider him equal to the Norse of Rouen, but those assembled might disagree.

He saw no sign of Bjornolf.

A few men in the front row murmured something about a woman addressing the *Thing*, but another man shook his head and clearly mouthed the word, "shieldmaiden," which calmed his companion.

Halla brushed her hair aside, exposing her gold torc. "Men of Rouen, I am Halla, daughter of Skidi, *høvding* of Lillebonne at the mouth of the Seine." She spoke with the strong voice she had used on the aldermen. "Today, I charge the warrior Bjornolf with raiding farmers loyal to Jarl Rollo."

Taurin's ears tingled at the dangerous ripple that spread through the hall as the crowd repeated her words for the listeners in the back. Too many words came too quickly for him to translate. Though they carried the unmistakable hint of outrage and disbelief, he couldn't discern whether it stemmed from Bjornolf's actions or her charges.

"Shortly after the army left for the Bessin on this year's raids, Bjornolf and those he departed Rouen with last year attacked four farmsteads within my territory. They slaughtered livestock, burned buildings, and killed a Frankish farmer."

Both he and Orderic had suggested she detail the misery caused by the raids, but Halla had insisted on quantifying only the damage. Emphasizing his brutality might impress the other Norsemen.

"He violated Rollo's edicts and flaunted our jarl's authority." She rested her hands on her belly. "I ask that he be punished according to our laws."

"How do you know it was him?" A lanky man with a long face pushed himself to the front of the crowd.

Taurin stepped forward to join his wife. "He sold his plunder to a Frankish trader. I and my companion Orderic tracked the trader to Bjornolf, but he escaped when we tried to seize him."

The lanky may sneered, "Why should we value the word of a Christian?"

"As my husband, he has the right to speak," Halla said.

A murmur spread through the crowd as they considered his

testimony. Even the Norseman who had challenged him nodded and returned to his place in the crowd. Only then did Taurin realize he had simply intended to gather information, not to defend Bjornolf.

Vikarr stepped forward and raised his chin. "I am Vikarr, *hirdman* of Lillebonne and warrior of Rouen. I heard Bjornolf boast of attacking farms in the Caux and saw him save his own life while his men died for him."

The murmuring, tinged with disgust, grew louder.

"You're certain it was Bjornolf?" Jorund asked.

"Yes. I fought with him at Bayeux and Saint-Lô and know him well."

Jorund craned his neck and pitched his voice over the crowd. "Bjornolf, present yourself!"

The murmuring softened as the crowd glanced around at their neighbors. Taurin held his breath, searching the crowd for the telltale movements of someone approaching.

Standing in the open space before Rollo, Halla rested her fists on her hips as if daring anyone to challenge her claim.

What would he do if Bjornolf called him a liar? He halted his hand part-way up to clench the cross at his neck. Halla had insisted that no one could challenge him to a duel once she made her accusation, but would Rollo follow that tradition if he could simply allow Bjornolf to kill Taurin and settle the matter for him?

Yet, after a few moments of relative silence, no one appeared. Taurin released his breath, letting his shoulders slump.

Rollo nodded to Jorund. The *stallari* asked, "Lawspeaker, what say you?"

The lawspeaker placed both hands on his staff and closed his eyes. Lips moving slowly, he nonetheless made no audible sound.

Aware of a sudden tension in the hall, Taurin opened his mouth to speak. Halla shot him a glare that silenced him.

Finally, the lawspeaker opened his eyes. "As jarl, Rollo had the right to extend his authority over the lands and people north of the Seine. No Norseman challenged his right to his title or position. As a result, that declaration passed into law. Violating this protection became a crime against the jarl." He cleared his throat before continuing. "However, the law does not specify a punishment for violating this protection."

"What?" Rollo straightened.

Conversation spread through the hall. Orderic leaned toward them and asked in Frankish, "What is happening?"

Halla answered, "They'll have to decide Bjornolf's guilt without knowing the punishment." She studied the crowd. "Many are uncomfortable with this."

Orderic frowned. "Why?"

"If they find him guilty, Rollo could apply any punishment, even one as severe as condemning the families of everyone involved. No one wants to grant the jarl that authority." She growled deep within her throat. "Rollo or Jorund should have foreseen this."

"Unless they intended for this to happen," Orderic retorted.

"Seal your lips or I'll sew them shut!" Halla hissed with enough venom to make Orderic recoil.

Taurin repressed a smile. It served him right for his constant animosity.

But his mirth lasted only a moment. Halla's words suggested some of those present might exonerate Bjornolf even though they believed him guilty.

"Silence!" Jorund shouted. Slowly, the murmurs subsided. "We must decide the matter. Is Bjornolf guilty of violating Jarl Rollo's oath of protection to the Franks?"

Taurin closed his eyes and prayed that God watched him in this heathen place. Surely some residue remained of the prayers offered in this city before the Norsemen profaned it. Some stone or shard of a holy cross must have endured.

Deafening shouts of agreement and dissent vied with each other for dominance in a hall that was suddenly too small to contain them. Taurin cupped his ears to protect them from the noise. He couldn't anticipate which way the *Thing* would decide.

Neither, it seemed, could Jorund. Waving them off, he instead called for a division. The shuffling of hundreds of feet scraping and sliding across wood replaced the shouts. While the women shifted to the rear, the men and shieldmaidens split into two roughly even groups. Orderic remained close, but Taurin couldn't bring himself to remind his friend that his opinion didn't matter.

Men poked their heads out to conduct their own estimates as Jorund made his way down one group and back up the other. For a few hundred heartbeats, no one moved.

The *stallari* returned to stand beside Rollo. "By a margin of twenty-eight, the *Thing* agrees to punish Bjornolf."

Victory!

"We won," Taurin breathed in Frankish.

Though he yearned to celebrate, he restrained himself. Their victory would seal Bjornolf's fate, and he could not laud the death of anyone, even a Norse raider.

But Orderic dropped to his knees and folded his hands before him. The nearest Norse pointed and laughed. One bearded man even raised his hands in mock prayer before chortling.

For months at a time, Taurin had endured the cold glares of betrayal from his neighbors. Until this moment, a pang of doubt had nagged at the corner of his mind. Now, it transformed into delight. This strange Norse justice had worked. All the raiders throughout the Norse world would see the punishment due to those who terrorized the Pays de Caux.

The jarl paused to cast his eyes over the assembly that had suddenly fallen remarkably silent. Finally, his gaze settled on Jorund and remained there for some time. Rollo's eyebrows knitted together so deeply that they shaded the tops of his eyelids.

He abruptly turned back to the assembly. "Bjornolf must repay his victims double the cost of the damage he inflicted. He will also pay the family of the murdered Frank a sword-weight of gold and is banned from raiding for five years."

Taurin gasped and raised a hand to his mouth. Rollo's idea of protection, of justice, was a pathetically small restitution?

"What was the punishment?" Orderic rose. "Taurin?"

This punishment would only encourage more raids. More of his people would die. Bjornolf himself would raid again. Indeed, he would have to, now that Rollo had forbidden him from joining the army. It would all happen as he had feared that day when three Norsemen had walked into his town.

Orderic had been right after all. These Norse didn't care about stupid, foolish Christians who always fell for the same deceptions. Their promises counted for nothing.

"Let's feast!" Rollo strode toward the assembly with arms outstretched.

Taurin glared at the big Norseman. He had pledged to defend the jarl's authority. He had married one of them. Despite it all, Rollo had lied.

Eyes narrowing, he glared at his wife so she might see his fury. She had promised. Rollo had promised!

But she had already stormed off toward the jarl. "Stay here!" he commanded to Orderic as he set after her.

"Taurin, what was the punish—"

"Stay here!" he repeated, rushing to catch Halla.

He was a step behind when she grasped the much larger jarl's arm and tugged hard enough to force him to turn.

"I told the Franks they'd find Norse justice here." She pressed a hand to her belly.

Grunting, he twisted out of her grip and clasped her arm in return. Blood burning, Taurin leapt to free her but halted when he realized the jarl merely led her further from the crowd.

No one else paid them much attention. Thralls carrying trays of food and goblets of mead had arrived to begin the feast. The hall filled with laughter and song as the Norsemen abandoned the business of the day and surrendered to revelry.

Rollo released her near the wall and squared to them. "You saw the close division. I can't turn all those people against me."

Taurin's eyes widened. "You gave your word. Does your promise only matter when it's convenient?" He flung the words as if they were daggers.

"Watch it, boy," Rollo glowered.

Despite his anger, Taurin fell silent. He was still surrounded by hundreds of Norsemen.

Halla placed a hand on his shoulder and pushed down enough to convince him to subside. "You're not stupid, Rollo." Halla's voice sounded soothing despite the content of her words. "This punishment will encourage attacks, not deter them."

At least Halla understood the danger.

"If I'm no longer jarl, my promise is worthless." Rollo's hushed voice nonetheless carried urgency. "I won't sacrifice my city for one dead Frank. Bjornolf has my disfavor and the *Thing* reproached him. Be content with that." With surprising deftness, he circled them and disappeared into the crowd.

It didn't matter whether Rollo had betrayed them by design or out of necessity. Taurin had collaborated with a pagan and had gained nothing in return.

He was ready to shout after the jarl when he noticed the confusion upon Halla's knitted eyebrows. She cradled her belly with her hands, rubbing it absently with a haunted expression.

The objection died on his lips. His eyes rested on that bulge. Their child would be half Norse and half Frank. Rollo's judgment threatened the only fragile home where it could grow in peace.

He had gained something precious, after all. Without his pledge to Rollo, he would have never basked in her comforting touch, never known her love.

Even if he couldn't trust Rollo's word, he could always trust her. She would never betray him.

CHAPTER FIFTEEN

Halla

ORDERIC STORMED OUT after learning of Bjornolf's punishment.
With a raised hand, Halla cut off Taurin's objection before he could voice it. "Whatever comes from this, we will deal with it. But I need time to think." She gestured toward the doors. "Make sure he doesn't do anything stupid."

As he departed, her thoughts lingered not on the punishment, but on the problem of finding a private place to relieve her bladder. The baby had started kicking during her accusation, and she had very nearly pissed herself when she'd tugged on Rollo's arm.

She passed three streets before finally finding a sufficiently private place to crouch down and exhale in blessed relief.

Her growling stomach and an overwhelming urge for cherries compelled her to waddle back to the feast. If the gods ever saw fit to inflict another pregnancy on her, she hoped they would time it better and spare her having to travel to the *Thing* heavy with child.

The scent of roasting meat made her salivate the moment she entered the feast hall, but she found the cherries first. She stuffed them in her mouth in quick succession, separating the pits with her teeth and spitting them on the floor. Eventually, someone would clean it up.

The craving passed as quickly as it came, and she turned to the nearest meat. A roasted boar, she suspected. Drawing her knife, she sliced off a chunk and plopped it into her mouth, juice running down her fingers. She moaned in delight as her tongue cheered the moist offering.

A well-tanned warrior with immaculately combed hair turned at the sound and gasped.

She glared at him, even as the juice dribbled down her chin. "You wish to say something?"

His outrage faded when his eyes dropped to her belly. Reaching for the table, he presented her with a honey-glazed sweet roll. "My wife was fond of these while bearing my son."

Smirking, she tasted a corner of the offering. The flavor tickled the back of her throat. Delighted, she devoured the rest in a great bite. Before she could thank him for his recommendation, the warrior had disappeared back into the crowd.

A high-pitched voice cried, "Halla!"

She wiped her mouth with a finger and licked it clean before turning.

Poppa approached with outstretched arms. At the last moment, she noticed Halla's belly and leaned forward to wrap her in a loose hug. Unbalanced, Halla clutched her to avoid tipping over.

Thank the gods she didn't need to fight in this condition.

"Look at you!" Smiling, Poppa shook her head. "I'm guessing your wound healed nicely."

Halla sighed. "It still itches." She gestured helplessly to her belly. "But who can tell what's causing that these days?" Two days earlier, she had lost the ability to see her toes.

Poppa brightened and placed her hand on Halla's stomach. Normally, she hated the presumption of other women wanting to touch her belly. But Poppa had tended her stomach after the Vire and deserved to see its state now.

The other woman's mouth turned down. Her eyes carried a hint of something other than joy. Jealousy. They had married on the same day, and yet only Halla, who hadn't contemplated the possibility of children until the *læknir* had told her, had fallen pregnant.

"It will happen for you." She squeezed Poppa's shoulder affectionately. "The gods will not ignore your prayers."

She attempted a smile. "Yes, God's will."

A shout drew Halla's attention toward Thorwold and Audfinnr, laughing nearby in reckless delight as they danced. At the second pass, Thorwold stumbled and knocked a woman in a dark brown apron-skirt into Poppa. Instead of shielding herself, the countess threw her arms across Halla, absorbing the impact for her.

Though unnecessary, the tender gesture made Halla want to wrap her arms around her. Revna would have done such a thing. Taurin, too, certainly. But no other. She hadn't realized how much she'd missed friendship this past year. Poppa might be the closest friend she had left.

But the lady didn't notice.

"Damn you, Thorwold!" She jabbed a finger. "Don't waste my husband's mead if you can't handle it, or I'll name you Thorwold de Buitiléir!"

Those nearby halted and cocked their heads.

Rolling her eyes, Poppa made a drinking gesture and stuck her tongue out limply. "It means 'of the bottle' in Frankish!"

The two men turned to each other and erupted with laughter.

"De Buitiléir," Audfinnr cried. "Sounds fearsome!"

"Begone, drunkards!" Poppa laughed, shooing them away.

Halla laughed, though for a different reason. "You've really made a home for yourself."

Poppa glanced up at Rollo, who was leaning against one of the ravens on his throne with Jorund and Sigrun. "I'd like to think so."

Halla squeezed her hand. "It suits you."

She giggled. "I suppose it does. What would I have done if your people hadn't sacked Bayeux?"

"Our lives turn on such accidents." Halla swallowed. Taurin had understood when she had shared her fears. Perhaps she could confide in Poppa as well. "The Vire put me on a different path."

The muscles of Poppa's face relaxed. Her eyes softened. "So that's what did it."

Halla drew a sharp breath. "What do you mean?"

Poppa placed a reassuring hand on her forearm. "Rollo wondered why you chose to marry. He assumed you found Taurin attractive." She laughed. "Men see only passion in others."

Halla swallowed. "And what did you think?"

Poppa shrugged. "I knew you had a reason." She took a quick breath. "What did you hope to find with Taurin?"

The gods had pressed the memory of that moment into her mind like a boot in the mud after a spring shower. "A purpose."

Poppa chuckled with a gentle ease. "Don't we all want that?"

Halla eyed her. The poor woman didn't know how wrong she was. Most of the warriors around them plundered and gave little thought to the possibility of dying. Few planned beyond the raiding season. And they were content. The past was decided, the future impossible to know.

"Did you find one?" Poppa asked.

Taurin and Orderic entered the hall, the latter still glowering. Her husband looked tired. But as he met her eyes, his smile illuminated his face. He broke his gaze only when Orderic nearly collided with a Dane backing toward him.

"Yes." She offered a bemused laugh. "I think I have."

Poppa squeezed her hand. "Then have a cup of wine with me."

She winced. "Wine?"

A laugh. "Fine, fine. Mead, then."

Halla threaded her arm through Poppa's and they began to work their way through the crowds toward the barrels. She appreciated the escort, as the revelers already began to stumble from intoxication.

After only a few steps, they reached a gap in the crowd and could go no farther. "Oh, my…" Poppa gasped.

Within the clearing, Snorrun, who had lost his field to goats, galloped in a circle holding aloft a pair of goblets that sloshed mead on those encircling him. No one seemed to mind, for they were too busy pointing and laughing.

He wore no pants, and his manhood flopped up and down with every leap.

Poppa's suggestion had made Halla thirsty, and this naked man stood between her and its relief. She scowled. "Snorrun No-Breeches, what a tiny spear for such a big man!"

The crowd roared and took up her chant. "No-Breeches, No-Breeches!"

Snorrun gawked in surprise before breaking into fresh laughter and flopping himself back and forth.

Halla spared a glance for her husband. Neither he nor Orderic was laughing.

A woman yelled, "Skol!" and they all drank. Rivulets dripped down beards and soaked into tunics.

Someone nudged the long-bearded skald from the raid, who was watching the scene with a smile. "Sing us a poem of No-Breeches and his tiny spear!"

But the skald refused, pointing between Snorrun's legs. "I'd hardly call that worthy of song."

They laughed again, but the idea had taken root. Try though he might to deflect them, the crowd would not relent. Finally, he threw up his hands and stood.

Word of a recitation snuffed conversation and quieted the room. The skald took another drink of his mead and cleared his throat before beginning.

All-Father speak and share your sight
Of Midgard shadow-fixed.
For darkness folds your folk in night
Bereft of wisdom's kiss.
Welcome with wisdom's kiss.

You bid us sail across the sea
For glory and for gain.
To wrest this land from foolish folk
Destined to die in pain.
Desperate to die in pain.

Guide our hand, gild our hearts,
Hammer house and home.
For fortune lies in fertile fields
Reclaimed for you to roam.
Here the gods shall roam.

The words stirred her blood. She had thought the same! Surely, the gods watched from Valhalla with gladness. They would spread across this land and populate it with warriors to aid at Ragnarok. From each patch of claimed dirt, they would challenge the forces of Loki and the jotuns.

Harrowing Hrolf, hero of Rouen,
Cleaving 'cross the land,
Breaker of bastions, bane of kings,
Wind no Frank withstands,
No withered Frank withstands,

Extend across abandoned acres
Nourish fallow fields

Spread life where lords let dormant lie
And reap the harvest yield
Of gold and grain the yield.

As Shetland shores and Orkney obey
And Danelaw does defend
Bind the bent-knees and your brothers
As alloys interblend.
Rising power interblend.

Poppa's chest rose and fell faster. Her eyes glistened with pride as she gazed at her husband from across the room.

Halla searched until she found her own husband, watching the skald along with the rest of the crowd. Did he hear the wonder and mystery in his voice? Did the meter and rhyme affect him as it did her?

Perhaps it did. His heart beat for his god with the same cadence as the skalds' did. Perhaps, some experiences transcended dogma. If anyone could bridge the differences between their cultures, she and Taurin could.

She would have to listen more closely to Father Norbert's teachings. Perhaps the carpenter god could impart wisdom, as well.

The skald continued the recitation, his voice echoing through the silent hall, broken only by the occasional crackling of the fires. Each whisper drew tension on the air, each accent struck like a sword blow. He carried them through the battles to the south, including both the triumph and the losses, and named warriors of renown.

And then, he sang two verses that left Halla speechless.

And Halla Swift-Axe, shieldmaiden,
Whom Freya favored best,
Seducing Sigrun the stolid and strong
And watches well the west.
She governs well the west.

Defeated dozens, left them limp
On battlefield and in bed.
On enemies at Saint-Lô, Avranches
Bloody appetites she fed.
Lusty appetites she fed.

He was singing about her! The skald had enshrined her in song. Generations would listen in hushed silence to voices weaving magic with her deeds. Would they inspire warriors in the small hours before a red dawn?

She had worked her entire life for this moment, to do something worthy of remembrance. And all who listened—warriors and *hersirs* and *høvdings*—had heard these verses.

Halla joined a few warriors in turning to Sigrun on the other side of the gathering. Lip curled in a grin, he raised a goblet to Halla, setting off a round of excited chatter.

She raised her chin, accepting the gazes of amazement and respect. She was *hvatur, høvding,* and *hersir* all. No longer must she fear some warrior supplanting her in Lillebonne. None could threaten a legendary warrior of song!

Immortality. Her name would live on the lips of her people down to the last generation and the fire at the end of the world. Mothers named their children for heroes of old; would they now name their daughters after her?

Heart bursting with joy, she searched for the one man with whom she wanted to share her triumph. She wanted to bury herself in her husband's arms and make love to him until the morning.

Elation faded into a hollow cavern of longing for a desire unfulfilled. He had disappeared.

HALLA

Halla passed every dish a pregnant woman might desire, but her appetite fled soon after the recitation. She spent the remainder of the feast nursing a single plate of cheese. Around midnight, she returned home, stumbling not from too much mead, but from fresh blisters from the long day.

When she entered, Taurin was waiting by the hearth, the flames of the fresh fire painting half his face in an orange glow and the other in shadow. The draped light couldn't hide his angry glare.

Halla sighed, entirely too tired to argue about Bjornolf's punishment.

"I'm surprised to see you home so soon." The ice in his voice seemed stranger for his proximity to the fire. "I thought you'd end up in someone else's bed."

Her sore feet melted away, replaced by a surge of anger. "Excuse me?"

"Aren't you famous for leaving men limp and expended?"

His voice seared her with the stinging pain of a cauterizing knife, his tenderness replaced with eyes ignited by fury. Where was the man who had pledged his love and devotion? She saw only a sanctimonious Christian.

"When we met, I told you we didn't shut our women up like slaves. Did you think me a maiden, blushing and ignorant of the world?"

"I suspected you had…experiences."

She squared to him, suddenly very eager for an argument. "Then why do you risk such a dangerous tone?"

During the silence that followed, he opened and closed his mouth twice. She could not guess his thoughts, but nor did she care to relieve his distress by interrupting his impotence.

"You rutted with men during the siege of Avranches this spring." His words jabbed the air.

"My sleeping with Jarl Sigrun does not diminish your honor in any way."

"You admit it!" He strode across the room. "Do you feel no shame?"

She frowned. "I did what I had to. And he was a jarl."

"That doesn't matter!"

"Of course it does." She crossed her arms. "He's a Norse warrior and a leader of men. By seducing him, I increased my renown and proved myself worthy in the eyes of my people."

"You betrayed me for fame?" His fists opened and closed at his sides.

"I acted to maintain my position as *høvding* of Lillebonne. Every warrior who passed through your town imagined himself ruling it."

"You don't know that."

"Yes, I do. It's our way." She grunted. "I had to solidify my position."

"And that required shaming me before your people?" Droplets of spittle flew from his mouth, catching the light as they fell to the ground.

"It's the man I seduced who they care about, not my husband."

He stumbled back until he collided with the hearth. Reaching out for support, his fingers clawed the wood until they turned white. "Marriage is sacred. Neither person may lie with another."

Surely, he wasn't that naïve! She rolled her eyes. "Marriage is an arrangement. You were disgusted with me after the *blót*. At the time, did you feel any affection for me to offend?"

"That doesn't matter!"

"Of course it does. I'm not going to deny myself the pleasure of sex because you refused to give up your tantrum. If I could protect my position at the same time, why wouldn't I?"

He stomped to the other side of the hearth, his footsteps echoing in the small room. "Surely your people have laws against adultery."

"Yes, but they don't apply."

He halted and gasped. "Excuse me?"

"I am *hvatur*, not *blaudur*. I may do as I will. I must obey only my jarl."

"Oh, so now I'm *blaudur*? Weak?" He hissed the word.

He had forced Bjornolf to flight and thwarted raids from among his own people. Actions taken amid danger overrode all else. "No. But your family has no standing in Rouen. Your status derives through me." Surely he understood this. It was the reason he had a voice during the assembly.

He shifted and the fire's light illuminated his entire face. From his look of outrage and betrayal, he evidently hadn't considered that.

"We did not feel for each other as we do now." She spread her hands before her. "At the time, I saw no impediment."

"Every man would object to his wife lying with another!"

She had never seen him so angry before. His passion and vigor set her blood pumping. Were he not furious at her, she would have torn his clothing off and mount him despite her sore feet.

He wrung his hands, pacing back and forth. "How could you do such a thing to me?"

She had done it to Jarl Sigrun, not him, but she suspected he wouldn't react well to her pointing out that distinction.

"Is your child mine?"

She sucked in a breath. "What?"

"You heard me."

"Would it matter if it wasn't?"

"Of course it would! I'll not raise another man's bastard."

She cupped her belly. "I was already pregnant when I left for the raid. I did not bleed for two months."

"So you claim."

A flush of fury filled her cheeks. Where was the gentle Taurin who had professed his love? The Taurin who had made her want to share her deepest fears?

"The child is yours. If you don't believe the *læknir* who confirmed it, count backward when the baby comes." She backed up, opening distance between them, and released a scream that vibrated in her ears. "By the gods, I don't understand you!"

Clenching his fists, he charged for the door. Halla expected him to slam his fist into it, but instead he yanked it open. For a moment, he simply stood in the doorway, his back illuminated by the hearth.

When he finally spoke, his voice was a whisper. "Yes, I see that now."

"Taurin, where are you going?"

But he didn't respond. He had already disappeared into the night.

TAURIN

Taurin stared into the water as it lapped against the pier. The cresting early morning sun struck the waves of the Seine, interrupting the deep blue with fragments of orange. He supposed it was beautiful, but the dancing light couldn't warm his heart.

"What do I do now?"

Even when Rollo had proven his promises were only as good as the patience of his people, at least Halla had shared his frustration. But now...

Orderic placed a hand on his shoulder. His touch offered comfort without relief. "I'm sorry, my friend. You've sacrificed so much. You don't deserve this."

"I thought..." He shook his head, unable to speak the words. He thought something special had blossomed when they touched, despite all the blood and tears between their peoples.

"You wished for happiness with your wife. Who can fault such a desire?" Orderic's words carried no scorn, only soothing comfort. "But she is a pagan. Their settlers want our land. This assembly proves they care nothing for our safety. And..." He hesitated for only a moment. "Her actions prove she doesn't share our values. How can we ever live in harmony with them?"

Part of him, the part that remembered his longing for the strange

Norse woman who lusted after life, rebelled against those words. But that same lust had revealed the great divide between them.

He swallowed and turned back to the water. This used to be a Christian shore before the Norsemen came. Now, they were spreading west. A year prior, he had feared only their axes and swords. Now, he wondered if perhaps their traditions would cause the greater damage.

Halla had made him believe her people valued fairness and justice. She had made him believe many things. Many lies.

His shoulders slumped with his exhale, and he could not raise them again. "There's nothing we can do."

Orderic withdrew his arm and clasped his hands behind his back. "What if there was?"

Taurin stared at his friend. It took a moment for him to understand his meaning. His were dangerous words, uttered in an unfriendly city surrounded by Norsemen.

What would it matter? He already stood to lose everything his ancestors had built. "What do you mean?"

"Rollo has many enemies. Enemies with armies." He licked his lips. "I have spoken with one such."

He leaned closer. "Who?" His voice was barely a whisper.

"Berengar of Rennes."

Taurin fell back a step, separating himself from the treasonous idea. That man had nearly killed Halla on the Vire. He studied the darkened nooks around them, dread swelling that a set of unfriendly ears would discover and report them.

But no, they were alone, as alone as Lillebonne was among strange heathens with bizarre customs.

He rubbed his fingers through his beard for a few moments before stopping himself. When had he developed that habit?

"He would help?"

"He greatly wishes to eject the Norsemen from Frankia."

"We can't risk the fate of Fécamp," Taurin murmured.

Orderic shook his head. "They had no one to aid them. They were doomed to fail."

Halla had confided that she'd sought a purpose in coming to Lillebonne. What Orderic was proposing would destroy that. Could he truly consider this choice?

He clenched his jaw. She hadn't considered that sleeping with Sigrun would shame him or destroy his honor. Ignorance made her betrayal all the more dangerous. How many more injuries would she or her kind inflict without realizing it?

He inhaled the morning air. "I suppose I could at least speak to this Berengar."

HALLA

Eleven additional settler families joined them on their voyage home, occupying Halla with questions about the soil, the weather, and their new neighbors. That satisfied her well enough. Taurin needed time to forget his anger, and she had resolved to wait him out.

As the voyage progressed, her attitude changed. The nausea returned, so she spent much of the voyage leaning over the side of the longship. Though his rubbing her back on the journey in had done nothing to prevent her vomiting, she still missed his comfort. Its absence made her realize how soothing his presence had been.

He had shaved his beard. She understood the significance of that gesture well enough.

She sighed. He needed to move past this tantrum.

At least, with the bolts of cloth and new patterns from Avranches safely stored beneath the planks of the longship, she could please one Frank with her return. Then again, she could have misread Adella as badly as she had misread her husband. At least she had the gold that composed the remainder of her share. Gold would never disappoint.

As their vessel sailed up the Bolbec and approached Lillebonne, shouts offered the first indication of trouble on shore. Dagobert and the other aldermen must have already been meeting; they awaited the ship by the docks.

When the party disembarked, the aldermen offered no kisses of friendship to either Taurin or Orderic. Nor did they approach her.

Tight-lipped, Dagobert asked, "How did it go?"

Taurin grunted. "Rollo levied a fine, but refused to execute Bjornolf."

The aldermen exchanged anxious glances but accepted the news in silence. Taurin stiffened, and even Halla noted the mildness of their response.

"What is it?" her husband asked.

"A trader staggered in last night after being attacked on the road."

"Bjornolf?" Taurin pressed.

Dagobert glanced at Halla briefly before answering. "We can't be certain. The trader hid when he heard their singing. They stole his wagon and goods."

"Thank God for that luck." Taurin crossed himself.

"You may want to save your gratitude," Dagobert murmured.

"Something else?" Orderic asked.

"They attacked a monastery to the north."

Halla frowned. "I didn't realize you had any monasteries to the north."

"Four days' ride."

Before she had arrived, none of them had dared to venture four days from town.

Dagobert swallowed. "They burned everything. And they…" His mouth twisted into a grimace.

"What?" Taurin prompted.

Dagobert steadied himself with a breath. "The raiders…they removed the hands of the monks who didn't flee, and then they burned them alive."

Taurin hissed and glared at Halla. "It's getting worse, exactly as I predicted."

"Bjornolf doesn't know of Rollo's judgment yet," she maintained.

Orderic barked a laugh. "You think a man who commits such crimes cares about a rebuke?"

"Enough." Taurin raised a hand to silence him. "We'll spread word of his punishment and see if he presents himself." He turned to glare at her. "While we wait for you to accept that I'm right, we'll assemble our men to kill him and his raiders."

The aldermen nodded and grumbled their approval.

"He will present himself," Halla insisted.

Taurin grunted and turned to face the aldermen, joining their mumbled conversation.

After the debacle of the *Thing*, the Franks wouldn't tolerate continued raids. They'd expect her to kill those responsible. But Rollo hadn't declared Bjornolf an outlaw, so she couldn't simply kill him.

Between her *hird* and the three dozen families in the area, she might resist their demands. But that would mean turning her swords on the Christians, perhaps even on Taurin himself.

Bjornolf had to stop once he heard about his punishment.

He had to.

CHAPTER SIXTEEN

TAURIN

THE REMNANTS OF the farmhouse sat within the overgrown clearing of an ancient forest far to the west of town. A few jagged planks of wood from outbuildings poked up from the foliage that ran wild with no one to tend it. Like so many other ruins, it bore dark gray charring from the fire that had destroyed it many years earlier.

Young trees no more than a decade old reached out from the edge of the forest. One had even found fertile ground two dozen strides from the forest's edge, isolated among the grasses and occasional patches of rye, now grown wild, that lingered from better days.

As Seraphim picked her way through the grasses, Taurin considered that single tree. How had it strayed so far from the others? Did it realize it stood alone?

Taurin sighed. Of course it didn't. His own doubts twisted his thoughts. Trees knew nothing of life's dangers.

The air smelled salty from Oceanus Britannicus half an hour's ride to the west. If he sampled a handful of earth, he'd taste it there, too. The soil here had always been poor. After the fire, the family that lived here had chosen to move to an abandoned farm far to the east rather than rebuild.

That made this particular farmhouse the perfect location for a secret meeting. It was out of the way. After all, being caught here could lead to his execution.

He darted his eyes to the horizon again. Still empty.

He led Seraphim along the natural break where the rye met the grasses to conceal his passage. His path caused him to circle the farmhouse. On the far side, a single horse tied to a rickety fence post munched on grass between the ruin and the forest. Only those approaching from the ocean would notice it.

As he dismounted, the scabbard at his hip rubbed against Seraphim, provoking a neigh. Rubbing her hindquarter where it had struck, he soothed, "I'm sorry, girl," before tying her up beside the other horse. He regretted bringing her. Everyone knew Seraphim.

He heard no voices. Where were the others?

Hand on his hilt, he stepped through the opening that had once been a door. The ancient house matched the style of his manor, but it was much smaller. Crumbling stone walls separated the space into a main room and two minor chambers off to one side. Grass poked through the broken stone slabs of the original floor.

He crouched at a shuffling from one of the secondary rooms.

Orderic stepped into view. "Well met, Taurin."

Exhaling a breath, he straightened. "You terrified me."

"I'm glad. That means you understand the importance of this meeting."

"And that you intend no treachery," a new voice announced.

A clean-shaven man with long, back-swept black hair and coal-gray eyes stepped into view through the opening behind Taurin. He wore a fur-trimmed cloak over a deep blue pale linen tunic edged with black thread. The weave in the cloth of both contained no noticeable imperfections. Even his belt and boots—well-tanned and supple leather—proclaimed his wealth.

Berengar.

A pair of mailed men in conical helmets emerged behind him and took up positions on either side. Their eyes surveyed the perimeter.

Orderic gestured to the newcomer. "Taurin, allow me to introduce Berengar II of Neustria, Count of Bayeux and Rennes and Margrave of the Breton March."

As Berengar's gaze raked over him, Taurin anticipated every imperfection the count might notice. Mud still clung to his boots from when he had stopped to relieve himself on the ride over. The edge of his tunic had begun to fray, albeit not badly enough to require re-hemming. His fine Andalusi sword seemed out of place compared to his functional clothing.

"I'm told you invited the Northmen into your lands," Berengar said.

Taurin swallowed his rising anxiety. Why did he begin with an accusation? "They found us. We could not resist their army."

"I don't disagree. That decision probably saved your town. Others were not so fortunate." The count scowled and glanced away, but his attention returned quickly. "You married one of the heathens, yes?"

Taurin swallowed. "Yes."

"A proper Christian marriage or a pagan ritual?"

The nuance of the question surprised him. "A pagan ritual."

"At least you aren't truly married."

"I am." Up shot the count's eyebrows, but if Taurin hadn't lied to Rollo in Rouen, surrounded by his warriors, he wouldn't lie to this man in an abandoned farmhouse. "In my heart, I accepted my obligations. I'm bound to her, and she to me."

The guards shifted their weight and looked to their count.

Berengar's forehead wrinkled in obvious contemplation. "Your friend claimed you oppose the plague these pagans present."

Taurin wondered if Berengar realized he sounded like the Norse skald. "I'll do what I must to guard my lands from devastation. Once, that meant accepting Rouen's protection against raids by other Norsemen."

"And now?" the count prompted.

"If Rollo cannot stop the raids, we must look elsewhere."

The tension melted from Berengar's face. "You could have said what I wished to hear, yet you voiced your true feelings. Why?"

Taurin swallowed. "In all things, I am a man of God. Deceit is a sin, and I would not damn myself for either a Norse jarl or a Frankish count."

Berengar's smile twitched his ears and creased his eyes. "Good. I can treat with an honest man of faith, even if he married a heathen."

"God be praised," Orderic breathed.

Taurin chose to ignore the insult. "Orderic says you can help us. How?"

"We blockade the Seine, isolating Rouen from the ocean and its foreign supplies. The Norse will begin to starve and will have to either abandon the city or attack our blockade."

"His forces would overpower you."

Berengar clasped his hands behind his back. "Not if we act before the warriors arrive for the spring raids."

It was a bold strategy. If Berengar succeeded, Rouen would have no more than a few hundred starving warriors to defend itself. Taurin thought of Jarl Sigrun and his longships, wending down the Seine to return home the previous winter. He had been able to do nothing as the man who had cuckolded him sailed away with Frankish plunder. When they next returned, Berengar could be waiting to annihilate them.

"Why haven't you done this already?"

Berengar shook his head. "We need to control both sides of the river. Orderic tells me your town has fresh docks and carpenters experienced in repairing ships. We need your facilities to maintain the blockade."

Orderic's eyes carried an intensity Taurin remembered from every competition, horse race, and wrestling match over the years. He believed in this plan. But had he considered the price?

"What do you desire from us?" Taurin asked.

"I need to know the location of every heathen farm so we can sweep them all out at once. Also, support from within when securing your town."

"What if they try to recapture us?" Orderic asked.

"I must hold Lillebonne for the blockade to succeed. I'll send every soldier I can spare to protect you, but I expect your people to fight as well."

Taurin cared less about the logistics of invasion than the fate of his people. "And afterward?"

Berengar straightened. "I will make Lillebonne the jewel of my northern empire. Your town is well-situated. Imagine trading as far south as Italy and Spain and east to Germania. If you open the door to the Caux, you'll pay no taxes for the next fifty years."

Orderic whooped in delight.

Berengar pointed to Taurin. "I'll even name the landowners who provide men to my cause as barons. Nobility, my friend. All for restoring the righteous rule of our holy faith over these abandoned lands."

Such a generous offer! But it could go wrong a dozen ways. The Norsemen could come in greater numbers or disgorge on the northern coast and cross overland. Rollo could counterattack before Berengar reinforced Lillebonne and slaughter the townsfolk for supporting his enemies.

Slaughter. He had lived beside the settlers for more than a year.

"What will happen to the Norse farmers?"

Berengar's eyes hardened, reminding Taurin of the jagged stones of the ruin surrounding them. "Those within Lillebonne must die. I can't devote any men to guarding them. Those at their farms will probably escape back to Rouen, which suits me. The more mouths Rollo must feed, the faster he will fall."

They would probably enjoy the chance for a glorious death in battle.

And then he imagined his wife lying in a pool of blood and had to swallow a sudden rush of bile. "What of my wife? She is the leader of the Norse. She'll give birth any day now."

"She is?" Berengar flung a glare toward Orderic and hesitated before clearing his throat. "As your wife, she belongs to your household." His mouth twitched. "I can make arrangements for her."

The inflection of his words caused the hair on Taurin's neck to stiffen. While he would surely make arrangements, Taurin doubted they involved preserving the life of his wife or child.

Child. He recalled his very first meeting with this man's daughter. "My lord, Poppa is safe and well in Rouen. We can arrange to free her, if you wish."

The count pinned Taurin with an icy glare as his neck muscles tightened. "My daughter died at Bayeux." The corner of his mouth quivered in a barely restrained scowl. "The creature you know is a traitor who whored herself to a heathen."

Heart thumping, Taurin resisted the urge to flee this ruin and ride back to Halla. A man who held his own family in contempt would murder her and his child while believing his actions righteous. Standing before him made Taurin's skin crawl beyond anything he had felt in Rouen.

Berengar, however, had already turned back to Orderic. "Convey my plan to the leaders of your town. I will expect your answer shortly." With a nod, he disappeared through the opening in the ruined wall, followed by his guards.

Taurin exhaled a silent breath, draining the tension of standing so close to such a deceitful man. While Orderic crossed to the empty doorway and waved at the departing count, Taurin wiped beads of sweat from his forehead.

His grandfather had been right about the nobles.

Orderic returned with outstretched arms and a smile so large that it brightened his eyes. "I told you he had the strength to combat the Norsemen!"

Taurin shook his head. "No."

The excitement drained from Orderic's face. "What?"

"Did you hear him?" He scowled. "He disowned his daughter for marrying Rollo. For all Berengar knows, Rollo could have taken her against her will. If he'd do that to family, what would he do to us for willingly collaborating with those same men for more than a year?"

Eyebrows knitting together so tightly that the muscles beneath them bulged, Orderic stared with his lips parted, frozen between silence and speech.

"He would use us to punish his enemy and drown us in our own blood." Taurin crossed and placed his hands atop his friend's shoulders. "I said I would meet with him and learn about our options, and I have. But I will not deal with that man. I don't trust him."

HALLA

Walking helped when the baby decided to kick, and the baby kicked all the time. Adella and Audhild had separately promised the child would come any day now.

She was strolling among the orchards when one of her *hirdmen* galloped up to the manor. He didn't slow until the last possible moment. Sighing, she already knew what he would report.

"Another attack, *høvding*."

She forced her fingers to unclench. She should send someone else to investigate. What if she stumbled upon Bjornolf or—proving Taurin's fears true—another band of raiders emboldened by the *Thing*? In her condition, she could neither ride nor fight.

No, she had to go. The Franks needed reassurance that she opposed these attacks. Since her husband was still off on whatever errand had taken him to the west of town, she asked Leubin to drive her to the site of the attack in a horse cart.

The baby had dropped some days earlier, so every jolt of the wooden wheels sent a wave of agony up her spine. None of her duties easily accommodated pregnancy, and she tired of being carted around like a sack of grain. The gods meant people to ride horses, not endure the odors they released behind them. Every breath of wind carried more stink and made her want to retch.

As the smoke from the burning farmhouse came into view, she wondered when she had last trained with her axes. Several months, at least. The belt that normally held them no longer fit her waist.

Her nostrils flared at the familiar acridity of burned flesh. Visions of Avranches returned. "Leubin, head to the farmhouse," she instructed in a voice drawn tight.

They passed a pair of smoldering outbuildings on opposite sides of the road. Enough of the pyramidal roof remained to identify one as the smokehouse. The other, the slaughterhouse, contained old blood stains intermixed with charred wood. Fires had consumed most of each structure.

The farmhouse, on the other hand, still emitted columns of thick black smoke. Perhaps the raiders had believed the owners hid their valuables and spent time ransacking it before burning it.

She approached hesitantly. Three of her warriors were already searching the freshly sown fields for tracks. Two others studied the ground as they advanced on the woodlands.

She narrowed her eyes as she studied the farmhouse. The pattern of devastation was all wrong. Raiders normally attacked quickly, tossing a torch through a window and another onto the roof. They didn't need to destroy everything, only produce enough flames to keep the shades of the dead from following them.

But this house had been reduced to ashes. Burned torches sat at the base of the cindered remnants of the walls every few *ells*. Reducing it utterly had taken time, each moment risking discovery.

And the smell of burning flesh persisted. They had obviously offered a sacrifice to the gods before leaving, yet she saw no altar of stones or bowls to collect the blood.

Lifting her skirts, Halla picked her way forward over the fragments of the oak door. She found the door latch among them, still clinging to the piece of the door frame holding the bracket.

Her eyes widened in sudden comprehension. This was just like the longhouse burning in the warrior's story on the march.

A blanket of black and gray soot covered the inside, broken by chunks of brown thatch roofing that had fallen from above. Scorched remnants of a long dress with a decorative flower pattern stitched along the hem and a blackened chunk of wood that retained the unmistakable cross-guard and hilt of a child's wooden sword sat beside an overturned trunk. So, too, did the bottom half of a homespun doll that leaked singed wool stuffing.

Nearby, the burning flesh smelled strongest. She cupped her belly as her baby began to kick. She ventured no farther, knowing she would find charred bodies within.

As she backed away, the cinders she had so carefully avoided smeared her turnshoes with soot. None of the farmhouses she had visited during her rounds had underground storage rooms, but perhaps someone had escaped out a window while the raiders withdrew. She circled around the far side of the farmhouse to search for tracks.

And cried out in horror.

A man hung limply, suspended by ropes between a pair of poles driven into the ground. Slung over his shoulders, the pink, fleshy bags of his lungs dripped blood down his chest and legs to pool at each of his feet. So much blood. He had been alive when they had done this to him.

A blood eagle.

She raised a hand to her mouth at the horror of it. She had only heard of such a punishment, never seen it first-hand.

"My lady?" Leubin dismounted the cart.

She waved him off when she caught the scent of excrement wafting up from the body. "Stay where you are!" She placed a hand to her chest to repress the urge to vomit.

But Leubin had already seen. His mouth fell open. "Why did they hang meat from his neck?"

He didn't understand.

She circled around the body, unable to resist the hideous urge to look. She would probably never see such a sight again. It simply wasn't done.

Dried blood coated the remainder of his back and saturated his breeches and the ragged tatters of tunic that still hung from his shoulders. The skin on his back was peeled open, revealing five ribs roughly yanked free at odd angles. The rest lay on the ground around him. She couldn't see his lungs from this angle, only the empty chasms where they had once sat and the tubes that still connected them to his innards.

Bile erupted before she could stop it. She fell to her knees. One of them settled in a wet patch of blood that began to dampen her skirt. A stab of pain made her gasp between convulsions of her stomach. As the second wave of nausea struck, she dropped her hands to brace herself and one of them landed on a discarded rib.

She rose to her feet unsteadily, wiping her hands on her ruined dress. She shouldn't have looked. Gods, she would never forget the sight.

Raiding proved that a person possessed the courage, cunning, and strength necessary for Ragnarok. Killing was simply a result. But this was unconscionable. Unwarranted. A blood eagle punished crimes against the gods. How could a nonbeliever offend them?

She stumbled to the cart, passing the farmhouse without a second glance. She would find no footprints. A man who blood-eagled an innocent wouldn't permit survivors.

Did all the Franks view her people thusly, as monsters inflicting uncounted misery and torture upon their loved ones? Until now, she hadn't understood why they had resisted the opportunity Rollo offered. But this brutality justified all their fears. Arbogast had raided his own people and they had accepted him back among their community. But Arbogast would never do this.

The Bjornolf she remembered would never do this. Someone new had to be raiding here.

She rested a hand on her belly as her baby shifted. Her own child would straddle two peoples, forever enduring Norse contempt and Frankish fear. How would such a life twist her son? Her daughter? Her arms began to shake.

No. She was a daughter of Freya, a child of Odin. She was better than this. Her child would inherit that strength as well. Strife would only harden and sharpen. And she would stand beside her child against the entire world, if necessary.

But the shaking only worsened. After a few moments, she realized she shook not from fear, but from cold. She thought she had saturated her dress when she had knelt to vomit, but she saw only a small red stain at her knee that didn't penetrate to her shift. Her eyes widened as she realized the fluid came from within her dress.

"Leubin, take me home, now!"

The baby was coming.

TAURIN

Leubin intercepted Taurin as he returned from meeting with Berengar. Out of breath, the poor man leaned on his knees, gasping. "Quickly... baby..."

Kicking Seraphim's ribs, Taurin bolted down the path, leaving the breathless man behind with the trail of his horse's hot breath on the cool air. He dismounted in a single motion and rushed for the door, shoving it open hard enough for the handle to slam against the inside wall with an echoing thud.

Taking the steps two at a time, he heard neither agonized screams nor cries of a baby. He prayed that didn't mean the worst. He should have been here this late in the pregnancy, even if Adella and Audhild had forbidden him to witness the delivery. But at least he could say good-bye if...

He skipped the last step and strained his calf muscle as he landed. He felt no pain, only a weakness that forced him to limp the rest of the way. Heart beating loudly enough that he could hear it over his own ragged breathing, he paused at the bedroom door.

Please let them be well. The last of his hope began to dwindle. He should be hearing some noise from inside. God could not do this to him after everything he had endured to reach this point.

Inhaling a steadying breath, he opened the door.

Unfamiliar human odors filled the room. Halla lay on the bed, sweat-soaked hair matted on her forehead. Blankets pressed in on her, bundling her against the cold. He saw no blood or other bodily fluids to provoke his terror, but she looked pale and didn't move.

He gasped, choking on his wretched misery.

And then, she raised her eyes.

They twinkled with such wonder that he caught his breath. They held neither recrimination for his absence nor specter of death, only joy.

He rushed toward her and slid to a stop beside the bed. Within the blankets, a little baby suckled hungrily at her breast.

"Taurin," she murmured.

"I'm here. How…are you well?"

Her smirk returned some vitality to her face and filled him with relief. "As well as possible." She jutted her chin at the baby. "Come meet your daughter."

A daughter!

He sank to the floor beside the bed and reached a hand out, touching her soft skin. The little baby watched him with clear blue eyes and a pure gaze, unreadable and open. She shimmered like a vision in the mist of a cool autumn day, too ephemeral, too magnificent to be real. He hadn't believed something so precious could exist in this world.

Only when wet streaks dampened his cheeks did he realize she shimmered because of the veil of his welling tears. God had given this child into his care. What had he done to deserve such a gift?

Gazing into this little creature's eyes, he pledged to give her a home where she could flourish. All past oaths paled compared to the one that filled his heart.

Countless times over the past seven months, he had wondered what his child would look like. Would she have his father's nose? His mother's cheeks?

In this moment, only one question really mattered. "Is she healthy?"

Halla laughed. "Yes, and possessed of a good appetite." She shifted her to her other breast. "She has your nose, I think."

Taurin wiped the tears from his cheeks. He studied her face, treasuring each slope and gentle feature. "And your eyes."

Her sigh carried humor, not exasperation. "All newborns have blue eyes."

"No." She was a blending of them both. "I see you reflected in them."

The baby fell asleep after her feeding. His face hurt from all the smiling as he watched her nod and twitch in the grasp of newfound sleep.

He raised his gaze to his wife. Her infidelity didn't matter, nor their arguments. All that mattered was this pure treasure resting in her arms.

"We need to talk about..." He could not form the words. "About our argument in Rouen."

"You felt betrayed. I understand that now." A spasm of pain crossed her face. She shifted the baby to sit higher on her chest. "I didn't think you saw our marriage as anything but an agreement."

He brushed a lock of hair from her forehead. "I always did. Though the oaths were pagan ones, I chose to speak them."

She frowned. "Our ways are different. Sex is for pleasure, marriage for security." Her eyes brightened. "I didn't love you on our wedding night, yet I still intensely enjoyed myself."

His cheeks flushed. It was a memorable night.

"Love only grew after I returned from the raid. By then, it was too late." She inhaled a deep breath and straightened. "I seduced Sigrun only to secure my authority and prove I'm still fit to rule."

"It's hard for me to accept that." He took a deep breath. "But I can't deny how your people reacted to it. No one turned to mock me."

"I knew they wouldn't." She touched his cheek with her free hand. "I didn't mean to hurt you." Her eyes carried neither guile nor deception.

"I know." He reached up to squeeze her hand.

"Can we move beyond this?" She lowered her chin. "Can you?"

He brushed his fingers against the thin brown hair atop his

daughter's head. It felt softer than the finest cloth. He would forgive Halla anything. He loved her, and he treasured the child they had made together. "I can, but I can't live in fear of my wife cuckolding me if her feelings wane."

She shook her head. "It's different now. Our hearts have touched each other."

He forced himself to ask the question this once. "You would never again lie with another man?"

"No. It would betray our feelings."

The tears welled within his eyes yet again. Rising, he leaned over the bed, careful not to disturb her or the baby, and pressed his lips to her forehead.

"Can you love me without the taint of jealousy over what has passed?" she asked.

Asking that question while holding their daughter could not be easy for her.

"With all my heart, I can."

She smiled weakly and brought a hand up to his cheek. "Then perhaps we should seal that pledge by having Father Norbert marry us in your Christian way."

He gasped. "You would do that?"

She shrugged. "If it reassures you of my feelings."

"It means more than that." No longer would a man like Berengar claim he wasn't truly married, or that his daughter was illegitimate. He ran his finger over the little girl's forehead.

"It's settled, then." She shifted her posture and grimaced. "Now take your daughter. I need rest."

His concern returned. "Are you sure you're well? You're quite pale."

Her eyes hardened. "I will ignore that stupid comment."

Grimacing, he reached for the baby. "We'll need to baptize her." She was light, far lighter than he expected, but her delicate body fit perfectly in his arms, as if God had made him to carry her.

"Nothing that will injure her," she whimpered.

"It won't." He smiled at the child again. "What should we call her?"

Halla smiled faintly. "Runa."

"Runa?"

She nodded. "It means 'secret knowledge'. The gods understood what they were doing when they guided us to each other. They gave us this gift." She ran a finger over the baby's nose.

Runa. His little girl.

"Hello, my daughter." He feathered his lips against her forehead. "Welcome to the world."

III

PERILOUS IS THE PATH

MARCH, AD 892

CHAPTER SEVENTEEN

HALLA

HALLA SHIFTED HER weight to her front foot and brought an axe around in an overhead chop. Using its momentum, she twirled and dropped to a knee, offering a blind slash around her back with her other axe. The maneuver would deliver a wound like the one she had taken by the Vire.

Or, it would if she fought a real opponent.

Jutting her lip forward, she considered the sequence. She wielded axes because her reach was already too short to keep a male warrior at distance with a sword. She relied on speed, but she was moving a heartbeat slower than before her pregnancy.

It was her hips, she concluded with a scowl. They sat wider, making her old motions sluggish and unfamiliar. And despite all her practice, her abdominal muscles responded too slowly, as if she moved through water. Pregnancy had inflicted more damage to her fighting skill than even a sword to her gut.

It wasn't fair.

She intended to raid again, but she only had two months to recover her old speed before the ships departed, probably south again. She had already shed most of the weight.

A rider cantered down the road past the rye field. She shielded her eyes with her hand, studying its approach. A canter indicated a visitor, not a crisis.

Sheathing her axes in the loops at her waist, she crossed to a trough and washed the sweat from her hands. Dismounting, the rider approached as she dried her hands on her training tunic, one of Taurin's.

"Hail, *høvding*." Audhild raised a hand in salute.

"And to you, my friend." Halla embraced her when she approached. "What brings you here today?"

Audhild wrinkled her mouth into a pained smile. "Is your husband home?"

The question made the hair on the back of her neck tingle. "He's searching for Bjornolf with some of my *hirdmen*."

Audhild swallowed and picked at the hem of her sleeve. "I would have come to you sooner, but you were recovering from the delivery."

She reached out to halt the woman's nervous fingers. "What is it?"

Audhild's words came in a jumble. "Do you truly believe Bjornolf is responsible for the latest raids?"

Halla had asked herself the same question. Bjornolf had always rushed to the thick of battle. Though fearless, he was no berserker losing his wits among the enemy.

"It isn't like him," she admitted. "Yet we have no reports of other raiders the area."

"But you aren't certain?"

Halla sighed. She had no witnesses either to provide descriptions or to identify the direction from which they had attacked. "No, I'm not certain."

"But if he did these things..." Audhild stared into the distance.

"If he did these things, then we must stop him, or our laws have no worth."

Audhild dropped her gaze to Halla's feet.

The wind shook the trees, rattling their leaves in the sudden silence. Halla resolved to wait her out. The other woman had come for a reason. She would speak eventually.

"I know where to find Bjornolf's camp."

"What?" Halla sucked in a breath. "How?"

Audhild raised her chin. "We've been selling him food for quite some time."

Halla scoffed and stumbled backward, desperate to put distance between herself and this treachery. If Audhild—who had more cause to think kindly of the Franks—could do this, then how could she trust any of her people? Her cheeks filled with a warm flush, a tingling of dread.

She recalled Audhild's reassuring grip on her clenched hand during her delivery two months prior. The woman's draught had provided the only relief from the agony of those six hours. And yet, she and her husband had aided a man who threatened everything she sought to create here. She clenched her fists to restrain her building fury.

Now, she understood her husband's isolation and helplessness as his people had shunned him. At least they had worn their hostility openly. These Franks, who had hidden upriver for decades as her people passed them along the Seine, showed more honesty and courage than her own people. She swallowed, hating the taste of that bitter truth.

She returned to stand before Audhild and crossed her arms before her. "Why would you do that? The *Thing* found him guilty."

"He was fined." She scowled. "A fool could understand the meaning of such a light punishment."

"He attacks our neighbors. Your family has benefitted from their support, yet you feed him? If not for you, he'd have moved on by now."

"He follows Odin's call. There's no shame in that, no matter what Rollo says."

"He murdered people, Audhild."

"He raided." She raised a finger. "There is a difference."

"And what about the blood eagle? Do you consider that justified?"

Audhild withdrew her hand and made a protective gesture across her face. "No, that's different." She shook her head. "These people have been kind to us. They don't deserve that." She inhaled a shaky breath. "I never expected to pity them."

Halla recalled her own shifting emotions about these strange Christians. Leubin, Adella, and Taurin most of all had treated her with courtesy despite the kohl outlines she still wore around her eyes and the gold torc at her neck.

"Where is he?"

The other woman tugged at her skirts. "Promise me you won't turn him over to the Franks. He deserves to be judged by us, not Christians."

After this latest attack, the Franks would demand his execution, regardless of guilt. But, she had promised to bring Norse justice, not trample it underfoot.

"I swear it."

She and her *hirdmen* had simply assumed he would beach his longship near the coast, but the small clearing Audhild described was far inland to the east. Many streams ran in that direction; he must be using them to mask his movements.

"How many men did you see in his camp?"

Adella shrugged. "Perhaps two dozen."

Halla pressed her lips together. Bjornolf would leave once she realized she knew his location. Confronting them would require more warriors than she had. If Audhild and Steingrim had deceived her, she couldn't trust any of the Norse settlers. Nor could she rely upon the Franks. They would kill Bjornolf before she could confirm his guilt. That would break her oath to Audhild, and the Norse would never trust her again.

But Halla was developing an idea. She pinned Audhild with a glare. "I trusted you when you arrived. I didn't require you to swear an oath, but I require it now."

Audhild swallowed, but her eyes carried the comprehension that Halla had every right to ask after what she had just learned.

"Do you give your oath to defend all who reside in these lands—Frankish and Norse alike—and stand against those who wish them harm?"

Audhild sighed and reached to her throat, lifting a necklace out from beneath her shift. Dangling from it was a charm of Brísingamen, Freya's necklace. Holding it delicately between her thumb and forefinger, she raised her other hand to the sky. "On the goddess, I so swear."

Halla exhaled and rubbed the tension from her neck. No Norse woman would violate that oath and risk the anger of the gods falling upon her and her children.

She curled her mouth into a smirk. "Then I have a task for you. We need several barrels of mead."

TAURIN

Taurin and Halla tied their horses up next to the stream, hoping the trickling water would conceal the occasional neighs as the beasts munched on the abundant grass. She led her husband over the foliage by the shafts of the setting sun that cut through the forest. Taurin followed as quietly as possible a few strides behind, moving carefully to avoid snapping any overturned branches.

He reached down to adjust the hilt at his waist. It gave too quickly, and he needed an extra moment to remember it belonged to a dagger, not the sword Halla had given him at their wedding. Their business this night could ill afford a long blade clinking against a tree or rock.

She held a single axe in her hand and kept adjusting her grip on it. It comforted him that she, too, felt nervous.

Halla raised a hand, and he ducked to conceal himself in the surrounding bushes. Searching the trees, he saw nothing. Only the chirping of evening birds and the occasional rustle of a small animal along the forest floor broke the silence.

She listened for a time before waving her hand forward. He

followed for several dozen more steps, eyeing the fading dusk light on the horizon. They had to hurry, or they'd miss the cart.

A hearty laugh punctured the silence and halted them mid-stride. It came from the north. Halla glanced back at him and swallowed.

They advanced until they found the collection of tents serving as Bjornolf's camp. Thick trees hemmed in two sides of a clearing twelve horse strides wide. A fast-running stream bounded the nearest side, and the final edge abutted an overgrown yet passable path. The Norse raiders themselves surrounded a roasting boar suspended over a fairly impressive fire beneath a makeshift spit.

Bjornolf, the brutal murderer himself, was laughing among them.

Taurin clenched his fist around the hilt of his dagger. He could almost feel the resistance of his blade sliding into Bjornolf's chest.

Halla placed a hand on his shoulder and pulled down hard. "Taurin?" Though barely a whisper, her voice conveyed concern. "Are you with me?"

The sounds of the forest came surging back all at once: the water rushing over the rocks, an owl hooting somewhere off to the west, and the crackling of the fire in the distance.

He also heard a neighing horse approaching down the path beyond the clearing. He jutted his chin toward it. "Steingrim."

Sure enough, as the horse advanced, Steingrim came into view astride a cart filled with barrels.

Taurin offered a silent prayer of gratitude for Steingrim and Audhild. Despite the Franks' mistrust, those two settlers had offered to help capture Bjornolf. They had committed themselves to living in peace beside his people, right from the beginning. He'd welcome as many Norsemen like them as wished to come to Lillebonne.

The raiders gathered around the cart as Bjornolf gestured to the barrels. Steingrim dismounted and greeted him with words Taurin couldn't hear before embracing the raider.

Taurin marveled at their strength as the raiders began removing the heavy barrels from the back. He had been able to barely tilt one when Steingrim had loaded them at his manor earlier in the day.

A few others retrieved goblets from their tents while Bjornolf handed the farmer a coin pouch and draped an arm around his shoulders.

Halla led Taurin some distance downstream along the far shore before crossing with two splashing strides and snaking upstream again. They stopped within earshot of the camp beside the stream and crouched to conceal themselves in the bushes.

Steingrim and the raiders were drinking from one of the casks.

"What now?" he whispered.

"We wait for them to get drunk."

He studied the dwindling twilight, now no more than a faint glow on the horizon. He hoped enough moonlight would penetrate the trees for them to navigate by, but the night was too young to tell. The forest would remain a canvas of darkness as long as he watched the raiders around that big, bright fire.

Three goblets later, Steingrim swept his hand across the raiders and remounted the cart to a resounding cheer before retracing his route back down the path.

"How long?" Taurin asked.

She shrugged. "As long as it takes."

"You're sure Bjornolf will drink enough?"

The combination of her raised eyebrows and downward-tilting chin both reassured him and made him feel like an imbecile. Of course, he would drink. Every Norseman drank. The dozens of shattered goblets in his estate proved it.

Half of their muttered campfire stories recounted raids from years past. An alarmingly large number of the rest involved women who had scorned their advances and humiliated them. Despite his purpose, Taurin listened with awe. No Frankish man would celebrate a woman who emptied her chamber pot on him or forced him to stand in the rain all night to prove his love.

Halla would never do such a thing; she hadn't even lied about her dalliance. Her sincerity, he supposed, was a blessing.

The last light of the sun had long since fled when one of the warriors staggered toward the thick, gnarled trees that concealed Taurin and Halla. Just when Taurin thought he would discover them, the man turned toward the stream. Grunting as his foot splashed in the water, he fell silent for a time. After a few tense heartbeats, a thin line of urine trickled into the water.

They were standing in the latrine! He covered his mouth to restrain his urge to vomit and instead studied the ground to ensure he wasn't stepping in the previous day's food.

He eyed Halla in the darkness, simultaneously impressed and disgusted with her strategy. Bjornolf would eventually have to come this way to relieve himself. They need only wait. But, she had only given birth two months earlier; was it safe for her to stand here?

One by one, the raiders peeled off and availed themselves of the river. When they finished the first cask, they cracked open another, though it took a group of them some time to remember how. The songs began to slur and taper off into silence mid-verse. While a few retreated to their tents, others lay where they fell, draped over upturned logs or face-down in the dirt.

Taurin leaned close to Halla's ear. "We could kill them all right now."

She pinned him with an icy glare that made him long to shelter within the fading camp fire. "Then you'd be no better than them. We don't know that they're responsible."

That was absurd; of course they were responsible. What other reason could justify their presence? "You cannot—"

"No." She chopped her hand down between them.

He clenched the hilt of his dagger until his knuckles hurt. They would both die if he raised his voice, and he would assuredly raise his voice if he argued further.

Even if Bjornolf hadn't raided since escaping Taurin's ambush that autumn, he still deserved death for the farmer he had killed in the last raid before the *Thing*.

The fire in camp burned low. Eventually, Bjornolf rose with a grunt and dragged himself to the firewood. The Norseman added three more logs and watched the weak flames until they caught. After scratching his chin, he lowered his hand to his abdomen and bellowed a burp. When he began moving again, he passed his seat and shambled toward the stream.

Halla turned, her eyes bearing a silent warning. This was it.

Bjornolf's foot caught on a root, but he avoided falling by spreading his arms out to balance himself. Once stable, he giggled.

That giggle burned Taurin's blood. Had he giggled that way as he'd torn the lungs out of that poor farmer?

At the first tinkling of Bjornolf relieving himself, Halla offered one final glance at the silent camp before shifting her weight onto the balls of her feet and leaping forward.

She brought the back of her axe head down against the base of his skull. She struck true, and Bjornolf crumpled after a single blow. Taurin was there at the same moment, halting the big Norseman from crashing to the ground. His muscles screamed from the unbalanced weight, but he dared not release the grunt that might offer even the slightest whisper of relief.

Taurin lowered Bjornolf's unconscious form without a sound. Opening his mouth to suck in air as quietly as he could, he searched for danger, but no one seemed to have heard them.

At a sudden dampness, Taurin looked down. Bjornolf's limp body had continued to urinate on his feet.

He fingered the hilt of the dagger at his waist. He could end all their troubles by grasping the smooth wooden handle and thrusting the blade into Bjornolf's throat.

"He deserves to die." Surely God would condone murder, just this once.

"Will that stop the raids?" Each word stabbed the silence.

He took several silent breaths to regain his control. She was right. Only Bjornolf's disgrace would end the danger. And if he truly wasn't responsible…

"Help me with his legs," he whispered.

Halla slipped her axe beneath Bjornolf's knees and gripped the haft with one hand while using the other to hold his feet. Taurin slipped his arms beneath the unconscious man's shoulders. Lumbering under the weight, they withdrew downstream before crossing. His shoulders screamed from the exertion, and he couldn't fathom how Halla managed.

Though Bjornolf showed no signs of waking, Taurin tensed at every sound, fearing the other warriors would notice his absence and charge after him. A child could follow the damaged grass that marked their passage.

But eventually, they reached the spot where Steingrim awaited, dozing peacefully on his cart beside their horses. He woke with a start when they dumped Bjornolf in the back.

He yawned and rubbed his eyes. "Any problems?"

Halla shook her head. "Take him to Lillebonne and put him in the town hall. Leubin is waiting."

"*Hersir.*" He saluted before goading the horse forward.

Halla watched the cart recede. "That worked well."

"The first part, at least," Taurin agreed.

She raised an eyebrow. "Meaning?"

He turned to free Seraphim, who had eaten much of the nearby foliage down to the roots. "What happens now? We won't find justice at the *Thing.*"

"No." She approached her colt. "Not the *Thing.*"

Taurin halted and studied her. "Will you turn him over to my people for a trial?"

"Definitely not."

He frowned. He could conceive of no other option. "What, then?"

She patted her horse's neck. "First, we discover if he's guilty."

"How? He won't answer you."

"I'll see the truth in his eyes."

He suspected she was right. "And then?"

Her breathing caused the thin linen of her shirt to ripple, first one direction, then the other. "We should accompany Steingrim in case Bjornolf wakes." She swung atop her colt.

Seraphim offered an affectionate whinny as Taurin mounted her, but he didn't pat her in response. His thoughts lingered on fact that his wife had no idea how to deal with Bjornolf now that she had him in her clutches.

HALLA

It took some hours to ensconce Bjornolf, still unconscious, in the town hall. Mistrusting both the Norse and the Franks, Halla conscripted two townsmen and two *hirdmen* to guard him—and each other—through the night. She neither wanted Bjornolf to escape nor mysteriously die before she could speak with him.

She collapsed into the bed beside Taurin three hours past midnight. One moment, she was rubbing her bare feet over the soft blankets and warm furs. The next, the sun shone through the window and Taurin's body was pressed against hers. She had evidently slept through both his snoring and the rooster.

Taurin's slow breath tickled her neck. For a moment, she reveled in the simple comfort of a fine morning.

But the dilemma presented by the previous night's excursion came rushing back. The blankets suddenly felt stifling. Taurin was too close, and she itched where his body pressed against hers. Her feet wanted to pace, her hands wanted to busy themselves with something, anything.

A quarter-hour later, Vikarr reported that Bjornolf was awake. With a sigh, she nudged Taurin and crossed to the chest in the corner containing her father's mail shirt and her axes.

They departed as soon as they could ready horses.

Little Lillebonne had grown so much over the past six seasons that freshly constructed buildings added two more cross streets down the main road leading to the markets. But even that expansion couldn't explain the thick crowds surrounding the town hall.

One of those crowds included Steingrim, Audhild and score of Norsemen, along with some of her own *hird*. The other—much larger—included Arbogast, Dagobert, Orderic, and the rest of the aldermen and dozens of townsfolk. Most carried weapons.

Halla began to understand why Taurin's people had restricted arms to the aldermen. Perhaps expanding that right had been a mistake, after all.

While the Franks glowered, the Norsemen watched them with the grim silence that preceded battle. Each group had gathered to ensure that Bjornolf received the treatment he deserved. They simply disagreed on what that might be.

She considered the crowd. What would Rollo do?

Her lip curled into a smirk. He would give a speech.

She cleared her throat. "I, Halla Skidadóttir, *hersir* of Rouen and *høvding* of Lillebonne, will speak to the prisoner to determine his guilt."

"His guilt is certain." Orderic's clear voice rang out above the murmuring crowds. "We demand his death."

Of course he would challenge her. She couldn't fathom why Taurin valued this man. He caused nothing but problems.

"What proof do you have?" shouted one of her *hirdmen*.

"He is a raider," Orderic hissed.

"So am I." The warrior peeled back his lips in a feral grin.

Ill-timed humor tugged at the corners of Orderic's eyes. "Perhaps someone should execute you as well, then." His tone raised the hair on the back of her neck. He wasn't making an empty threat.

The warrior squared his shoulders and strummed the hilt of the sword at his hip. "I invite you to try."

"Enough!" Halla shouted. If she didn't satisfy both of these groups, either one could riot, perhaps even provoke a full-scale rebellion. She rounded on Orderic. "Is it the Frankish custom to execute a man without establishing his guilt? If so, slay Arbogast beside you. His guilt is certain."

Eyes widening, the named alderman retreated farther into the crowd. However, Orderic subsided.

Scowling, she turned to Taurin. "Keep them from killing each other until I return."

Her husband squeezed her hand, but his eyes carried as little faith in Norse justice as Orderic. She couldn't blame him, not after the *Thing* and the blood eagle.

She stepped into the town hall. The afternoon sun followed her through the door, peeking around her form and framing a mortal shadow. Bjornolf grunted and shielded his eyes in obvious pain. The previous night, she'd knocked him out in a single blow. She wasn't surprised his head hurt.

"Leave us," she instructed the guards.

The Franks sidestepped her the moment the words left her lips, but the Norsemen nodded respectfully before departing and closing the door behind them.

Bjornolf hauled himself to his feet and straightened his urine-stained clothes. She raised her hand to her nose to filter the stink. They had both had a hard night.

"I wondered if I'd see you. I hear you're responsible for this." He probed the back of his head. "Wasn't accusing me of murder at the *Thing* enough for you?" He spoiled the menace of his growl by slurring his words.

"You violated Rollo's oath of protection."

"An oath to Christians." With deliberate effort, he twisted to the side enough to spit on the floor. "These people are too weak to live beside us. I answer the call of the gods."

"You blood-eagled one of my people."

His eyes narrowed for only an instant, but that flicker provided all the certainty Halla needed. An innocent man would have reacted with outrage or confusion, not anger. The blood eagle, all the raids both before and after the *Thing*... Bjornolf had committed them all. She should have followed Taurin's suggestion and killed them the previous night.

No. Doing so without proof would abuse her authority. Even now, despite knowing the truth, she lacked the means to convince anyone of it.

"Your people?" he accused. "How can you count yourself among these cowards?"

"I honor my oaths."

"The gods little regard an oath to cattle." He scoffed, but the gesture made him wince and clutch his head. "They're beneath us."

"Does that include my daughter?"

Already, Runa could grip Halla's finger and suckle with such strength. She would become a fine warrior. Taurin's blood hadn't diluted her vigor one bit.

"I heard about that. Who's the father? A real man, or that mewling coward Targon?"

"His name is Taurin."

"His, then." His lip curled. "I pity your daughter, begotten by that half-man."

"He set you to flight last fall."

She delighted in his scowl. No one insulted her daughter.

"Norsemen from all over will see how easily we can crush these Christians. Others will raid. Rollo will have no choice but to abandon this foolish cause. Wolves do not lie with sheep."

"These Franks have more strength than you think," she warned. "If they rise up, they'll kill many of our settlers." Hopefully, Bjornolf's capture and Taurin's ambush the previous year hadn't already taught the Franks that what worked against a single warrior could work for Rollo's entire army. Her people could not withstand all the towns north of the Seine banding together.

Bjornolf rubbed his temple. "If they do, Rollo will scorch everything north of the Seine. Either way, his dream is dead."

She imagined her home aflame. Leubin and his sons lying blood-soaked along the road. Adella and the wives of their workers raped and sold in the markets to the north.

"So you admit to the raids?"

The words came too quickly, and she cursed herself for letting them slip with so little care.

Bjornolf bared his teeth. "You don't have any proof, do you?" He released a long, loud bellow that faded as he massaged his ear. "The *Thing* will never condemn me. Everything you've done today is meaningless."

She wanted to break his nose, but that wouldn't refute the truth of his words. Even if she could prove his guilt, she doubted Rollo would declare his warband as outlaws. It would cost the jarl too much support.

The Franks knew it, too. Orderic, though arrogant, spoke the truth. Bjornolf had to die.

She had given Taurin her oath to protect his people from raids, but if she handed this man to the Franks, her own people would revolt. They expected her to follow the law. They'd never trust her. Audhild's disobedience would become normal.

What could she do?

"Release me." He crossed his arms.

If the gods wanted slaughter, why had they set her on this path? She had been happy at Avranches. She would rather face her enemies in battle than deal with malcontents like Orderic or deception like Audhild's.

Battle.

She gasped. She had asked the gods for a meaningful death. Now, she understood. They had answered her prayers exactly as she had wished.

"Come with me."

Bjornolf watched her with an arched eyebrow that looked silly on his bearded and scarred face.

She pulled open the church door. Behind her, Bjornolf howled at the sudden wash of light but followed her, nonetheless.

The crowd fell silent as she halted just past the threshold. Halla smiled at the two pairs of guards, Frankish and Norse, standing near the doors with their hands upon their hilts. Did they realize how alike they looked?

"By our law, our people judge guilt at the *Thing* each year," she shouted. "The prisoner does not claim responsibility for the raids and I have no evidence that he committed them."

Smirking, Bjornolf directed a mocking wave at the Franks.

The townsfolk shouted and raised their fists in the air. A few of the Norsemen slid into a defensive posture.

"You cannot release him!" Orderic ejected each word alongside droplets of spittle. "He murdered our friends." Despite his words, he was smiling in triumph.

This was the second time he'd curried a mob against her.

"I agree with you."

Her words quenched their growing anger and left a profound silence in its place.

"What?" Bjornolf glared at her.

The delight on Orderic's face gave way to confusion. "But you said—"

"I said I have no evidence to present at the *Thing*."

Out of the corner of her eye, Taurin frowned. He was trying to anticipate her intentions. She spared a moment to bask in his confusion. Usually, his thoughts struck like lightning.

She turned to Bjornolf. Much had changed since she had mocked him for preening over his braid. "I gave my oath to protect these people. Bjornolf, I say you are a murderer for raiding these people and a coward for hiding from your guilt."

"Halla!" Taurin's mouth remained hanging open after the word erupted from his lips.

He understood, then.

"I challenge you to single combat. Let the gods show the truth of the matter."

No one spoke, not even Bjornolf. They all simply stared, her irrevocable words echoing in their ears. By both Frankish and Norse law, such a challenge, once made, had to be answered.

"I accept."

The intensity of his glare surprised her: he must truly hate the thought of their people living beside the Franks.

Taurin closed the distance in a great stride. "For God's sake, Halla, why?" The note of despair in his voice threatened to break her heart.

She raised a hand to his cheek. "You still don't understand our ways, do you?"

The tears began to glisten in his eyes. "You should have let me kill him last night."

Beside him, Bjornolf grunted.

"What would that say about Norse justice?" She gestured to the faces watching them. "And how could your people trust me if I violate my own laws?"

"But this?" He shook his head. "Think of our daughter." He clasped her shoulders. "I don't want to lose you."

He didn't think she could win. That would have angered her if she didn't agree.

She brushed her hand over his cheek, savoring the feel of his skin. "I'm doing this for our daughter, my love. She is both Norse and Frankish." Men like Bjornolf would only hold them back. They could not remain as they were and still rule this land.

Of course Taurin wouldn't understand. He had spent too many years among the soft embrace of his faith. But her people understood that, in the end, violence solved all problems.

While the Franks had heard of trial by combat, none of them had witnessed it. The Norse, however, began pushing the crowd back to create a circle amid the town square. They would have enough room despite the new market stalls built in the previous two years, if only just.

"Someone give me a sword and shield," Bjornolf demanded.

"*Hersir*, what weapons do you choose?" Steingrim asked.

She could no longer rely on quickness. She would need protection from his greater reach. "Give me a shield." She offered him one of her axes.

Taurin tugged at her elbow, whirling her around to face him. "You haven't fully recovered from your pregnancy."

He was right. "This cannot wait."

He eyed Bjornolf. "Let me fight in your place."

She squeezed his hand. "My dear, I know how our people think, how they move. I've seen him fight and know his tendencies. I stand the best chance."

"What happens if..." He swallowed and lowered his eyes.

She could not defeat Bjornolf. He was too strong to overpower and his reach was too long. Perhaps once, before Runa... No, not even then. Yet, even her death could protect her daughter's home.

"Then at least your people will know I honored my oath to my last breath."

He turned away. "That's not what I mean, love."

The sound of that word on his lips made her smile. "I know." While she would be in Valhalla, he would have the harder task. He would stay behind. "Then speak well of me to our daughter. Tell her..." How could she distill a lifetime into a few words? Others could teach her how to braid her hair or honor the gods. Taurin would teach her to make the hard choice instead of the easy one. "Tell her I died as a warrior for a cause I believed in."

He closed the distance and kissed her, enveloping her with his arms. His embrace pressed her mail shirt around her shoulders. The tiny whiskers growing once again on his chin tickled her lips.

Flashes of their time together filled her mind. The passionate nights filled with wild delight. The maddening confusion of his sensitive moods. The hungered longing when they parted. The first moments of wakefulness when their limbs intertwined. Sometimes, she would simply bask in the simple pleasure of his warmth and touch, hating the rooster for interrupting it.

She would never again feel any of it.

When they finally parted, she sought his eyes to remember the affection in them, only to find her own vision fractured from tears. She had wanted a cause worth dying for, but the gods had offered so much more that she almost regretted leaving this man that they'd given her.

Almost. If this was her time, she would face it with courage, no matter what she left behind. She wiped her tears.

Her *hird* had finished clearing the ring.

"Heed me now," she announced to the crowd. "If Bjornolf should prevail, then the gods find him innocent and wish him to depart in peace."

Narrowing his eyes, Taurin fell still. "You expect me to release the man who killed you?"

"I do." In a whisper only he could hear, she added, "After you slaughter his warriors. You were right. They were responsible."

His eyes widened. "Then why do this if you intend to deceive him?"

"For our daughter to have a future here, your people must trust mine. And I'm not deceiving him. Winning this trial would only exonerate him, not his followers. They are murderers. Destroy them."

Taurin shook his head. "I don't understand the distinction."

She smiled. "Yet you don't try to stop me. That means more than you'll ever know."

He inhaled and opened his mouth.

"Shieldmaiden, are you prepared?" Bjornolf interrupted.

She faced him. Better to be done with it. Dragging it out would only weaken her resolve. "Tonight, one of us dines in Valhalla."

They stepped into the ring. He carried his shield low, but because of his greater height, it sat even with hers. His sword shook slightly in his hand.

Back when they had captured Bayeux, he had cut down four Frankish soldiers in a matter of heartbeats. They had made the mistake of slipping inside his guard, thinking he would keep them at a distance. But Bjornolf always preferred to fight up close. He was a sight to behold.

No, she couldn't think of him as a worthy warrior. She had to remember Bjornolf the malcontent who had backed down from Rollo on the southern shore of the Seine. The Bjornolf who had apologized for his rude behavior in Rouen. Bjornolf, who had feared living beside the Franks so much that he'd mutilated a Frankish farmer and committed sacrilege. This man thought her husband deserved to be a thrall and her daughter was unfit to be the child of a Norse warrior. This man, who had fought beside her and embodied everything her people believed, represented the old ways that threatened her daughter's future.

He had to die.

The anger built within the pit of her stomach, transforming fear of his sword into a burning need to paint the dirt red with his blood. She adjusted her thumb on the haft of her axe to index it properly.

She circled to the right, forcing him to do the same to keep her before him. But something was wrong. Every time he stepped, his sword and shield dipped. Was he luring her into a hasty attack?

As she shifted her weight to take her next step, he brought his sword down in a quick chop. Well-timed but poorly aimed, it carved through the air to her left as she danced out of the way. She countered with a slash of her axe that deflected off his shield.

They were close now. She cocked her axe to strike, but he moved faster, chopping from above. Though she raised her shield to ward it off, the force of the blow knocked her arm to the side.

Before she could cry out from the searing pain in her shoulder, he slammed the face of his shield into her much-abused abdomen, knocking her backwards. She whimpered as her tailbone struck the ground. Though she tried to push herself to the side, her stomach muscles refused to obey.

Bjornolf was too far away and had to shuffle closer. She barely scampered out of the way of his sword. It struck the dirt where she had fallen as she rolled to the left twice, opening enough distance to scramble to her feet.

She sucked in deep breaths and gritted her teeth at her screaming muscles. Numbness spread across her right leg. Those muscles would stiffen before long. She might not parry the next attack in time.

But he was moving slower than she remembered. She should be dead now.

Halla advanced, feigning a thrust with the edge of her shield before backing away. He charged again and swept his sword from right to left. This time, she ducked and swung her axe as his momentum carried him past her. The edge sliced through his tunic and traced a line across his torso.

He growled and lashed out wildly. She barely raised her shield before his sword struck it with an echoing thud that vibrated her entire arm.

He felt the reddening wound with the back of his hand and gave a great bellow. He charged again, bashing at her with his shield. She fell back to avoid it, but her back foot caught on a rock. Gasping in panic, she hopped to keep upright.

The maneuver raised her up half a head. From that angle, she noticed something she hadn't seen before. As Bjornolf thrust his shield, he closed his eyes. When he opened them again, his eyeballs rolled around for an instant before focusing on her again.

She backed away and regained her balance. As he recovered his stance, he absently cocked his head and blinked.

No veteran warrior would close his eyes when attacking. Something was wrong. She had hit him hard the previous night. Such blows to the head could make a warrior sluggish.

Maybe the gods didn't intend for her to die this day, after all.

He raised his sword for another strike. Gritting her teeth, Halla raised her shield again. But instead of bracing behind it, she shifted her right foot and axe hand forward.

With a mighty swing, he brought the tip of his sword around in a great arc. When Halla deflected it up and away with her shield, he bashed with his shield. She had left herself too exposed for him to try anything else. For the briefest of moments, he closed his eyes as before.

Seizing the chance, she threw herself to the right. She wasn't quite fast enough though, and he slammed into her left arm with enough force to rip her shield from her grip. She would have cried if she could.

Yet his shield had also knocked her further to the right. By the time he opened his eyes, she was past his defenses. Falling, she chopped at his exposed side with her axe. The slurping sound of the blade finding soft flesh gave way to a cracking. The force of the impact yanked the weapon from her grasp.

She struck the ground hard, driving her shoulder into the dirt. Her left arm flopped against her body a moment later with a searing tear of agony. With a cry of pain, she cradled it.

Metal struck the ground with a dull clang. Her axe must not have embedded itself as deeply in Bjornolf as she had thought and had instead fallen to the ground. Both of her shoulders throbbed, and try though she might, she couldn't slip her right elbow beneath her to push herself upright. She could only flop onto her back and push herself away with her feet before Bjornolf countered.

But the Norseman wasn't advancing. He knelt in the dirt, back turned. She had a moment to recover.

With a whimper, she slid her right arm beneath her. She could still move her left hand, but only with extreme pain. At least it wasn't broken.

She needed a weapon. Pulling herself to her knees, she searched in vain for her axe.

In the dirt, sunlight reflected off something metallic. Staggering to her feet, she rushed for it despite the screaming protests of her muscles. As she came closer, she realized it was a sword.

Bjornolf's sword.

Grasping the hilt, she whirled to confront her opponent, expecting him to set upon her. But he was still kneeling, moving his left arm back and forth awkwardly. She circled him for a better look.

He had fully extended his arm when he had bashed his shield forward. The head of her axe had imbedded itself in his side between his ribs, and the haft stuck out awkwardly, preventing him from lowering his arm. Shards of rib stuck out from the wound and blood coated his entire side.

A mortal wound.

None of the Franks spoke. Rosamund buried her face in Tescelin's chest. Halla wouldn't have expected pity for the man who had butchered and flayed one of their neighbors.

A few of the Norsemen gestured around their faces, while Audhild raised her eyes and murmured to the sky. A prayer for the warrior about to join them.

But that prayer wasn't for her. She had won.

She searched faces until she found Taurin's glistening eyes. Shaking, he was clenching Orderic's tunic with both hands. Even that irritating man gazed at her with amazement.

"Halla?" The word limped on Bjornolf's exhaled breath.

Her shoulders throbbed under the weight of the sword. She stepped forward, dragging the tip in the dirt. "The gods spoke to me in Rouen, Bjornolf. They showed me my path."

With slow determination, he rasped, "I can't...believe...they want...this."

"When you dine with them tonight, you can ask them."

Tears rolled down his cheeks as his smile reached his eyes. "With... Revna."

She bit back her own tears. She was glad Revna hadn't lived to witness this day.

She raised the sword and laid it across her left arm to steady her aim. Even holding it up was agony. "Are you prepared?"

Raising his chin made his breath rasp louder. "I...face death... without fear."

He was still a warrior, worthy of respect, no different than the Frankish archer at Avranches. How strange, she thought, that one would dine in Valhalla and the other would ascend to his heaven.

"May the gods honor your courage."

She thrust the blade forward, piercing his neck with a single, smooth stroke. The force tipped him over, pulling the sword from her hand. She lacked the strength to keep her grip.

In that last moment, Bjornolf tried to smile, but with his neck muscles severed he could only open his mouth in a bizarre gasp.

Halla wondered at that expression for several heartbeats after he fell still. Had he seen the Valkyries arrive to take him to Odin? She prayed it was so.

Faces stared back at her. Amazement. Respect. Disbelief. She had killed a man who should have easily killed her. She had their attention and couldn't afford to squander this chance.

She pointed to Bjornolf's body. "This man was my friend in Rouen. In Lillebonne, he is my enemy. I swore to protect you. If it costs me my life, I will honor that oath. This is my home. I will either live here or die here."

Slowly, she shuffled over to the body. The effort of bending over nearly unbalanced her. She yanked on her axe, sticking out of Bjornolf's ribs, three times before it came free. Sliding it into the hoop at her waist, she cast a silent plea to Taurin.

His supportive arms surrounded her almost immediately.

"I can barely stand," she murmured. "Take me home?"

He lifted her into his arms and carried her toward the edge of the ring. Though he approached the side with the Franks, they parted obediently to permit his passage.

As he walked through them, Emeline brushed against Halla's left shoulder with a delicate touch. Her eyes glistened above a pained smile.

A man did the same with her foot on the other side.

And another.

Taurin continued through the narrow corridor. One after another, the Franks honored her for killing the man who had burned their farms. Each touch sent a burst of pain through her body, but she bit her lip to keep from whimpering.

She had endured their glares and suspicion for so many months. Now, she slumped against her husband's chest as they offered their humble gratitude. These arrogant, intolerant Christians had accepted her.

CHAPTER EIGHTEEN

TAURIN

FATHER NORBERT STOOD before the congregation with raised arms, his voice echoing through the church. "Oh, Lord, we thank you for delivering us from the depredations of the wicked and showing us your boundless will."

Taurin glanced at the small group of Norse in the audience. What did they think of Norbert ascribing his wife's actions to God's will? She hadn't challenged Bjornolf a week prior for Christ, but rather for Runa, a half-Norse, half-Frankish child who Norbert once would have preferred never to exist.

"We ask that you keep our defender in our prayers as she…as she recovers from the injuries she sustained doing your great work." Norbert began making an exaggerated sign of the cross in broad motions. "*In nomine Patris, et Filii, et Spiritus Sancti.*"

Taurin frowned at the catch in Norbert's voice. The priest could accept primsigned Norse settlers—many of whom had surely raided before—in his church, but not salvation at the hands of a woman.

With mass concluded, the congregants filed out. Orderic withdrew to the side of the church when an unfamiliar man approached and whispered something in his ear. Taurin offered a valediction to the other aldermen before departing.

Emeline tugged at his shoulder with a grip strong enough to halt his progress. "How is your wife?"

Though Halla could barely lift her left arm the day after the duel, she hadn't broken it. Yet, he couldn't view the black and purplish bruises that riddled her body for very long before turning away in agony. He had nearly lost her.

"She is healing. Thank you for asking."

The tension drained from her forehead. "Please tell her my prayers are with her."

Taurin stared after her as she departed. Norse had burned that woman's house, yet now she prayed for one of them. Nor was she the only one. Guntramm, who had been so eager to attack the raiders. Tescelin and Rosamund. Huebald. One by one, they all asked after Halla's health.

Once Taurin stepped outside, Orderic clamped down on his arm and began to drag him down a side street. "Come."

Taurin had to jog to keep up. "What are you—"

"Not here." Orderic continued farther from the crowds. Only after they ducked around another corner did he stop.

Taurin straightened his tunic and massaged his upper arm. "What agitates you so?"

Orderic peered down the street before answering. "I have been your friend for many years, since we were young boys."

Taurin stopped fussing and laid his hands flat against his stomach. His friend's eyes burned with an intense mix of anger and excitement that ignited a sudden rush of panic.

"If my sister had lived, we would be brothers now," Orderic continued. "In honor of the bond, I give you this warning. Keep yourself and your child away from town three days from now."

Taurin now recognized where he had seen such intensity. In

Rouen, Philbert had looked the same when he'd spoken of the massacre of Fécamp.

"Why?"

"I've received word from our friend to the south."

It had been two months since he had met with Berengar. Watching his wife whimper in her sleep, he had thanked God for the impulse to ask the count about his daughter. It had prevented a terrible mistake.

"I told you I don't trust that man."

"You did," Orderic agreed. "But I never agreed to stop communicating with him."

Taurin sucked in a breath. "What have you done?"

His friend's eyes danced. "You've paid a great price for protecting our people, Taurin. I couldn't ask you to do that again. This time, I will care for us."

Dizzy and disoriented, he steadied himself with a hand on Orderic's shoulder. Fingers digging into his friend's flesh, he repeated in a voice no louder than a squeak, "What have you done?"

"Berengar is sending a hundred fifty men-at-arms in three days to wipe clean the Norse stink. They've taken much from you, Taurin. Now, we take it back."

His hand came up to cover his mouth as visions of Halla and Runa being surrounded and abused by a gang of Breton soldiers filled his mind. He had only wanted to learn about his options by meeting with Berengar. He never intended to invite massacre.

"Three days." Even if a rider left now, he wouldn't reach Rouen in time, let alone return with help.

Orderic could risk this warning because it was no risk at all. The Bretons would outnumber and overwhelm the Norse.

"His men will cleanse the town of every pagan they find, then he'll arrive with the rest of his army to secure the countryside." Orderic placed a hand on Taurin's shoulder. "I've arranged for you and your child to be safe, but you must stay away. Controlling soldiers in battle is difficult. I don't want you coming to harm."

Taurin knew better than to trust that the count would safeguard his family. He had disowned his daughter for collaborating with the Norse. He would punish everyone who supported them here in Lillebonne.

Nor had Orderic claimed he would spare Halla. He couldn't. Halla was *hǫvding*.

Orderic gave a contented sigh as a smile curled across his lips. "Your long punishment is almost over, my friend. We won't have to tolerate these heathens profaning the earth with their foul rites any more. You'll finally be free."

Taurin searched his friend's face for some sign that he didn't mean those words. His wife had conducted those rites. His daughter carried their blood in her veins.

Halla could never understand why he had repeatedly defended Orderic's intransigence. Taurin had told her she didn't see his heart. He had believed Orderic would eventually see that while their gods were different, they still loved and laughed and dreamed.

You can know a man for years, yet only meet him when you share danger.

He was meeting Orderic—the true Orderic—for the first time. This Orderic hated and resented the Norse. He hated everything Taurin's wife and child represented.

He had invited in their executioner.

Orderic offered one last squeeze. "Three days. Stay home." Eyes distant, a smile curled across his face for a moment before he strode back toward the church.

Taurin didn't want to imagine what visions had evoked that smile.

Once, he had worried that the Norsemen had deceived him to subjugate his people. But now, he only feared the loss of his child and her mother.

One hundred and fifty men-at-arms were coming to shatter a dream he desperately wanted to believe in.

HALLA

Halla woke as Taurin unlatched the door to their bedroom. She was still running a hand through her hair and wiping a thin line of drool from her cheek when he entered. He carried a clay mug in one hand and a crock in the other, with a few lengths of cloth draped over his wrist.

He settled on the edge of the bed. "How are you feeling?"

Her body felt like she had lost every wrestling match she had ever witnessed at feasts in Rouen. "I'm alive."

He frowned and handed her the mug. "Some mead for the pain?"

Fingers twitching, she accepted it and downed half before stopping for breath. "Just the thing."

He raised the crock. "And some poultice for the bruising."

She nodded and slipped her right arm out of her shift. Setting the crock onto the floor, he helped her pull it over her head. She winced as the fabric grazed her battered left arm, but after a quick tug, she was free of the garment.

A single glance at the thick bruise stretching from her shoulder down her arm was all she could bear of the mottled splash of color across her skin. If Bjornolf's shield had struck even a hand-length farther down her arm, she could have broken it.

Taurin began applying the poultice. The slimy mixture felt strange, but she had used it often enough to know it would work wonders in a few minutes. Already, the coolness on her skin began soothing the pain.

He tied a strip of cloth around her shoulder and applied some more to her abdomen. She drew a breath. Her muscles weren't as tight as they had been before the baby. When his fingers paused along her stomach, she suppressed a flare of anger that he would notice.

His finger traced a path laterally along her stomach. She peeked down. He was only studying her scar from the Vire.

"This is where it all truly began," he murmured.

She laid her head back against the pillow. Without that scar, Runa wouldn't be sleeping in the next room. Bjornolf might still be alive. And, very likely, someone else would rule this region and Taurin and many, many Franks would be dead.

"The gods knew what they were doing."

"Do you truly believe this is divine will?" His eyes carried some deeper intent that made the hairs on her skin tingle.

She reached for her shift and forced her left arm through it despite the pain. "Do you not?"

Taurin rose from the bed and hesitantly crossed the room. Reaching the window, he stopped and stared out it. "I had my doubts."

"But no longer?"

He shook his head. "No, but the effects of suspicion can linger on and hurt us still."

She sighed. "We've spoken about this. If you can't accept my sleeping with Sigrun—"

"I've made my peace with that." He waved a hand limply. "But much has happened between Rouen and Runa."

Something in his tone caught her attention. "What do you mean?"

He turned to face her but ventured no closer nor attempted to sit. His chest heaved with each breath.

Worry began to claw at her. "Taurin?"

He raised his hands before him. "You married me to reconcile my people to your rule, yes?"

"Yes…"

"And I agreed because you and Rollo promised protection," he continued. "It was a simple agreement."

"I thought it became more than that," she murmured.

He nodded quickly. "Sigrun and the *blót* wouldn't have pained me if it wasn't." He rubbed the stubble along his chin. "But when the time came, Rollo didn't honor his pledge."

She frowned, not understanding his intentions. "Taurin, what's all this about?"

His deep breath filled his chest. "Orderic suggested that we explore whether anyone else could protect us. He arranged a meeting with Berengar of Rennes. That's where I was the day Runa was born."

Her fingers curled into fists around the blankets. "You met with the man who nearly killed me on the Vire while I was delivering your child?"

"I didn't realize you were in labor at the time."

"Taurin!"

"Rollo broke his word."

"He meant everything he said, as did I."

"Good intentions don't exonerate a person for breaking their oaths. Surely your people have consequences for deceit."

She swallowed and looked away, unable to refute him. Rollo's limp punishment of Bjornolf had angered her for that very reason. She had warned Rollo that Taurin would always do what was best for his people.

She met his gaze again. "So you conspired with Berengar."

He raised a hand. "I spoke with him, but afterward I told Orderic I wanted nothing to do with him or his intentions."

She forced her fingers to relax. "Why?"

He released a long, slow breath. "I asked if he intended to recover Poppa." His eyes tightened until she could barely see his pupils. "He acted like she was dead. He disowned her. How could a man do such a thing to his own daughter?" He swallowed and met her eyes. "I could not treat with such a man."

First, Audhild had betrayed her, and now this. "You should have told me."

"There was nothing to tell," he insisted. "He said he needed our support, and I refused to give it. I thought I put an end to it."

She lowered her chin. "You *thought* you put an end to it?"

He rubbed his hands together before him. "Today, Orderic told me to stay away from Lillebonne three days from now. Berengar intends to send a hundred fifty men to massacre your people."

"By Odin!" She bolted upright in the bed, ignoring the stab of pain surging through her arm and into her chest.

All the horrors of the Vire were coming to claim her, Audhild, Steingrim, and even little Runa. Three days. And the Christians dared to call her people barbarians!

"You brought this upon us."

"If I'm responsible for Orderic and Berengar, then you're responsible for Rollo and Bjornolf." His eyebrows pinched together. "I had a conversation. That's all. When he advocated massacre, I put an end to it."

"Or so you thought."

The vigor of his defense faded. He nodded weakly. "I never dreamed Orderic would do this on his own."

She had passed Orderic off as a summer storm, fierce-looking but posing no real danger. "I should have killed him months ago."

Taurin rubbed his whiskers with both hands. "Perhaps you should have."

She stared at him in disbelief. That admission would have cost him dearly. He had once claimed he cared for Orderic as she loved Revna.

"You should have seen his face." He stared through the window again. "He delighted in the thought of murder. I've known him a long time, Halla. Or, I thought I knew him. In that moment, he was a stranger."

Studying the torment on her husband's face, she recalled her own disgust at Bjornolf. She still couldn't imagine him pulling the lungs from that farmer's body. She hadn't believed him capable of such grisly horror.

Yet, while she had known Bjornolf for six years, Taurin had known Orderic his entire life.

"I'm sorry I met with him," he whispered. "Had I known this would happen, I wouldn't have."

He always wore his thoughts on his face. Judging it now, she saw only sincerity. She believed he had chosen not to participate in this scheme. And he was choosing again by confessing to her now. Surely he knew his admission doomed his friend.

Those choices mattered.

She released a long sigh. Orderic probably would have approached Berengar without Taurin. But now, she had a warning about their plot.

"You never really know a person until you see how they react to hardship," she muttered.

He inhaled, breaking the silence. "You showed who you were when you risked your life to protect my people. You persuaded Steingrim to help capture Bjornolf. Today, my people asked after your health. They're offering prayers for your recovery. You won them over."

"You give me too much credit. I didn't do it for them. What home does our daughter have if not here?"

"That's why I met with Berengar. I envisioned warriors terrorizing every settlement of the Caux. How long until they burned our estate or set upon us as we traveled to town? How long until they carried off our daughter to the slave markets?"

His words settled in the pit of her stomach. The kind of raiders who would attack Rollo's lands wouldn't care whether they killed Christians or the Norsemen who chose to live among them. In her homeland, men raided each other all the time.

Would she lock her daughter within their estate her entire life? Even if she did, their manor was a tempting target for any warband. How would Runa claim her place in Valhalla if she couldn't earn renown?

Taurin always saw the consequences before anyone else.

She narrowed her eyes. "What exactly is happening in three days?"

Taurin settled on the edge of the bed. "A hundred fifty Bretons will take the town. From what Orderic said, Berengar will arrive later with the rest of his army."

"Only a hundred fifty?" Berengar could muster many hundreds, perhaps thousands.

"That's what he said."

Though they were fewer than she feared, they were more than she could repulse. The gods did not give her an easy path, but she would walk it regardless.

"He said nothing else?"

"No." Taurin rubbed his chin again. "When I spoke with Berengar, he proposed a blockade of the Seine, but he needed to control Lillebonne to protect his ships. If his strategy hasn't changed, I doubt he'd risk sailing right up the Bolbec. He'd be vulnerable while unloading. They'll probably unload to the west, then march overland."

She shifted to release some of the tension in her muscles. They'd both be dead before Freya's day if they didn't discover a way to counter the Bretons.

"How many trustworthy men can you muster?"

He swallowed. "Perhaps twelve or thirteen."

The Norse would bring her another two or three dozen. She could lay ambushes along the roads and position bowmen through the woods, but that would scatter her people. Anyone she assigned to harry the Bretons likely wouldn't regroup fast enough to defend the town. She needed more warriors, preferably good, strong Norse raiders who would never run from greater numbers.

With a start, she realized where she could find them.

Casting the blanket aside, Halla ground her teeth at the pain in her shoulder and crossed to the chest containing her padded tunic and mail shirt. An idea began to snap into place like the planks of a longship's hull stacking from the keel.

She would have to sacrifice a snake, exactly the kind of profane offering Loki preferred. She had never knowingly offended the trickster god in all her years, and she would need his help.

Time was short, and she had many tasks to assign.

HALLA

The next morning, Halla sent her *hirdmen* to deliver the same message to each of the Norse settlers: attend your *høvding* at her estate at sundown.

They arrived one household at a time. Fathers and mothers

exchanged anxious glances as they ushered their children inside. They were right to be nervous, she thought as eyed the road. She would need every one of them. Berengar would send skilled warriors from his own *hird*, not farmers pressed into service.

Chatter and laughter seeped out of the manor and broke the silence. Its volume continued to increase as the stable filled and Leubin started a second row of carts flanking the road. For some time, no further groups arrived.

She eyed the horizon. Only the faintest brush of sunset reached over the manor to light the trees in the distance. Travel at night was dangerous, and she wanted to send her people on their way as soon as possible to begin preparations.

And then she saw Seraphim galloping down the road.

With a quick prayer for Hermod the messenger, she met Taurin as he dismounted near a water trough beside a pair of visiting horses. The mare stamped and whinnied at the intrusion of unfamiliar animals, but she settled quickly and lapped at the water, washing away the foam clinging to her muzzle.

"Thank the gods," Halla breathed. "I was about to start."

Taurin clasped her hands and kissed her on the forehead. He smelled of sweat and dirt, like the scouts during the march.

"What do they say?"

He answered between breaths. "Ten of my people will fight. Many more offer horses."

She led him toward the manor. "How many horses?"

"Four dozen worthy of battle."

"Very good." She pushed open the door and stepped inside, with Taurin panting from behind.

The several dozen Norsemen abandoned conversation and lowered their goblets as she halted before them.

"In my time as your *høvding*, I have yet to command your presence," she began as Taurin settled behind her. "I do so now because we face a grave threat."

Light expressions dropped into grimaces.

"Berengar of Rennes is sending a hundred fifty men to take Lillebonne. He intends to destroy our farms and kill every Norseman he finds."

Her words produced a few gasps and anxious murmurs.

A redheaded farmer whose holding abutted a stream feeding into the Bolbec rubbed his beard. "When do we leave?"

"We don't."

No one spoke. Faces turned grim, and several heads swiveled to count their numbers.

"We cannot win against such numbers." The redhead's hushed voice thundered in the silence. "But we can get out families to Rouen and return to crush these Franks with Rollo's warriors."

"Bretons," Taurin corrected.

The farmer scowled. "Whoever."

"We'll find no relief in Rouen," Halla said. "If Berengar takes Lillebonne, he'll blockade the Seine, destroy our settlements, and ambush the staggered ships arriving for the summer raiders. Rollo will have neither the warriors nor the supplies to dislodge him."

Steingrim rose and swept his eyes over the other farmers. "Then we must stop him. And if we do not, then we at least prove our worth unto our last breath."

Taurin gasped beside her.

A few heads nodded. Husbands looked to wives. Parents clasped their children's shoulders. Someone cried, "Skol!" and they raised their goblets.

Though they were surrounded by Franks and threatened by Bretons, her people hadn't lost their strength. Her heart swelled with pride.

"If we die, we will die well," Steingrim said to his children loudly enough for all to hear.

"We may not need to die at all." She gestured to her husband. "Taurin and a number of his men will join in defense of the town."

The Norsemen shifted their weight and lowered their goblets.

She had expected gratitude, not recalcitrance. "You've been living and planting beside them. Will you now hesitate to fight beside them?"

"I don't mind fighting beside a Christian," Steingrim interrupted. "Nor do I suspect any of us does." He waited, gathering nods. "But they've never fought a battle, never withstood a charge against a shield wall. You ask us to trust our lives to their inexperience."

Halla recalled the Christian rider who had almost killed her on the Vire. "Even the most inexperienced warrior is dangerous on horseback."

"Horseback?" one of the farmers cried with alarm. "We do not fight on horseback."

"We must if we wish to overcome their numbers."

"How can we maneuver horses in town?" another asked.

Halla curled her mouth into a grin. "I have a plan." She swallowed, wetting her lips. "Give me one good charge, then you can dismount and fight as you will. Agreed?"

No one spoke. Behind her, Taurin's boots scraped against the marble floor as he shifted. If they refused to follow her, she and Taurin would have to ride off with Runa immediately, abandoning all their efforts of these past six seasons.

"Horses!" Downing the rest of his mead, Steingrim slammed the goblet on the dining table. "At least the gods will hear us with all that racket!"

They broke into a frenzied laughter fueled by tension and anxiety. Clasping each other on the shoulders and arms, they started to sing of Odin and his fateful encounter with Fenrir.

Halla smiled in relief. They knew their path and were content.

Taurin squeezed her shoulder. "I need a drink."

With raised eyebrows, she watched him pour a goblet of mead. He usually only drank it when nothing else was available. But she supposed she could understand his need: now that she had her warriors, he would have to face Orderic.

Halla crossed to Audhild and tugged on her arm. Sparing a quick glance to confirm that no one observed them, Halla led the other woman up the stairs to her bedroom.

Audhild arched an eyebrow but spoke only when Halla latched the door. "Do you truly have a plan for overcoming such numbers?"

"I do, but whether our people live or die depends on you."

Audhild drew an unsteady breath.

"If the raiders learn we've left Lillebonne unprotected to engage the Bretons, they will seek revenge on the town, yes?"

The other woman nodded. "They wouldn't linger unless they wanted vengeance. You grabbed Bjornolf from right under their noses. They cannot let that go unpunished."

"I assumed as much." Halla pressed her lips together. "Are you still in contact with them?"

Audhild straightened and set her jaw. "Even after I swore to Freya, you fear I'd expose the town to a sack? Halla, what must I do to convince—"

"Stop, stop!"

Halla placed her hands on Audhild's shoulders as the other woman steadied herself from a rage not yet extinguished.

"You misunderstand me. I want them to attack Lillebonne. I need those raiders to be in town at sunset in two days."

TAURIN

Taurin had traveled to Orderic's estate so often that Seraphim knew the route even in full darkness. Yet this time, he imagined Bjornolf's warriors, still at large, hiding behind each tree. The route filled him with a heavy dread.

Dismounting and tying Seraphim to the hitching post, Taurin fussed with the alignment of his tunic and took a cleansing breath. "God, give me strength."

He was about to betray someone he loved.

He rapped on the door twice, paused, and repeated. The patter of approaching footsteps mirrored the rhythm of his racing heart.

The latch squeaked as Orderic opened the door. He craned his neck to peer into the emptiness beyond. "Taurin? What are you doing here at this hour?"

"I must speak with you." He gestured inside.

"Of course, of course." Patting him on the shoulder, his hand lingered for a moment on the tense muscles of Taurin's arm. Closing the door, Orderic eyed him. "Is all well?"

"You need to gather your men and leave town." Taurin rubbed his hands together to conceal their shaking.

"No, it can't be done. I need more time. I've yet to approach some of the other aldermen."

"Halla knows Berengar is coming and that you arranged it."

He hissed. "Taurin!" Grabbing him by the shoulders, Orderic pushed him roughly into the wall. "You betrayed me?"

"Peace." Taurin wrapped his hands around the other man's wrists. "I have not betrayed you."

Orderic narrowed his eyes but didn't release him. "Explain yourself."

"I knew Halla would gather the Norseman. She cannot afford to lose this town and see Rouen blockaded."

Orderic shook Taurin's cloak and tunic where his hands gripped it. "They will be waiting for us. We needed surprise. Surely you understood that!"

Taurin held his ground. "You have more than a hundred men. You don't need surprise. But you do need to destroy them all at once so they don't hide in the wilderness and attack when Rollo arrives." Orderic's eyes widened. "They know the land, Orderic. Bjornolf had fewer men than she can gather, and look at the damage he caused."

He raised his chin but clung to his suspicion. "Why would you betray your wife?"

Taurin shook his head slowly. "You were right. I put us in more harm. You witnessed Rollo's betrayal for yourself in Rouen. I…I have to make it right."

Taurin endured his scrutiny for a long while. As he did, he recalled how they had cried over the death of Orderic's sister, how they had always supported each other through the long years. This was his dear friend.

Suspicion displaced the anger in Orderic's eyes. "You shouldn't have done this without speaking to me."

Taurin rested his hands on his friend's shoulders. "The opportunity presented itself as I spoke to Halla. I had to act when I did."

He scowled at mention of her name. "What does she know?"

"The Bretons are coming in three days. That's all I knew."

"What about the other aldermen? They could contribute men."

Taurin shook his head. "I saw her numbers when she gathered her people. They don't stand a chance. Let the Bretons risk their lives while our people remain safe."

"She can warn Rollo." Orderic's protest was softer than before.

Taurin shrugged. "Let her send riders away. It'll only ease Berengar's task."

His hands released Taurin's cloak. "What are her plans?"

Taurin resisted the urge to straighten his clothing, wrinkled from Orderic's grip. "She will gather the Norse in town at sundown and ride out to attack when the Bretons make camp for the night."

"Ride?" Orderic's breath quickened. "I didn't think they fought on horseback."

Taurin shrugged. "She thinks it'll make a difference."

Orderic rubbed his chin. "If they catch us unprepared—"

"They won't, not if the Bretons force a march and surprise her before she's ready. They'll face only a few dozen Norsemen on foot in a confined space."

"That's a long way to march. They'll be exhausted," Orderic muttered.

"How much devastation will the Norse inflict if they're allowed to retreat?" Taurin's voice rose louder. "They could burn the town rather than let the Bretons control it. We invited Berengar in to save our people, not see us ruined. You saw what they did to that farmer, the blood eagle." He crossed himself.

Orderic rubbed his hand over his mouth. "Quite right," he murmured. "Better to put down all the dogs at once." He raised a finger. "But no more changes to our plans without my approval, understood?"

Taurin swallowed his frustration at being given orders; now wasn't the time for pride. He had his chance to make decisions. This was Orderic's plan now. "I understand."

His friend softened. "I understand your thinking now. I'm sorry if I was angry," he mumbled. "I thought…"

Taurin squeezed his shoulder. "You thought I had betrayed you for my wife."

"Yes."

"I understand." Taurin bit his lip. "Could any heathen ever mean more to me than my dear friend?"

Orderic smiled as brightly as when he had reported Berengar's success a year and a half earlier. "I will go tonight with what men I can gather." He clutched Taurin in a tight embrace. "I'm glad I don't have to do this alone."

Taurin squeezed his eyes shut to block out his swirling feelings. He remembered Halla standing in the square, covered in kohl, mail, and leather. Orderic had warned him then of the danger the Norsemen presented. Had Orderic planned, even then, to use the sword to drive them away?

Like a fool, Taurin had believed he could somehow stop the bloodshed. He'd been wrong, so very wrong. Some things simply could not be.

And now, he would have to kill someone he loved.

HALLA

The next morning, the clear, sonorous ringing of Lillebonne's church bell surmounted the surrounding buildings and reached into the woodlands beyond. The traditional cadence of danger gathered the townsfolk until, by noon, whispering denizens packed the church and spilled into the street.

The bells hadn't sounded in warning for over fifty years.

Steadying herself with a deep breath, Halla ran her hands over her braids, checking that no tendrils escaped. She had spent two hours polishing her mail so it would reflect the light. She would need to be the consummate warrior.

She had shared her reasons for this gathering with Father Norbert when she had asked to use the bell. He fidgeted beside her, the constant movement of his hands signaling the conflict in his heart. Two years earlier he would have unequivocally supported a Christian plot against Norsemen. But he now knew they didn't breathe fire and devour infants, after all.

Children's stories. Now, they faced real danger.

Halla studied these faces from the pulpit. Though the hair was darker and shorter, their faced showed the same uncertainty and fear as the candlelit Norsemen the night before. She shared their fear. A hundred fifty men was no small force.

Taurin shifted beside her. "I don't see Orderic or his wealthiest tenants."

The crowd now contained most of the aldermen and many of the *pecunium*-holders.

"I suppose he's gone to await the Bretons. How many are missing?"

Taurin rubbed his beard. She started to chuckle.

"What?" he asked.

"Nothing." She dimpled her lips into a faint smile, eyeing his whiskers. "How many?"

He searched the crowd. "Perhaps ten?"

Ten more men she would have to kill, when she faced too many already.

She raised her hands to draw the congregation's attention. Her shoulder seared with a blistering ache where Bjornolf's shield had smashed into it, but she clenched her jaw to keep the pain from showing on her face.

A hush descended upon the front rows and slowly worked its way backwards, snuffing conversation throughout the church. She waited until the chatter seeping through the open doors hushed and gave way to the clucking of chickens and the bleating of goats outside.

"Rollo of Rouen tasked me with defending this region. Last week, that meant killing one of my own people. Now, we face another threat. A hundred and fifty Breton soldiers will arrive tomorrow. They plan to occupy Lillebonne, kill every Norseman they find, and blockade Rouen from supplies and warriors."

While a few murmured, the majority of the assembly dipped their heads and brought their hands together before them. Several made their crossing gesture. Father Norbert had joined them, muttering something about salvation.

She had hoped they'd tear out their hair and wail in grief. Even a Christian army posed a serious threat; men possessed by the frenzy of battle rarely distinguished between enemy and bystander. Surely, they had to know the dangers they would face.

The strange ritual unnerved her, and she gripped the pulpit to steady herself. She felt like she was intruding on something private.

Beside her, Taurin gestured for her to continue.

"This is our home. My warriors and the Norse settlers intend to defend it."

The whispering ended as heads rose to listen. The desperation in their eyes unnerved her. No Norseman would look at her like that. "I have a plan that may yet see us prevail." She paused, inhaling another breath. "I cannot guarantee we will succeed. I advise everyone to remain at your farmsteads until you determine how they intend to treat you."

"What does that mean?" asked Huebald in a high-pitched tone. "Why would they harm us?"

Halla was relieved that someone asked that question and spared her from having to broach the subject herself. "You've worked beside us in peace for many seasons. The leader of these Bretons, Berengar of Rennes, disowned his daughter for marrying Rollo. He may condemn you as collaborators and traitors."

Now, even the aldermen began to whisper with an edge of desperation. That the leader of the army approaching them would disown his own child—a daughter, no less!—did not sit well in the hearts of these humble people.

"We know what armies do," cried Rosamund. "They steal our food and ravage our daughters."

"Rollo's army didn't," shouted one of the farmers from the west.

"Our champion wouldn't let them." A tall man near the front pointed at Halla. "She will preserve us now."

Halla gasped. Taurin had said her duel with Bjornolf had affected them, but she had never expected such faith.

"I will do what I can, but this town will not be safe. Stay with friends throughout the area. Those who linger in Lillebonne risk their lives." When no one moved, she commanded, "Go. Prepare yourselves."

She withdrew to the side of the church as the crowd dispersed amid frenzied chatter and frenetic activity. Taurin followed closely behind, as did Father Norbert, after a brief hesitation.

"We've done what we can," Taurin muttered.

"Now, we see if it's enough," Halla said.

"Do you truly believe these Bretons will seek retribution against us?" Norbert's voice wavered.

"How would you react if, two years ago, someone suggested you would cooperate with a Norseman?" Taurin asked.

The priest's eyes widened. "I thought…" He turned to face the crucifix behind him. "I feared…"

"You treated us as the demons you believed us to be," Halla said as she watched Huebald and a group of Franks who hadn't dispersed.

Norbert frowned. "Forgive me."

"There is nothing to forgive." She reached a hand out to touch his shoulder but halted when he flinched. He might tolerate her, but the thought of affection from her still unnerved him. "You did as you believed to be right. None can expect more than that."

Beside her, Taurin folded his arms. He, too, had acted as he'd believed was correct. Despite his intelligence, he could still be a fool. But he was an honest fool.

"But the world changes around us, and our ways must change with them. Orderic chooses not to accept this." Her lips quivered into a scowl. "I will teach him the cost of his intransigence."

"I cannot condone the murder of one of my flock," Norbert said.

Halla remembered a conversation many months earlier about that topic. "Then consider his death a mere consequence of battle."

Norbert's eyes clung to their uncertainty. "You did not tell the crowd that he had joined the Bretons."

"Nor did you," she noted.

"Their thoughts should be for their families' safety," the priest defended.

"I entirely agree."

Huebald and the group of townsfolk approached. She recognized a few of the faces, including Guntramm and Tescelin, from the blended training.

Though Huebald stood straight, he curled his fingers into a fist and released them repeatedly. "Halla?"

Perhaps two dozen men stood with him, blocking her escape through the church doors. Had Orderic suborned them? This would be their last chance to ambush her before the Bretons arrived.

But they stood awkwardly as they waited behind Huebald, shifting their weight and seemingly unsure what to do with their empty hands.

She rested her palms on her axes, dangling from her belt. "Yes?"

"We wish to join your warriors and fight for our home."

Her arms fell to her sides. "Excuse me?" Had she imagined the words?

The blacksmith shifted his weight and glanced at Taurin. "We wish to fight with you."

In all their planning, neither she nor Taurin had expected the townsfolk to stand against their own kind.

"Why?" Her voice wavered with disbelief.

"Five decades ago, the King of the Franks did nothing when Norsemen burned our town. This Berengar never cared about us in all these long years. But you"—he pointed at her—"risked your life for us."

"You would kill fellow Christians?" Norbert asked, wide-eyed.

Huebald raised his chin. "I would defend my town beside those who would risk their lives to protect us." He raised his arms to encompass the group. "We all will."

Nods and mutters of agreement bubbled up through the group.

Guntramm said, "The traders Rollo brought let me afford an extra set of clothes for each of my children. And I can build a new water mill on my land."

"Steingrim helped clear my land so I could plant another field," Tescelin added. "He and his wife are as kind as any Christian."

"Can we join you?" Huebald asked. "We aren't cowards."

She had arrived in Lillebonne expecting to execute some of these people. Now, they wished to fight for her. When had that happened? Was it when she had welcomed the mob of angry Christians into her home after that first *blót*? Or when Adella had helped her endure her pregnancy? Or was it when she had killed Bjornolf?

No, it had happened gradually, in the tiny spaces of each insignificant conversation, each trip into town for supplies, each ride to check on the settlements. They had become a community, all of them, Christian and Norse alike. She wondered if even the gods had anticipated that.

She had once told Taurin she could never conceive of living in one place, of being bound to land as he was. Now, she couldn't imagine living any other way.

She and her daughter belonged here, among these people.

"Assemble here tomorrow at noon," she instructed. "Each of you should bring a sword, what armor you have, and a horse capable of a good gallop."

CHAPTER NINETEEN

TAURIN

HALLA'S SUGGESTION THAT they rest on the eve of battle seemed sensible. Yet though they adjourned to bed shortly after twilight, retiring early only gave Taurin more time to listen to the insects chirping in the darkness outside. His thoughts simply refused to stop long enough for him to drift off to sleep.

For fifty years, his people had looked to the sea with terror at the threat of longships disgorging marauding heathens. And yet, those heathens had finally arrived in trading *knörrs*, not raiding *snekkes*, and the only threat facing Lillebonne came from a Christian army.

Halla shifted and burrowed against him. Her rapid breathing suggested she was also awake. She said nothing through the long hours, but her presence comforted him. Eventually—he didn't know when—he finally drifted off.

He woke shortly after dawn when Halla stirred next to him, and they began to dress. She grunted when she forced her wounded shoulder into her padded tunic. Taurin noted the stitching that sealed up tears in the fabric from past battles, including the sealed rip from her wound along the Vire and the short tear in the forearm from Avranches.

344 | K.M. BUTLER

How many more tears would it have before the day ended?

He dressed in a leather tunic, stiffened leather breeches, and rawhide strips at his wrists and ankles. Finally, he positioned the leather cuirass one of the Norsemen had offered him.

He had never needed mail or metal armor before. None of his people had. He should have purchased some in Rouen when he had visited. Selling his surplus at the *Thing* had earned him the money, but instead of preparing for difficult times, he had made repairs around the estate and purchased more seed and animals.

If God granted him another chance, he pledged not to squander his good fortune again.

When he descended the stairs, the household had already begun assembling the wagons. So far west of the city, his estate lay near the Bretons' likely route. Berengar's men might decide to stop and punish his servants for collaborating with the Norse over the previous two years. He had to evacuate everyone on the estate who wouldn't be fighting.

Taurin walked along the column, reassuring the frightened women and crying children saying goodbye to their husbands and fathers, perhaps for the last time.

"It's just a precaution," he assured. "I'll send a rider the moment it's safe to return home."

The tension around their eyes suggested they didn't believe his words either. The Bretons would do their best to prevent him from ever sending that message.

Halla was giving instructions to the Norseman who would lead them to Rouen, a thirteen-year old boy who had made the journey several times with his father. Despite all their careful preparations, her eyes carried the same doubt.

They met back at the door to the manor when the last of the men had finished preparing the wagons and said their own goodbyes. Adella kissed her husband one last time. As she embraced her eldest boys, tears rolled down her cheeks.

The wet nurse, bundled in one of Halla's finest wool cloaks, emerged holding little Runa swaddled in a linen blanket. Halla accepted her from the nurse and leaned over her, whispering something too softly for him to translate. A single tear fell from Halla's eye, disappearing within the bundle.

Taurin circled to see his little daughter, etching every slope and curve of her tender features into his memory. Taurin smiled at those blue eyes, so like her mother's. Runa giggled as she reached up to her parents. Eyes filling with tears, Taurin took her tiny fingers between his thumb and forefinger. Her skin felt so soft, innocent.

He refused to cry, instead forcing a smile that squinted his eyes. If she never saw him again, he wanted her last memory of him to be a happy one.

Stirring, Halla crossed to the lead wagon and passed her precious parcel off to Adella as the wet nurse climbed into the back. The other woman waited for some instruction, but Halla simply rejoined Taurin in silence.

The first wagons began moving in a long, noisy line down the road past the growing rye. Beside him, Leubin waved at the retreating form of his wife. Once they were clear of Lillebonne, they would head east to the old Roman bridge crossing the Bolbec before continuing on to Rouen.

Taurin rubbed his shoulders when he lost sight of his bundled daughter. He might never see her again.

"Whatever decisions led to this moment no longer matter." Halla's voice was low but steady. "Regrets will make you hesitate. Lay them down before you pick up your sword."

"If I hadn't met with him—"

"Then we would not know these Bretons were coming. You didn't invite them here." She turned back to the wagons. The last one had nearly disappeared down the road. "Our fates are already written. Meet yours with courage."

Taurin lowered his eyes. He suspected that this pagan wisdom of a warrior people would serve him better than any of Father Norbert's teachings in the upcoming battle. "I will try."

She inhaled a deep breath, still watching the now empty road. "If I die this day, will you make me a promise?"

Taurin recalled the last time his wife had departed for battle. "I swear Runa will know of your deeds."

She exhaled a weak laugh and shook her head. "I'd rather you tell her of my heart, of the woman I am." Vulnerability and pain showed within her eyes. "And that I love her very much."

The words sundered his heart and threatened to drown him in the sorrow of a shattered life. He leaned his head against hers. "She will know you as I know you. All your passion. All your honesty. All your faith. I swear it."

She wrapped an arm around his waist and leaned into him. "Then I can fight beside my husband without fear."

She stepped back with eyes closed. When she opened them again after a cleansing breath, they were dry and flint-edged.

"Now, let's teach these Bretons to fear when Frank and Norseman join together."

HALLA

In a typical raid, Norsemen would shout a war cry before attacking to warn the gods of valorous deeds. Quite often, it terrified the hapless victims. Men and women did not make sound decisions when gripped by panic, and the first moments of an attack usually decided an outcome.

Halla heard no such shriek before Bjornolf's raiders descended upon Lillebonne in the waning light of dusk.

They moved slowly until they passed the outlying buildings, freshly constructed over the previous month. Fanning out, the two dozen raiders spread from building to building. The sharp groans of wooden doors being kicked open marked their progress.

A few determined Franks had refused to evacuate. The raiders dragged them out into the streets and hacked at them wantonly. The shrieks of Frankish agony rising from the town blended with the raiders' laughter as they rained blow after blow designed to wound but not kill.

Halla, concealed alone within the fresh growth of the edge of the forest to the south, watched the gruesome scene in silence. She had warned them as strongly as she could. Those who chose to stay deserved their fates. Some had no doubt greeted her news of the Bretons with guarded delight. Dying by the hands of Norsemen served them right.

In fact, her heart leapt. They were a necessary sacrifice. Their deaths meant Audhild had succeeded in her deception. These raiders were discovering exactly the undefended town, ripe for pillaging, that they expected.

Just as Halla had intended.

The screams grew louder. The added noise would give the impression of a much larger force.

Beside her, the scout who had just arrived from the west still panted as he tried to catch his breath.

Any minute now.

A tongue of orange flashed as the raiders set the first fire. Slowly, the flames crept up the side of a building and grew larger. Only when they cast the town in a hazy glow did she realize the raiders had started with the church.

Three more buildings caught fire. The flames cast enough light to outline the rapidly expanding clouds of smoke spreading across the sky. At least the flames would prevent the shades of the dead from lingering nearby.

For a moment, she thought she saw a winged figure cloaked within the shadow. She inhaled a few breaths to steady the flush of nervous excitement. The gods were watching.

She closed her eyes and smiled. She had asked them for the chance to die in a worthwhile cause. Too late, they were granting that wish.

Now, Halla yearned only to return home with Runa and Taurin, dear Taurin.

Movement beyond the western meadow obstructed the setting sun. Men were approaching on foot, interrupting the light behind them and casting dancing shadows over the tops of the grass. She lost count after the first fifty men wearing identical conical helmets. All but a handful wore cloaks with a large black cross on a field of white. She remembered that cloak from the Vire.

The Bretons had arrived.

The raiders had noticed, too. Someone shouted in Norse and the raiders formed a solid barrier of interlocking shields.

The Bretons approached slowly until they reached the town. As the buildings funneled them down Lillebonne's main road, they began to charge. They looked like ants converging on an anthill.

The groups met with a grinding collision peppered with the clangs of metal on metal and the occasional scream. The buildings blocked Halla's view of the impact, but the shield wall obviously held. Neither victorious Bretons nor broken raiders trickled back toward the church.

Halla breathed a sigh of relief. She was relying on Bjornolf's raiders not dying easily. She needed them to kill as many Bretons as possible before they finally fell.

She turned and darted into the forest, raising her arms to protect her face and neck against the sharp branches. The scout followed behind obediently.

Her *hird* and the Norse settlers awaited several dozen *ells* deeper among the trees. At her approach, they began checking their armor and donning their helmets. The Frankish horses they rode jumped in agitation at the distant screams and grinding metal. The poor animals weren't used to the sounds of battle. Hopefully, they would last through a charge.

Audhild, wearing layered leather armor and kohl over the left side of her face to ward off the spirits of the dead, held the reins of Halla's colt. Swinging atop it, Halla goaded it forward and pulled around to study her warband. Angry faces stared back at her. That was good. Anger would serve them well.

"Stay close!" Silence no longer mattered; the Bretons would be busy with Bjornolf's raiders. "It's a short ride, so don't spare your mount."

"We're with you." Steingrim assured before nodding to his wife. Protective runes and kohl symbols of Thor and Odin covered his face and neck.

Halla pointed toward the town. "These invaders desire our land. They think they will easily kill us. But I know they will not, because the gods witness what you do here tonight. Now is the time to earn your place in Valhalla." She drew her axe from its loop at her belt. "You are the hammer of the gods! Make them tremble with your fury!"

They cried out as one, banging their swords and axes against their shields, as she kicked her horse forward. The others followed in her wake, horses carefully picking their way through the forest brush until they reached the grassy field surrounding Lillebonne.

The raiders' shield wall had disintegrated. Individual battles filled the town square. One by one, the market stalls rising above their heads fell, hewn by an errant sword or a collision between combatants.

Halla cantered forward at the head of her warriors. The raiders were losing, but the Bretons paid a dear price. Each raider who died took at least two Christians with him. They continued to hack and slash even as their death strokes fell. Neither the Bretons nor the raiders had yet turned to face the oncoming charge.

So long was the Breton column that, off to the west, some hadn't yet filed into the main street. They might be tired from the long march, but they weren't yet exhausted from battle. Halla's spirits sank as her horse passed out of the meadow and headed north onto the main street. They would devastate with this charge, but the Bretons had plenty of fresh soldiers to surround them afterwards.

The gods had answered her promise after all. She would die for a worthy cause.

Her horse took another two strides. Most of the raiders were dead now, their blood intermingling with Breton blood as if such a blending were utterly natural.

A single Breton turned his head to the south. His eyes widened as he recognized the three dozen riders bearing down on him.

At the last moment, she pictured Taurin sitting by her birthing bed, holding little Runa with that contented smile that softened his features. She hoped Taurin, somewhere to the southwest, would honor his pledge to tell Runa about her.

"By all the Aesir!" She slammed her axe down as her horse struck the first shocked Breton.

TAURIN

Taurin held his hand to his mouth to stop himself from vomiting as Halla and the other Norsemen struck with an audible crack. He swore he felt the vibration from the collision from his position in the marsh to the southwest of town.

That was his wife, fighting for her life.

The Bretons were too great. The end of their column had only just finished entering the town. Sixty or seventy hadn't yet engaged Halla's Norsemen, who had now dismounted.

The ribbon at his neck felt too constricting. He tugged at it for a moment, then forced himself to stop and instead tighten the knot.

He kicked his horse forward and gestured for his men to follow. Hooves stuck in the gooey mud with each step. No one bothered with this marsh anymore, which made it the perfect place to lie in wait.

He raised his fist to halt once they reached the meadow. A few horses stamped the ground to shake the muck from their hooves.

Taurin brought Seraphim around. All of his men wore a deep red ribbon around their necks. He had known most of them his entire life. How many would sleep in Heaven this day?

Father Norbert had blessed them all before withdrawing with the women and children, but Taurin felt he should say something as well. When he crossed himself, the others did the same.

"Almighty God, watch over us in our hour of need. If it is Your will that we prevail this day, grant us strength. If it be not, we ask for Your forgiveness for our trespasses." He crossed himself again. "Amen."

There. The rest was in God's hands.

He turned and drew his sword. The scraping of the metal blade rubbing against the wooden sheath echoed as his men did the same. "May God keep you all."

Seraphim rushed ahead after only a gentle tap. The other Franks—Huebald and Tescelin, Leubin and Guntramm, and all the others—cantered behind, forming a column two abreast.

"Steady. It's not a race," Leubin called out to one of his sons, who was crowding too close.

Taurin led his to enter town by the western road behind the Bretons. The rear of Berengar's column noticed their approach. When Taurin made the sign of the cross with his sword, they waved a cheerful greeting and called for the men in front to allow them past.

Orderic had evidently done as he had promised and informed them to expect Taurin. Naturally, he couldn't part from Halla before the battle, since she would notice his absence and change her tactics.

Or so they believed.

Four strides from the back of the Breton line, Taurin goaded Seraphim into a full gallop, speeding through the corridor between the still-cheering soldiers. He brought his sword down on the neck of one with enough force to rattle his own arm with the impact.

He had dreaded this moment since Halla had shared the plan that required him not only to deceive Orderic, but to kill Christians with his own sword.

But as he brought his sword down again, he felt no guilt, only the desperate need to strike before the Breton closest to him could.

Screams of terror and disbelief spread quickly. Seraphim rushed forward, bowling over any stray men who interposed her path. Faces passed in a blur, but Taurin continued to strike again and again as they did. Each blow vibrated into his arm. Each strike twisted another Christian face into a look of pain and horror.

Any one of these men would kill his wife and daughter as heathens.

As he raised his sword again, drops of blood splashed against his cheeks. He jerked and Seraphim obeyed the accidental command, rearing her head to the left and knocking two Bretons to the ground. As Taurin wiped his face clean, his mare stamped at the downed soldiers with a sickening crunch.

Swinging Seraphim's head around to clear space, he risked a glance behind. His men had stalled and were fighting for their lives among the Bretons. As he watched, mailed hands hauled one of his tenants down.

Had they gone far enough? The flaming church loomed in his vision. He was near Huebald's blacksmith shop. It, too, burned. The heat permeated his leather armor and warmed whatever fluid—sweat or blood—caked his face.

The warriors he had pushed aside with Seraphim's head were rushing forward again from his left. He managed to slash the shoulder of one before they hauled him down. Freed of her rider, Seraphim reared back before bolting down a side street, far from the madness of steel and blood and sweat.

Goodbye, Seraphim. He wished he could run to safety with her, but this was his end. He would die here in the town he had failed to defend.

One of the Bretons raised his sword. His eyes burned with fury. Taurin tugged at his weapon, but a body atop it pinned it in place.

He remembered the grim determination on Halla's face even as Bjornolf had knocked her to the ground during their duel. He had thought she would die then, yet she had shown such great courage. He could do the same.

He met the man's eyes as the Breton started his downswing.

Goodbye, Halla. Goodbye, Runa.

The blow never fell. Instead, blood sprinkled Taurin's face again as a sword poked through the man's chest. Taurin scrambled to avoid the weapon falling from the man's grip. His attacker crumpled to the ground, revealing Vikarr behind him, bashing his pommel into another Breton and kicking a third aside.

The charge had worked! His men had reached the town square.

"Wait!" Taurin cried in Norse as Vikarr prepared to stab him. He shook the red sash around his neck. "Allies."

"Ha!" The *hirdman* lowered his sword and instead hauled Taurin to his feet. "No resting yet!" Vikarr waded toward the rest of Taurin's Franks, who were surrounded now that their charge had stalled.

A few more Norse followed him, descending on the Bretons engaging Taurin's riders. With a moment to collect himself, Taurin glanced around. If this was the town square, where was Halla? The flames, now burning out of control, provided more than enough light to see. More buildings had caught fire, including the town hall.

In front of it, a trio of Bretons had pinned Halla against the burning façade.

Struggling for solid footing among the slippery bodies and pools of blood, he ran for her, ignoring a passing pair of Bretons fighting a Norseman. Only Halla mattered.

She was parrying their blows, but the injuries from her duel with Bjornolf were slowing her down too much.

Just a little further…

One of the Bretons had maneuvered behind her and raised his sword.

"No!" He stumbled as his foot caught on a sprawled limb. He wouldn't reach her in time. Desperate, he flung his sword, sending it end over end at her attacker.

It missed the man's chest, but struck his arm with a spray of blood, knocking the Breton's sword from his grasp. Taurin lost his balance and crashed into the stunned Breton. They fell in a tangled heap close enough to the burning edifice that the heat seared his face and threatened to singe his beard.

He scrambled to his feet, searching for his sword among the wreckage of the market square. The Breton grunted and raised himself onto an elbow, reaching for his own weapon.

"Taurin!"

He turned, and Halla tossed him one of her axes. Catching the light weapon, he brought it around in a single motion, faster than he could ever swing his sword.

It settled firmly in the Breton's chest with a sickening gurgle. Eyes frozen in disbelief, the man slumped over and fell still.

Taurin tugged at the axe, but it wouldn't dislodge. Abandoning it, he scrambled over to his sword and clamped down on the moon-carved hilt.

Drawing it defensively before him, he rose to help Halla, only to see her back rushing deeper into the melee. Her remaining attackers lay lifeless where she had stood. He started after her.

"Taurin!"

God save him, he knew that voice. He turned.

Orderic stood with shield and sword in hand by the alley abutting the church, the same alley where he had warned Taurin of the Breton attack. The same alley where Orderic's frenzied expression had terrified him.

He had dreaded this confrontation since lying to Orderic about betraying his wife.

His friend's gritted teeth and curled lip announced his comprehension that Taurin had never intended to help destroy the Norse, that he had goaded the Bretons into a long march so they would fight exhausted and nauseated after a sea voyage.

Orderic was his friend, and he had used him.

He glanced to his left. His riders and the Norsemen were fighting together now, pushing the Bretons back. He couldn't tell whether any of Bjornolf's raiders had survived, but he need not fear an attack from the writhing casualties strewn throughout the square, screaming and dragging themselves away from the carnage.

"You betrayed me." Orderic's voice seethed with anger. "I embraced you as a brother. I told you how much I valued your support. And all the while, you were lying to me."

"I betrayed you?" Taurin scoffed. "You've undermined me from the moment I returned from Rouen. Were you being a brother when you incited Father Norbert to march on my home? Or when you whispered poison against Halla? Where was your support?"

"You sold us to them."

"You're selling us to Berengar."

"He's a Christian." Orderic's lip rose in a sneer. "I wonder if you remember what that even means."

"I am as Christian as you are," Taurin insisted. "As Christian as the lords who abused us before abandoning us. Lords like Berengar."

Orderic shook his head. "You gave up everything for them. For her." The flames from the church reflected off the blade in his hand as he adjusted his grip. "She spread her legs and turned you into a heathen."

"And yet, they're fighting to protect our farmers while you seek to slaughter women and children." He wiped sweat from his eyes. The fire's heat was intensifying. "I stand by the oath I swore at my wedding."

Orderic pointed the tip of his sword at Taurin and peeled his lips back to expose a toothy grin. "Then you will die as a traitor and a blasphemer."

Orderic charged forward, cocking his sword back. Taurin had no shield, but he crossed to the Breton he had killed and yanked at the haft of Halla's axe again. This time, it pulled loose as Orderic's sword came down.

Taurin deflected it with his own blade and retreated to adjust his grip on the axe. Its unbalanced weight felt awkward, but he preferred it to an empty hand.

He abruptly recalled that Halla had given him both: the axe moments earlier and the sword at their wedding.

Orderic slashed at his neck with frightening speed. Taurin leapt backward but felt the tip trace along the top of his cuirass. Eyes widening, he wiped the back of his hand over his throat, but it came back free of blood.

His friend meant to kill him.

They had helped each other through the pain of losing a father and a sister. Memories of every shared laugh and cup of wine, every private dream for the future voiced on long summer days twisted into yawning chasms of regret as Orderic readied himself again.

That Orderic was gone. The dream of massacre had consumed him.

Orderic advanced again behind his shield, opening his defenses only when he stabbed for Taurin's chest. Taurin batted the sword aside and followed up with a slash of his own, but the other man snapped his shield back into position too quickly, leaving no opening to pick apart. Fatigue made Taurin's muscles heavy. His arm throbbed from when the Bretons had pulled him from his horse.

His eyes widened. Halla had claimed he fought too defensively. Orderic had called him a heathen.

He needed to fight like one.

As Orderic raised his sword and shifted his weight to his back foot, his shield arm dipped. Taurin charged, but instead of striking, he kicked hard at the center of the shield, sending Orderic sprawling backward.

The alderman struck the ground hard. The impact spun his arm within the straps until the shield faced toward his own body.

Taurin continued his rush. Shield useless, Orderic raised his sword, but Taurin hooked it with his axe and flung it aside before stabbing. The tempered Andalusi blade penetrated the leather armor and buried itself deep within Orderic's chest.

Orderic stared in wide-mouthed disbelief at the blade poking out of him. A Muslim-crafted sword, wielded by a Christian married to a heathen.

Taurin released the blade with a shaking hand. Blood began to pool around the wound. Orderic's blood, blood he had shed.

Halla had killed one of her own people, a friend, for his crimes.

Now, he had done the same. But even the man who wished to kill his wife shouldn't die alone.

Kicking Orderic's sword out of his reach, Taurin knelt beside his friend.

"I only wanted...to preserve...our world," Orderic wheezed. "You've...destroyed us."

Taurin cradled his head. "The world you fought for was already gone. You just refused to let go of the memory."

Orderic gasped at a spasm of pain. More blood pumped from the wound. "They will...erase...who we are."

Oh, how much like Bjornolf he sounded! In the end, that same fear had destroyed them both.

"They will change us," Taurin agreed. "They'll make us stronger, give us back a future."

Orderic's lips began to pale. It wouldn't be long now. "I'd...rather die...than...live in...that future."

It was a sentiment worthy of Valhalla. Taurin had once feared that the Norsemen would infect his people with bloodlust. But that hunger had simmered beneath the surface since the first Norse raid. His people had lacked only the means for retribution, not the desire for it.

Taurin closed his hand over his friend's mouth in a desperate attempt to keep Orderic's last breath from escaping, but the warm air leaked between his fingers with a shivering finality. Helpless, he could only stare at the eerie stillness of Orderic's body.

There was no going back. The world had changed too much, and it had no place for those who refused to acknowledge that truth.

HALLA

The final two dozen unwounded Bretons threw down their weapons as Halla and her Norsemen advanced on them. Raising her hands to the gods, she released a great bellow soon picked up by not only the Norse, but also the relieved Franks.

It was over. They had won.

Audhild and Steingrim collided and felt each other for injuries. Frantic probing of blood splattered on each of their faces gave way to relieved kisses. Halla smiled in gratitude that the gods hadn't called either of them away this day.

"Divide them," she ordered.

Her surviving warriors recruited the Franks to collect the weapons and search the prisoners.

She had first seen the square empty nearly two years earlier, and then filled with bustling traders breathing life into Lillebonne. Now, bodies and sundered limbs sat in bloody pools that reflected the flames consuming that square.

Four of her *hird* and eight of the settlers were dead or had passed beyond the help of even a trained *læknir*, if they'd had one. Ten Franks had also died in their devastating charge, including Guntramm. Fortunately, Huebald the blacksmith had survived; she would need his skill to forge chains for these prisoners in the coming days.

But Leubin and two of his sons cried over a lifeless body, slain by a deep gash to the neck. For a moment, their tears surprised Halla, and she had to remind herself they didn't believe in Valhalla. She did not envy her eventual reunion with Adella.

Taurin approached from the ruins of the church. He was alive! His solid stride suggested no great injuries. Tears stained the soot and sweat on her cheeks. She would sacrifice to each of the gods for their good fortune.

She ran to him as fast as her feet could find solid footing among the shattered merchant stalls, bodies, and wreckage. He reached out and took her in his arms. Buried beneath all the odors of battle, she smelled him, that scent she remembered through all their nights together. She closed her eyes and released a soft sigh.

She felt his hand against her neck, then the pressure of his lips on her head. For a moment, she forgot about the work still to be done. Her family was safe. Whatever his conversations with Berengar,

Taurin's actions had shown his true loyalties. He had killed for them. That mattered, more for him than it would for any Norseman.

She pulled back when he stiffened. His eyes focused on something off to her left. She understood without needing to follow his gaze.

"Leubin's eldest," she said. "It was quick."

His eyes began to glisten as he watched their steward's grief. She would turn his face away if it would prevent the pain within them. If her husband were a Norseman, she would remind him that the boy joined the victorious dead and that this was no time for sorrow.

But he wasn't a Norseman. If he were, she would have married someone else to bridge the gulf between the Franks and her people, and Orderic and Berengar's men might have triumphed.

Orderic. "Where is Orderic?"

Taurin swallowed and lowered his head. "He's dead." He offered her the axe. Blood still clung to the blade. "Thank you for lending it to me." The strain around his eyes told the tale.

"I'm sorry the task fell to you."

His eyes lost focus. "It could be none other."

While his meaning eluded her, she decided not to press the matter, not after what he must have endured.

He raised his head and studied the scene around him. "Lillebonne is lost."

The smoldering flames had reduced whole neighborhoods to cinders. While the outlying buildings survived, the church, the town hall and the entire core of the town continued to burn.

She sneezed as she breathed in a piece of ash floating on the breeze. The smoke on the air tickled her throat and made her want to swallow.

"It's not the first time," she reminded. "But now, my people can help rebuild."

His voice grew solemn. "Would you?"

She squeezed his hand. "We won't give in to the Bretons by abandoning our farms just because the town burned. There are many ways to fight for one's land."

His eyes brightened. "Then this isn't the end."

She kissed him on the cheek. "It's only the beginning."

One of her *hirdmen* saluted and gestured to the prisoners. Only three of Orderic's men and one of the Norse raiders had survived. Most of her people guarded about four dozen Bretons, including the wounded.

She turned to address them, but Taurin halted her with a hand on her wrist. "Rollo forbade enslaving Franks, but we can't go through this again." He lowered his chin and fixed her with a gritty stare. "End it."

It was not a Christian comment, but that of a virile Norseman. A ripple of excitement raced up her spine, filling her with a flush of arousal.

"I will."

She halted before Orderic's three surviving supporters, watched by a trio of her *hird*. Their eyes carried hatred, not defeat.

"You gleaned the benefits of working with Rouen, but chose to take arms against us," she said in Frankish.

"Save your words," shouted a black-haired man with a pinched face. "You won't convince us to support you."

"I'm not trying to." She smirked. "I'm simply explaining why I'm going to dispossess your families and exile them from Lillebonne."

He jumped to his feet, but collapsed when the closest *hirdman* slashed a red tear in his calf. "You cannot punish them for our actions!"

"You should have considered that before you opposed me. I will not harbor insurrection in my midst."

At her nod, her warriors brought their swords down on the prisoners' necks. They struck the sodden ground with three sickening slaps.

A sacrifice for the future.

Her husband nodded in approval. He had changed.

A few of the Bretons whimpered and scuttled helplessly for an escape as she halted before them. She offered her most ferocious grin, baring her teeth and savoring their fear. Perhaps she would tell their lord how they had cowered before a woman to extract some retribution for his disowning his dear Poppa.

Terror was a wonderful thing.

"Soldiers of Berengar." She pitched her voice high so it would carry. "If you were Norsemen, I'd kill you so your deaths might redeem your shame at surrendering and earn you a place in Valhalla. But you are Christian, and your ways are different. I will allow your lord Berengar to ransom you. If you try to escape, I will flog and behead you."

A pair of Norsemen distributed several coils of rope and her warriors began to bind the prisoners. She heard a few grumbles that they wanted to butcher the lot, but she silenced them with a glare. She was both *høvding* and *hersir* and would not tolerate disobedience.

Taurin approached, his brow furrowed. "Ransom?"

"Why shouldn't Berengar pay to rebuild the town his men destroyed? We can also sell the weapons and armor we stripped and the lands of Orderic and his men."

Eyes widening, he stroked his beard. "The victims of Bjornolf's raids will need proper compensation, as well."

The Norseman in her disliked forcing raiders to repay their victims. She had participated in too many raids herself. But she was *høvding* now, and most of her people were Frankish. Taurin had proven willing to accept some of her people's ways. Perhaps she should do the same.

She eyed the surviving raider. "I have an idea."

The man stood as she approached. None of her warriors would stop him from meeting death on his feet.

She halted before him. "You fought well today against a much greater force."

He gave a smug smile. "I go to Valhalla with a light heart. Strike true."

"I can give you death if you wish, but you will not awaken among the gods."

His expression hardened. "Why not?"

"You are an outlaw, and the gods do not accept outlaws at their table."

He lowered his eyes. The skalds were very clear on the fate of criminals.

"I have a suggestion," she offered.

His eyes narrowed. "What is that?"

"If you tell me where Bjornolf stored his plunder, I will absolve you for your participation in his crimes. You will be an outlaw no longer and may join any warband, even Rollo's or mine, if you wish. Your heart is fierce. You will assuredly earn your way to Valhalla."

Breath quickening, he narrowed his eyes. "You would swear to this?"

She made a reverent gesture around her face. "I swear I will do as I say with all good faith, by Freya, by Thor, and by Odin All-Father."

His eyes widened as she completed the oath. He licked his lips. "I will do as you ask."

She trudged back to Taurin, who was watching the prisoners. The Bretons were standing, bound at the wrists and tied together by a long length of rope. The Norsemen and Franks arranged them in a marching line.

"What do we do with them? I'd recommend the church, but…" A shadow passed over his face as he studied the cinders that remained of the holy building.

"We have to keep them at our estate for now. One of the corrals, perhaps?"

He nodded slowly. "Orderic said Berengar would only sail once his soldiers reported success, but what if he still comes?"

Defeating his first army had seemed impossible enough of a task that she hadn't thought beyond it. "I don't know."

Somehow, she doubted a lord like Berengar, who faced fresh raids every year, would risk his warriors if such a large force didn't report back. Anything could await him. Surely, he wouldn't leave his own lands undefended.

She hoped he wouldn't. She wouldn't have Bjornolf's raiders next time.

HALLA

Halla stared out of her bedroom window toward the long road leading east. After two days without Berengar's ships arriving, she had felt secure enough to recall Runa's convoy. Leubin had insisted on telling Adella about their eldest son, so he volunteered to ride after them.

That was three days past. Two days later, the treasonous thought that perhaps Berengar had found and massacred the convoy had wormed its way into her mind. She had thought of nothing else all through the night.

She gripped the window frame to still her shaking hands. She wanted her little Runa now.

Her husband wrapped his arms around her. "They'll be along soon."

She wanted them here now, not soon. "I know."

"I want to hold her, too."

She nestled into his embrace. "When did you start knowing my thoughts?"

"Maybe I'm starting to understand you." He leaned in and kissed her cheek. "Just a little."

Not very long ago, she had doubted that would ever happen. That thought had filled her with as much despair then as his simple words of reassurance warmed her now.

"You've changed."

"I suppose I have."

Would the woman who had raided Bayeux with Rollo and Revna appreciate the subtle contentment of a husband understanding her desires? She had been so small back then. Yet during the previous two winters, she had endured such difficulty. Perhaps she shouldn't judge her younger self so harshly.

She wouldn't return to that life for any reason. The orchards and fields flanking the road outside her window were home now. "I have as well."

When he inhaled a breath, his chest pressed against her back and filled her with a sense of security. Her worries began to recede.

"Maybe that's why we're still here when so many aren't."

"What do you mean?" she asked.

"Orderic and Bjornolf clung to a past that doesn't exist anymore. It destroyed them."

The same could also be said for dear Revna. If not for her pregnancy, perhaps she would have died beside her friend. She thought the gods had offered her a good death by guiding her to this land north of the Seine. But now, she understood they had offered her a new life.

"I love you," she murmured. "I'm glad I met you."

He kissed the tip of her ear. "And I love you."

In the distance, the first wagon crested the hill, flanked by Leubin atop his horse. Halla held a tight breath until they came close enough that she could recognize Adella and the wet nurse, carrying little Runa, sitting in front.

They were home.

EPILOGUE

AUGUST, AD 892

TAURIN

A MIX OF A dozen clean-shaved Franks and bearded Norsemen pulled on the woven rope in rhythm. Slowly, the massive wooden frame rose into place. It halted flush against the walls already erected and craftsmen swarmed in to tie it down until they could affix it permanently. Releasing the ropes, the workers sank to the ground, sucking in deep breaths.

Taurin sighed in contentment. The new town hall was coming along nicely.

He studied the several buildings under construction throughout the town square. Had his grandfather felt a similar mix of anxiety and excitement when he had relocated Lillebonne up river so many years earlier? Had he imagined, in the aftermath of that terrible raid, that it would survive more than five decades?

Halla and Taurin had shocked Rollo when they had arrived in Rouen with fifty prisoners. Amazed that they had thwarted the invasion, the jarl had eagerly agreed to use the plunder and ransom as Halla wished. He had even provided coin from his own treasury to rebuild the town, on the condition that they rebuild at the site of Old Lillebonne. He wanted fully equipped docks along the Seine, not the tiny Bolbec. After all this time, Lillebonne was coming home. Taurin took great satisfaction at the prospect of Norsemen rebuilding the town they themselves had burned.

Taurin had also pressed Rollo to resolve the matter of the Franks' status. Eager to encourage such displays of loyalty, Rollo had granted all the Franks in his domain full rights as Norsemen. Any who raided them would be committing murder and theft.

Taurin stepped aside for a burly Norseman carrying another load of timber from the *knörr* anchored nearby. Able to accommodate twelve ships, the new docks occupied more riverfront than the width of the old town.

He wondered how long it would take to grow used to this new view of the Seine. He could barely make out the features of the distant southern shore. The Bolbec was a tiny sliver compared to this mighty river.

He used to fear seeing longships on the water. Now, he welcomed them. Three would remain permanently stationed in Lillebonne to guard against Breton incursions. Berengar wouldn't get another chance to invade.

Halla approached from the berthed *knörr* with a smile. He slung his arm over her shoulder as she squeezed his waist. "They raised the frame?"

"Only just."

"Good. They should finish before winter."

He smiled in appreciation of the similar path of their thoughts. Sweeping his gaze over the buildings, he considered the church. The original stone foundation had survived largely intact these past fifty years. They had already finished repairing the walls, but the roof remained open to the elements.

Father Norbert was making the sign of the cross over the workers resting before the partially erected town hall. Both Norsemen and Franks bowed their heads as he spoke.

Taurin nodded toward him. "He'll be intolerable until he has a new church."

Her laugh sounded like the tinkling of rain on the roof. "I doubt it." She tossed a thumb back toward the docked *knörr*. "I just heard. Poppa convinced Rollo to allow an archbishop to return to Rouen. A man named Witto. Rollo will send him to bless the church when it's finished."

Taurin shook his head in disbelief. Two years earlier, he had feared that the arrival of the Norsemen would see the end of his town and his people. In a way, it had. But that end was only the winter that led to spring growth. Seasons changed, but his people would endure.

A smile curled onto his face as he let his eyes wander. A patrol was setting out to search for brigands reported in the wilds along the Seine. Two of them were clean-shaven Franks with short hair, but the third was a braided and bearded Norseman with kohl-stained eyes. As they passed, he heard snippets of conversation about a drinking contest the previous night.

Chopping axes echoed from one of the construction sites. Beside their apprentices, Frankish and Norse carpenters started arguing over technique. After a few exchanges, sharp gestures and rapid words gave way to satisfied nods as they returned to work.

And in the center of the new, larger town square, Huebald was entertaining a rapt audience with a tale embellished by broad motions. After watching for a few moments, Taurin realized he was recounting the battle that spring with the same vivacity as the skald in Rouen.

The old Lillebonne had belonged to the Franks alone, a testament to their perseverance against ruin. This new town would belong to all, Norse and Christian alike. It was a fitting home for his daughter.

Whether due to his god, hers, their toils, or accidents of fortune, he no longer cared. The knot of fear about the future had uncoiled from around his heart.

He threaded his fingers through his wife's. She turned and smiled before leaning her head against his shoulder. They weren't alone anymore.

MAJOR CHARACTERS

NORSE

Halla Skidadóttir, a Danish shieldmaiden serving Rollo of Rouen

Jarl Rollo, Norwegian warlord who controls the formerly Christian city of Rouen

Revna Viksdóttir, Halla's friend and fellow shieldmaiden

Jorund the Raven, Rollo's most trusted advisor and friend

Bjornolf Didriksson, a traditional Norse warrior in Rollo's retinue

Sigrun Shieldbreaker, Norwegian jarl who raids annually with Rollo

Oleg Ygrinsson, a trader who supplies Rouen

FRANKS

Taurin, a landowner in Lillebonne, a quiet village north of the Seine

Orderic, another landowner and Taurin's friend

Arbogast, another landowner caught raiding his fellow townsfolk

Norbert, town priest of Lillebonne

Leubin, Taurin's steward

Adella, Leubin's wife

BRETONS

Berengar, Count of Bayeux

Poppa, Berengar's daughter and Rollo's captive

GLOSSARY

alderman – a powerful landowner in Frankish society who exerted political power in the absence of counts or other nobles

Bessin – region of northern France between Brittany and Normandy

blaudur – the opposite of *hvatur*, *blaudur* is weak, submissive, or subject to the will of others

blót – a Norse ritual sacrifice; the most important was made to Freyr in January or February

Bragi – god of music and poetry, esteemed by poetic skalds

Bretons – residents of Brittany, a duchy in northwest France

Brísingamen – Freya's necklace, her most beloved possession

chlamys – a short cloak common to the Carolingian Franks

dalmatica – Byzantine outer garment featuring long, flaring sleeves

demesne – portion of an estate retained for cultivation by a landowner, usually worked by tenants in a rotating schedule

ell – a unit of length used to measure cloth, roughly 20 in (50 cm)

Freya – goddess of fertility and overseer of Sessrúmnir, a feasting hall in the Norse afterlife

Freyr – god of the harvest to whom the important winter sacrifice was dedicated

Frigg – goddess of marriage and motherhood, wife of Odin

gythia – a Norse priestess who performs sacrifices and oversee *blóts*

hersir – leader of a group of warriors who owed allegiance to a jarl

hirdman – loyal warrior and bodyguard of an important Norse leader (group: *hird*)

høvding – a term of respect for a chieftain or community leader

hvatur – a virtue characterized by strength, virility, renown, and the ability to exert one's will upon others; *hvatur* and *blaudur*—not gender—determined social rights in Norse society

knörr – a trading vessel wider than a longship with a shallow draft

læknir – healing woman (pl. læknar)

Laugardagur – Saturday, the traditional Norse bathing day

Loki – god of trickery and mischief, who preferred profane sacrifices

manse – a parcel of land rented to tenants in exchange for a portion of the tenant's crop and labor in the landowner's fields

Oceanus Britannicus – Viking-age name of the English Channel

Odin All-Father – king of the gods who sacrificed an eye to gain foreknowledge of Ragnarok

Pays de Caux – the northern part of modern-day Normandy, stretching from the Seine River to the English Channel

pecunium – a right in perpetuity to farm a parcel of land and to pass it down to one's children

skald – Norse poets who recited sagas immortalizing famous warriors of the past

snekke – a military longship that could both travel up rivers and on the open ocean

stallari – a trusted aide combining the duties of a marshal, advisor, and military chief of staff

Thing – a multi-day assembly of all free Norse citizens to settle disagreements, dispense justice, and pass laws

Thor – warrior god and defender of mankind associated with blacksmiths and thunder

thrall – the Norse word for slave

víkingr – "to go raiding"; often misused to refer to the Norse people

ABOUT THE AUTHOR

K.M. Butler studied literature at Carnegie Mellon University and has always had an avid interest in history. His writing influences are *The Lions of al-Rassan* by Guy Gavriel Kay and Colleen McCullough's *Masters of Rome* series.

He lives in Philadelphia with his wife and two daughters. His wife is his first and harshest editor, while his daughters always want his stories to feature more blood and talking animals, but never at the same time.

Contact K.M. Butler at *kmbutlerauthor@yahoo.com* or on Twitter at *@kmbutlerauthor*.

Made in the USA
Las Vegas, NV
11 May 2024

89838810R00225